AGAINST
THE LOVELESS
WORLD

ALSO BY SUSAN ABULHAWA

Mornings in Jenin
My Voice Sought the Wind
The Blue Between Sky and Water

AGAINST THE LOVELESS WORLD

— *A Novel* —

SUSAN ABULHAWA

BLOOMSBURY CIRCUS

LONDON • OXFORD • NEW YORK • NEW DELHI • SYDNEY

BLOOMSBURY CIRCUS
Bloomsbury Publishing Plc
50 Bedford Square, London, WC1B 3DP, UK

BLOOMSBURY, BLOOMSBURY CIRCUS and the Bloomsbury Circus logo are
trademarks of Bloomsbury Publishing Plc

First published in 2020 in the USA by Atria Books, Simon & Schuster, Inc.
First published in Great Britain 2020

A catalogue record for this book is available from the British Library

ISBN: HB: 978-1-5266-1879-5; TPB: 978-1-5266-1880-1;
eBook: 978-1-5266-1878-8

2 4 6 8 10 9 7 5 3 1

Text design by Jill Putorti
Printed and bound in Great Britain by CPI Group (UK) Ltd, Croydon CR0 4YY

To find out more about our authors and books visit www.bloomsbury.com
and sign up for our newsletters

In memory of Mame Lambeth, my person. And in memory of Aminah Abulhawa, the person I always waited for.

GLOSSARY

abaya
: A simple, loose overgarment or cloak, worn by some women in parts of North Africa and the Arabian Peninsula. In Kuwait, they are traditionally black and are worn by both men and women.

adan
: Muslim call to worship.

ahlan
: One of the many forms of "welcome" in Arabic.

alhamdulillah
: Gratitude to God.

alhamdulillah assalameh
: Gratitude to God for your safety (safe arrival).

Allahu akbar
: God is bigger. This phrase is used in every conceivable situation to invoke a belief that God is bigger than any circumstance, and God is all-knowing in whatever afflicts or blesses humans.

Allah yustor
: God protect.

almas
: Diamond.

ammi, ammo
: Palestinian colloquial for "uncle," used to address older male relatives or any elder men as a sign of respect.

argileh   Hookah, smoking pipe.

aseeleh   A woman rooted in tradition and good manners.

babbour   A type of kerosene camp stove.

bismillah   In the name of God.

bizir   Roasted watermelon seeds.

booza   Ice cream. Booza dhahab is a popular ice cream in Kuwait.

dabke   Literally means "stomping of the feet"; it is a native Levantine folk dance performed by Palestinians, Lebanese, Syrians, and Jordanians. The dance combines lines or circles of men and women, dancing in coordinated movements that vary from one region to another.

dawali   Grape leaves.

dhuhr   Noon.

dinar   A unit of currency; the Kuwaiti dinar (KD) is roughly three times stronger than the US dollar. One KD equals approximately 3.37 USD as of late 2019.

dishdasha   A loose, ankle-length garment, usually with long sleeves, worn throughout Africa, Persia, the Levant, the Arabian Peninsula, and Iraq. Men's disdashas are simple, traditionally white or gray, whereas women's dishdashas vary from simple to ornately patterned and colorful.

diwaniya   A large room where men in the Gulf region receive male guests to conduct business or socialize. Traditional diwaniyas boast seating on floor cushions

	that line the walls around the room. Sitting or hosting a diwaniya is an important feature of the social and economic fabric of male life in Kuwait.
dua'a	A prayer to God.
dunum	A unit of land equivalent to approximately one quarter of an acre.
el hilw ma byinsa el halawa	The sweet do not forget the sweets.
enshallah	God willing.
fajr	Sunrise.
fajr salat	Sunrise worship, the first of five daily worships in Islam.
fallahi	Singular masculine form of *fallah*, which refers to the peasant class.
Fatiha	Generally means "the opening," but specifically refers to the opening Surah in the Quran. In the context where it's mentioned in the prose, the Fatiha is traditionally recited for the souls of the dead.
fattoush	A Levantine salad common to Palestine, Lebanon, Jordan, and Syria. It typically includes lettuce, tomatoes, cucumbers, radishes, and fried pieces of pita bread. Some families also like to add green peppers, green onions, and parsley. In Arabic, the word *fattoush* is derived from *fatteh*, which literally means "crumbs" (which is also the origin of the word *feta* for cheese).
frangie	Westerners.
fuul	Fava beans, usually in the form of a paste dipped with spices and olive oil.

ghada	Lunch, the biggest meal of the day in Arab societies.
ghutra-o-egal	Traditional headwear of Arab men. The ghutra is the cloth head covering, which is held in place with an egal, a black chord, worn doubled on the crown of the head.
habibi	Singular masculine form of "my beloved."
habibti	Singular feminine form of "my beloved."
haader, ya sit el kol	The literal translation—"present, lady of all"—is an affectionate way of saying "yes, ma'am."
ha'ek alay	A way of saying "my bad" or "please forgive me." The literal translation doesn't make sense in English: "your justice is on me."
hajjeh	A title of respect for an elderly woman, particularly if she undertook the Haj pilgrimage to Mecca.
hammam	Public bathhouse associated with Islamic culture. Bathers begin by relaxing in steamy hot rooms, where they are then lathered and scrubbed with special loofas to remove layers of dead skin, followed by a massage with essential oils and a cooling period. Variations include dips in ice-cold water before the massage, or relaxation on hot tiles in dry rooms.
hara	Neighborhood, typically in poorer areas.
haram	Sinful.
hawiyya	Identity, ID card.

hummus	A protein-rich paste made with tahini (ground sesame seeds), garbanzo beans, garlic, olive oil, lemon juice, and salt. For centuries, hummus has been a staple food in Levantine societies—Palestine, Lebanon, Syria, and Jordan—though it is common throughout the Arab world.
ibriq	Coffee- or teapot.
immi	Palestinian colloquial for "my mother."
istaghfar Allah	Literally translates to "I seek forgiveness in God." It is often uttered in proximity to transgressions, misdeeds, or evil as supplication. It is also used in humor.
jafra	A popular dabke style that encompasses an entire genre of songs, which can vary significantly but still keep a basic rhythm that is recognizable from one song to another, lending itself to consistent forms of dabke dances.
jameed	Hard, dry, salted yogurt made from sheep or goat milk. It is the main ingredient in mansaf. The milk is filtered through fine cheesecloth to make thick yogurt, to which salt is added daily to further thicken the yogurt and drain away the whey. When it is sufficiently thick, it is balled into spheres and dried for days in the shade.
khala	One of the many ways to say "auntie."
Khaleeji	Of or pertaining to the region of the Arabian or Persian Gulf.
khamr	Literal translation refers to a fermented or brewed substance. In the prose, it means alcohol.

khaneeth	Faggot.
khanjar	A traditional dagger with an extremely sharp curved edge, originally from Oman. Often ornate, they are worn by men for ceremonial occasions.
kheir	Blessings. Can be used as a question—*Kheir?*—meaning "What?"
khobz	Bread.
knafe	A cheesy dessert.
kuffiyeh	Checkered scarf, traditionally worn as men's headdress, but popularly around the neck among young people of all genders. The black and white version is typical among Palestinians, and has come to symbolize Palestinian nationalism. A red and white version is also worn among Palestinians as well as Arabs throughout West Asia and North Africa.
kuzbarat el ajooz	Literally meaning "spice of the old lady," but specifically refers to wild Venus-hair, an herb.
labneh	A type of soft cheese made by straining yogurt (laban). Typically eaten as a snack or light food in the Levant region (Palestine, Lebanon, Syria, and Jordan).
mansaf	Popular Levantine dish of lamb cooked in a jameed sauce (fermented dried yogurt) and served over rice, with nuts and other garnishes. It is the national dish of Jordan, but also common in Palestine, Iraq, Syria, and some Gulf countries.
maqlooba	Traditional Palestinian dish eaten throughout the Levant. It consists of layers of meat, rice, and vegetables in special

spice mixtures. The name translates to "flipped" or "upside down," because the pot is flipped upside down when served.

mashawi
Grilled meats.

matchboos
A national dish of Kuwait, Bahrain, and Qatar, it consists of rice cooked in a special spice mix (cardamom, peppercorns, cinnamon, coriander, cloves, cumin, nutmeg, paprika) with black lime and topped with a browned and spicy tomato sauce.

mezze
Snack foods or appetizers, typically consisting of various cheeses, salads, and spreads (such as hummus, mhammara, labneh).

mhammara
Translates to "reddened," and refers to a dip originally from Syria. It is made from roasted Aleppo peppers, garlic, crushed walnuts, olive oil, pomegranate, and breadcrumbs.

mistika
A resin obtained from the mastic tree (*Pistacia lentiscus*). Also called Arabic gum; used to flavor foods and desserts.

mitkawteen
Non-Kuwaiti natives who are granted Kuwait citizenship.

mlookhiya
The leaves of a jute plant, typically eaten as a stew by the same name. The dish is thought to have originated in ancient Egypt or India. It is traditionally cooked with chicken or chicken stock and garlic, and served with rice and squeezed lemon.

mo'akhar
Part of Islamic marriage contracts, which list two types of mahr (dowry): The muqaddam is paid up front to seal

the marriage. The mo'akhar is a deferred payment in the event of divorce or death of the husband.

msakhan   A traditional layered Palestinian dish, with a large piece of taboun bread at the base, covered with heaps of caramelized onions and generous spicing with sumac, topped off with roasted chicken, toasted almonds, and pine nuts.

mukhtar   The "chosen," refers to an elder elected by the village council as a leader and arbiter of dispute.

Nabulsi cheese   A white brined cheese that originated from Nablus, Palestine, 7000-9000 years ago.

nahr   River.

ney   A wind instrument similar to the flute, traditionally made from hollow cane or reed with holes for the fingers and thumb. It is one of the oldest musical instruments still in use.

niqab   A face veil that leaves openings only for the eyes.

osool   Derived from the word "origin" or "roots," it refers in the prose to having principles and traditional good values.

qabbah   Embroidered chest piece of a thobe (caftan).

radah   Embroidered shoulder piece of a thobe (caftan).

Rashida, habibit Baba   Rashida, Daddy's beloved.

Romi   Refers to the era of the Roman Empire.

sabaho	Mornin'. Shortened way of saying "good morning."
salamtik, alf salamah	Literally means "blessings on you, a thousand blessings," but is meant to convey gratitude to God for someone's wellness, especially after being ill.
salat	Worship.
shabab	The youth.
shabka	Literally means "binding" or "web." It refers to the gold jewelry, including the wedding ring, that's meant to "tie" the newlyweds. It is considered an important part of weddings in Arab societies, as it is also meant to offer some financial security for the bride.
shakshouka	An Arab dish that originated in Morocco, whereby eggs are poached in a tomato base with chili peppers, garlic, cinnamon, cumin, cayenne, paprika, nutmeg, and other spices. Shakshouka is among a long list of Arab cuisines being appropriated as "Israeli food" even though these dishes predate Israel by hundreds of years.
sharmoot	Whore, singular masculine form; in context, "sharmoot, ibn sharmoota": whore, son of a whore.
sharmoota	Whore, singular feminine form.
sidi	Palestinian colloquial for "grandfather" or "papa."
sirwal	Baggy trousers made from light material, typically worn under a dishdasha in Arab countries. Different forms of

	the sirwal are also worn in Iran, India, and Pakistan.
sitt	Ms.
sitti	Palestinian colloquial for "grandmother" or "granny."
souq	Market.
subhan Allah	Praise God.
taboon	A clay oven used for thousands of years in Palestine to bake bread. It has an opening at the bottom where the fire is stoked. Traditionally used communally by villagers or large families. The flat bread made in a taboon is called by the same name.
takht	Literally means "bed," but refers to the musical ensemble typically from Egypt and the Levant and consisting of the oud, qanun, kamanjah, ney, riq, and darbakka instruments.
taqseem	Literally means "division," but refers to instrumental improvisations that precede traditional musical compositions.
tarab	There is no equivalence to this word in the English language. It describes the emotional, even spiritual, transformation that occurs when one feels a convergence with music. The phenomenon of being "transported" by music is epitomized by tarab. Appreciating classical Arabic songs involves an understanding of this concept.
tatreez	Embroidery.
tfadaloo	Welcome (plural).

thobe	Traditional embroidered caftan.
thuhr	Afternoon.
um	Mother of.
waleh	A versatile word in colloquial Arabic that can range from an insult to an endearment, depending on context. *Waleh* is the feminine form of *wala*. An English equivalent might be the urban use of the words *girl* and *boy*. Said among friends, "girl" is familiar and endearing. But said by a white supremacist to a black or brown woman, it is an insult. The context in this book is the former.
wudu	Ablution. Ritual cleansing in Islam before worship practices.
ya Sater	O Protector. Referencing God to call for protection, it is an expression meant to convey caution, trepidation, or generally fear of the unknown.
yalla	A versatile word in the Arabic language. Translates to "let's go" but can be used in a wide range of contexts with different meanings. For example, it can mean "get over it," "forget it," "do it," or "get moving."
yaqoot	Ruby; gem.
yis'ed soutik	Literal translation is "may your voice be happy." It is meant to convey love and joy at hearing the voice of a dear one.
yumma	Palestinian fallahi (peasant) colloquial for "mother."
za'atar	Thyme, often crushed and combined with sesame to be consumed with olive oil and bread.

zaffa

Traditional wedding procession leading the newlyweds and wedding party through the streets to the wedding reception. Typically the procession is led by dancers and a musical ensemble of bendir drums, bagpipes, and horns.

zaghareet

Ululations—long, high-pitched vocal trilling produced by emitting a loud tone accompanied by a rapid back-and-forth movement of the tongue. It is typically practiced by women to express great joy.

zakira

Memory.

zeit

Oil; usually refers to olive oil.

zeit-o-za'atar

Olive oil and za'atar (thyme), a snack commonly eaten in Palestinian society.

I.

KUWAIT

THE CUBE, EAST

I LIVE IN the Cube. I write on its glossy gray cinder-block walls however I can—with my nails before, with pencils now that the guards bring me some supplies.

Light comes through the small glass-block window high on the wall, reached only by the many-legged crawling creatures that also reside here. I am fond of the spiders and ants, which have set up separate dominions and manage to avoid each other in our shared nine-square-meter universe. The light of a world beyond, with a sun and moon and stars, or maybe just fluorescent bulbs—I can't be sure—streams through the window in a prism that lands on the wall in red, yellow, blue, and purple patterns. The shadows of tree branches, passing animals, armed guards, or perhaps other prisoners sometimes slide across the light.

I once tried to reach the window. I stacked everything I had on top of the bed—a bedside table, the small box where I keep my toiletries, and three books the guards had given me (Arabic translations of *Schindler's List*, *How to Be Happy*, and *Always Be Grateful*). I stretched as tall as I could on the stack but only reached a cobweb.

When my nails were strong and I weighed more than now, I

tried to mark time as prisoners do, one line on the wall for each day in groups of five. But I soon realized the light and dark cycles in the Cube do not match those of the outside world. It was a relief to know, because keeping up with life beyond the Cube had begun to weigh on me. Abandoning the imposition of a calendar helped me understand that time isn't real; it has no logic in the absence of hope or anticipation. The Cube is thus devoid of time. It contains, instead, a yawning stretch of something unnamed, without present, future, or past, which I fill with imagined or remembered life.

Occasionally people come to see me. They carry on their bodies and speech the climate of the world where seasons and weather change; where cars and planes and boats and bicycles ferry people from place to place; where groups gather to play, eat, cry, or go to war. Nearly all of my visitors are white. Although I can't know when it's day or night, it's easy to discern the seasons from them. In summer and spring, the sun glows from their skin. They breathe easily and carry the spirit of bloom. In winter they arrive pale and dull, with darkened eyes.

There were more of them before my hair turned gray, mostly businesspeople from the prison industry (there is such a thing) coming to survey the Cube. These smartly dressed voyeurs always left me feeling hollow. Reporters and human rights workers still come, though not as frequently anymore. After Lena and the Western woman came, I stopped receiving visitors for a while.

The guard allowed me to sit on the bed instead of being locked to the wall when the Western woman, who looked in her early thirties, came to interview me. I don't remember if she was a reporter or a human rights worker. She may have been a novelist. I appreciated that she brought an interpreter with her—a young Palestinian woman from Nazareth. Some visitors didn't bother, expecting me to speak English. I can, of course, but it's not easy on my tongue, and I don't care to be accommodating.

She was interested in my life in Kuwait and wanted to talk about my "sexuality." They all want my pussy's story. They presume so much, take liberties with words they're not entitled to. She asked if it's true I was a prostitute.

"You think prostitution has to do with sexuality?" I asked.

Fleeting confusion passed over her face. "No, of course not," she finally replied. "Let's move on."

She was tall, her brown hair loosely tied at the back. She wore jeans and a simple cream blouse, a jacket, and comfortable black shoes. No makeup. I didn't like her. I liked the interpreter, who was short and dark, like me, and wore red Converse shoes with fourteen black dots on the white rubber toe caps. One dot, then a group of nine dots, then four dots: 194, the code we used to evade Israeli surveillance. Hidden messages were thus assembled from every first, then ninth, then fourth word. That's how I knew she was more than an interpreter. *Her* name, I remember, was Lena.

At first I was confused. The 194 method only works with written messages. We couldn't count, listen, interpret, and speak at the same time. Then I realized Lena was tapping her pencil on certain words as she translated. She must have recognized the moment I figured it out because she smiled slightly. The words she kept tapping were variants of "eat the note," "mouth the paper," and "notepad food."

The interviewer looked down, as if unsure about her next question. "What would you like to talk about?" she asked.

On this particular day, I had been roaming the shores, deserts, and malls of Kuwait in simpler times.

"*Zeit-o-za'atar*," I blurted.

"Is that the Palestinian bread dip?" she asked Lena.

Lena nodded, and the woman jotted down some notes, though I could tell she wasn't interested in the story. I told it anyway.

"When we lived in Kuwait, the Tawjihi scores of the graduating high school class were always published in the newspapers, and Palestinians dominated the top ten graduates every year. Kuwaitis were especially perturbed the year when the top five were *all* Palestinian, and rumors began circulating that Palestinians were smart because we ate so much zeit-o-za'atar. The whole country went on a zeit-o-za'atar eating binge. Stores could barely keep za'atar stocked on shelves." I laughed.

The Western woman fidgeted as she listened to Lena translate. Ignoring her growing impatience, I continued: "I knew it wasn't true, because I ate a lot of za'atar and never did well in school. I got held back in ninth grade for failing both religion and mathematics the same year my brother, Jehad, was invited to skip fourth grade." Although those had been happier times, I recalled them now with a sense of tragedy and a desire to assure my younger self of her worth and intellect; of her capacity to learn, to believe she was not dumb, as the world had convinced her she was.

The Western woman tried to interrupt me, but I went on: "For a while, I tried to do better and let my little brother tutor me. But once a school believes you're stupid, no amount of good work will convince them otherwise."

"Your brother . . . I read that he was—"

I didn't let her finish. "My brother *is* brilliant," I said. She looked down at her notepad, though she had quit taking notes. I knew she wasn't interested in these reveries of my childhood. "I don't care what you read about my brother. Jehad was gentle and vulnerable. When he was in middle school, I found out two boys were bullying him. I gathered my girl posse, and we waited for them outside the school gate and gave them a good hiding. It made Jehad look up to me even more. One summer—"

The Western woman put her hand up. She glanced down at her notepad, covered her written questions with both hands, inhaled deeply, and blinked one of those exaggeratedly long blinks—as if she were breathing through her eyelids—then said, "I read somewhere that you were gang-raped the night Saddam Hussein invaded Kuwait."

I raised one eyebrow, which seemed to make her uneasy. In my peripheral view, Lena's lips turned up almost imperceptibly.

The woman continued, "I can only imagine the horror of that night, and I'm sorry to bring it up."

"What makes you think it's okay to ask me these things?"

Lena hesitated but faithfully translated.

The woman appeared exasperated. "You agreed to be interviewed. That's why I'm asking questions," she said, pausing to take another breath through her eyelids. "I had to go through two months of vetting just to have this hour with you. I provided all my questions to the authorities in advance," she added, almost desperately.

Lena repeated her words in Arabic but communicated something else with her eyes.

Finally I responded: "Ah, the authorities did not run them by me. Rest assured that I shall reprimand them accordingly." My sarcasm reduced her nearly to tears, which softened me. I added, "But I'll answer your question: No. I was *not* gang-raped the night Saddam invaded Kuwait."

She seemed disappointed, but moved on to ask how I became involved in the resistance. She called it "terrorism." She asked about my prison cell, which she called a "nice room," then qualified, "But I know it's still prison."

"Are you Jewish?" I asked.

She made another long blink. "I don't see how that matters."

"It matters."

"I'm here as a professional, not a religion."

"And yet most professionals wouldn't call this place a nice room," I said.

Her eyes bore into me. "Considering what you did, I'd say it was nicer than you might deserve. You wouldn't fare so well in any Arab country. They'd have flogged and hanged you by now."

She folded her notebook and rose. "I think I have all I need," she said, motioning to the guard to let them out.

The guard—who had been standing over us, ensuring that neither the Western woman nor the translator touched me or handed me any object—locked my security bracelets to the wall before opening the door.

The woman turned to me. "I just want you to know that my grandparents—"

"—survived the Holocaust," I finished her sentence.

Her eyes filled with contempt. "As a matter of fact, they did. And they taught me to always be fair. That's what I was trying to do here," she said.

Lena started to translate, but I interrupted. "That's not what you're doing here," I said in English with enough scorn to mask the indignity of being shackled to the wall. The guard ordered us to stop speaking and I was grateful, for it allowed me to have the last word. Such a small sliver of control meant everything—*everything*—to me.

Later came the whistle signaling that my next meal was being pushed through the slot. But as I approached the door, someone on the other side whispered, "Inside the bread."

I sat down with the tray, tore small pieces of the pita bread, and carefully peered into its pocket, mindful of the ceiling camera. There it was, a tightly folded paper wrapped in plastic. I waited until dark to open it and put it in one of my books, which I pretended to read when light came again.

Stop speaking to reporters. Israel is selling a story that Muslim men abused you your entire life, then forced you to join a terrorist group. They claim Israel saved you, and prison has given you a better life. You're the only prisoner who gets international visitors. They're allowed into your cell. That's unheard of! Think about it. They're publishing pictures of you in a clean cell with a lot of books to show that Israel is a benevolent nation, even to terrorists. Your family is well. They send their love. We are still fighting to get them a chance to visit. Eat this note.

I didn't need a signature to know it was from Jumana. This was the first indication I'd had that she was okay. I could barely remember her face, but I missed her. I wished she had written something about Bilal. Some news. Or just his name. Or simply the first letter of his name. *B is alive and well. B sends his love.* Or just *B*.

When it was dark again, I put the note in my mouth, chewed, and swallowed. I imagined how terrible I must look in those photos in the press. I am not allowed a mirror, but I knew my hair was frizzy without a blow-dryer. It hadn't yet turned gray as it is now, and I hadn't stopped caring about such matters. The fuzz over my lip hadn't been waxed and my eyebrows were bushy. I probably looked exactly how Westerners imagine a terrorist—unkempt, hairy, dark, ugly. But those weren't the photos that bothered me. It was the ones in the Arab press during my trial, taken in Kuwait all those years ago. I imagined my family seeing them. How much it must have hurt my mother.

But now even that no longer moves me. Nothing can move in confinement, not even the heart.

I didn't have visitors for a very long time after Lena and the Western woman left. My hair had grown nearly five centimeters when I saw the next human—a guard. She entered the Cube holding a notebook and two mechanical pencils. She could have just slipped them through the door slot, but she chose to enter the Cube, announcing herself over the speaker so that I could lock myself to the wall. I wondered if she was the one who had slipped me the note. She wasn't allowed to speak, but she smiled, I think, when she saw how excited I was by the delivery on my bed.

I had waged a long battle to gain these writing utensils. But now I wondered what to write. A letter? A story! A journal! Maybe poems? As soon as the metal door slammed shut, and I was unlocked from the wall, I picked up one pencil and opened the notebook.

I stare at the blank pages now, trying to tell my story—everything I confessed to Bilal and everything after. I want to tell it as storytellers do, with emotional anchors, but I recall emotions in name only. My life returns to me in images, smells, and sounds, but never feelings. I feel nothing.

DANCE, RUBY RIVER

I DON'T REMEMBER the first time I danced. Women of my generation were born dancing. It was just something we did when we gathered. We'd form a circle, clapping and singing as each of us entered the middle to roll our hips. But I knew early on, by the way people watched me, that the way I danced was enchanting.

When the music plays, my body moves as it wishes. I never tried to control anything. It was complete surrender to music and all the unseen, unknowable forces it inspired. I let rhythm rub against my body and wrap around my breath. Maybe that's what people saw, because dancing is the nearest I've ever come to true faith.

Eastern dance, what people who don't know better call "belly dancing," might look like controlled, orchestrated movement, but it's exactly the opposite. Our dance is about chaos and anarchy. It is the antithesis of control. It's about relinquishing power over one's body, bestowing autonomy on every bone, ligament, nerve, and muscle fiber. On every skin and fat cell. Every organ.

I suppose this is true of every form of native dance, but all I know are the rhythms of the Levant, Babylon, el Khaleej, and North Africa. This is the music that rooted in my body as it matured from infancy, then settled in my bones. The lyrics of Um Kulthum, the plaint of a ney, the melody of a *qanuun* or the rasp of an oud are the sounds of my life. They echo inside me, through time and with the stories those ancient instruments made. As much as I love the sounds of India—the complex resonance of the sitar or the high-pitched strings of a *tumbi*—or the deep percussion and multilayered rhythms of African drums and the piercing precision of a xylophone, though they move my body, they do not reach the depths from which music transports me, because they are the sounds of other peoples and stories I only heard as an adult.

Music is like spoken language, inextricable from its culture. If you don't learn a language early in life, its words will forever come out wrinkled and accented by another world, no matter how well you memorize or love the vocabulary, grammar, and cadences of a new language. This is why foreign "belly dancers" have always bothered me. The use of our music as a prop to wiggle and shimmy and jump around offends me.

Eastern music is the soundtrack of me, and dancing is the only nation I ever claimed, the only religion I comprehend. When I see women "belly dance" to music they do not understand, in clothes of a people they do not know—or worse, disdain—I feel they are colonizing me and all Arab women who are the keepers of our traditions and heritage.

My life began in a two-bedroom apartment in Hawalli, a Kuwait ghetto where Palestinian refugees settled after the Nakba. Although I grew up hearing stories of Palestine, I didn't get the politics, nor did I care to learn. Even though our father took us there every year to "renew our papers," Palestine remained the old country in my young mind, a distant place of my grandmother's generation.

In fourth grade, Gameela, an Egyptian classmate, taunted me once with "Palestinians are stupid. That's why the Jews stole your country." I yanked her to the ground by her braids and beat her up good. The school suspended me, entrenching my reputation as a troublemaker. It was one of the few times Sitti Wasfiyeh said she was proud of me. No one in school dared cross me after that.

I never told anyone, until I met Bilal, that I beat up Gameela precisely to get suspended in advance of national school testing. I was barely literate. More than anything, I feared being outed as dumb. Up until then, I had gotten by in school by cheating on tests, through my superior memorization skills, and by fighting. But then my brother, Jehad, began tutoring me when he advanced enough to be almost in the same grade as me. He did it in secret and told me often that I was "really smart." With his encouragement, I began to read poetry, and in time, I could recite some of the greatest and most erotic love stories in Arabic verse. It was through them that I found a command of the written word.

Mama kept a box of black-and-white photographs from her life in Haifa. Her family had been well-off, but European Jews stole everything when they conquered Palestine in 1948—right down to their furniture, books, and bank accounts. Her family became penniless overnight, then scattered to different corners of the world or died. She didn't like to talk about it. "What's the point of picking at scabs?" she'd say, except when I told her what Gameela had said. She called up Gameela's mama and told her she'd better tie up her loose Egyptian tongue, or she'd cut it out of her face.

"Woman, you better put your hands on your head when you talk about Palestine, or I'll put my shoe in your mouth," she yelled into the receiver. It thrilled me to hear my mother berate Gameela's mother, and I couldn't stop giggling.

My paternal grandmother, Sitti Wasfiyeh, Hajjeh Um Nabil, lived with us. Unlike Mama, she'd never really left her village in Palestine. Just as I do now in the Cube, my grandmother roamed Ein el-Sultan in her mind. She bored us with tales of her childhood and about people we didn't know. She was sure we would return someday.

"It's the oldest city in the world, you cow," she said to me. "Way long ago. Older than Jericho, even. If you were any good in school you'd know that." I looked it up later with Jehad's help, hoping to prove I was smart. "Sitti, I know Ein el-Sultan was established in 7000 BC."

"You don't think I know that?" Sitti said. "Maybe you should work on losing some weight. No one is going to marry a cow."

Sitti Wasfiyeh had moments of kindness too. Braiding my hair in grade school. Teaching me to roll grape leaves, carve zucchini, and bake bread. But she could be mean for no reason at times, which nearly always coincided with calls to her daughters, aunts I had only heard of who lived in Jordan. To make matters worse, my brother could do no wrong in Sitti Wasfiyeh's eyes, which made her insults all the more wounding. Mama would tell me not to be so sensitive: "She's an ornery old woman, what can we do? She doesn't mean any of it."

I gave it back to Sitti Wasfiyeh when I was fifteen and already believing I was bad. I was the leader of a gang that pulled pranks on teachers. I regularly stole candy from the corner store and one time let a boy kiss me on the lips. I back-talked adults and once even made Sitti Wasfiyeh cry.

"You're a mean old woman," I yelled. "That's why your daughters haven't asked you to live with them. It's not because they're moving, or their houses are too small, or whatever other lies they feed you. It's because you're a nasty old woman nobody wants around, and if you don't learn how to speak to us better, we're going to throw you out too. All three of us are crammed into one bedroom so you can have your own room. You should be kissing my mother's feet for what she has done for you. If it was up to me, I'd throw you out on the street. And you know very well your stupid daughters don't send us a dime. The next time you accuse my mother of taking your money, I might personally throw you the hell out." No one my age spoke to their elders in such a manner. I was bad.

Mama whacked me with her rubber slipper. "Don't you ever speak to your grandmother that way," she screamed, the stings of her slipper on my skin punctuating each word. "If your father, may God rest his soul, were here, he'd put stripes all over your body with his belt." I was glad my father wasn't around then. He probably would have done exactly that.

"How can you possibly defend her? She treats you even worse!" I cried.

My mother dropped her slipper, breathless from the effort. She didn't have much fight in her since Baba died. She took a deep breath, let it out slowly, and led me toward the veranda, but only after I apologized to Sitti Wasfiyeh, kissed her hand three times, and kept my mouth shut when she said, "You're like a wild animal. Not raised right."

Mama gently put her hand on my shoulder. "Let's sit outside and talk, *habibti*," she said. That's how it was with us. An argument or a whupping was over in seconds, and we were back to habibti and other love words.

"You have to understand. We're all she has in the world. Somewhere deep inside her, she knows what you say is true. That's why she's in there crying. But if she can pretend that I'm the reason her daughters don't answer her calls, or why they don't visit or ask her to live with them, then she never has to face the truth that her children have thrown her away. That's a terrible fate."

I listened, realizing I was hearing something from the silent depths of my mother. We were a family with secrets, things that lurked in the corners of our lives, unseen, unspoken, but felt in the texture of arguments, the extra length of a pause, the focus of a stare. For example, I didn't know until many years later that I was probably conceived before my parents married; my father asked for Mama's hand to avoid scandal and shame. I don't know if the rumor was true. But it might have been the reason we barely knew her family.

I met them when my maternal grandmother died in Syria, and we traveled to their refugee camp in Yarmouk for the funeral. Everyone was nice to me, my brother, and Mama. But I could tell, from the warmth and love they exchanged with each other but not with Mama, that she had somehow always been on the margins of her family. She didn't say, but I thought it was because of me or because her father, who died when they were all kids, had loved her most.

"I need a cigarette, habibti. Go inside. Open the third drawer. In the very back, there's a pack rolled up in socks."

Mama was always between a pack-a-day habit and "trying to quit" periods. I was the only girl among my friends who wasn't trying to sneak a smoke at that age. I had read in a comic book how Western companies were using tobacco to kill us slowly and take all our money and resources in the process. Refusing to smoke was an act of rebellion, and I liked to lecture others about the Western conspiracy, but I didn't want to spoil the moment with Mama, so I dutifully fetched her Marlboro stash as the tea boiled in the kitchen.

"May God bless you for all your days, my daughter," she said when I returned with the hot pot, two cups, a cut of fresh mint, sugar, and her stale pack of Marlboros. Normally we could see kids playing in the narrow street below our balcony, but it was laundry day, and our clothes hanging to dry obstructed the view. As Mama had taught me, I had hung my brother's jeans and shirts on the outer lines facing the street, then Mama's dishdashas. My pants, dresses, and shirts were on the middle lines, hidden from the lustful eyes of adolescent passersby, and finally, on the inner lines close to the edge of the balcony, we hung our underwear. Instead of looking out at the goings-on in the street, all I could see were our panties fluttering in the wind under a blue sky.

Pouring the tea, I said, "Mama, you have to stop her. She's awful."

"Sometimes I want to take her to Amman to live with her daughters, but it's not right." She lit the cigarette and sucked, closed her eyes, and lifted her chin with satisfaction, releasing a cloud of smoke from her mouth. "Your father, may God rest his soul, made me promise to care for his mother, no matter what." Promises to the dead were sacrosanct.

My mother would stand up to Sitti Wasfiyeh when she wanted, but most of the time she just let things be. Unlike me, Mama was never one for drama, unless it involved someone hurting her children, which was why she once threatened her mother-in-law with a kitchen knife. I was maybe seven years old and had just come in to eat before going back out to play, but Mama insisted I stay in. "Besides," she teased, "I think you might be getting too old to play with boys. They might think you're sweet on them."

I didn't hear what Sitti Wasfiyeh said, but my mother went to the kitchen and came back with a knife. "By God and His Prophet, I will cut your tongue if you ever utter such a thing again."

Later I asked her what Sitti Wasfiyeh had said. Mama shooed me away. "Mind your business and don't meddle in grown-up affairs," she said.

I stayed indoors that day thinking loud arguments would explode when my father returned from work, but when he arrived, Mama sent me to the neighbor's next door. Whatever was going on, it had to do with me. There was something that I, in particular, could not know. Of course, knowing what I do now, Sitti Wasfiyeh probably brought up the rumor of my birth and said something like "the apple doesn't fall far from the tree," or worse.

According to Mama, Baba wasn't much for housework. "I'm a man! What do you expect?" he'd say. But I know he wiped down our glass coffee table with Windex, which was fancier than using dish soap and indicated we were middle-class in the slums of Kuwait. "*Yalla*"—he'd motion for me to join him—"sing what you learned."

I'd begin the Fattooma song by Ghawwar el-Tousheh. On weekend mornings when Mama went to the neighbor's house for coffee, he'd teach me a few more lines of the lyrics, and I'd sing while he wiped down the coffee table. The Windex would form a rainbow across the glass, which amazed me. Baba said it was the magic of Windex. It only happened twice, but memory has somehow stretched it to the whole of my childhood, as if he and I sang and cleaned every day.

I wasn't allowed to sing the Fattooma song around Mama.

"Why?" I asked Baba.

"She really hates this song, and we'd both be in trouble if she knew you sing it."

I was torn between love for my father and loyalty to my mother. But I kept my mouth shut because that's the kind of person I am. I also knew, without knowing that I knew, that Fattooma was probably his new girlfriend's name, and that Mama knew it too.

I should recall more about my father. I was old enough to have accumulated memories by the time he died. For a while I invented memories of things I wished he'd done—brush my hair, teach me to fix cars, visit school on Parent Day, tell my stupid teachers to kiss his ass, swim together in the ocean, read to me, carry me on his shoulders, take my side against Mama on report card day, and put Sitti Wasfiyeh in her place when she said I was stupid as a donkey or when she made me wash my mouth out with soap for cursing. I imagined him being as fed up with Mama's Singer sewing machine as I was, insisting that she stop sewing our clothes and take us shopping in the Salmiya souq.

But all that is left of my father is a man who sings the Fattooma song and wipes the coffee table with Windex until he dies and fades into the looming absence of a face in the framed photo hanging on a wall in a long-abandoned Kuwait apartment in a country that abandoned us.

Mama was pregnant with me when Israel made her a refugee for the second time. After fleeing Haifa in 1948, she had made a home with my father in Sitti Wasfiyeh's ancestral village, Ein el-Sultan. Fleeing once more in June 1967 with only whatever they could carry, they walked more than eight kilometers to cross the River Jordan at the Allenby Bridge. When they got there, the bridge was overwhelmed with bodies and eventually collapsed just as Mama was about to cross. Some people fell and had to be rescued. Some didn't make it out. But people kept walking on the collapsed bridge, holding on to its cables and broken pieces as they waded through the water. Mama told me: "I just prayed to God as your father and I crossed, and I made a deal with the river. I said I'd name you after it if it didn't swallow any of us."

But calling me Jordan would have been too strange. That's how I got the name Nahr. *River.*

My father made the dangerous journey back into Palestine after he got us to safety in Jordan. Palestinians learned the first time in 1948 that leaving to save your life meant you would lose everything and could never go back. That's why Baba stayed alone in our empty house for months under curfew while Israel consolidated power over the whole of Palestine. To be alone in the eerie quiet of the emptied home, where he and his siblings had grown up amid the daily bustle of a large family, must have been painful. Still, he stayed and got a *hawiyya*; he could thenceforth remain in Palestine as a "foreign resident" in his own home. He said it was better than being a refugee.

Baba joined us as soon as he could. But his long absence had fractured our family, and by the time I was born, my parents had already made their way to Kuwait, where my father was fucking the first of many girlfriends. Her name was Yaqoot and that's the name he recorded on my birth certificate—not Nahr—without consulting my mother. He was probably with Yaqoot the night Mama went into labor, probably a little drunk when he reached the hospital and still basking in the glow of a romantic evening when he impulsively named me after his new lover, perhaps underestimating Mama's intuition and rage.

Yaqoot is an unusual name for Palestinians. One finds it more among Iraqis, which is why I figure my father's lover was a daughter of Babylon. It means "ruby," and everyone agrees it's a rich and resonant Arabic name. But when Mama saw the birth certificate, she screamed and cried and hit my father. She smashed all the plates in our house, hurling a few at him as he ducked left and right. He let her vent, apologized, swore Mama was the only woman he loved, and promised he wouldn't do it again. They probably made love afterward, had a good run together for a while, then the whole scenario was repeated with another woman.

When she was pregnant the second time, Mama threatened to

kill my father if he named the baby after one of his "whores," but she didn't have to worry when she birthed a boy. My father named him Wasfy, after his mother, Sitti Wasfiyeh, which was just as bad as far as Mama was concerned. Needless to say, Mama never used the names recorded on our birth certificates. She kept her promise to the river and called me Nahr. My brother Wasfy was Jehad, a name Mama chose, which became yet another point of contention between her and Sitti Wasfiyeh.

Only my family and some administrators at my school knew my real name was Yaqoot, which had an element of fate to it, because when the Americans ousted Saddam, Kuwaiti police asked about someone named Nahr, but my identification card said Yaqoot.

My brother wasn't as lucky. People called him by either name, or both, Wasfy Jehad. When the Kuwaiti police went on the hunt for Palestinians to exact revenge because Yasser Arafat had sided with Saddam, they knew who they were looking for.

Jehad was only three years old when Baba died of a heart attack in the arms of another woman. Mama lied and said Baba was home when it happened. She made up an elaborate tale that shifted each time she told it. "He was wearing the red flannel pajamas I bought for him," she would say one moment. The next, he'd be in the green pajamas or just his underwear. In that version she had to dress him quickly before the ambulance came. Mama was a terrible liar, but the truth was too humiliating, even though everyone knew, and Mama knew they knew. The lie wasn't just to protect her and us from shame. I think she wanted to protect Baba too. Despite everything, Mama loved my father very much. And he loved her, in his own way.

Once, in the heat of a fight over money (it was usually about money), Sitti Wasfiyeh blamed Mama for the death of my father, her only son. "If you had been a better wife, he wouldn't have had to go to other women," Sitti Wasfiyeh had said casually as she ate the food Mama had prepared.

"If you had raised a man who knew how to keep his dick in his pants and spent his money on his family instead of on whores, we wouldn't be having this argument," Mama fired back. That night, I heard her on the balcony apologizing to my dead father for what she had said. "I forgive you, my love. I miss you," she spoke softly to the ether.

———

Palestinians who had been chased out of their homes in Jerusalem, Haifa, Yafa, Akka, Jenin, Bethlehem, Gaza, Nablus, Nazareth, Maj-dal, and every major Palestinian city found a place in Kuwait. The oil boom offered opportunity to build a new life there. Although Kuwait never allowed us more than temporary residency—making it clear we were always guests—Palestinians prospered and had a major hand in building Kuwait as the world knows it now. We participated and contributed in nearly every sector of life, but we remained an underclass.

I knew that, but it didn't matter. I loved Kuwait. It was my home, and I was a loyal subject of the royals. I lined up every day of school with the other students to sing the national anthem. I sang with passion and allegiance to Kuwait's successive ruling emirs. I grieved when Emir Sabah Salem el-Sabah died in 1977. And every February 25, we partied like mad to celebrate Kuwait's Independence Day as if it were our own.

I loved everything about Kuwaitis—their delicate Khaleeji *thobes*, their *matchboos* with browned chicken and hot sauce, their *diwaniyas*, pearl diving traditions, and tribal ways. I even taught myself to speak their dialect and could dance Khaleeji "better than their best." That's what someone told me. In eighth grade, I was even selected to be part of the official troupe that danced on a televised celebration for the royals during Independence Day. But unlike the rest of the group, I wasn't included the following year because people complained, insisting that such an honor should be reserved for Kuwaiti kids.

"They don't like seeing Palestinians excel at anything," Mama said to make me feel better, but she only managed to annoy me. I didn't appreciate her speaking ill about Kuwaitis; but for her, everything came down to being Palestinian, and the whole world was out to get us. It wasn't until I had survived time, war, and prison that I understood why.

"You see how the whole country is eating zeit-o-za'atar, trying to be like us?" She laughed big. I could see the fillings in her teeth. Now, alone in the Cube, I laugh at the memory, and it's as if the silver fillings I remember are my own. I tell Mama how much I loved it when she guffawed like that. The guards are accustomed to the conversations I have with the walls. I know I'm alone here. I'm not delusional. But the way memory animates the past is more real than the present. I see and feel and hear Jehad, Sitti Wasfiyeh, Mama, Baba. Most of all, I am with Bilal here.

<hr />

There were no cell phones or computers when I was a kid, and television offered just two channels—one in Arabic, the other in English with subtitles. Programming started in the evening and lasted until midnight. Both channels opened and closed with readings from the Quran, which we kids waited through impatiently before we could watch cartoons (Tom and Jerry or Road Runner), followed by soap operas. Once a week, each channel showed a movie, heavily censored to remove any hint of physical intimacy, which meant I never saw images of lovers even holding hands. It was obvious where the cuts were made. One moment actors would be looking deeply into each other's eyes, leaning in for a kiss; next thing they'd be standing farther apart than when they started. The film would spasm, which encouraged us to fill in the cut with a kiss or more. But I wasn't even good at that. I could only imagine what I already knew, which was simply a peck on the lips, until Suad Marzouq informed us, a group of stunned fourteen-year-olds, that adults kissed with their tongues. We thought she was lying, but we practiced on each other anyway. By the time I was sixteen, I thought I knew everything there was to know about love. My friends and I had managed to get our hands on one or two dirty magazines. Once we even snagged a VHS porn video.

I was a natural flirt and got a lot of attention from boys, but I never had a real boyfriend like some of my friends. They would meet their boyfriends in secret, just to hold hands in the park. We thought we were bold and daring, but the most any of us did was kiss a boy. I believed what my world taught—that God intended one man for me, and my life would begin when I found him. My body would turn to fire at the thought of being married and making babies, just like the actors in the porn film.

I was seventeen when I first met Mhammad. He was twenty-five. He lived in the homeland but was in Kuwait visiting his aunt, Um Naseem, our neighbor one floor up. We had all seen him on the news when he was released from an Israeli prison a month earlier, and my friends were envious that he was now living in our building.

"Is he as handsome as he looks on TV?" one asked. I hadn't seen him in person yet, but I thought he looked ordinary and old on TV.

"I hear he's looking for a wife after being in prison for seven years," another said.

"Nahr, can we hang out at your house?" asked a third.

"What's wrong with you? Did the world run out of boys our own age?" I shooed them away.

They looked at me as if I were crazy.

Mhammad Jalal AbuJabal was a bona fide hero, a guerrilla fighter responsible for resistance operations. My friends said he was captured after killing two Zionist soldiers single-handedly after they killed two of his friends, martyrs, God rest their souls.

"He killed one of them with a knife, then took his gun and shot the other one," they explained.

"So?"

"He's not a boy. He's a man. A famous freedom fighter," Sabah said, sucking through her teeth, mocking my ignorance. I hated when she did that, especially in front of the other girls.

Sabah lived in the building next to ours, and we had known each other as long as I could remember. Ours was a friendship forged from rivalry and jealousy as much as from love and familiarity. We knew each other's secrets, had history, and stuck up for each other against outsiders, but we consistently tried to outdo each other and sometimes competed for the attention of the same boys.

"He did some badass stuff. Since you don't care about what happens to Palestine, I guess it doesn't matter to you. But most of us appreciate what he sacrificed for the struggle," Sabah continued.

Sabah didn't know shit about Palestine. None of us did, except sound bites from the news and conversations of adults who used to live there. Truth be told, we didn't care either. We were daughters of Kuwait, even though we could never be citizens.

"Eat shit, Sabah. Maybe he'll marry you. Give it a try!" I said.

Once I realized that Sabah was interested in this new man, I wanted him too. I was prettier and a better dancer, even though she wasn't bad looking and was smarter than me. She played the guitar, which annoyed me because she could captivate anyone when she'd start on it. Luckily, she was insecure and shy and mostly played in private or just around our close friends.

Over the next few days, I pieced together Mhammad's story from a conversation among Sitti Wasfiyeh, Mama, and the neighbors. Mhammad came from a well-known family with vast land holdings, though most of it had already been confiscated by the Zionist entity—that's how people referred to Israel, like it'll go away if we don't say the name. They had captured and tortured him for eight days before he finally signed a confession, typed up in Hebrew, which he couldn't read, stating that he had been one of three men who attacked three soldiers, killing two of them. The surviving soldier hadn't seen him during the attack, but there were other witnesses who, also under torture, confessed to seeing him near the site of the assault. He was tried in a military court and sentenced to life in prison. They said he could get a reduced sentence if he gave up his younger brother, Bilal, who had escaped to Jordan. But he maintained that his brother had nothing to do with the killings; that Bilal's departure had been mere coincidence. In the end, he had confessed to the murder of two Israeli soldiers, blowing up a military supply warehouse a month earlier, and plotting to carry out attacks on civilians. Seven years later, they released him in a strange prisoner swap brokered by Israel's recent darling, Hosni Mubarak of Egypt. That's when he turned up in Kuwait.

No one believed Bilal had nothing to do with that fateful day. He had been imprisoned already at fifteen for protesting a Jewish-only settlement and was gaining a reputation as a natural leader. In exile, while attending university, Bilal agitated for resistance. Israel wanted him badly. They tried and failed to assassinate or capture him. Ultimately, it was Bilal himself who offered a deal for his surrender—Mhammad's freedom in exchange for his. To everyone's surprise, Israel agreed. It became clear that Bilal was a bigger prize to them than most had realized. I suppose Israel knew what I would learn years later—that nothing in Mhammad's confession was actually true.

To ensure that Israel would not rearrest his brother, Bilal demanded that Mhammad be released to the Red Cross and transferred to Lebanon, Kuwait, Jordan, Tunisia, or any Arab nation that would have him, except Egypt, because Egypt might hand him back to Israel.

Mhammad went through several countries before landing at his aunt's home in Kuwait. We didn't know why. Some said it was the best place not to be rearrested after Israel got Bilal, because Kuwait was a real haven for Palestinians. Some claimed the deal meant he could never return to Palestine, and no other place would have him. Others said he was in Kuwait for a job offer. Sabah was sure he came to find a wife. "I heard his mama in Palestine is anxious to see him married," she said.

But I know now that going from place to place is just something exiles have to do. Whatever the reason, the earth is never steady beneath our feet.

—————

I flirted shamelessly with Mhammad that spring of 1985. It was a game at first, an unspoken competition between Sabah and me. When he showed no interest, I obsessed and stalked him long enough to engineer repeated "chance" encounters in the stairwell of our building. He was handsome indeed, and I found myself constantly thinking about him despite our age difference.

"Congratulations, Nahr." Sabah rolled her eyes. "You said hi to him in the stairwell. That's groundbreaking."

I enjoyed what I thought was Sabah's envy. "More than just hi," I said, and added that he was planning to attend an upcoming wedding party in our neighborhood. "He said he wanted to see me dance," I lied.

Our friends squealed, but Sabah said nothing.

My plan worked. Even though my mother made me stop dancing at the wedding after a few songs—"It's too much, Nahr!" she said—I knew I had caught his attention. He couldn't take his eyes off me that night. I don't remember much else from that summer, except that I told my friends I had found the man God intended for me.

Mhammad and I met regularly, at the beach, parks, and malls. My friends, even Sabah, covered for me with Mama. He told me stories about Palestine much different from my grandmother's and parents'. In his version, there was a nightlife for young people, where they danced and partied, went to cafés, parks, and clubs. Palestinians were still allowed to access the Mediterranean beach back then, and we talked about our shared love of the ocean. He wanted to know about my life. He was not fond of the desert heat and was struggling to adjust in Kuwait. He said he would have left weeks ago had he not met me. "Your friendship means the world to me," he said. He seemed vulnerable, and his need for me made me believe that I loved him. I told him so. Months later, he and his aunt's family were in our home, asking for my hand.

I fantasized about fairy-tale love and sex, about having my own house, children, and a job like modern women—maybe as a smartly dressed secretary like the ones on the covers of women's magazines. I was preoccupied with finding the latest appliances to suit the life I imagined. The kind of semimanual washer at our house—where we fed each item through rollers to squeeze out the water—would not do. Some people even had dishwashers that cleaned, rinsed, and dried their dishes. I wanted one, and Mhammad promised I'd get it. I imagined being the envy of all my friends.

Sitti Wasfiyeh was delighted, although suspicious about the appliances. "I don't trust a machine to clean dishes. It won't scrub things clean. You'll get bugs in your house. I'll never visit you," she warned.

Mama counseled me not to rush into making such a big decision. She thought Mhammad too old for me, and admitted, years later, that she almost forbade the marriage, but the force of my enthusiasm and joy made her doubt her instincts. "You had the biggest personality in the family, and without realizing it, we all deferred to you," she told me. I thought Mama's reservations were the misplaced concern of a woman whose marriage hadn't worked out, and I rationalized that my story was beginning differently from hers.

My brother, Jehad, was uncomfortable in the role of man of the house, which tradition obliged him to accept, even though he was only eleven. "Whatever. I don't care, Nanu. Just get it over with one way or another. I don't think I can stand another one of these courtship formalities!" he said at first. Later, when he realized I would be moving out of our apartment, he tried to assert himself.

"As the man in this family, I insist that Nanu continue to live here. She can visit her husband, but she cannot live with him," he declared on the eve of our engagement. Our guests were amused. "How sweet," someone said. He had an asthma attack that evening and I slept in his bed through the night, letting him cry on my chest, promising I would never be far, and would always be there when he needed me.

Jehad wasn't really the only man in the family. My mother's brothers showed up to fulfill their social duties to represent me in the formal conversations about my dowry and other practicalities of marriage. My family didn't believe in the excesses some people demanded, but they couldn't just give me away for nothing. They didn't want to break my young suitor, but I wasn't some nobody who wasn't worth a decent dowry. Mama said we had to consider what the young man could afford. "But we need to make sure you will be cared for. So his family must show us they're serious," she said.

Before the negotiations were settled, Mhammad's aunt dropped a bombshell that almost unraveled everything. "We expect the wedding will cost at least eight thousand dinars, and we're prepared to pay ten thousand. But we have to wait for a while."

"A while?" Mama asked.

"His brother, Bilal, was just imprisoned, and his mother cannot travel to Kuwait for a wedding, because Israel might confiscate her home if she leaves. It would be wrong and disrespectful for the eldest son to hold a wedding celebration under these circumstances," Mhammad's aunt said.

It was hard to argue with her logic, but they also understood the humiliation I could suffer getting legally married but forgoing a wedding party. Mama suggested we postpone the marriage, but the ultimate decision was mine. In the end, I went for one thousand dinars, a gold *shabka* worth two thousand dinars, and a two-thousand-dinar *mo'akhar*. Mhammad's family also rented and furnished the marital apartment, and set up a joint account with ten thousand dinars, to be spent on our wedding in a few months, when Hajjeh Um Mhammad, my mother-in-law, could travel to Kuwait, *enshallah*.

I was satisfied. He loved me. Forgoing an immediate wedding party was the price of marrying a national hero. Our job as women was to sacrifice, and I was a woman now. I imagined a beautiful life for us in Kuwait. We would make memories on the beaches and in the desert, on vacations in Cairo, Amman, Beirut, Damascus, and Baghdad. I would take our children to Palestine to visit our families

there. "It's a sacrifice I'm willing to make for the man I love," I declared, and refused to let Mama talk me out of the marriage. Then
I listened impatiently as she instructed me to call her if Mhammad
was too rough on our first night together.

"It's normal for it to hurt the first time," she said, as I rummaged
through the new clothes from my dowry. I didn't dare tell her that I
already knew about sex from the porn video.

"Should I wear the black one or the white one?" I asked her,
holding up two negligees.

Her face reddened. "Whichever one you like most," she said, and
left the room.

We were married by an imam, our marriage certificate wit-
nessed by my uncle and by Jamil, Mhammad's dearest friend in Kuwait. Mhammad smiled and squeezed my hand.

It's hard to remember suppressed disappointment, especially
when I didn't acknowledge it at the time, not even to myself. I had
always dreamed of a wedding, hundreds of eyes upon me with love
or envy, or maybe lust. But there was none of that. Just a muted celebration, a small gathering, some cake, and a cute dress—this event
a placeholder for the grand wedding I believed was still to come. Or
maybe I just pretended I did.

———

In hindsight I see that Tamara's ghost was there all along. The first
time I heard the name was on our wedding night. Our families delivered us to the threshold of our new apartment, their faces fixed
in the kind of nervous happiness that comes with anticipating
some profound transformation of one's child. His aunt and family
and my family showered us with hugs and congratulations. Before
they left, Mama hugged me one more time, whispering in my ear,

"A thousand congratulations, my love. May God protect and guide you always. And remember what I said."

Alone in our beautifully furnished new apartment, I had expected—hoped—he would push me against the wall with passionate kisses, his hands hungrily finding their way up my thighs, the way I'd seen in the illicit movie. Instead, we turned to each other, smiling awkwardly. I asked if he'd like me to make us a drink, and he nodded. As we sipped tea on our new sofa, he pulled me to him.

"We don't have to do anything if you don't want to," he said.

It startled me that he would say such a thing. I immediately blamed myself for being too demure. I look back now on so many moments in my life when I instinctively took responsibility for the actions and feelings of those around me.

"Oh, but I want to," I said. "Wait one moment." I got up and went into the bedroom, where I had already unpacked my clothes days before, opened my special drawer of "marital wear," and chose the white negligee, because I had read in a magazine that men preferred women who were both pure and sexy. I freshened my makeup, admired the full glory of my womanhood in the mirror, and was ready. Fire ignited my body as I ran my hands along the curves from my breasts to my hips. A sinful smile crossed my face as I emerged to stand before him, ready to be devoured by my husband, who would surely be overcome by his great fortune to have such a beautiful bride.

He smiled, turning his eyes away, as if embarrassed for me. My smile, curves, fire, beauty, and sexiness melted into a naked blob of shame. Tears filled my eyes. I held them back as best as I could, but he must have noticed. When he finally approached me, it was with sympathy.

So it was that the first time I was touched sexually was with hands of pity. He wiped my tears away and kissed my cheeks. He said I was beautiful. I kissed him back, but I could not recapture the heat of moments past. He led me into the bedroom, turned out the lights, and laid me gently on the bed before he went into the bathroom. I waited, a confused spectator to my own life, until he returned, slipping next to me in the darkness. His erection and nakedness awakened my body to move in complement to his. He stopped to reposition himself a couple of times, clumsily, as if executing a chore. Whatever had stirred in me was gone, and I resolved to do the best I could to get through the night, sure that I had done something wrong. Finally he slid inside of me, and I began a performance, determined to overcome his disappointment and make him love and want me.

Moaning the way I had seen actors do in that old porn tape, I faked pleasure through the discomfort of being penetrated for the first time. I was waiting for it to feel good, hoping nothing was wrong with me, wanting it to be over, wondering if this was what it would always be like. Thinking about having a baby. Whether my body was beautiful. And if I was doing it right. Mama had said it might hurt, and she was right. But I thought it would feel special and sweet too. I gritted my teeth and clenched my fists. He was mostly quiet, sometimes instructing me to relax. He struggled, unable to keep an erection until he turned me on my stomach and entered me from behind. I had seen this in the porn video too, and tried to mimic what the actress had done. I was in pain as he began to breathe harder and moved faster inside of me. Finally he whispered, "Tamara!" and collapsed and rolled off.

I woke up a few hours later to find him naked on the balcony, crying softly to an indifferent moon, a cigarette burning between his fingers. I went back to bed quietly, knowing his tears had something to do with the name he had uttered tenderly into the air above my back. Alone in our bed, with my head under the sheets, I whispered the name to myself: "Tamara." But sound lodged in my throat, and I swallowed it back whole, so now Tamara lived in me too.

———

Mhammad and I both worked. He managed a local restaurant, and I did light bookkeeping for a hair salon where I also threaded eyebrows and did manicures. I've always been good at stuff like that, and having a job made me feel like a modern woman. But in truth, marriage was not what I'd imagined. I'm sure Mhammad and I shared many tender times. But I can only remember one. We had gone to the beach together and lain in the sun, then gone to the home of some friends to drink alcohol they made. Jugs and jugs of horrible-tasting dark liquid. They thought my aversion was cute and encouraged me to give it a chance. I couldn't get used to the taste, but I went along, wanting to feel as sophisticated as the other wives appeared to be, and eventually I liked the way it made me feel sexy and worldly. Mhammad said he was happy that I wasn't up-tight about drinking. He said modern women smoked and drank. But I still refused to smoke and repeated what I had read in the comic book years ago about a Western conspiracy to kill us with cigarettes. They laughed the way adults do when a small child says something silly. Marriage had made me smaller.

We ate and danced and laughed, first at the beach and later with his friends. My shoulders were slightly sunburned, and Mhammad rubbed aloe on my skin. We were tired, barely able to stand by the time we finally made it to our apartment. I thought we would go right to sleep, but Mhammad insisted we finish off the night with what little was left of his own contraband liquor stash. He took out his oud and began strumming, tuning it first. My hips took hold of the music and made love to its notes. I was swimming in the joy of it, took off my top and brassiere until I was dancing naked, only a scarf around my hips. He kept playing, I dancing, neither of us wanting to stop. Eventually we succumbed to the alcohol and exhaustion, and later we made love. I learned that evening that we could love each other best if we were drunk. But even then, on that fine day, he didn't look at me, flipping me onto my stomach, and I knew he was making love to Tamara, not me.

I tried to duplicate the closeness of that night on other occasions, encouraging him to drink at home with me and play his music. But we'd just flounder through the awkwardness until we went to sleep drunk and disappointed.

The next months are a blur of a few images and sounds, mostly arguments, followed by tears and a slammed front door. Like my father, he'd come back in the middle of the night, telling me he had been at the coffeehouse with his friend Jamil. But unlike my father, Mhammad did not love his wife. He did not want to be with me and did not enjoy touching me. And in time, I didn't want him either, but not before something tender inside of me hardened.

I was nineteen when my husband walked out. It was not a fight, nor was it the first time I'd accused him of leaving to go find his precious Tamara. But this time he left and didn't return, not even to collect his things. He didn't show up at his job, and I spent the first week of his absence searching for him in hospitals and police stations. Jamil, Mhammad's best friend in Kuwait, didn't know where he had gone either.

Jamil's face was like nothing I had ever seen on a man. He looked devastated, as if he were the one who had lost his spouse.

"I believe he's made his way back to Palestine, maybe to look for . . ." Jamil hesitated. His eyes welled up. "Tamara. He went to Tamara, I think."

My heart sank. There was that name again—a name with no face, voice, or story.

"He told you about Tamara?" I asked. "Do you know her? Who is she? Where is she?"

Jamil looked away. "I'm sorry, Nahr. I hope he will at least give you a divorce so you can, enshallah, remarry and not live in limbo."

Divorce? I hadn't even considered the possibility until Jamil said the word.

I have revisited that moment with Jamil many times. Knowing what I do now, I see in his face what was not evident to me then. I know now the meaning of Jamil's tears, the secret in the furrows of his brow. Tamara meant something to him too.

———

I met Um Buraq in the wreckage of my marriage. I was at the wedding of a former classmate, who was a distant relative of hers. I didn't know this classmate well and only went because Sabah begged me. "If you don't want to leave the house for your own good, then do it for me. I really want to go, but I'm too shy to go alone," she told me.

"Liar. Lots of our friends are going."

"Well, you're the most popular, and everyone will want to see you dance. It'll give me status if we go together."

"Still a liar." I stared at her, half smiling. She knew me well enough to know that I had already given in. And I knew her well enough to know that she was sincere. Sabah was truly sorry that my marriage was over.

"Great! It's settled. I'll pick you up in the morning. We'll get a scrub at the *hammam*, then we'll get lunch, get our hair done—"

"No! I'll go to the wedding, but I'm not going through a long salon day too. It's not like I'm part of their family," I protested.

"It's not for the wedding, Nahr! You look terrible. And you smell!"

It was the middle of the afternoon and I was still in my nightgown. My hair was an unwashed, frizzy mess. I hadn't bathed in days.

"Fine. Since you're paying!"

For many years, I have wondered what my life would have been had I not agreed to go to that wedding. It was the first time I'd been outside the house in weeks. I had taken too much time off from work and expected to be fired soon.

Sabah and I passed the day getting groomed and pampered. The steam and hard scrubbing of a Moroccan hammam reawakened my skin. I felt renewed, reinvented by water. We lay side by side through the scrubs, massages, and body oiling. We got facials, manicures, and pedicures. Our hair was blown out and styled. And after we ate lunch, we took a nap and went back for makeup, then got dressed and headed to the wedding.

I don't remember much about that evening except that the more I danced, the less my heart hurt. The music was mostly pop Khaleeji, Egyptian, and Lebanese. But they played some of the classics with a *takht* orchestra and some instrumental *taqseem*. There were enough of us from the Levant that they even played a *jafra*, and we lit up the dance floor, stomping out a high-stepping *dabke*. I dragged the bride into the middle as we dabke'd around her, and she liked that. I only stopped dancing when the DJ paused for the women of both families to exchange compliments and declare what an honor it was to give away and to receive the bride.

An older Kuwaiti woman sat down at our table and squeezed into a chair next to me, introducing herself simply as a relative of the bride.

"It's a good thing Khaleeji weddings are segregated. All these women would have torn you to pieces if you were dancing like that in front of their husbands. Palestinian weddings are mixed, right?" she asked.

"Usually. But it depends on the family. Some are more traditional and keep things separate. But usually they're mixed. Except for the henna night and sometimes the *zaffa*."

"Does your husband let you dance at mixed Palestinian weddings?"

I hesitated, unsure if I could still claim to have a husband. "He doesn't mind."

"I hear your husband is a Palestinian hero," the woman said.

It was the way she said it, like she knew something. I nodded and turned away.

"Pardon me for being nosy," she said. "I tend to run off my mouth, but I mean no harm. I'm sorry if I offended you."

"What did you say your name was?"

"Um Buraq. It's nice to meet you, Yaqoot."

It seemed this bitch knew a few things about me. My legal name wasn't a secret, but not many people knew it.

I stared her down.

"Oh! There I go again, running off at the mouth. I know what you're thinking. You're wondering how I know your name. I'm sorry. I was intrigued watching you dance. I asked, and the bride told me."

I didn't respond, unsure what to make of her.

She smiled. "I know I'm older than you, but I am just trying to strike up a friendship. A few of us are going to finish out the night at another party when this one breaks up. I wanted to see if you'd like to join us."

To my twenty-year-old eyes, she looked ancient, but I know now that she was barely forty. "The wedding party will go on well past midnight. Who is even still awake at that hour?" I asked.

I'll never forget her reaction. Her lips widened more than

seemed possible, expanding over large teeth with a prominent gap that was off center from her nose, and she laughed—a frightening, high-pitched cackle. "Oh, darling! A whole part of Kuwait comes alive only after midnight," she said. I must have recoiled, because she closed her enormous mouth and stopped laughing.

"Here, take my pager number in case you change your mind." She handed me a card. It surprised me she had a pager. Only doctors and businesspeople used them. I thought maybe she was someone important, and that changed my attitude. I accepted the card with gratitude and gave her my home number.

"Why's an old woman giving you her pager number? It's weird," Sabah said, watching Um Buraq walk away.

Going to that wedding got me out of the house and finally helped me create a new rhythm in my life. Or rather, I just reverted to the way things were before my brief marriage, as if it had never happened. I stayed in our marital apartment as long as I could, pretending Mhammad was away on business whenever the landlord came to collect the rent, trying to hold out as long as I could in case he decided to return, or at least send money. After two months the landlord's wife told me the whole building knew my husband had walked out on me and said I had better pay up or be hauled out by the police.

Mama and I went with Um Naseem, Mhammad's aunt, to withdraw money from the joint account they had set up for our wedding, only to find that Mhammad had emptied it months ago. He left me nothing. Um Naseem was deeply apologetic and gave me a few hundred dinars, which I knew she couldn't afford. Then Hajjeh Um Mhammad, my mother-in-law, called me from Palestine. She cried through the phone and promised to help me however she could. I know it broke her heart too. I wouldn't accept her money, because I knew she had already sold so much of her inheritance to pay legal fees and Israeli fines just to keep her home. She was a widow living alone, and I wasn't going to add to her burdens. She sent a thousand dinars anyway, and Um Naseem insisted I take it. I didn't tell Mama at first because she would have made me use the money to pay back rent. But I was being evicted and didn't want to stay in that apartment anyway. I didn't share Mama's moral sensibilities and was happy to rip off the landlord. I even broke the handle on the bathroom fixture on purpose.

Jehad and Mama helped me move in the middle of the night. Mama made me leave the furniture in lieu of rent. She wouldn't accept that I could just skip out on paying, because "stealing is *haram.*" She said God would punish me eventually for it, as if being an abandoned bride when I was barely twenty wasn't punishment enough. It turned out that my nice appliances weren't even mine. Mhammad had been renting them from the landlord. I'd have to go back to hand-washing the dishes and using the semimanual washing machine. But I took comfort in imagining the landlord's face when he saw the broken bathroom fixture.

Before long, I had a new job as a clerk at a private school, and my life continued as it had been before I got married. I still threaded eyebrows on the side. Occasionally I did makeup and nails for weddings and partygoers. The familiarity made me wonder sometimes if my marriage had not just been a dream. Mhammad slowly faded from my thoughts. I might have put him out of my mind completely had not Sitti Wasfiyeh reminded me occasionally that I'd failed to keep a husband for even one year; or had not the inevitable question of why I wasn't pregnant yet come up when I ran into someone I hadn't seen in a while. Sabah was usually with me when this happened, and she would intercede.

"This is the 1980s. A woman doesn't have to have kids right away," she'd say, or "Nahr is a modern woman. She doesn't want children just yet."

Sabah had my back, especially when it came to outsiders. So I trusted her when she confirmed my unease about Um Buraq, and I didn't return the old woman's call when she left a message on our machine at the apartment shortly before I was evicted. I thought Um Buraq was just overbearing (though intriguing), but Sabah detected scandal.

"Good thing you're not at that number anymore," Sabah said. "You know I don't like repeating things like this, but I heard that her husband married a second wife because she can't have kids. She goes by Um Buraq to have a veneer of respectability at her age. But since her husband doesn't visit her much anymore, there's no one around to keep her in line. I heard she sleeps with other men. *Istaghfar Allah!*"

"Well, of course! How else is she going to cool her fires?" I joked. I had heard those rumors too, but that's what made Um Buraq interesting. Sabah shoved me good-naturedly.

"What?" I protested, and assumed the wisdom reserved for women who've actually fucked before. "Someday you will know that bliss," I said, pretending my experience with sex had been anything but traumatizing.

I remained curious about Um Buraq. The unapologetic confidence she exuded, despite her compromised standing as an abandoned first wife, made me respect her. Somehow she got our family's telephone number and left a message with my mother. Sabah was unusually harsh because I planned to call back.

"People are already gossiping about you because of your lousy husband. Why would you consort with someone like Um Buraq?

She's also not even a native. She's Iraqi but pretends she's Kuwaiti because her husband is," Sabah said.

"How do you know they're gossiping unless you've participated in the gossip? And what does her being Iraqi have to do with anything?" I shot back.

"Come on, Nahr. You know I'm just trying to look out for you," she said, and I did. But I hung up on her anyway. Usually Sabah and I would reconcile within a day or two after an argument. But that would not happen this time. It would be a long time before we rekindled our friendship, because I decided that day to call Um Buraq. I didn't care if the rumors about her were true. I thought she would understand me; that she would know how it felt to be a discarded woman.

UM BURAQ

HERE IN THE Cube, I contemplate every decision I made. Turning to Um Buraq stands out as pivotal in altering the course of my life.

"Well, well. What a nice surprise, and great timing," Um Buraq said. She was going to a party with friends that evening, and she'd love it if I could come. I said I'd like to but couldn't. "My family wouldn't believe a wedding could go on that late," I said.

"Don't worry. You'll stay with me. All my girls do," Um Buraq said. Had I been more sophisticated, less naïve—had I been smart, prudent, more like Sabah—I might have wondered what she meant by "all my girls."

I asked what I should wear. "Something sexy," she said.

"Is it a mixed party?" I asked.

She chuckled. "Yes, it's mixed."

I assumed it would be mostly couples, since that was the only kind of late-night mixed party I had ever been to.

"I'm not comfortable being at parties with couples," I said. "Will there be other single people?"

Then came her enormous laugh. Even through the phone, it was shocking. I imagined the big teeth, the wide gap, the fat lips. She realized I was starting to back out and immediately said, "You have nothing to worry about. I'm going without a husband, aren't I?"

———

"I'm glad you're making new friends and moving on with your life," Mama said. But Sitti Wasfiyeh warned, "People are going to talk. Someone in your position shouldn't be staying outside of the home."

"Leave her alone," my mother said. "All she does is work. At the salon, at the school. Sabah is her only friend. She needs to live her life." I still hear Mama's words in my head.

Jehad was on his way out to play football when Um Buraq's driver beeped the horn under our balcony. He and I descended the stairs together, and he glimpsed Um Buraq, who was dressed in a traditional black abaya in the passenger seat. "You're hanging out with old Kuwaiti women now?" he teased, and went on his way as I walked to her car. I was surprised to see two other women in the backseat when I got in. We exchanged greetings, and Um Buraq introduced us. Their names were "Susu" and "Fifi." I could tell from their accents that Susu was Lebanese and Fifi was Egyptian. They were my age and quite beautiful.

"We have to find a good name for you too," Um Buraq said.

"What do you mean?"

At a traffic light, she turned to me. "Pick a name other than Yaqoot," she said.

"Almas," I blurted out spontaneously. Diamond. I have thought much about that decision to choose another name. Was I making a commitment to something? To a rebellion, perhaps. A rejection of the script to achieve a respectable life—modesty, a husband, children, social status, money? Was I wanting to try life on the margins of all that was unnaturally proper? And if so, why? Was it the excitement? A desire for relevance? Attention? Unfettered sexuality? Or maybe something less interesting. I had already been rejected and abandoned by my husband before I was twenty. I hadn't even had a proper wedding, which only cheapened me in the eyes of others and intensified their scorn. Maybe I turned to Um Buraq because I thought she could understand the shock and heartache of my fall from grace.

Um Buraq beamed and raised her eyebrows approvingly. "So it is! Almas. A fitting name for a gem like you."

Now I had three names—four, if you count Nanu, which my brother sometimes called me.

Um Buraq's house was a modest but elegant home in the Rumaithiya district. A South Asian woman in her fifties opened the door. Deepa was one of two servants in the home. The other was Ajay, the woman's husband, our driver. People in Kuwait were often harsh and unkind to their servants, but Um Buraq, though demanding, seemed to relate to her housekeeper as family. I was surprised to hear her speak a few words in their language.

"Do you speak Hindi?" I asked.

"No! Malayalam," Um Buraq snapped, perturbed that I didn't know the difference.

Deepa had come to Kuwait for work some twenty years before when Um Buraq was first married, and had seen her through the heartbreak of miscarriages, then abandonment. Deepa herself had been childless and escaped the shame of it to work in Kuwait. Only later, after her husband tried to conceive with another wife, was it revealed that he had been infertile, not her. Ajay begged Deepa to take him back, and Deepa begged Um Buraq to bring him to Kuwait. But since Um Buraq could not afford another servant, she brought him on the condition that she could hire him out and take a portion of his earnings. He agreed and abandoned his second wife to escape his impotence, and the three of them lived together in childlessness and the unspoken shame of it. They were all around the same age, but both Deepa and Ajay called Um Buraq "Mama."

"The dress you brought will not do," Um Buraq said, and she gave me a few skimpy things to try on. One little red dress she chose clung to me, accentuating my curves. I ran my hands over my body, watching in the mirror how it slid from my breasts to my waist and glided over the arches of my hips. I felt glamorous. It was probably the most expensive clothing I had ever worn. In this dress, I could be someone other than a twenty-year-old failure, who'd only learned to read well enough in her teens, fallen in love with and married the first man who came along, then wound up little more than gossip fodder. I could be Almas, a diamond, in this dress.

"Take this too." Um Buraq handed me a sparkly little purse to match my dress.

I applied heavy makeup for Almas, creating an alluring and sophisticated version of myself. I liked this woman in thick kohl, mascara, and red lipstick staring back at me in the mirror.

"Do you prefer Red Label or Black Label?" Susu asked.

I thought she was talking about my dress, wondering why she'd say the words in English. "I don't know. No one can see the tag," I said, twisting to see the dress label in the mirror. They all laughed. Susu almost spit out her soda.

"What's funny?"

"Here." Susu held out her soda. "This is Red Label."

I recognized the smell. "It's alcohol! I thought you were drinking cola."

Still laughing, Fifi said, "Just drink it. Don't pretend here. We know all you Palestinians drink alcohol."

I remembered Mhammad. And my father. I could almost hear Mama yelling that he reeked of *khamr* and sin. That he should go back to whatever whorehouse he had been to. I took the glass from Susu, sniffed the fumes, and swallowed a large gulp. This alcohol wasn't like the stuff Mhammad had introduced me to. It wasn't even the same color. Fire spread through me. I thought I would vomit. I coughed it up, my eyes watered, and snot shot out my nose. They all laughed.

I ran to the bathroom. The makeup I had admired moments before was smeared, kohl and black mascara running down my face.

"You look like a cat that just ate her kittens," Um Buraq said, standing at the bathroom door. Deepa was smiling next to her. "I'll fix it for you, darling." She seemed almost maternal.

"Do you drink that terrible stuff?" I asked Um Buraq.

"Not me. But I don't judge. I'll show you how to drink it," she said, and Deepa added in broken Arabic, "Not drink like water, Almas. Drink slow."

Deepa fetched a damp towel and handed it to Um Buraq, who dabbed it gently on my face. My head was already spinning.

"Just let go. Trust me. You will have the time of your life. We women deserve to have fun in this world," Um Buraq said softly, even lovingly, as she reapplied my makeup. "God didn't make us just to have babies and serve the needs of men while they run around and do whatever they want." I thought about Mhammad again, and the sting of abandonment shot through me. She went on, "They're vampires who leave when they've sucked your last drop of blood."

"Mama, Ajay needs me," Deepa interrupted.

Um Buraq waved her hand. "Make him wait. Let's get this girl together."

I would learn over time that Um Buraq tolerated Ajay for Deepa's sake, even though she took half his earnings every month. Um Buraq would have taken all of it were it not for Deepa. Ajay could do nothing about it. He had been disgraced in India and had nowhere to go but Kuwait with Deepa. His work permit was held in Um Buraq's name. She owned him and was making him pay for leaving Deepa, a kind of proxy punishment of her own husband, who had taken a second wife and abandoned her. Um Buraq's husband had told her to be grateful to him for sparing her the shame of divorce. But Um Buraq knew that it was simply cheaper for him to keep her as a first wife than to pay her mo'akhar, the divorce dowry, which is intentionally exorbitant in some marriages to prevent divorce.

Until I met Um Buraq, it had never occurred to me that patriarchy was anything but the natural order of life. She was the first woman I met who truly hated men. She said it openly and without apology. I found her persuasive.

Deepa brought me a bottle of sparkling water. I gulped it down and let out a satisfying burp that made us all laugh. Then Deepa handed me a glass. "Scotch with fizzy water," she said, bobbing her head in the way of South Asians, smiling. "Sip, sip only. No drink."

I sipped. It was awful. Then it wasn't that bad. We joined Fifi and Susu in the living room, grabbed our purses, and walked out together.

"Wait." Um Buraq took the little red purse from my hand, looked inside, then handed it back. "Good girl. You don't want to take any ID with you," she said.

That moment, too, stands out in my memory. Putting a wallet and my ID in the new purse would have been the natural thing to

do. Was there some part of me that knew I should not have anything on me that could reveal my identity? Had I imagined, somewhere in the recesses of my mind, that we could be stopped by the
police? Or was I just drunk?

My body was relaxed in the car, my heart open to the world,
warm and full of love. I felt affection for Um Buraq and Deepa.
Maybe even Fifi and Susu, whatever their real names were. The
three of us were wrapped in black abayas over our little dresses
in the backseat of Um Buraq's Lincoln Continental. She sat in the
front, next to Ajay, who kept his hands on the steering wheel, occasionally looking at us in the rearview mirror.

I liked the dress hugging my waist, squeezing my tits together
like they were going to burst. It wasn't really me, but Almas. I put
the window down to let the cool wind of the desert winter blow
against my face.

"Girl! Close it! The heat is on!" Um Buraq yelled, and the girls
giggled. "Deepa gave you too much to drink," she said, warning,
"Do not forget that your name is Almas. Try to sober up. Understand?"

"How?" I asked.

"How what?"

"How do I sober up?"

She thought about it and said, "Do arithmetic in your head.
Count things. Count everything around you. It'll help you focus."

It was nearly eleven when we arrived at the seaside chalet. My
head was light. I wobbled in the ill-fitting high heels Um Buraq had
given me as we approached a grand, ornately carved wooden door.
It opened before we reached it. Out came a middle-aged Kuwaiti
man, welcoming us with exaggerated delight. He wore a traditional
dishdasha, but without a *ghutra-o-egal* on his head. Inside, we were

met by the cheers of a small group of men in a vast diwaniya room. *"Ahlan ahlan ahlan!* Welcome, all you beauties. Now the party can start!"

We were the only women there. "You kept us waiting, ladies! But you are well worth it. Come, have a seat. What can I get you to drink?"

Count things to sober up, I reminded myself.

I counted ten men, then four bottles of Black Label scotch and six bottles of Red Label scotch, three of them empty, two partly consumed, and five still sealed. Ten packs of cigarettes, three *argilehs.* One piece of mirror glass with two lines of a white powder. Ten ashtrays full of smashed cigarette butts, six bowls of nuts, two fancy silver buckets of ice, three bottles of Pepsi, two bottles of ginger ale.

"Welcome, beautiful. Have a seat," someone said, and I realized I was the only one still standing. The men introduced themselves as Abu this or that, and soon they were showing photos of their kids.

As the music grew louder, Fifi and Susu got up to dance with the men, then pulled me up to join them. I lifted my arms and my hips twisted and curled around the air. The music rushed into me, eclipsed though by a growing unease.

Count, Nahr, I said to myself. Two pictures on the wall, one of the emir, the other of his successor. One inscribed sword resting below the photos. Six Persian rugs lining the long diwaniya; three hanging chandeliers, one large, two smaller, all dimmed. I closed my eyes. My body danced. Three men began raining many banknotes over me. *When my father was away all those nights, is this the sort of place where he went, doing what these men are doing? What are they doing? What am I doing? Just dance, Nahr. Dance, Yaqoot. Dance, Almas. Almas. Almas. My name is Almas.*

One. Two. Three names. Four: Nanu. Jehad. Drink a little more Red Label. Sip, sip. No, drink. Count.

I don't know how long I was dancing, but at some point the middle chandelier had been turned off and the others dimmed even more. Fifi had gone off with one of the men. Susu was snuggled on the sofa between two men. Um Buraq was playing backgammon at a large table in the corner with the eldest man at the party, while the rest watched and bet on who would win. The room was clouded with smoke, and I suddenly felt nauseated. One of the men who had been dancing showed me to a bathroom. There I came face-to-face with Almas in a large mirror. I was barefoot, my skin glistening with sweat, hair limp and makeup slightly dissolved but not smeared. The toilet, bidet, gold faucets, marble tile, Jacuzzi tub, and glass shower floated around me as I rushed to the toilet, vomiting the acid of scotch and mixed nuts. I heaved until there was nothing in me but bile. The same man was crouching next to me, holding my hair. *I thought I locked the door.* He handed me a warm, wet towel, then a cold glass of water, then guided me to the sink, gave me a toothbrush and toothpaste, stroked my hair. "*Salamtik, alf salamah,*" he kept saying, soothing me.

I cleaned myself up and asked him to please give me some privacy. He turned to walk out, and when I heard the door close, I sat to pee. As I washed and dried myself in the bidet, I realized, to my horror, that he was still in the bathroom, his back turned, but staring at me in the mirror. He smiled when I saw him. A rush of fear added to my confusion, and now I could barely walk.

"Let me help you," he said. "Maybe some fresh air will do you good." He guided me through a separate entrance that opened to the beach. I could hear the ocean, but it was too dark to see much except a slice of moon and the glory of endless stars. He pulled me down to sit with him. I hadn't noticed that he had already spread a blanket on the sand next to an outdoor gas fireplace. "You're beautiful," he said, fondling my breasts, pushing me onto my back. "All the others wanted you the minute you started dancing. I can't believe how lucky I am."

The stars were thick in the sky, a web of eternity. I had only ever seen the sky like this when Jehad and I were young and our father would take the family for weeks to camp in the desert. The whole country would set up tents for the winter. *How did I forget those days? How many times did we do that as a family? Such wonderful memories of my father, even better than the Windex rainbow on glass and Fattooma song. No. This isn't the sort of place my father went on his long nights away. Not possible.*

The Persian Gulf air moving in and out of my lungs was salty, dry, and cold. The same air in and out of his lungs as he moved in and out of me. Something sharp, maybe a rock or a shell, dug into my back under the blanket with every thrust he made. I had to pee again. The stars were watching me, daring me to move. But I didn't. I endured and waited, because that's what girls do. Even bad girls like me. We endure and wait, and cater to the whims of men, because sometimes our lives are at stake . . . until we get even.

I peed where I lay on the blanket and felt the warm wetness between my thighs. "You're worth every penny," he said. "Can I get you anything?"

He nudged me. "Are you okay?" Exhaustion pressed on my chest and held me down. He nudged me again, and I closed my eyes to the stars.

When I opened them again, I was on my stomach, lying on a hard surface, the voices of men and women talking around me. I saw the bare legs of a woman whose painted blue toes I recognized as Fifi's. The lights were bright in the room and I tried to turn over, but someone held me down. Fifi crouched to meet my face. "It's okay, a big shard of glass was stuck in your back from the beach. There's a doctor here fixing you up," she said. Then she whispered, "Didn't you feel it? Anyway, we couldn't take you to a hospital because . . . you know."

I slept at Um Buraq's house. Sharp pain would shoot through me when I tried to move my arm on the side where muscles in my back had been sliced by the glass. In the morning I cleaned myself up in the bathtub as best as I could with one arm. Deepa helped me wash my hair without getting the bandage wet. The other girls had left, and it was just Um Buraq and me.

"You caused quite a ruckus last night. You should be more careful next time," she said, pushing a tray of fried eggs and *labneh* in front of me while she pawed leftover matchboos. The traditional Kuwaiti dish of saffron rice cooked with raisins and nuts, topped with golden chicken and spicy tomato sauce, was typically an afternoon or evening meal, but she would eat it at any time of the day or night.

"No thank you. I'm not hungry."

"Here, Deepa squeezed some fresh orange and ginger for you. Drink it. And take these two Panadols for your headache."

I sipped the juice, my hair still wet.

"It all worked out better than I expected," Um Buraq said, scooping up a fistful of golden rice. "Fetch me that over there." She pointed at a fat blue envelope bound with a rubber band.

"I don't work for you. Get your own envelope," I said.

"Well, it's for you. But I'm happy to keep it if you want," she said without looking up from her food.

I reached slightly with my functional arm, but even that movement was painful.

"Open it," she said.

I winced, barely able to move.

"I'll do it." She took the envelope, licked the rice from her fingers, pulled out a stack of notes and counted two thousand dinars with her greasy fingers, then put it all back and gave it to me.

"They felt bad and gave us some money for the trouble that boy caused," she said. Those men had paid her five hundred dinars for me, then gave her five thousand for the damage the nephew did. I wanted to give the money back and never see this woman again. But I made three hundred dinars a month working full-time, and here she was offering me two thousand.

"Where's the rest?" I asked.

She almost choked on her food.

"Why are you keeping three thousand five hundred dinars?" I persisted, faking courage.

"That's the deal," she said, taking another bite without looking at me.

"There's no deal," I said, trying to harden my voice and stifle the pain.

She smiled, her large lips stretching nearly to the ends of her face, a piece of parsley stuck to her teeth and the vulgar gap between them mocking me. "I like you," she said, and reaching her greasy hands into her bosom, pulled out a cloth purse full of large banknotes. She counted one thousand dinars and pushed them to me. I didn't pick them up, continuing to stare at her, at that gap. The smile faded. She counted another five hundred, and that was it. "Fair is fair. I have to eat too. Now go get dressed. Ajay will drive you home."

I took the money and left, hoping never to see her again.

I made up a tale about twisting my arm, until I needed Mama's help getting dressed for work one morning and she saw my bandage. She insisted I show the wound and tell her what had really happened.

"Mama. It's not a big deal," I tried to dissuade her. But she wouldn't let up. "I fell down the steps at Um Buraq's house and landed on a piece of the glass that had been in my hand. I didn't tell you because I didn't want you worrying."

"You should be more careful. Lucky you didn't break your neck," she sighed. Sitti Wasfiyeh added, "That's what happens when you don't watch where you're going. I keep telling you to watch where you're going. No one listens to me. You're clumsy and don't listen to your elders."

My arm slowly recovered as the wound in my back healed. I didn't know what to do with the thirty-five hundred dinars I had tucked away in my safe, where I kept the gold shabka from my wedding, ten gold ingots remaining from the twenty Mama had bought in secret when Baba was alive, and a one-thousand-dinar college fund for Jehad, from the money Mhammad's family gave me after he left, and which we kept dipping into to pay bills. It would not be enough to get Jehad through the door of most universities, but with this new stack of bills, I began to imagine that one day I could pay for him to have a good university education and become a rich doctor who would support us in turn. There was still a year and a half to come up with the rest.

Um Buraq left several messages at the house over the next two months, but I didn't return her calls. Sabah thought I was still mad about whatever stupid argument we'd had, which I didn't even remember. I didn't answer or return her calls either. By sheer luck, my grandmother was having coffee with a neighbor one flight up when Um Buraq showed up at our apartment. I saw her through the peephole, pretended no one was home, and let her knock until she gave up and left. But I worried she'd return and provoke a scandal.

I got a second job as a retail clerk at a clothing store. My routine was: school clerk job, evening retail job, home, repeat. On weekends and free hours here and there, I took in customers for eyebrow threading. I was robotic, impervious to the memory of that terrible party. I liked being busy, exhausted, and numb. I didn't want to think or feel until I had something worthwhile to show—maybe a savings account to help send my brother to college, or a good job that would bring me respect and social standing. In the quiet, hidden parts of me, I even dared to imagine getting a degree myself, or reciting poetry in public. But my exhausting determination alarmed my mother. "Look at you. What do you mean, you're fine? You look like you've lost at least ten kilos," she said.

I didn't hear from Um Buraq again until she showed up at work, insisting I accept her invitation to talk before heading to my second job. At Juice King in Salmiya, we ordered two tall glasses of freshly squeezed juice cocktails delivered to her car, where I sat looking straight ahead.

"I should have told you more about the party. I'm sorry that I didn't. I was only trying to help," she said.

"I didn't ask for your help. Why are you harassing me at my job?"

"I want to make you an offer."

"I don't want anything from you."

She sighed. "Look, just hear me out. I'm not a bad person. Women like us—"

"I'm not like you."

She took her time before answering. "If you're married in name only, abandoned and humiliated by your husband in the prime of your life, without a legitimate means to support your family and yourself in any meaningful way in this materialist culture that spits in your face if you're not driving the right car, then you are *just* like me."

She stared until I turned to look at her. I didn't know what to say. I thought about the contents of the safe at home, the stranger on top of me at the beach, glass pushing into my back. The knot in my stomach I'd had since that night tightened its grip. I wanted to vomit. Was she right? Was this my fate?

"What do you want from me?" I asked, concentrating fire in my eyes, but actually feeling defeated.

"I want us to be friends. We can help each other, and I believe in time you will see things differently. I know your brother is one of the top students in the country and has been every year."

I went cold. My anger was suddenly real and powerful. "Listen to me. I will gouge out your eyes if you mention my family again. Do you understand?"

But she continued as if I hadn't said anything. "Your brother deserves to get a good education. I know your family cannot afford to send him to university. But I can help."

It's true I wanted Jehad to become the surgeon he dreamed of being. And I wanted to be the person to make it happen. To be my family's savior and protector. But the reality of what she was offering made my stomach churn again. "I need to go back to work," I said, stiffening, trying to hold my gut together.

The waiter walked by our car and took Um Buraq's empty glass. I motioned for him to take mine. "Was something wrong with the juice?" he asked, seeing it nearly untouched.

"She's not feeling well," Um Buraq answered for me, reaching over to tip him. After he left, she said, "I am offering you a chance to make a month's salary in one hour."

"And if I say no?"

She shifted in her seat, stretching her body to open the glove compartment. It was full of junk and papers. "Open that," she ordered, pointing to another blue envelope.

"I don't want your money."

"It's not money. Open it."

I did. And there I was, in that tight little red dress, a glass of liquor in my hand, dancing between three men ogling my body, showering me with money, money all around my bare feet on the floor. "You took these pictures? You planned this?"

I opened the car door, retching. If those photos ever got out, I would never be able to show my face anywhere. I could also be imprisoned for prostitution. *Prostitution!*

"Take some time," she said grimly, and started the car.

Two months later, I went to another party with her, Susu, and Fifi. Again, married men without their wives, showing off photos of their kids.

I would learn that Um Buraq always asked to see photos when the men were drunk enough, not because she wanted to see their kids, but so she could collect the four-digit codes for their bank cards. "Men like this have several accounts. They're too stupid to remember the codes, so they keep little pieces of paper in their wallets with the numbers," she explained. She taught me how to steal the bank cards that went with those codes. We'd withdraw as much as possible, without raising suspicion. For men with that kind of money, a thousand dinars was like pocket change. They wouldn't miss it at all, she taught me.

Um Buraq had an apartment in Hawalli for her girls. We went there when she told us to. We kept it clean, stocked with food and lingerie. We also went there sometimes to be alone. Fifi was a student, and I often found her there with her books spread on the table. She'd hurry to gather her things and leave. It's strange, but I never got to know much about her or Susu, not even their real names. I kept my clerk job and went to the apartment only a few hours a week. It was easy to hide it from my family, because I had many legitimate reasons to be out—eyebrow-threading clients, going to the mall, seeing friends, running errands.

Susu gave me a pill to relax the first time in the apartment. She also advised me to lie about my age. "Tell him you're sixteen years old. It'll make him finish faster. The younger they think you are, the faster they get off," she said. I did as she suggested. He lasted 173 seconds (I counted), paid four hundred dinars (I counted twice), and left. A few weeks later, he returned with an expensive gold necklace and paid the same amount for less than half an hour. There were others. Each bought a little piece of me and took it away forever. I remember them all.

Abu Nasser was the most pathetic. Married with five kids. From a wealthy family. Generally thought pious, a pillar of his community and an upstanding public figure. He spoke on platforms about virtue, caliphates, and better times when morality was woven through social and legal fabrics that wrapped tightly around women. He repulsed me initially, but in time I came to pity him. Now, in the Cube, I am grateful for him. Abu Nasser showed me what lived beneath public piety. From him I learned who those legislating morality and pretending to be more virtuous than the rest of us really were.

I was one of the few, if not the only one, privy to the stagnant cesspool behind Abu Nasser's eyes. He believed the devil was weakening his resolve. He always rationalized violating the rules of God by using technicalities. He said it wasn't technically a sin if he didn't touch me. He always came to me when he knew I had my period. All I had to do was hand him my filthy panties, lined with a bloody menstrual pad, and leave him be. He'd pay more if I had worn the same pad all day without changing. Even more for two days' worth of my body's sludge. The nastier the better. He'd hold it like a precious gift and slowly bring it to his face, inhaling while he jerked off. I had to sit in the same room but could not look at him (another absolving technicality for the Day of Reckoning). But he made sure I heard him. Little-man noises, like a whimpering dog, that made me hate myself. As soon as he finished, he'd start crying, his face smeared with my blood. Then he'd curse me. "Temptress! May God punish you for luring me here." He'd beseech God, "O Lord, I call upon your mercy to keep the devil and the devil's temptress away." Then he would throw money on the floor and run out, surely to the mosque to purge his soul. But on schedule, he came back in twenty-eight days, at the peak of my heaviest menstrual flow.

Once, when I didn't have anything for Abu Nasser, he accused me of carrying someone's bastard child, called me a whore, and left. He came back three days later to apologize for having committed the sin of disparaging a woman's honor without evidence. In his apology, he exonerated himself since "technically" I wasn't an honorable woman to begin with.

His timing was impeccable because I had just begun to bleed. I went to the bathroom and came out with a dirty pad dangling from my fingertips. He paid extra that time. If nothing else, he was generous.

Abu Moathe was a bank branch manager who alternated between violence and sentimentality. He wanted me to fight him, to act out rape scenes. Only, I was never acting, because even though

I was getting paid, it felt like rape, my screams muffled by his hand. Sometimes he went too far and left bruises on my body.

Abu Moathe was one of the rare *mitkawteen*, Palestinians who had been granted Kuwaiti citizenship, because his father had been a high-ranking military general before Kuwait struck oil. Most mitkawteen were intellectuals and high-born merchants who took pride in being Palestinian. But Abu Moathe hid his Palestinian origins and went out of his way to deny it. Once, he slapped me hard enough to knock me out because I asked what village in Palestine his family was from. The swollen left side of my face turned out to be a fractured cheekbone.

Um Buraq never liked him and warned me to stay away. "Don't get me wrong. Money is money, but not at any price. That man is crazy," she said.

But after he broke my cheek, Um Buraq paid him a visit at the bank. She had good timing too, showing up just as his father, the general, was there with several men to congratulate Abu Moathe on the birth of his second son. Um Buraq pretended to apply for a loan, but by her presence, she was really delivering a message that she could create a scandal and ruin him.

"His face went white when he saw me," Um Buraq later told me.

Concerned about explaining my swollen, bruised face to my mother, the morning after it happened, I sneaked out of the house before my family awoke and went to work early at the school. I made myself fall in front of the guard, Abu Zhaq, a kind, elderly Palestinian man who wore Coke-bottle glasses and dentures and passed the time reading the Quran and Sufi poetry. He rushed to help me, but he didn't ask how my face bruised that quickly. He knew my fall was for show and played along. I could tell he pitied me, which made me all the more ashamed.

"May God give you long life, Ammi," I said. "I'm fine. It was just a minor fall."

Abu Moathe apologized, tearfully. He always did that. He would tell me he loved me. That I was the first woman he'd ever really loved. That his Kuwaiti wife could not understand him the way I did, on account of my being Palestinian. He would kiss my feet, sobbing, and I would feel sympathy for him, which made me think I loved him too—that perhaps it was possible love could be nestled between revulsion and hatred. It wouldn't be long before he would hurt me again. But after Um Buraq went to him, he changed. There was a plan in his remorse. He asked me to marry him, confessing a fantasy of walking around with two wives, one on each arm.

It is difficult now to admit that I thought this a reasonable thing to want; that I imagined—even fantasized about—being his second, preferred wife. I wanted to be chosen, maybe loved. I wanted out of my life, out of my skin, and his offer seemed like the best someone like me could hope for.

"But I'm already married," I reminded him.

"I can take care of that," he said. Wanting to seem purer to him, I confessed how Um Buraq had coerced me into this work. I told him how she had blackmailed me with photos, and he promised to end it all and take care of me forever. I told him I loved him too, and confessed that my real name was Yaqoot, though I kept Nahr to myself.

Abu Moathe threatened Um Buraq in the same way she did to him. He visited her estranged husband on pretense about some business. He was letting her know that he knew who her husband was and could just as easily ruin her. As he expected, she was waiting for him at the apartment on his next visit to me. He had a triumphant smirk as he jabbed his fat finger into her shoulder.

"Yaqoot doesn't work for you anymore," he said, demanding she hand over the photos.

Um Buraq looked mockingly at me. "You told him your name, you stupid girl? And you want *him* to have the photos?" she said, incredulous. She turned back to him, laughing her terrifying laugh like she had already squashed a million bugs like him before. I thought that would enrage him, but it confused him instead, and it taught me an important life lesson: when you don't react predictably, it throws people off, hopefully long enough for you to get the upper hand.

That's what Um Buraq did that day. She said she wouldn't ever call me again. And when I insisted she turn over the photos, she shook her head and repeated, "You stupid, stupid girl," and agreed to everything, provided Abu Moathe paid her for them. She made him feel like he had won, and he stupidly agreed to her conditions. Then she could just name her price—any price—because a man's word is unbending. There were codes of honor among degenerates. He paid her handsomely.

That's how Abu Moathe became my sugar daddy, for a while anyway. I no longer had to face Um Buraq, and my days became more predictable, but now I had to let him slap me around. He agreed never to strike my face or neck where marks would be visible, as long as he could bruise the rest of me.

His secret apartment was also in Salmiya, where I'd go whenever he paged me. I'd pretend to be an unsuspecting housewife or maid going about my day cooking and cleaning, and he would play my rapist, who'd sneak in when no one else was home. I had to fight back at first, to provoke him into beating me into submission, then I'd succumb to him and beg for more. This theater happened once or twice a week. It's how I paid all our bills and began to build up

Jehad's college savings. Abu Moathe even taught me about investing in the stock market. I tried it out for a while with a bit of money.
Although I didn't gamble my money in the market, stocks would
provide an easy cover to explain extra income to my family.

Abu Moathe showered me with gifts of jewelry, clothes, shoes,
and purses. But I had to leave those at the secret apartment because Mama was already perplexed by our change of fortune. She
didn't know about the college savings, and I kept my previous jobs
to account for my income and time out of the house. For the first
time, we didn't teeter on the verge of eviction, and Mama could
spend her sewing earnings on herself. "May God bless you, my
daughter. You are worth more than all the gold in the world," she'd
say. She believed my stories, because what I was really doing was so
far from her imagination.

I teased Abu Moathe once about his promise to marry me, and
he said, "Um Moathe would probably cut off my balls in my sleep if
I went through with it." I never mentioned marriage again, and he
soon stopped paging and changed the lock on his apartment. He
had moved on to another woman.

That's what I told Bilal years later. But it isn't the whole truth.
Abu Moathe didn't just stop paging me. I let myself get pregnant,
thinking I could trap him into marrying me. I thought he could
help me get a divorce. But he took me to Egypt instead, my first
trip on an airplane. There, we went to a clinic. Two elderly women
assisted me onto the table in a filthy room. A nurse stuck an IV in
my arm, and when I woke up, I had thick bloody pads between my
legs. The same elderly women walked me out of the filthy room. I
bled for two weeks straight, got a fever and terrible cramps. Terrified to go to a doctor, because what they'd find could send me to
prison, I turned to Um Buraq, and she took care of everything. She

brought me to her home and fetched a doctor, who said I could die of sepsis if they didn't get me to a hospital, but agreed they could wait one day to see if the intravenous antibiotics would kick in. I barely remember any of this, but it's what happened. Um Buraq brought a traditional healer after that, and they nursed me back to health. She covered for me with my mother, telling her that we were camping in the desert where there were no phone booths. It took me a week to regain my wits and some strength. The doctor said my pussy was messed up and scarred inside; he said I was no good for kids anymore.

Abu Moathe's callous dismissal helped to crystallize the reality of my life. I tried paging him, but he didn't return my calls. After I called his office several times, he rang Um Buraq to deliver a warning that he would destroy us both if I continued to harass him. I curled my body around my hollowed womb and lay there, encrusted in profound loneliness. I felt small in the world, unlovable and worthless. I bore stains that could never be washed away, and I had a true desire to die, until Um Buraq shook me one day from the bed, Deepa standing next to her with a drink.

"Listen to me!" she demanded. "First thing, you drink this herbal tea. And then you climb out of whatever pit you're in." Deepa put a pillow behind my back as Um Buraq lifted me. I took the glass of tea and sipped slowly. The taste of sage and cinnamon filled my head as the warm liquid slid down my throat, into my excavated belly. I stared at Um Buraq blankly.

"Now, you listen to me," she began. "Abu Moathe is shit. Every man is shit. The sooner you accept this truth, the easier your life will be. I thought you knew this by now. What were you thinking? He was going to marry and make you respectable? You take what you can get from them. They have all the power in the world, but it's possible to have power over them. This is what you must learn."

I leaned forward and let my head fall onto Um Buraq's shoulder. She put her arms around me, then pushed me gently back. "You get one more day of self-pity, but tomorrow morning you get out of bed, clear your head, and decide how you will live. It is that simple. You make that one decision. Then you make another, and another. There are no forces holding you in this pathetic state. You are young, beautiful, and healthy. You have a home, family, and friends. Start from there."

Deepa nudged me gently to drink more of the tea before they both left the room. I lay there through the night, watching memories and imagination play on the ceiling, much the same as I do now in the Cube.

Before sunrise, I made the decision to roll out of bed at the call to *fajr* prayer. My scarred, empty womb felt like a boulder in my abdomen as I walked to the kitchen to make coffee. To my surprise, Deepa was already awake, boiling an *ibriq* of coffee. She poured two cups and pushed one toward me where we sat at the table, sipping in silence, because words had no place in that moment. I made another decision to pray, performing the ritual *wudu* cleansing, then donning the prayer robe Um Buraq had left for me and performing the fajr *salat*. It felt good to pray. I made another decision to wash my hair and shower, scrubbing every inch of skin on my body. Then a decision to dry and style my hair. A decision to apply light makeup. When Um Buraq awoke at noon, I sat down to eat with her and Deepa.

"You look good," Um Buraq said, taking a large bite of eggs and bread. "What have you decided to do?" The chewed-up eggs tossed around in her mouth as she spoke.

"I want to be normal," I said.

"You have always been normal, girl," she said. "Normal isn't what other people do. You make your own normal."

I knew what she meant. Um Buraq was always railing against social propriety, pointing out the layers of hypocrisy everywhere, hating on men.

"I don't want to do this anymore. I just want to work as a school clerk and a saleswoman at the mall, and support my family," I said.

Um Buraq looked at me and I held her gaze, refusing to be the first to look away. She moved her eyes first, running her tongue over her teeth and sucking air to dislodge food from the crevices of her vast mouth. "Then that's what you shall do, my dear. I am here if you ever need me," she said.

We held each other in a stare again. "Thank you for taking care of me these past days. I'll pay you back for the doctor bills," I told her.

"You're welcome. And you don't need to worry about the doctor bills. I took care of it and that's that," she said.

The contradictions of our relationship cemented. I felt affection for this woman who had blackmailed and prostituted me. The force of sharing unspeakable secrets created a closeness with her, at the same time that I had an urge to get away from her and never see her again. More paradoxical was that Um Buraq loved me, at the same time she used and exploited me. I can't explain that, but I know it's true.

———

I resumed my life as I had done when Mhammad left me, as if the past had not happened, and I was simply carrying on uninterrupted. I went back to my school clerk job and picked up more evening hours at my retail job and more clients for eyebrow threading.

Fridays were reserved for family, and a sense of contentment slowly crept into the physical exhaustion of my routine. My salary was much less than I had led my family to believe in months previous, and I was forced to use some of my savings to cover bills. But every day I made the same series of decisions, and life went on.

It was Jehad's final year of high school, and much of our home life revolved around ensuring him the privacy, quiet, and nutrition he needed to get through the grueling exams every quarter and also to complete university applications. At the midterm results, one bit of good news followed another. Jehad was poised to be in the national top five of his graduating class. Then came university acceptance letters from England, Italy, and Russia, and I was confronted with the cost of university. One year's tuition was more than I thought all four years would be. The savings I had wouldn't be enough.

Mama and I took all our jewelry to get it valued, but selling would only cover a fraction of what we needed. Jehad had saved some money too, from working odd jobs here and there, and assured us that he could get a job wherever he landed to cover the rest. But it was an unrealistic plan that we all knew couldn't work, given the amount needed. I tried getting a bank loan, but they said I didn't earn enough to get more than a small personal loan of one thousand dinars.

"I got the loan," I lied to Mama, and she made us a celebratory meal for Jehad, the first person in our family to go to college. "The loan combined with the money I made investing in stocks will cover nearly everything," I lied again.

So I returned to Um Buraq, on the condition that I would only go to parties and dance, nothing more. No alcohol, no pills, no sex. I would just be a dancer. Only a dancer.

"You don't have to do anything you don't want to. Men would pay gold just to watch you dance," she said. "What happened was for the best, I think, because now you can't go around telling people that I'm forcing you to do what you want to do anyway. You see, I only showed you those photos back then to ease your conscience about choosing what you wanted to do in the first place. I would never have revealed them. I wouldn't do that to another woman. But you went and made a deal with the devil, and now the devil has those pictures. Anyway, what's done is done. But let it be a lesson for you. Never trust a man, girl. Never trust a man."

I made only one exception to my new rule with Um Buraq, because I needed to show a large sum of money to legitimize the lie I told my family about the bank loan. I agreed to meet one more man. He came dragging his seventeen-year-old son to the apartment, instructing me to "take care of the boy." He turned to his son with threatening, angry eyes, put money on the table, and left, closing the door with a soft thud that made his intensity all the more menacing.

The boy looked near tears. "Do you smoke?" I asked, grabbing a pack of cigarettes I kept handy for times like this. He nodded. "I don't usually allow people to smoke in here, but I'll make an exception for you," I said, and led him to the balcony.

He lit a cigarette, and after a few puffs said, "Let's just get this over with."

He wasn't much younger than me, but I felt I could be his mother. It made me realize how much I had aged in only a couple of years. I was twenty-two but felt twice that.

"I say when, and if, anything happens," I said. "What's your name?" I stepped into the kitchen and began filling the teakettle.

"Mohsin." He put out the cigarette and followed me.

"Are you a virgin?"

"No!"

"Do you like boys?" I could see my question startled him and I took delight in that, but he didn't answer.

"Don't worry. It's not like I'm a holy woman. It's okay to like boys, Mohsin. Everybody has a little bit of love for the same sex, some people more than others." I hadn't realized my own thoughts on the matter until I spoke them.

"I didn't say I was a homo," he said.

"No, you didn't." I poured us some sweet mint tea. "But I'm saying that strict heterosexuality is probably a small minority of humanity. If you take society and religion out of the equation, we're probably all a little homo." I went all-in with my theory, making it up as I went along, amazing myself.

Mohsin smiled at that. We went back on the balcony, where he lit up another cigarette and watched life on the street ten stories below. We spent two hours like that. I lectured him on the dangers of smoking, imparting the Western conspiracy to poison us all, though I wasn't sure I believed that any longer. He told me how his father had caught him in the act with an older man. It was my job as an expert in matters of love to assure his father that his son was not a faggot but an insatiable lover and admirer of the female form. Mohsin found in me a place to unburden his soul.

"Can you just assure him that I'll make my future wife a very happy woman or something like that? And, I don't know, maybe hint that I just have a lot of hormones and always need it . . . but say it . . . maybe in a crude way so he believes?" His brown face got redder as he spoke.

I put my hand on his. "Don't worry. I'll protect your secret and convince him you're a ladies' man."

He smiled, relieved, and thanked me. No therapist or clergy can substitute for the confidence of a whore, because whores have no voice in the world, no avenue to daylight, and that makes us the most reliable custodians of secrets and truth.

"You know my biggest secret. Tell me one of yours," he said.

I gave him a side glance and a smile. "Son, we are not friends, and this is not a secret-sharing session."

"Please."

"Why do you want to know my secrets?"

"Not all of them. Just one. I'll never tell anyone."

I thought for a moment and told him a nonsecret secret. "I have three names. Almas, of course. But I'm also known as Nahr and as Yaqoot."

"Which one is your real name?"

"One secret. That's it."

He smiled. "I'll never forget you," he said.

As I found out years later, he was true to his word, and would do a remarkable favor for me in turn.

———

Jehad graduated from high school in June of 1990 and chose Moscow State University from the list that accepted him. He told me that Moscow used to bring hundreds of Palestinians to study in Russia free of charge, but all that changed when the Soviet Union dissolved. He felt it was only right that he go there instead of a Western country. His first year would be spent learning Russian and taking basic classes in culture, or he could do an intensive language course in Amman for half the cost, then go straight to university in Moscow.

In addition to the supposed loan of five thousand dinars, I revealed a ten-thousand-dinar savings account. I named a random company at the top of the stock exchange, which I had read about in the newspaper. "I bought stock in it two years ago and it tripled my investment," I said.

Jehad picked me up and twirled me around. Sitti Wasfiyeh pulled me to her and kissed my face. But Mama reacted differently. "Who gave you a stock tip?" she asked.

"Um Buraq." It was the first name that came to mind. Mama seemed to relax.

"I can't figure out if that woman is a devil or an angel," Mama said.

"Who cares? Jehad is going to university!" I said, wrapping my arms around her.

Mama kissed me, tears welling in her eyes. "My darling daughter. You have done so much for this family."

The past year of working two jobs—three, if you count freelance eyebrow-threading and dancing at clandestine weekend parties—was worth it to see my family so happy. Mama was also relieved that she didn't have to suffer the humiliation of asking her brothers for money, as she had had to do in the years before I was able to pitch in.

Jehad decided to do his language prerequisites in Amman, instead of Moscow, to save money. He set off in mid-July for a summer course that began in August. The money I had was still not enough to support us, plus all four years of Jehad's university, so I continued to dance at parties, determined my brother would become a surgeon, the first ever in our family. As I say this, I know it wasn't my only motivation. It's true that I lived my own dreams through him to some extent. But I liked dancing at these illicit parties. There was something alluring about living on the margins, in secret disrepute. It freed me from the drudgery of respectability—the low-paying jobs, social pretenses, children. I could have some autonomy without a husband. I could be my family's breadwinner, the powerful woman who took care of others. And all I had to do was what I loved most of all: dance.

On the night of August 2, 1990, Um Buraq sent three of us to a party at a beach chalet where high-ranking Saudi military officers were visiting. We arrived after midnight to find a gathering of eleven men, most already drunk. I had a bad feeling immediately. The chalet was secluded. Armed guards greeted us at the door, perhaps a normal thing for important military men, I reasoned. The host, an intimidating man, was irritated to see only three of us and complained that he had requested "at least fifteen girls."

"Yes, I know. I heard you tell her to spare no expense at all. You are her most generous customer." I flattered loud enough for all his guests to hear. This pleased him, and his guests chimed in about his hospitality.

Um Buraq was always clear that I was there only to dance, and the hosts honored her conditions. It was rare that Um Buraq did not accompany us, but this time she was home ill, and her absence may have emboldened the men to be more aggressive. It seemed our host had also lied to Um Buraq about how many men would be there. She would not have sent us had she known. The girls and I exchanged quick glances and surveyed the room for bathrooms, windows, doors. But it was no use. With sober guards outside, there was no way to leave.

The variety of booze on hand was more than the usual black-market scotch. Wine, beer, vodka, and many other liquors I'd never heard of filled the bar. The other women already had glasses, but I refused, requesting sparkling water instead. The men laughed, but one of them brought me a glass of water, which I did not drink. The two women and I communicated with our eyes. We would go along to buy some time, and they would slip Valium into the men's drinks. Drugging them to slip away was a stupid plan, because there were still guards by the doors, but it was better to be stuck there all night than be mauled by drunk, offensive men. I did my part and got up to dance. One of the women dropped a pill into one of their drinks, and I began to believe the threat would pass if we could subdue them through the night. But before too long, four men surrounded me, pawing and pushing up against me.

I could not fight them off. Nor could the other girls help. I had always wondered if such a day would come, though I didn't believe it would. I began silently praying, begging God, the angels, the heavens for help. The men ripped my clothes and pinned me down. Four or five of them. One of them lifted his dishdasha, lowered his *sirwal*, and pushed himself between my legs. His dishdasha fell over my waist, concealing his limp member as he pretended to thrust himself in and out of me, while the others fondled my breasts and pushed their erections against my face. I heard the other girls crying, beseeching God, begging them to stop. Memories flashed through my mind. All the choices and circumstances that had brought me to that moment.

I thought I was going to die that night and lashed out with all the force I could, digging my long, manicured nails into someone's skin enough to draw blood. "Whore, daughter of whores!" one of them cried, slapping me so hard the room spun. It was no use. I stopped fighting, thinking I had a better chance if I didn't resist. I lay there, tears falling down the sides of my face. I watched the second hand of a clock on the wall jump fitfully from one second to another, round and round. The clock watched me back. And I began to count.

One hundred thirty-two seconds ticked on the clock until it read four minutes past 2 a.m., when new voices, slamming doors, ringing phones, and alarmed faces began to fill the room. The men were scrambling, fleeing out the doors. I thought it a police bust and panicked, though I didn't move. But the police wouldn't dare go against such powerful men. I lay there, frozen, eyes and legs wide open. One of the girls finally came in and pulled me off the sofa.

"Almas, the men are gone. We have to get out of here," she said. "Saddam Hussein is invading Kuwait! Iraq's army is in the streets!"

II.

IRAQ

THE CUBE, WEST

VISITORS AND GUARDS have told me that the Cube is a technological marvel, the first of its kind. As an almost completely automated solitary cell, it has made me famous in "security circles"—private prison corporations, surveillance tech companies, and various ancillary suppliers of bondage.

The bedposts are concrete, but the bed platform is made of thick plastic straps attached to the posts. There are no springs. In fact, there's no exposed metal, except the door. They say there's not even a metal screw. Gray sheets and a gray blanket cover a thin foam mattress wrapped in plastic, a cream pillow stained yellow from my body's oils.

A concrete sink sits partially inside the western wall (opposite the wall where light enters from the glass-block window, which I decided was east), under a hole that delivers water when I press a small button next to it. It runs for three seconds at a time and the button can be pushed up to ten times a day before it stops working. I stick my finger inside the hole sometimes. I wish I could put my head under it and drink directly from the hole, but the sink opening isn't big enough.

The shower abuts the sink. This is the truly revolutionary part of prison technology. There is no visible showerhead, just a horizontal slab that juts overhead from the wall, like a corner shelf with small holes from which water emerges, much the same concept as the sink. This shower rules my life. It is my friend, my lover. I named my shower Attar. I have no way to turn him on or off. Before water falls from his small concrete holes, a red light will buzz, its glow tinting the whole of the Cube. I don't think of it as a light anymore. They are Attar's eyes, his warmth, his arrival and presence. I watch it sometimes, waiting. And when his eyes make my body and the room one in red, I quickly remove my clothes and stand to receive him. I never know if his water will be cold or warm or hot or scalding. Before he was Attar, when he was *it*, the strange shower, I would stand away, my hand stretched to feel the water temperature. Now I don't care. I love him whether the water is hot or cold. When it is perfect, I imagine Attar loves me. But it does not last. Attar stays only seven minutes. I counted the minutes several times. I never know when he will return. Sometimes he is absent for days. Sometimes he comes while I am sleeping, and I rush to disrobe.

I have one bar of soap. Occasionally guards push small shampoo bottles through a slit in the metal door. I have not given a proper name to Metal Hole.

I tried to keep a sleep and waking regimen, to structure and account for my days, but that's not the nature of time in here. There are no days or nights. Light and dark, just like Attar, come and go randomly.

I dance. Attar just came and left, and I am still wet, dancing. Music plays in my head as if at a wedding with my family, or with the men who paid to watch me dance, then to touch and own me.

Those men, I hated them all. Maybe I loved them too. I pitied them. Perhaps predators in particular deserve pity, if only for the spiritual sewage of them.

A journalist was here the last time Attar came on and my hair was clean. He asked about the lines I had drawn on the wall, not the ones marking days, those had already faded.

"The paths of ants," I explained. "They roam in single file."

He looked back at his questions and changed the subject to Iraq's occupation. I wonder if there might be some being somewhere tracing the journey of my small life, as I do the ants'.

"Are you still with me?" the reporter asked, stretching his neck to my line of sight.

People think Iraq's occupation of Kuwait was some kind of massacre, but that isn't true. The real horrors happened when Iraq left, and I suppose it hasn't stopped. I tried to explain to the interviewer, but he wasn't interested. He even argued: "But surely you understand why Kuwaitis would be upset with Palestinians? Yasser Arafat betrayed them by siding with Saddam Hussein."

I find that reporters and writers who come here don't actually want to listen to me or hear my thoughts, except where I might validate what they already believe.

SIX MONTHS

KUWAIT BEGAN AS a village in the Basra Province of the Ottoman Empire, which reigned for more than six hundred years. Realizing Kuwait's potential for oil, the French and British carved it out as a small, independent country they could easily exploit. That's what Jehad told me. He tried to explain the illegality and human rights aspects of Iraq's occupation of Kuwait, but I didn't want to hear it. I didn't care if Iraq had a right to invade, whether Kuwait had been slant-drilling for oil under the border, or if Yasser Arafat was a son of a bitch for siding with Saddam. All I knew was that Saddam Hussein had saved my life that night, and for the duration of Iraq's presence in Kuwait, I was a liberated, happy woman.

Kuwaitis used to look down on us foreigners. Whereas Kuwaiti policemen sometimes took liberties with female drivers they identified as non-Kuwaiti, Iraqi soldiers gave me a sense of camaraderie and empathy. They did not stare at my breasts and tilt their heads toward my ass upon seeing my ID card. It wasn't because Iraqi soldiers were better men. Rather, because they didn't want to be in Kuwait. They were a tired army that had just come off the battlefields against Iran, and the soldiers I met were simply homesick.

Still, I had not understood the extent of our subordination until I knew what it meant to be respected, not in spite of being Palestinian but precisely because of it. We all felt it, and it was hard not to revel in it. We simultaneously loved and resented Kuwait, just as Kuwait both loved and resented us.

The rich fled the country, leaving their belongings in unguarded mansions. I was right there with the looters who broke in and took whatever we could carry. It wasn't just us non-Kuwaitis. Poorer Kuwaitis did the same. Iraqi soldiers were also stealing. Um Buraq took me with her to pick through a mansion belonging to one of the al-Ghanim families. I already knew how they lived, but it was still shocking to see such ostentatious wealth. Um Buraq and I opened a bathroom closet with cosmetics worth at least ten thousand dinars. There were even bags of unopened makeup from London. One bag with twenty Chanel lipstick tubes still had the receipt in it. One thousand two hundred British pounds spent on lipstick in one day. These people deserved to be robbed. One house had gold faucets in the master bathroom. It looked as if someone had tried to pull them out. We gave it a try but couldn't shift them. The toilet seat had been removed, and we figured it too must have been gold. Why else would someone steal a toilet seat? The vulgarity of excess was on full display. We thought Iraq's invasion of Kuwait was God's punishment on them, and we were all too happy to be agents of the Lord.

The real valuables—diamonds, cash, gold bars—were long gone, but we managed to get decent spoils. Um Buraq even hauled away a lush set of sofas and other furniture. Those were good times. Six months of feeling powerful and safe. As long as Iraqi soldiers roamed the streets, I felt in control of my fate. That's what Saddam gave me, and I loved him for it. I don't care what anyone says about him. Saddam was my hero, and many years later, when the Americans saw him hanged, I wept wretched, bitter tears.

Unlike Jehad, I hadn't been one for watching the news. When powerless, following world events only highlights your impotence. But during those six months when Kuwait was again a province of Iraq, I thought I could affect the course of our lives; that my opinions could be relevant. I consumed political news and analyses for the first time in my life, and Jehad and I spoke about current events over the phone several times a week.

Allegiances at the Arab League summit were split between those aligned with Saddam Hussein and those supporting Saudi Arabia's move to allow United States troops to amass on its border.

Jehad said, "It's not that Libya, Yemen, Morocco, and others are siding with Saddam. They just don't want American military bases all over the Arab world."

"Exactly," I said. "And the minute they're here, they'll never leave until they kill Saddam and destroy Iraq. They'll take out Gaddafi and then el Assad, and probably move on to Iran."

"I agree completely, Sis." Jehad was surprised, but also proud that I had acquired a critical analysis. His approval meant alot to me.

"In concert with Israel, they will plunge the whole region into chaos and death. The Saudis are all too happy to appease. They're as bad as Israel. It wouldn't surprise me if we don't wake up in a few years to learn they're working hand in hand with Zionists, probably against Iran," I said.

I also spoke regularly with Sabah. She and her family had been among the masses who fled with whatever they could when Saddam invaded. I went to see her before they left. Her mother let me in, but Sabah had locked herself in her bedroom. So much separated me from her and from the person I was before we drifted apart, but she mattered to me, and I didn't want to lose our friendship forever in the chaos of political upheaval.

I sat against the wall and spoke to her through the door. "I don't blame you for being mad at me. I haven't been a good friend," I said. That was all it took for the door to swing open. She hugged me, and we went into her room, where she had been packing a small suitcase. "Mother said to take only what I absolutely have to. She said we'll come back when this is over, but my father reminded us what happened in Palestine, so we're taking things we can't do without."

"You can't live without that?" I asked, pointing to the stuffed toy in her suitcase.

Sabah blushed. "It was a present."

"From a boy?" Much had happened in her life too.

She filled me in on the details of how they'd met, their late-night phone calls when her parents slept, the love letters. I envied her innocence and shared in her happiness too. We talked for a while, getting caught up as I helped her pack. Then she asked if I was still friends with Um Buraq.

"Yeah, why?"

She looked away, but I pressed her to explain.

"I defended you a lot over the past few months," she said.

"Defended me from what?"

She sat me down. "People talk. Look. People say things about Um Buraq. That she goes to late-night parties and things like that." Sabah hesitated. "Some people said she was taking you with her."

I remember that moment well. I wasn't upset with Sabah for confronting me with my reputation. I don't think she would have participated in such harmful gossip. But the hurt and bitterness taking root in me tightened my throat and made my belly cramp. As

I look back from the Cube, that physical expression of my humiliation was a kind of hinge between the tenderness of the girl who still
craved acceptance and the hardened woman who was much older
than Sabah, jaded and maybe wiser—more like Um Buraq.

"As if I give a shit what people say," I said.

Sabah and I promised to stay in touch no matter where we
ended up.

I kept my promise and made regular calls to her in Jordan, even
though Mama worried about the cost of long-distance calls. The
Iraqi occupation put us in an economic bubble. Utility companies
were barely functional, and money had no value. It was just paper.
In this strange new order, I thought we could afford to "waste
calls," especially since I was wearing expensive Chanel lipstick. I
had saved the receipt showing I had twelve hundred British pounds
worth of lipstick. Perhaps as proof of my worth.

My retail job vanished as stores shuttered during the occupation, but the shortages of food, electricity, and drinkable water did
not lessen the number of women with bushy eyebrows. In fact, with
most salons closed, I had more customers than I could handle and
I used a room in Um Buraq's house as a makeshift salon. In part, it
provided a small income for her. She loved my company as much as
I did hers, and our friendship grew in the common ground on the
margins of honor. There was also the matter of her having saved my
life after the abortion. She never spoke of it again, which made me
appreciate her all the more.

Um Buraq's house became known as "Yaqoot's Salon." I abandoned Almas. Nahr was for the purer part of me. And Yaqoot was
everything in between.

I did hair, makeup, wax, and eyebrows, while Um Buraq and
Deepa served coffee and tea to customers. We women passed the

time in gossip, idle chatter, and dirty jokes. None wanted to talk about the occupation, the military, or war. Few knew anything about politics anyway.

But, of course, it was unavoidable. Usually I was the one mentioning something I had read in the newspaper. I might say, "I heard that the Americans are lining up tanks on the Saudi border." Someone would respond, "God help us," then we'd move on to stories about rich Kuwaitis partying it up in London nightclubs. Or, "The deadline for Iraqi withdrawal is in three weeks." God help us. "Iraqis just executed two Kuwaitis in the resistance." God help us. "Saddam said he's going to give the Americans the mother of all battles." God help us. One woman said once, "Palestinians will pay dearly for betraying Kuwait, even though most have nothing to do with it." I said, "God help us."

Um Buraq and I began making body butters and facial moisturizers from olive oil, goat's butter, herbs, myrrh oil, and frankincense. It was a craft she'd learned as a little girl from her grandmother in Basra. We sold everything we made.

Saddam imposed Iraqi currency, and Um Buraq and I split whatever came in. We didn't know it then, but the money we made from threading all that facial hair and cooking up toiletries would become worthless overnight. I kept those green banknotes emblazoned with Saddam's portrait, a reminder that the world can pivot at any moment. It wasn't much, just a few hundred dinars, because I often accepted noncash payments, such as bread, produce, looted appliances. And when we had more than we needed to live on, Um Buraq and I shared with those around us. I made sure our home had enough food and clean water. Mama in turn shared with our neighbors. Um Buraq also took care of her neighbors, ensuring they had bread and water when the shortages hit. We didn't need much money in those days. Our lives became wonderfully simple, clearer somehow in the fog of occupation. Folks with money—the creditors and landlords—had fled the country, leaving the rest of us with a new freedom to exist. We didn't have to pay rent for six months; no one was there to collect it.

Almost daily, Mama and Sitti Wasfiyeh would gather with the women in our building who remained in Kuwait. They'd bake bread rather than wait in the bread lines. Despite the uncertainty, people socialized without the weight of financial responsibilities. Iraq's occupation had the effect of a natural disaster—it allowed us to take a break from the contrived necessities of money. There was a deeply felt dignity in the sense that one's shelter and sustenance were not mortgaged. We went where we could not have afforded before the invasion, walked into homes where we'd never have been invited, and into establishments that would not have welcomed us during normal times. No one was poor. No one was rich. We just were. And we shared. We ate. We drank. We laughed. We danced. We cried. We dreamed and imagined a better world. Then we waited for fate to fall on our heads from American warplanes.

Newspapers and television pundits spoke of the United States military buildup in Saudi Arabia, but I could not imagine war. I thought it only happened far away, in "war zones" deep in the desert or beyond the orange cones bobbing in the ocean where swimmers were not permitted to go. I was a daughter of refugees chased out of their homes in Palestine, not once but twice, yet I could not conceive of bullets and bombs coming so close. But as time passed, the louder and more animated the pundits became. People who previously spoke only in whispers now spoke openly about the United States destroying Iraq. On the other hand, those who had been emboldened by Saddam Hussein began to shrink. Then they began to flee.

Most foreign workers fled in the early days of the Iraqi occupation, but Deepa stayed almost until the end. She had little to go back to. Parents gone, no kids. Then Um Buraq told her to leave. All those years Um Buraq had been taking half of Ajay's money, she was actually putting it aside in a savings account for Deepa. She gave it on the condition that Deepa use it to build a house in India, in her home state of Kerala, and she made Deepa promise to put the house title in her own name, not Ajay's or the name of any man. Since all money had changed to Iraqi currency, the value of the account was half of what it had once been, but it was still more money than Deepa had ever owned—Ajay too—she told me, crying.

I went with Um Buraq to the airport on the day Deepa and Ajay left. It was October 20, 1990. We waited five hours for two available seats on Indian Airlines, which set a world record for the most people evacuated by a civilian airline. Um Buraq bade farewell to her faithful friend and companion; it was the only time I ever saw Um Buraq cry.

About six weeks after Deepa and Ajay left, my brother returned from Amman. Jehad's university was closed for winter break, and the United States had given Saddam one month to withdraw from Kuwait. Jehad warned us that the United States would attack and probably wipe us all out if Saddam stayed. I disagreed. I thought Saddam was invincible. I believed he'd be the Arab leader who would finally defeat Western imperialists and Zionist colonizers. My recent interest in politics made me feel smart to speak with my brother with such a vocabulary.

When an American invasion was clearly imminent, I stopped reading and watching the news. I kept myself busy to stay out of the house, because I could not bear to listen to Mama, who was cheering for the Americans to come. "People just can't go around stealing other people's countries," she said. "It's wrong. For better or worse, Kuwait is our home. It's our duty to defend it. When did you stop loving this country? Don't you know the only tax collected in this country is for the Palestinian resistance? We cannot deny that!"

I left without answering and stayed more and more with Um Buraq, coming home as little as possible, until our home boiled and evaporated and then vanished with history's disappeared bits. But that wouldn't happen yet.

There was something else. I had a secret life during those months. No one, not even Um Buraq, knew. I took up with an Iraqi soldier. I wasn't yet ready to give up on men. Part of me wanted to know if men could be good; if it was possible for physical intimacy with a man to be something honest, loving, nurturing, powerful, and passionate. I wondered, too, whether I was lovable. I needed to know, because I thought we might all die soon.

His name was Mubshir. He manned a checkpoint I passed frequently. A few glances and flirtations later, he gave me a number and time to call a public pay phone, where he would be waiting. At first we met by the sea, but as things developed, we began meeting in an abandoned apartment in the Salmiya district. We found a kind of refuge in each other, especially when it became clear that he would be forced to fight the Americans soon. He thought he was going to die and worried how death would come. But we didn't talk about that much. We fucked with little respite to keep from thinking about it.

Mubshir was beautiful. He was the first man who ever made me climax. I told him I loved him, and he said the same to me, but we were pretending, and both knew it. We wanted a love story. It made our imminent demise romantic. He had a girl back home in

Baghdad. I think all he ever wanted was to be her husband, her provider and protector, the father of her babies. He didn't lie or try to mislead me, and the way he spoke of her made me love her too. I didn't mind when he called me by her name, or that he pretended my body in his arms was hers. Sometimes I imagined I really was her. I thought it was the closest I would ever come to being loved by a man.

Then the Americans rolled in on their monstrous tanks, smiling from their perches, flowers thrown at them from all sides. I don't know what became of Mubshir. I'd like to imagine him with his girl, but I've seen enough of our world to know better. Charred corpses of fleeing Iraqis burned stiff in every conceivable configuration littered the desert sand for miles and miles in what became known as the Highway of Death.

Jehad had been back from Amman less than a month when American soldiers swarmed our streets. He was a few centimeters taller and his whiskers had bloomed into a proper mustache and beard. I wanted to hear about university, but in that month he was preoccupied by our situation and spoke of little else.

"I think the Americans orchestrated all of it and our stupid leaders, especially Saddam, are playing right into their hands," he said, taking a hit from his inhaler. I noticed he was doing that more frequently now. He wanted to help the resistance defend Kuwait, but he felt the same kinship with Iraqis as he did with Kuwaitis. He could not fathom harming Iraqis and cursed Saddam for bringing such division among brothers. He cited historical examples of American treachery, spoke of Iran's shah and several CIA coups against Arab leaders. The malice of it all vexed him.

I was both impressed and annoyed with him. I didn't want my brother to be engulfed in politics the way so many men were. I was so emotionally invested in his future that I neglected to examine my own ambitions. I too wanted to learn. I wanted to leave and love and live something else. I didn't yet know what, mostly because I needed to ensure that Jehad could find his way first.

"Teach me something in Russian," I begged. "Please?"

"*Kak pozhivaesh?*"

"What does it mean?"

"It means, how are you?"

"No. I want to know dirty words."

I learned several fabulous words that day but forgot them all except one superb line: "*Otva'li, mu'dak, b'lyad!*" It means: Fuck off, you asshole, fuck!

Jehad's second semester started at the end of January, and he tried to persuade us to go with him to Amman. But none of us wanted to leave. For my part, it was perhaps a false sense of security, an inability to truly fathom war at our doorstep. I also wasn't keen on being in Jordan. Sabah had painted a bleak image of Amman as an economically depressed and corrupt place. But it was Sitti Was-fiyeh who persuaded my brother it was pointless to try to make us flee. She had been listening to us, uncharacteristically quiet, then she asserted, "I'm not going anywhere. I'm tired of being chased out of wherever I am in the world. Out of Haifa, then out of Ein el-Sultan, then Jordan, and now Kuwait? No. I'll just die here instead of facing another exodus. I'm too old for this shit that these shit people keep doing to us. Shit. All of it—shit!"

My brother begged, but it was no use trying to persuade my grandmother. Jehad despised Iraq's occupation of Kuwait, but he feared American intervention and decided to stay with us rather than leave. I was furious. "Mama and I work day and night to make it possible for you to study, and you think you can just decide not to go? As if your life is yours to do as you please without regard to your family?" I yelled.

Jehad stiffened. "I'm not leaving my family in this situation. So you can just stop, Nahr!"

Jehad's insistence eventually brought Sitti Wasfiyeh and me around to leaving, but by then it was too late. The American invasion was already under way. We stayed put, waiting for our future to emerge from the blasts, news reports, and innuendo. I could feel the sun setting on our lives in Kuwait, and when the Americans arrived, the sun indeed was gone. For months it was blacked out by blankets of soot. From the Highway of Death, Iraqis had managed one last act of defiance. They set flame to oil wells, which heaved unstoppable plumes of smoke into the sky that not even the sun could penetrate. It looked and smelled like the end of days, an apocalypse sucking us into hell.

With Iraq out of Kuwait, the United States paraded its military through our streets. By then we had already heard enough of Kuwaiti rage against Palestinians to know that we were not welcome to join them in street celebrations—not that I wanted to welcome the Americans. But Mama did.

In one way or another, Palestinians would have to pay, not only because some collaborated with Iraq, but also because we were a convenient proxy for vengeance against Saddam. Despite warnings from everyone, Jehad refused to leave or go into hiding. "I didn't do anything," he said. "What do I need to hide for? I wasn't even in the country during the occupation. I've only been back a few weeks."

No matter what reason or evidence we presented, despite the stories of disappeared Palestinians, my brother's belief in the essential goodness and fairness of human beings blinded him to danger.

"Kuwaitis aren't monsters. They're not going to do anything to me. I can prove I wasn't even here," he insisted. "Come on! Iraq arrested five thousand Palestinians for joining the Kuwaiti resistance. They know the difference."

"How can you be so smart and so stupid at the same time?" I cried. I knew more about the nature of humans—of men, in particular.

A day later, I saw from my window the police and a military jeep driving on our street. I ran to fetch my brother but by the time I reached the bottom of the stairwell, they already had him on the ground in handcuffs, beating and kicking him. I tried to intervene. An arm swung in front of my face against a black sky in the middle of the day. My heart throbbed. My cheeks pushed against glass. A car window? I bit my tongue. Then I lay stiff with pain on a plastic chair at the police station. I knew some time had passed, but only later understood it had been ten hours. I had no memory of being beaten, but my body bore the evidence. They gave me an injection and demanded to know where my sister Nahr was. But I—Yaqoot—swore I only had one brother. That is all I remember, except for the occasional faces that appear in my dreams reenacting disjointed versions of that day. When it was over, Kuwaiti authorities had my fingerprints, in lieu of a signature, on a document testifying that my brother had collaborated with Iraqi authorities during the occupation.

Somewhere during that time at the police station, I awoke to the sound of men screaming in other rooms, and later to Mama crying, beseeching the police. Sounds are what fill those days in my memory. They echo through the facts, the images, the pain of a fractured rib, the desire to take my brother's place in their torture dungeons, the anguish of unmistakable endings—the end of innocence, of a home, of health, of days with daydreams and nights without nightmares.

They released me, but not my brother, and I returned to the police station the same day with Mama in the hope of talking them into releasing Jehad. The station walls were painted green. American military personnel milled about, and Kuwaiti police seemed to want to impress the Americans. They shooed us away. I yelled the Russian words I remembered: "Otva`li, mu`dak, b`lyad!"—Fuck off, you asshole, fuck!—hoping my brother could hear me to know that we were there.

Policemen shoved us out, warning us not to return.

"Please, my sons, may God's mercy and His blessings fill your lives with success and joy," my mother begged. "Please give him these." Mama put several inhalers in one officer's hands.

As we left the police station, from the corner of my eyes I saw a hand drop the inhalers into a trash bin.

Our landlord was waiting for us when we returned. We had three days to pay six months' back rent or he would come with the police to evict us.

"Most people in the country have been pardoned from paying their rent during the occupation," I protested.

"Not Palestinians. Your Iraqi friends gave you jobs. You have money to pay."

Mama tried to explain that we did not have work. But I stopped her. I could see it was no use. This was not about rent.

Police barged into our apartment the next day. The landlord used his master key to open our door without knocking. I was on the phone, speaking with a lawyer about getting my brother out of jail. Mama was nervously smoking a cigarette and Sitti Wasfiyeh was praying the noon salat. I dropped the phone receiver and left it on the floor, afraid to bend down to pick it up. Mama was screaming.

"We still have two days to pay rent!" I reminded the landlord, confused why they were there.

The officer brushed his finger across my lips. "We don't care about your rent. We are looking for traitors."

"There's no one here but us," I said.

"Well, then. Maybe you're the traitors."

When I think of that day, what I remember most is Sitti Wasfi-yeh's face. She looked up from her prayer mat at the stampede of soldiers and police searching our apartment, overturning furniture, spilling drawers, gutting cushions, and breaking things. My grand-mother's face was ashen, her mouth open, though no words came out. I rushed to her, worried she was having a heart attack, and when she felt my arms around her, she began to sob. My mother yelled, "We are not collaborators. You're making a mistake. We've been in this country for twenty-five years. We love Kuwait."

It pained me to see my mother beg. I hated those men. Now I hated Kuwait. I hated their emirs and their people. I hated that I had pledged allegiance to them in school, danced for their Inde-pendence Day.

"Look at this!" one of them shouted, holding up the bag of Chanel lipstick, reading the receipt. "They shop in London for expensive makeup." The rest of them went to look at the bag.

"Open this!" another barked, pointing to the safe. Mama and I looked at each other. I kissed Sitti Wasfiyeh and got up to open it.

Most of what I had saved over the past year had already been de-posited in our bank account for Jehad's university, and just the day before I had used most of what was left in the safe to pay the lawyer. The police took what little remained, along with my gold shabka.

"You clearly have plenty to be shopping in London for lipstick. You probably don't need this," an officer said, smiling as he took the bag of Chanel lipstick, tucking our money and gold into it. He picked up the few notes of Iraqi currency and balled them in his fist. "You can keep these," he said, throwing them at me.

My grandmother cried like I'd never seen. She looked so small, vulnerable and helpless, the creases on her face filling with tears, like small rivers. As the men were leaving, she said in a quivering, tired voice, "Why, my sons? Why did you do this? This is haram, my sons. It's *haram*. Why do you treat us like this?"

One of them, a young man who had seemed uncomfortable in his skin, turned to her, his eyes downcast. "I'm sorry, *khala*," he said. I'm sorry, Auntie. But he was quickly shoved aside by the man who had confiscated our savings. "Go ask Yasser Arafat why!" He spat on our floor and left.

The landlord stayed behind to remind us, "Two more days. Six months' back rent. All of it or you're out. No partial payment."

———

As the banks slowly unfroze accounts, hordes of people pushed and pried their way into the branches, and most ATMs were out of order or out of money. Remarkably, the restored Kuwaiti government announced that all bank accounts would be replenished to what they had been on August 2, the day time stood still, as if the past six months never happened. Some banks managed to get people to form lines, but mostly it was chaos. I waited five hours without success to access my account. The second day I camped outside the bank and managed to get a turn when it opened, but they would only allow me to withdraw a small amount, not enough to pay the landlord.

I left the bank and went to ask Um Buraq for a loan.

"Nahr," she said. Um Buraq only called me by that name when she communicated grave matters. "I wish I could help. But I don't know if I'm safe right now, and I need to hold on to every penny. My husband came this morning and made me give him all my gold jewelry. That cunt of a man wants to take a third wife, to 'celebrate liberation'! He said he would turn me in to the police as a collaborator if I didn't. The way things are right now, they'll believe him, since I'm sure some of my cousins in Iraq have kids in the military. The government's announcement to replenish accounts to what they were the day before the invasion means they will deposit back the money I gave to Deepa. But it's going to take some time. I'll give you whatever I can then, but for right now, I just can't. But if I were you . . . I hate to say this . . . you should ask Abu Moathe for help. At a minimum, he could make sure you got all your money out of your bank account."

It sickened me to turn to Abu Moathe, but I was out of options.

I called first to gauge his mood. If I didn't get a good vibe, I planned to call Abu Nasser, the panty sniffer. But Abu Moathe seemed happy to hear from me and said to hurry over. He would tell the guards to let me into the bank.

Two armed guards managed the throngs of people pulsing impatiently outside, allowing only a few in at a time. I shoved my way through to the guards, flashing my ID. "Abu Moathe is expecting me," I said.

Inside, I was shown to the manager's office, where Abu Moathe walked around a large wooden desk to greet me.

"Salaam, my friend. Your visit honors me," he began with the customary flattery, then called on someone to bring us drinks. "What can I offer you?" he asked. "I recall you prefer tea to coffee."

"Tea would be lovely. Thank you very much, Abu Moathe," I said, and he ordered the old woman standing timidly at the door to bring two glasses of tea.

He walked around me to close the door, brushing his fingers across my shoulder. "To what do I owe the honor?" he asked.

The old woman came in with the tray of hot tea and placed it on his desk as I explained that I needed to withdraw my money to pay our rent and to get my brother out of jail. I told him my brother was innocent, arrested even though he had been in Jordan studying during the occupation.

"Then how could they arrest him if he was out of the country?"

I stuttered, "He, he, he came back at the end of the first semester, a few weeks before the liberation war."

"You lied," he said, smirking, offering me a cigarette. I declined, feeling like prey in a trap.

"I didn't lie, Abu Moathe. May God forgive you for saying that."

He lit a cigarette, saying to himself, "She dares to mention God."

"I'm sorry, Abu Moathe. I'll just go." I got up to leave.

"Sit down!" he barked. "You must have forgotten who I am. I will tell you when you can go."

I did as he ordered, glancing around surreptitiously for something with which to protect myself. There was only a mess of papers and files on his desk. Some pens, an empty demitasse, and a paperweight—a drop of oil embedded in a glass cube, nothing that would harm him much. He reclined in his leather chair, smirking again, a cloud of smoke foaming from his mouth. His large belly protruded in front of him.

"I always found it strange that a woman like you didn't smoke."

"What do you mean, a woman like me?" I tried to gather the courage to walk out, at the same time noticing a bank card attached to a paper on his desk.

"You know what I mean," he said. "Anyway, I looked up your account after you called. It never occurred to me to look you up by the name Yaqoot. I never believed it was your real name." He paused. "But I guess whores tell the truth sometimes."

I wiggled my toes inside my high heels, still mustering the will to get up. I tried not to glance at the paper with the attached bank card. When banks sent new account cards, they came with preset PIN codes, which could be reset at any ATM. It was probably his bank card with the code. The glass cube paperweight was next to it.

"You got a nice amount of savings from this country, didn't you?" he said, sipping from the glass of tea in his hand. He set it down, then stood and walked around the desk toward me.

"Please, Abu Moathe . . ."

"I'll give you the money from your account. But what's in it for me? Or do you just want to take and take and give nothing? That's what Palestinians do. You eat, then bite the hand that fed you." I thought better of reminding him of his Palestinian origins.

I got up to leave, but he pulled me back by my hair. I remembered how much it used to give him pleasure to yank my hair. "Bend over and pull up your dress, whore." He pushed me, warning me what would happen if I didn't keep quiet.

"I will toss you out of this door and yell for everyone to hear that you came in offering to suck my dick for money. And you'll be in jail right next to your brother, the filthy dog son of a whore."

I steadied myself, lifted my dress, and lowered my panties. They were white with blue lace trim. I bent over the desk slowly, over the glass cube paperweight and bank card, which I could see now had his name. He pushed my legs apart. I curled my toes inside my shoes, my fingers around the paperweight in one palm, and my nails into the flesh of the other. He pushed himself inside me. I clenched my teeth, dug my nails deeper into my skin, and watched the ripples in the glass of tea as he panted behind me. "You fucking ungrateful Palestinians. Did you think that was it? That Saddam was going to rule Kuwait? You thought you could betray us like that? Here's your reminder, bitch. This is what Palestinians are good for. Cheap labor and cheap whores. We buy and sell people like you here."

I loosened my fists, left one palm on the paperweight and grabbed the bank card with the other, memorized the PIN code printed in small numerals, and stuffed the card into my brassiere.

"This is what you get now, whore."

I repeated the number in my head over and over, until he discharged himself inside me. I pulled up my white underpants with the blue lace trim. Pulled down my dress. Straightened myself and waited, plotting my revenge.

He buzzed his assistant. "Bring Madam Yaqoot's file.

"Sit," he told me. I sat, feeling his semen slip out of me. "And drink some of that tea," he added. I picked up the glass, sipped the tea, repeating the PIN code to myself: 3254, 3254, 3254.

A knock on the door was followed by a young woman with a file. I avoided looking at her. She waited while he opened the file, then handed it back to her. She gave me a few forms from the folder to sign. I handed her my ID, and she returned with the balance of my bank account. It wasn't the restored value, as promised by the government, but I didn't press for it, especially since Abu Moathe's bank card was snuggled between my tits.

I thanked Abu Moathe as if he had not just raped me. He told me I was welcome as if he had not just raped me.

Walking into the crowd still waiting outside, I felt more semen trickle down my inner thighs and I imagined withdrawing all his fucking money from his fucking bank account with that fucking bank card tucked in my breasts. *3254, 3254.*

I made it home. But it wasn't home. The apartment where I had lived most of my life was alien now. We had not been able to put it back together since the police turned it upside down. Mama had been busy caring for Sitti Wasfiyeh, who was taken to the hospital because her "head was exploding," as she said. Her blood pressure was dangerously high. She would have had a stroke if Mama hadn't gotten her to a doctor in time. But I had the money from my account, and it helped Mama and Sitti Wasfiyeh sleep that night, secure in knowing we would not be thrown out of our apartment, our possessions dumped in the street.

Emptying my bank account gave us enough to pay the landlord, the lawyer, and bribes to whomever the lawyer suggested. "They know he wasn't in the country," the lawyer said. "But there's no rule of law right now. We just have to convince them to let him go."

I wondered how much money Abu Moathe had in his account, and I began to panic thinking what might happen if he realized his card was gone. He could inform the authorities that I'd taken it. But I recalled how careless and disorganized he was. He probably didn't remember the card was on his desk and would blame his secretary for misplacing it.

The next day and for the following two weeks, Um Buraq and I drove all around the country with Abu Moathe's bank card, in search of available ATMs, where we began withdrawing as much as we could from each location, every day.

Our lawyer enlisted the help of an international human rights organization, which was successful in getting Jehad transferred to a hospital. The combination of pressure from the media, bribes, and legal channels finally persuaded the authorities to release him.

Mama and I got to work cleaning and putting the apartment back together in anticipation of Jehad's return. We glued and nailed broken drawers and cabinets as best we could, refolded clothes, stacked belongings on shelves, and filled four bags of trash. We cleaned the windows, wiped the furniture, scrubbed the bathroom and kitchen, swept, mopped, beat and aired out the rugs, washed bedding, and did laundry. Sitti Wasfiyeh wanted to help. We put all our knickknacks and cutlery in front of her to wipe and shine. She had the most comfortable mattress and swore by God that her grandson must sleep on it until he was healed. "You're welcome to take my bed," I offered.

"I'm not sleeping with you cows," she said, waving me off. "Arrange me a bed on the floor next to my grandson."

Mama and I looked at each other. "No. That will not work. Your snoring will keep him up," I said.

She hesitated, moving her dentures around in her mouth with her tongue. "Okay. I didn't think about that. I'll sleep in your bed," she said, and went back to shining a spoon.

Exhausted that evening, we went to bed early. Sitti Wasfiyeh wanted to keep the clean sheets on her bed fresh for Jehad, so she had gotten a head start on her new sleeping arrangement in Mama's and my bed. Still, she complained we hadn't washed the sheets properly, had not fixed the bed comfortably enough, that the dinner we ate had been too greasy and, therefore, she probably wouldn't be able to sleep, would get sick and not be able to go get her grandson from the hospital, all because of me. Or because of Mama. Or both of us. It was a conspiracy against her. She was sure of it, until she fell asleep.

We were all up before the sun, waiting in the lobby of the hospital for permission to see Jehad and, we hoped, bring him home. Sitti Wasfiyeh looked small and frail as she sat there patiently, counting her rosary beads for hours.

Finally the lawyer walked in, a small stack of papers in hand, and motioned for us to follow him. Jehad's release had been secured. "*Alhamdulillah*," we all sighed. Thank you, Lord!

I helped Sitti Wasfiyeh to her feet and we followed the lawyer to a hospital room, where Jehad sat in a wheelchair. We rushed to him as the lawyer negotiated with the guards, going through the stack of papers he had brought. Heavy bandages covered half of Jehad's face. Doctors had been unable to save his eye. His arm was in a cast, with fourteen screws in the bones of his right hand and forearm. The official record stated that he fell, hitting stationary objects in such a way that caused severe trauma to his optic nerve, secondary to deep ocular lacerations and fragmentation of the orbital bone and optic canal. There was more medical jargon I didn't understand—multiple metacarpal and phalangeal bones comminuted at the level of the metacarpophalangeal joint. But Jehad got up when he saw us and kissed Sitti Wasfiyeh's hands, our mother's, then me. I understood a new kind of joy that day. It was the sort of happiness that comes only when life takes everything and leaves you only the people who matter most. Being with my family in the relief of Jehad's safety that day brought us back to life.

Jehad wanted rest when we got back to the apartment. We had a small meal together. He ate very little and said even less. Seeing Jehad so defeated was hard to bear. He had been spared, but we could not be sure any of us would survive in Kuwait much longer. The emotional toll of the day had exhausted us, and we went to bed early. Mama tucked Jehad into bed, taking all of our pillows to make sure he was propped up as the doctors had ordered, to reduce the pressure on his remaining eye.

I watched him sleep from the doorway, knowing I would never forgive myself. Jehad had stayed in Kuwait because I'd sided with

Sitti Wasfiyeh and refused to leave. I will carry his broken dreams for the rest of my life.

I'd like to tell what happened to my brother. What they did to him. The ways they violated and broke him. How Kuwaiti police and military colluded with the Americans to empty him of himself. I'd like to tell because I want the world to know what they got away with, what the powerful always get away with. But it is not my story to tell, and Jehad has found solace in silence.

We were one of a few Palestinian families from our neighborhood still in Kuwait. Street after street of apartment buildings stood empty. The corner stores that once flashed with lights and colorful FOR SALE signs were now dim and shuttered. The kids who played ball in the street had disappeared. The young men who used to gather on corners to watch and harass us women were no more. The balcony clotheslines that once decorated every building with laundry were bare.

We had stayed because we could not leave Jehad behind. Now that he was back, we packed up what we could carry of our lives: clothes, a few kitchen items, the framed photo of Baba on the living room wall, and Mama's Singer sewing machine. There were two more families left on our block, one in our building and another in the adjacent one. They came to welcome Jehad back, and we decided to all leave together in the early morning, believing there might be some safety in numbers to get through the checkpoints on the way to the airport.

We wanted to take our cars on the fourteen-hour journey to Amman, but they had Iraqi license plates—we had been forced to change them during the occupation, and now Kuwait would not allow Palestinians to get new car plates. Um Buraq promised to sell our cars for us and send the money. And to my surprise, she showed up at four o'clock on the morning of our planned departure to drive us to the airport.

"I want to make sure the paperwork for the cars is in order," she said.

"Liar. We already did that," I said, hugging her. "You came because you love me. Admit it, you old bat."

There had been times when Mama tried to forbid me to see Um Buraq, believing she was a bad influence. But now she embraced her and thanked her for helping us get out of the country.

While Mama cooked up a breakfast to start us on our journey, Um Buraq and I made one last run to an ATM with Abu Moathe's card. "I'm a little scared that this might be the day we get caught," I said.

"How are we going to get caught? It's four in the morning," Um Buraq said. She had a point. "Plus, it's a savings account. So he's obviously not checking it regularly. I'm sure he has another card for his daily account." By that point, we had withdrawn nearly 12,000 dinars, which we split evenly between us. The account still had a balance of a little over 9,860 dinars.

At last it was time to go. Our neighbors waited in three taxis as the five of us squeezed into Um Buraq's Lincoln Continental. Mama asked Um Buraq how she'd gotten all those dings and scratches on her car. "People in this country can't drive," Um Buraq explained, and we set off.

Ajay had mostly been the one who drove her car. In the short time since he had left, she had managed to crash into sidewalks, a streetlight pole, and the side of a building. She was so tiny, she had to crane her neck to see over the steering wheel and swerved in and out of lanes.

Jehad didn't say much, but Um Buraq went on apologizing for

what the police had done to him. She said Kuwait would suffer a loss for not embracing a young man as smart and passionate as him. To spare Jehad, I changed the subject by asking about Deepa and Ajay.

"I can't believe I forgot to tell you!" she exclaimed, bumping the car into the sidewalk, jolting us all. "Deepa bought a house!"

"Stop!" Sitti Wasfiyeh yelled. "Stop the car!"

Um Buraq slammed on the brakes in the middle of the road. "*Bismillah!*" she yelled. "What's wrong, Hajjeh?"

Our neighbors in the taxi behind us also slammed their brakes, almost ramming into us.

"I want to sit in the backseat," my grandmother demanded. "I didn't survive four wars just to die in a car accident. Help me out of here!" she ordered, opening the door.

I had grown accustomed to Um Buraq's crazy driving over the past months, but Mama and Sitti Wasfiyeh were bracing themselves. Um Buraq seemed puzzled. Jehad smiled, almost laughing, and that made me so happy I laughed too. I couldn't stop, which made Mama laugh. Sitti Wasfiyeh was delighted to have provoked it all. "I've always been funny, even when I was a little girl. I could make people laugh like this," she said. And that turned Jehad's smile into laughter too. Even Um Buraq was laughing, all of us inside her banged-up Lincoln Continental at the head of a four-car caravan on an eerily quiet road, heading away from a deserted Palestinian city inside Kuwait.

"This country will never be the same without Palestinians. Look at all these empty buildings," Um Buraq said when we all quieted down.

Mama began sobbing in the backseat. Sitti Wasfiyeh chimed in, cursing Israelis and Yasser Arafat. She raised her hands in prayer. "O God, my Lord, destroy the Jews for making us endless refugees and condemn Yasser Arafat for causing another Palestinian exodus. O my Lord, burn the Americans and burn the Jews. They are behind all these wars."

"Amen," Mama said.

Jehad remained silent, watching the world speed by his window.

We were stopped at two checkpoints along the way, but thanks to Um Buraq we passed without incident. She showed her ID, clearly listing her as Kuwaiti, and lied that we, along with the caravan behind us, were Palestinians who had sheltered and saved her entire family during the occupation. She spoke to them with the authority of a public auntie, and they responded with due deference to an elder, waving us all through after checking our IDs.

"Um Buraq, I don't think we could have gotten through these checkpoints without more humiliation if it hadn't been for you. May God bless you, keep evil away from you, and bring brightness and joy to all your days," Mama said.

Sitti Wasfiyeh joined in with prayer and appreciation for Um Buraq. I listened to Jehad's silence. He was somewhere else.

Um Buraq took me in a warm embrace at the airport before we left. She kissed both my cheeks several times, wished me Godspeed, and whispered in my ear, "I'll send customers your way if you need money. Just let me know. And you can probably use that card in Amman. Give it a try. God be with you, Sister."

I kissed her again, and when we pulled back, she cupped my face in her palms and said:

"Whatever happens in this ungenerous world, we will meet again, my sister."

III.

JORDAN

THE CUBE, NORTH

THE NORTH SIDE of my universe is a gray wall with three protruding items. The first is a small toilet made of thick plastic, which flushes when it pleases. I try to coordinate my body functions with its timing, but it's random, so it smells in here, which I prefer to the disinfectant they spray from little holes in all the walls.

There are also two electronic receptacles where my prison bracelets fasten. Two small spots blink yellow when I must insert my bracelets to shackle myself. Robotic innards in the wall shriek and mechanically grab my bracelets, locking me to the wall. Then the yellow light turns green and an earsplitting alarm goes off, alerting the guards that they can safely enter. One of the "improvements" Israel made was to lower the volume on the alarm. When visitors come to survey the Cube, they are shown this feature to demonstrate how conditions are adjusted for my comfort and convenience.

But even the best inventions for confinement and subjugation cannot account for life's resolve to freedom. These high-tech shackles are meant to hold me in place with my arms behind my back, but I fasten myself facing the wall, to my jailers' great annoyance. I remain that way until visitors leave. In the meantime, sometimes I sing, and when possible, I fart. Their discomfort gives me pleasure. In this way, the north side is both the domain of bondage and the direction for defiance.

I waged my fight for writing utensils on the north wall. The guards had ignored all my requests for pen and paper until I used bodily fluids to write on that wall. In menstrual blood I wrote: *Long live Saddam Hussein*, and in feces: *Israel is shit*.

They made me clean it, but gave me a pencil to keep. I won.

Except for prison-industry guests, Israeli law allows only immediate family to visit Palestinian prisoners. My husband is gone. I have no children. That means only my mother and, possibly, my brother could come, but Israel revoked Jehad's hawiyya and put his and Mama's names on a visa blacklist. They cannot even enter the country, much less visit me in the Cube.

I have a recurring dream that I'm drinking coffee with Saddam Hussein. I am desperate to speak to him, but we sit in silence, staring at each other. We turn our cups over to allow the coffee grounds to paint our fates. Um Buraq arrives to read our fortunes, but I insist we wait for Jehad to arrive. Then both Saddam and Um Buraq point to an olive tree in our midst, and I am satisfied Jehad is with us. But the tree is also Bilal. Um Buraq contemplates Saddam's cup and after a moment laments that Jehad should have left Kuwait before the Americans came. Saddam shrugs and motions to my cup. I turn it over and, to my horror, I see faceless men beating my brother. I seek Bilal for help, but the olive tree is gone. I wake up in panic, sweat, and regret. Then I try hard to get back to the dream to rescue my brother, to leave Kuwait before the Americans come.

UNSTEADY EARTH

ONE OF THE families in our caravan had a home in Amman, where we stayed for a couple of weeks until we could find a place. We eventually rented a one-bedroom, furnished apartment. It was the best we could afford at the time. Sitti Wasfiyeh got the bedroom. The rest of us rolled out our bedding in the family room. In fairness, Sitti Wasfiyeh urged Mama or Jehad to take the bedroom, but we insisted it was hers. She was our elder, after all.

"May God bless you, my children. Um Jehad, you are the only real daughter I ever had," she said on her way to bed that first night, leaving us shocked by her sincere gratitude. I think it broke her heart that her daughters, who lived in Jordan, had not insisted she live with them. The three of us watched Sitti Wasfiyeh's small, hunched body shuffle to her new room. Jehad jumped up to help her walk, and for the rest of the night, even in my dreams, I thought of my grandmother, her anguished life in a world that could not spare a space for her.

Amman felt like the worst place in the world, even though I had rarely traveled outside Kuwait, and never beyond our region. The small buildings with shops, passed off as malls, were uninspiring and overpriced. The quality of everything from food to clothing to hair salons was inferior to what I was accustomed to in Kuwait, yet cost nearly twice as much. I tried to find work, but unemployment in Jordan was already high before half a million Palestinians displaced from Kuwait descended on the country.

Everywhere I turned in Amman there was a reminder of loss. My favorite Kuwaiti television series—of Um E'leiwi and Bu E'leiwi, Suad Abdullah and Hayat elFahd and Maryam Saleh—were now painful to watch. I missed Kuwait's ocean, the warm blue immensity that accompanied us wherever we were, even when we camped in the desert during winter. The Arabian Gulf lapped at all my memories: its salty air brushing against our skin, threading our hair, and infusing our lungs when we sat at beachside cafés or evening concerts; the tide revealing and hiding tens of thousands of scampering crabs; the scorching sand blistering our feet; the boys we watched watching us on the beach, its warm water washing away our worries; ice cream from Ala'a Eddin in Salmiya, frozen *booza dhahab* cooling us in the heat. I was so far from those shores that held everything I knew in the world. I had not yet imagined a future for myself, but somehow I knew it had been derailed. I suppose I had always assumed that whatever dreams I thought to follow would unfold in the familiar landscape of Kuwait. Now the land had been pulled from under my feet and I wobbled in the unsteady terrain of refugees, struggling to carry on.

It wasn't like that for Mama or even Sitti Wasfiyeh, who had sworn she would never recover from becoming a refugee again. It amazed me to see how quickly they got comfortable in the new apartment and settled into a routine, as if their lives had simply been excised and replanted elsewhere, intact, with just a dusting of grief they shook off before returning to the business of living.

Maybe it was easier because the trauma of forced displacement was already well-known to them, and they understood how idleness and purposelessness could dull the mind, droop the eyelids, and seep too much sleep and despair into the day. They were experienced refugees, better equipped to handle recurring generational trauma.

Mama soon struck a deal with a local tailor to take up his extra work, filling our apartment with the familiar hum of her Singer sewing machine. She started with simple hemming and mending jobs, then got an order for traditional *tatreez* embroidery, which was followed by a few more such commissions. I had watched my mother embroider now and then over the years, but I'd never paid much attention to it. To my young eyes, embroidered caftans belonged to another generation, and I foolishly thought them unrefined compared to modern European clothes. But in Amman, in the haze of my exile and idleness and through the lens of loss, the spectacular intricacy of tatreez crystallized as I watched my mother create gorgeous caftans, and I finally realized hers was a masterful testament to our heritage and her own artistry. She would spend hours upon painstaking hours hunched over her lap, needle and thimble pulling and pushing threads in and out of fabric, creating patterns that told the stories of our people in a pictorial language conceived by Palestinian women over centuries. Mama was fluent. She knew which patterns came from which village, what they meant, and how that meaning might change next to another pattern. She'd tried to teach me when I was a little girl, but I had wanted no part of it.

Now, in the Cube, I recall the day she gave up trying to teach me. She said, "I don't blame you. If I had a chance to go to school like you, that's what I would have done instead. You're a smart girl. Someday you'll have a desk job, not like me, who only knows how to embroider a past we cannot recover."

Mama was more skilled than most, and before long she had carved out a niche in Amman embroidering wedding thobes—the most delicate and expensive tatreez commissions. One such dress would ordinarily require six to nine months to create, but our financial situation pushed Mama to work even longer hours, producing one every two to three months. Each of them was a work of art, meticulously embroidered to tell stories, and it pained me to see them sold.

Her first customer was a bride who wanted traditional tatreez designs on silk, an impossibly difficult material for embroidery. She specified that the design speak to the place of her heritage in Palestine and to that of her groom, and she wanted my mother to copy designs from the *qabbah*, *shinyar*, and *radah* parts of a tattered caftan that had belonged to her mother's great-grandmother. But Mama suggested combining the old and the new, incorporating actual pieces of the ancient caftan's tatreez into the bridal gown. The woman agreed once she saw Mama's drawings, and the final product was stunning.

The bride-to-be twirled before the mirror in her gorgeous new dress, saying, "You are a genius, Um Jehad! Better than all those fancy designers. Their gowns can't hold a candle to this. My friends will die of envy when they see me at the wedding, and I know my groom will love it too."

The fitting and sewing room doubled as our family room, which was also our bedroom by night. I had nowhere to escape that woman's happiness. My heart ached as I watched the bride admire herself in the mirror. Mama had wanted to design my wedding gown, but I went shopping for "modernity." I'm sure I said something insensitive to her about being stuck in the past; that thobes were for a bygone world. I'm sure it hurt her, although she never let on. This moment with a stranger twirling in the gorgeous gown my mother had created should have been mine to share with Mama. I had to become another person, someone at the other end of disgrace, rape, and exile, to fully appreciate that my mother, a simple widow with an elementary education, was an extraordinary artist. My mother was a maker of beauty, a brilliant custodian of culture and history. And I was the ungrateful daughter who had not understood until now.

"I'll bet my friends are going to ask you to make their dresses for them too," the woman said. "But no matter what, please don't tell them what I paid. If they want you to make a dress, I suggest you charge them at least four times what you charged me."

"If you think it's worth it, why don't you just pay that much for your own dress?" I said, but Mama's look told me to mind my own business. She smiled at the woman, who pretended not to hear me, and I left them to answer the phone in the hallway.

"Um Buraq! *Yis'ed soutik.* Hello, my friend," I said as soon as I heard her voice.

"Darling, listen. My phones are probably bugged so I'm calling from a public phone and don't have much time," she said, sounding out of breath.

"*Kheir . . . ?*"

"You-know-who called me a few days ago. He thinks you stole his bank card and withdrew money from his account. I told him you would never do such a thing," she said, pausing to take a breath. "He tried to make me give him your address in Amman, but I told him I had no idea where you were. I don't want to know. You need to watch your back. He said he will destroy you if it's the last thing he ever does."

"He can have at it, the whore son of a whore. Fuck his mother's pussy," I said. Um Buraq brought out the vulgarity in me, and I liked the way it sounded on my tongue.

"I'll call you later. There are people waiting for the phone. He reminded me that he still has those pictures and I'm worried he'll do something stupid. I'll see what I can do here. God be with you," she said, and hung up.

I wasn't concerned about the photos. There was no one to show them to, because my family had all left the country. I was more worried about money. I still hadn't been able to find a job and what I'd withdrawn from Abu Moathe's account was spent on a down payment for a car. I had tried to use his card in Amman, but it didn't work. Now I knew why.

A week later, Mama was making final adjustments on the bride's wedding dress.

"Mama, I'm sorry I was rude to that bride. I didn't mean to interfere in your work. It's just that she has unlimited money and she is still happy to cheat you. The dress is fit for royalty." My words weren't nearly adequate to express the love and torment I felt.

"You have to let me do this my way. I'm just trying to keep the rent paid and lights on," she said, squeezing my hand lovingly. I knew she didn't say that to remind me that I needed to get a job, but I felt it nonetheless. I had been the breadwinner and caretaker of the family. That was my identity. But there was nothing for me in Amman. Mama had a unique skill, but administrators and beauticians were a dime a dozen.

I looked at Mama's face, that thing in my chest squeezing again, and it occurred to me that she had been around my age when she was forced out of her home in Palestine. She had come to Amman then too, before journeying on to Kuwait with my father. It seemed to me that fate was inherited, like eye color. I wondered if she had felt the same disorientation that now ruled my days. Had it been all she could think about—the incomprehensibility of forced, permanent displacement?

I threw my arms around her and buried my face in her neck. "I was stupid before not to appreciate your tatreez, Mama. I promise I am going to find work. I want you to rest."

"Darling, I don't mind tatreez. It gives me something to do. Makes me feel useful. Maybe it also reminds me of when I was a girl," she said, stroking my hair. "Don't worry. I know you'll find the right job soon. In the meantime, you deserve some rest. You're the one who has been carrying this family for years. If it hadn't been for your hard work and smart investments, we would never have made it out. You're the one who managed to earn enough to send your brother to college. He'd still be there if it wasn't for Saddam, son of a bitch. But alhamdulillah, my daughter. Everything will be fine. We take what God gives us, good and bad, and trust in His wisdom."

I sobbed harder on her chest. I had told so many lies and kept secrets that stood between us, a darkness where images lurked of who I really was. I felt dirty in my mother's arms, wishing I could be the strong, resourceful woman she thought I was. She held me, stroking my face with one hand and wiping my tears with the other. "I am going to make you the most beautiful dress I've ever embroidered for your wedding, because you will find the right man to love and marry," she said.

She kissed my forehead and wiped my tears, then picked up an embroidering spool. "Right now, I have to get back to this. I've got another small job before I finish the wedding dress."

"I can help if you want," I offered.

Mama set me up next to her with some thread and a chest piece that would be sewn to a thobe once it was embroidered. I followed her instructions for the cypress tree and pasha's tent motifs and managed to accomplish about four centimeters of stitching before I realized it was all wrong. I unraveled the mess and started over, already bored and frustrated. But I pushed through, wanting to prove something—I don't know what. Mama would look over at me occasionally and smile, making small talk about things she wanted to buy for the apartment, people we needed to visit soon to pay respects for a death or offer congratulations on a birth, upcoming wedding invitations. "And Ramadan is just around the corner," she added.

"Is this right, Mama?" I showed her my second attempt. She leaned over my work, then looked at me. We both knew I was useless at anything requiring patience, but we pretended anyway, and now faced the inevitable. We held each other with our eyes. She grinned. I did the same, and irrepressible laughter rose in us both.

"You actually lasted longer than I expected," Mama finally said. "Why don't you go make us some tea while I do this."

"Tea coming up. And I have an even better idea. Wait." I went to the kitchen to start the kettle, then filled a small plastic tub with warm water and heaps of black salt. I gathered a few towels, a bottle of nail polish, two small volcanic rocks from the bathroom, and a jar of body butter I had made the day before from olive oil, coconut butter, rosewater, eucalyptus leaves, and thyme.

I returned with the tray of tea glasses and fetched the tub and cream. "Close your eyes and don't open them until I tell you," I instructed. "And just lift your dishdasha to your knees."

She did as I said, exposing her lower legs. I lifted her feet one by one and gently placed them into the warm black-salt water. She let out a long, satisfied sigh as she opened her eyes. "This feels wonderful, my daughter. God bless you and bring you love and happiness."

"Keep the prayers going. There's more. Get ready for my specialty pedicure!" I said.

I rubbed Mama's feet in the salt water, scrubbing off the dead skin with the volcanic rocks. She put her embroidery aside to enjoy the pampering. I wrapped her feet in hot towels, cut away the cuticles on her toes, cleaned the nails, buffed and painted them red, then massaged my special butter into her feet and calves. It pleased me to watch her relax—tension and aches dissolving in my hands.

"I don't know why you don't just open your own salon. You've always been so good at these things. I don't know anyone who knows more about beauty and health. You do everything. Eyebrows, waxing, haircuts, blowouts, nails, feet, makeup, skin care. Everything! And you're the only person I know who makes natural cosmetics. People would pay a lot of money to feel as good as you're making me feel right now," she said.

"You really think that could work?" I was daring in many things, but not with what little money we had.

"Of course! When have you ever known me not to tell the truth?"

Sitti Wasfiyeh, who had just returned from a visit with her daughters, was hobbling through the door on her cane as Mama spoke. "You lie all the time," she said casually. "What did you two make to eat today? I hope it's good."

Mama and I laughed quietly, and she called out, "Welcome back, Hajjeh! We missed you all day. I made *mlookhiya*, soupy, the way you like it."

And I added, "Didn't my aunts feed you?"

We waited to hear the lie and complaints we knew were coming.

"Oh. That's nice. But I wanted *msakhan* today, and you know my daughters' cooking is shit since they moved in with their in-laws. They're not allowed to cook the way I taught them," she said, rekindling our laughter, which made Sitti Wasfiyeh even grumpier.

"She's going to make me do her feet now too, isn't she?" I whispered to Mama.

"You may as well get it all ready or else we won't hear the end of how terrible her feet look and feel," Mama said.

As I got up to carry the dirty water away, Mama remembered to ask me, "Oh, by the way, have you heard from Um Buraq?"

"No. She called me last week, but I haven't been able to get an answer on the phone since. Why?"

"It must be true, then," Mama said. "I heard she's in jail."

"*What?*" I almost dropped the tub of dirty water.

"I don't know the details. I heard that someone, maybe her driver, turned her in to the authorities for collaborating with the Iraqis." Then Mama whispered, "Actually, they apparently said that she was having an affair with an Iraqi officer. It's hard to believe, though. A woman of her age . . ."

"Are you talking about Ajay? He went back to India, him and Deepa, his wife, when we were still in Kuwait. This doesn't make sense."

"Nothing in the world makes sense. I'm just telling you what I heard. It's in the newspaper, but I didn't read it yet. I could never figure out that woman. She was too crass for my taste, but she was always so kind and generous. Regardless, she doesn't deserve to be in prison," Mama said, adding, "You never know who you can really trust in this world. Look what her driver did to her after she kept them in her house all those years."

Buried in the Arab World section of the newspaper, below an article about new word processors with Arabic script, I found an article about an electronic web called "the Internet," which would soon connect the world through machines and television-like monitors.

It sounded like science fiction to me, so I thought the article next to it, about a Kuwaiti woman collaborator, might also be some kind of fiction, particularly because it didn't mention her name.

I called around to our old crew, some mutual friends in Kuwait, and some of the ladies from our makeshift salon during Iraq's occupation. The story that emerged was that Um Buraq had indeed been arrested and put in jail, along with another woman, on charges of treason.

Sometime after Deepa and Ajay left for India, Um Buraq's neighbor demanded payment from her, claiming Ajay had gotten her housekeeper pregnant. The neighbor insisted that, as Ajay's employer, Um Buraq was responsible for the financial loss incurred from having to send the housekeeper back to Sri Lanka. Of course, Um Buraq did not pay. She made it known that Ajay was impotent. An argument ensued, and Um Buraq didn't hold back. "Do a blood test. You might find out your husband is the father," she told her neighbor.

A few short months later, police broke down Um Buraq's door, arresting her in the middle of the night. At her trial, the prosecution produced sworn witness statements that she had collaborated with the Iraqi occupation and had violated various virtue and decency laws. The neighbor woman and her husband testified that they had seen Iraqi officials coming and going from her home late at night. They said she and a Palestinian friend were both collaborators. I guessed they meant me, so I made sure to hide the paper from Mama.

The prosecution was also able to obtain a corroborating statement from Ajay. He testified at the Kuwaiti embassy in India that he personally drove her to and from an Iraqi military center, where she informed on a Kuwaiti member of the resistance. Ajay had found a way to take revenge on Um Buraq for withholding half his wages for years and, in the end, turning the money over to Deepa.

Everything Ajay told them was true. Um Buraq had indeed informed on a Kuwaiti, but it was to save the man's wife, whom he
had beaten so severely she was unrecognizable. The woman had
been a regular customer at our salon. When she didn't show up for
a week, we found her in the hospital, recovering from three broken
ribs, a punctured lung, a busted jaw, a broken nose, black eyes, and
various cuts and bruises. Not long after the woman was released
from the hospital, Iraqi forces arrested her husband. He died under
Iraqi torture, and now both his wife and Um Buraq were facing life
sentences for his death.

————

Geopolitical news was a staple in local conversations, especially
among the two hundred fifty thousand Palestinians who were kicked
out of Kuwait. Even the least informed knew the headlines, and I was
no different: "US Secretary of State James Baker Asserts 'New World
Order'"; "Madrid Conference: Is This the Beginning of Peace?"

Under the new American president, Bill Clinton, Yasser Arafat
signed a treaty with Israel called the Oslo Accords. There was mass
euphoria, but Jehad said, "It's a disaster." He also saw it as an opportunity. "It might help us restore our hawiyyas," he said. "We had
our residency cards through Baba when we were little, but Israel
revoked them since we couldn't afford to go back to renew after
he died. I have a connection in the PLO who said he can get them
reinstated for us."

"First of all, what the hell are we going to do in Palestine? We
don't know anyone! Second, how do you have a PLO connection?"
I asked.

"We still have a lot of family there," he said, ignoring the second
part of my question.

"That we barely know!"

"Trust me, Nahr. We should really try to get residency cards. We are unwanted in the world. It couldn't hurt for us to have another option, even if we don't use it. How long do you think we've got before something happens here and Jordan kicks us out to God knows where? Anyway, you don't have to do anything. I'll take care of the applications. It has to be done now, because they're only allowing a few people back and just ones who had residency cards in the past, or rich people who can help the economy."

"Fine. Tell me how to help," I said, though I still didn't see the point.

But then he added, "Besides, Mama wants you to get a divorce. The only way to do that is in Palestine, since Mhammad will not come here." Everyone in my life who knew my situation had been urging me to get a divorce. The assumption was that the only decent life I could have would be through a second marriage, and the only way to achieve that was to officially end the first one.

"You too? Why is everyone in my business?" I said.

"Nanu, Mama is right. You might want to get married one of these days."

"Listen, little brother. I appreciate your concern, but you should concentrate on yourself. Do you even like girls anymore?"

"We're not talking about me. And yes, I do. But I don't want to get married now."

"Neither do I."

He laughed. "I should know better than to argue with you."

I laughed too, kissed him, and made us a bite to eat. It was one of the few lighthearted moments Jehad and I had shared since we came to Amman. His time in Kuwaiti jail had changed him forever. Jehad had become a man of compressed, dense quiet. He refused to speak of what had happened to him, left his story embedded in the scars on his body, in the blinded left eye and lame right hand. I respected his choice, especially as I saw how gentle a life he created. Jehad did not become the surgeon he'd dreamed of being, but an artist, a talented and sought-after gardener in Jordan, landscaping some of the most beautiful homes in Amman.

Although I made some attempts to find steady work, I was mostly relishing the sweetness of grief and self-pity. The seduction of sleep was potent, but I managed to crawl my way through each day, busying myself as much as I could. I earned some money here and there threading eyebrows and doing henna designs, but that work was sporadic. Being idle in such a miserable city cleared space in my head for a theater of memory, like choppy movie clips replaying over and over behind my eyes. They had begun to feel less like memories and more like talons ripping at my entrails. The endless work with which I'd populated my time in Kuwait to keep thoughts at bay was gone. Now Abu Moathe in his office at the bank, the men panting and laughing around me like hyenas the night Saddam rolled his army into Kuwait, Abu Nasser the panty sniffer, the filthy abortion clinic in Cairo, the thick bloodied pads between my legs, clawed at me whether awake or sleeping.

Mama's embroidery and Jehad's landscaping work kept a roof over our heads and food on the table. The housekeeping tasks naturally fell to me. I did the cooking, cleaning, and shopping. And I took over caring for Sitti Wasfiyeh. I hadn't realized how much Mama had done for her over the years. She could not, or rather would not, bathe herself. As a child, Sitti Wasfiyeh had bathed her own grandmother, and expected the same from us. She'd grown up in a time when one had to heat bathing water over a flame, and she could not conceive of doing it differently, despite having hot water from the tap. "I don't trust it," she would say.

As Mama used to do, I had to heat large vats over the stove and carry the water to the bathroom, mix it with cooler water, then scoop and pour it over her as she scrubbed herself with olive-oil soap, the only kind she trusted.

Sometime in late December of 1993, Jehad came home early from work.

"I got them!" he said, excitedly brandishing a folder. He had been successful in getting our hawiyyas reinstated, which would enable us to return to Palestine. Only Jehad and I could get them, since we'd had them as children. Mama and Sitti Wasfiyeh would have to get visitor visas if they wanted to go back. None of it made sense to me, and I wasn't particularly eager to go to Palestine. But Jehad was.

Mama and Sitti Wasfiyeh were happy too. In fact, the whole world was. Yasser Arafat got a Nobel Prize, an actual airport was being built in Gaza, and real Palestinian passports were being issued.

"I never thought I'd see the day," Sitti Wasfiyeh said, tearing up. But she still refused to apply for a visitor's visa from the new Israeli embassy in Amman. "I've waited this long, I'll wait a little more until I can go as a citizen in our own state. I'm not going to ask those sons of bitches for permission to go home. I have underwear older than the Zionist entity. The newsman said this Oslo thing means there will be a state in five years. Enshallah, I will still be alive in five years. Alhamdulillah."

Mama didn't mind getting a visitor's visa. "Let them think they own the land. I know better. I know the land owns us, her native children."

I kept quiet, hoping they wouldn't notice me.

Mama turned to me and said, "Praise God, my grandchildren will be born in Palestine."

"Wow. You skipped right to grandchildren. And here I was worried you were going to lecture me again about getting a divorce and remarrying," I said.

"Why are you always sarcastic?" Mama snapped. "Everything is a problem for you. What's wrong with getting married again? Being normal? You're like two different people. One minute you're nice, the next you're vicious."

"I didn't realize you thought I was abnormal or vicious."

Mama narrowed her eyes, a habit that preceded an outburst. Growing up, I had watched it when she fought with my father, or on the days when I brought my report cards home, or when she argued with merchants she thought were ripping her off.

"Yes, I do!" she began, one hand on her hip, the other pointing a finger in my face. "Because it's not normal to choose to be alone this way. The way you talk about men as if they're all devils is not normal. You are still young and beautiful. If you don't find a man soon, you're going to be alone for the rest of your life."

"Be quiet, both of you!" Sitti Wasfiyeh yelled. "You're giving me a headache. My show is about to come on. Go fight outside."

"If you think men are essential to life, then why don't you go find yourself a husband and leave me alone," I yelled back, immediately regretting it.

"Shut up, Nahr!" Jehad scolded me as Mama walked off, mumbling curses.

———

I stayed in Amman to care for Sitti Wasfiyeh while Mama and Jehad went to Palestine. Part of me wanted to go, to get the divorce and have a fresh start. I wanted, too, to visit Palestine as an adult; to see my husband's mother, Hajjeh Um Mhammad, and finally meet his famous brother, Bilal, about whom we had all heard so much over the years. But I told myself I wasn't ready. I realize now, in the silence that echoes off itself in the Cube, that I didn't want to face rumors about me that had likely already traveled there. In the long, idle hours since we came to Amman, I had begun to idealize Palestine as others did, and I secretly imagined a fresh start, maybe opening my own salon there as Mama suggested I do in Amman.

"My daughters are happy to take care of me!" Sitti Wasfiyeh said, adding, "But you should stay here to keep the house clean."

I knew it wouldn't be long before Sitti Wasfiyeh made up an excuse to come back. As much as she tried to be part of her daughters' families, she was rarely more than a burden to them. It took just one day for her to call me to come get her, claiming she had forgotten her blood pressure medicine.

"I can bring your pills to you, Sitti," I said.

"Just do as I say and come get me," she huffed, and hung up.

I chatted a bit with my insufferable aunt Latifa when I arrived. She told me Sitti Wasfiyeh had complained that she had to go back to the apartment "to keep watch over you since you are there alone." I didn't contradict her, because I wasn't about to bad-talk my grandmother to her. I only trash-talked Sitti Wasfiyeh to my mother and Jehad. I noticed, too, that my aunt began rushing me out the door after her husband called to tell her he was returning home early.

Before we left, I said to Sitti Wasfiyeh, in front of Aunt Latifa, "I'm lucky to have a grandmother like you who doesn't leave me alone in the apartment." Sitti smiled with her loose dentures and dancing eyes. All my life I had heard Sitti Wasfiyeh claim how much her daughters wanted her to live with them, how we were lucky she chose us instead, and how poorly we compared financially, in beauty, in housekeeping and cooking skills, which was directly tied to our inability to please our husbands. She'd always blamed geography, but now we were in the same city, and they still weren't doing much for her. It broke her heart, though she wouldn't admit it, not even to herself. Mama would lie that my aunts had called to check on Sitti Wasfiyeh. An argument would inevitably ensue, with Sitti Wasfiyeh accusing Mama of intentionally not answering their calls until she was away, taking a bath or a nap, to keep her from her daughters. But we didn't mind her insults and accusations, because we preferred my grandmother ornery rather than heartbroken.

Mama and Jehad were in Palestine for two weeks. It was the first and only time Sitti Wasfiyeh and I had been alone together for more than a few hours, and although I dreaded it initially, they turned out to be lovely, memorable days. Sitti Wasfiyeh was different without my mother and Jehad around. Or maybe I was. She had always loved smoking argileh in outdoor coffeehouses. We used to take her to beachfront cafés in Kuwait, and like a child in a toy store, she'd have to be coaxed and prodded to leave. Since we'd moved to Amman, she had taken to smoking on our balcony overlooking a trash-strewn street, but it was "better than nothing," she said.

One evening, while we sat together on the balcony of our small apartment watching children in the street, their clothes stained with the day's play, my grandmother told me about the time her father caught her smoking. "I was about thirteen or fourteen, shortly before I got married. My grandfather, who would be your great-great-grandfather, used to leave his argileh still lit for us to clean. I would smoke a little if no one was around, before washing it. One day when he went to mosque, my cousins and I took turns finishing it off. We smoked until the charcoal was all ash, but just as we got up to empty it, my father walked in." Sitti took another puff on the argileh pipe. "He didn't see us actually smoking, but the room was full of smoke, and he knew. We lied, but that only made him angrier. We all got a beating."

"What about Sidi?" I asked. "Did he mind you smoking?"

"Your grandfather loved it, because he thought I was naughty. Good girls didn't smoke back then. The two of us smoked together, only in private, of course. We had a great time," she said, her eyes moistened by the long-ago time and place that still lived within her. "I never thought there would come a day when women could just sit in outdoor cafés and smoke like the men," she added, turning to me, grinning. "That's the best part for me. But I'm old and it's okay. For women of your generation, it just makes them loose and do bad things."

"Oh, Sitti, don't start with that," I said.

"I'm not talking about you. I know you're a good girl. You don't even smoke at home," she said.

I left it at that, watching her profile, the wrinkles on her cheek moving and changing with every puff on the argileh, and I tried to imagine her on the cusp of marriage, still a little girl sneaking a smoke with her cousins in Palestine.

"You know, I always had a bad feeling about that no-good dog you married," she said. My grandmother had a knack for revisionist history. Back then she'd said he was too good for me and urged me to accept his proposal to make an honest woman of me. She had told my mother she'd better marry me off before I let someone puncture my hymen and destroy my reputation. She'd said I was already too old and the marriage window would soon be closing. But not now. "I'm glad you got rid of him," she said.

Our extended family in Palestine had heard about Jehad's imprisonment in Kuwait and received him as a hero, welcoming him with feasts in his honor in the homes of cousins we had only heard about or met once or twice as children. Mama was grateful, but it seemed neither she nor Jehad felt at home.

"Everything is different," Mama told me upon their return to Amman. "All the checkpoints, Jewish settlement construction, foreign Jews everywhere. I hardly recognized the place. I felt like a stranger in my own country."

Mama had refused to talk on the phone about her trip to her childhood home in Haifa, but now I pressed her.

"What can I say, my daughter," she said, an unfamiliar new grief suffusing her expression. "Foreign Jews were living there like they were the real owners." She waved her hand as she often did to shoo away pain.

"What was it like? Did you go inside? This is important, Mama. Why are you waving it off?" I prodded.

Mama threw an orange she had been peeling onto the floor. "Why don't you know when to stop?" Her chin quivered.

We were quiet for a while, until Jehad started on politics, our panacea conversation to mask whatever needed masking. Oslo was the topic of the day. From all the hoopla on the news about peace and that Oslo deal, I had thought life would be different there.

Jehad said, "It's true people feel hopeful. But Oslo is just for show. Something terrible is happening behind it."

"What do you mean?" I asked, but he waved me off too and changed the subject.

The big news was mostly about Bilal, the brother-in-law I had never met, who'd been imprisoned in exchange for my husband's freedom and only recently freed in the prisoner release part of the Oslo Accords.

"He's taken to tending sheep in the hills. Strange. A very quiet man," Mama said, happy to move on to gossip, just as the rhythmic thud of Sitti Wasfiyeh's cane arose in the hallway in tempo with her unsteady steps.

"From a fighter with a Kalashnikov to a sheepherder with a stick," Sitti Wasfiyeh said ruefully. "They're breaking our fighters. If ever there was a symbol of what those Zionist dogs, sons of sixty dogs, are doing to us . . ." Sitti Wasfiyeh shook her head and let the words hang over us.

"Sitti, how do you know what we're talking about?" I asked.

"I was listening by the door!" she said, matter-of-fact. "I wanted to see if you were talking about me."

Jehad got up to help her onto the floor mat. "God bless you, son," she thanked him, and reached for the bowl of cherries and pomegranate arils we were snacking on.

"I don't think it's like that, Sitti." Jehad went back to talking about Bilal. "He's decent and smart. Nothing like his brother. Plus, he hasn't abandoned the resistance."

This piqued my interest, not because of Bilal or the resistance, but because of the way Jehad said it. I knew my brother well enough to know when a larger story was hidden in the folds of a few uttered words, but it was futile to probe him in front of Mama and Sitti Wasfiyeh.

"Your grandmother is right, Jehad. The smart chemist and great fighter Israel was hunting all those years wasn't at all what I expected. Bilal was small and meek. Didn't have much to say. I was not impressed." Mama sucked in air through her teeth.

Jehad fidgeted with the pomegranate arils in his hand, then looked up at Mama. "Small, meek, and quiet describes me pretty well," he said. Mama protested, but he stopped her. "And as unimpressive as I may seem to you, going from a medical student to a simple gardener, I assure you that you have no clue what is inside of me."

Jehad got up and left the house, ignoring Mama's pleas, and I knew that whatever was stirring inside him, it had to do with Palestine. I suspected he knew more about Bilal and resistance activities there than he was letting on.

"Let him go," Sitti Wasfiyeh told her, and mumbled prayers for his safety, peace of mind, and blessed future with a wife and family of his own. Amen.

"Mama, you have to lay off Jehad. He's not interested in going back to school. He's content in his job and earns a decent living. You have to stop nagging him about studying, working, and marriage and kids and whatever. All he hears is your disappointment," I said.

"How do you know what he hears? Did he tell you?"

"No, Mama. He didn't tell me. I know because that's all I hear when you nag me every day about my life and what a failure you think I am."

"I never said that!" she protested, then began to cry when I walked away into the kitchen. She followed me there. "Why does everybody walk away from me when I say something is wrong with this family? What's wrong with wanting more for my children?"

Mama took me by the arm. "Never mind your brother right now. There's something I need to ask you." She paused. "People heard things about you."

I raised one eyebrow to her.

"They didn't mention Um Buraq by name, but they said there

was talk you spent a lot of time with an older Kuwaiti woman with a bad reputation," she said.

"Who said that?"

"Your aunts," she said.

"Of course it would come from those bitches," I said. "While you were away, Latifa hurried me out of her house before her husband came home, like she was afraid he'd see me there."

Mama made a face like she was holding back a question.

"What?" I demanded.

"Well, I mean, I've always found that friendship odd," she said.

"Um Buraq has been good to all of us!" I feigned outrage. "You know better than anyone how people love to talk about any and every woman who ends up without her husband."

Mama recoiled, probably remembering the humiliating days after Baba died in another woman's arms.

"Mama, Um Buraq is a good person. She doesn't deserve what people say about her. And she has been a good friend to me."

"I know, habibti. I'm sorry," she said.

Without consulting me, Jehad had made arrangements for my divorce while he was in Palestine. "I spoke with Bilal about it. His brother agreed to give him power of attorney to execute the divorce on his behalf," Jehad told me. "But you have to do it, Nahr. Mama is right about this. You can't stay tied to that man."

Jehad could barely say Mhammad's name. It wasn't only that he had abandoned me and disappeared without a word, but there had been rumors that Mhammad had become (and might have been all along) an Israeli informer. Few believed it because of his history, and of course because of the respect his brother, Bilal, commanded. But there had been enough sightings of him in Tel Aviv to refute the story that he was living in exile somewhere in the West.

"Really? How do you know? You're hiding something from me. I can feel it," I said.

"Nanu, I'm not. That's all I know," he said.

"Are you working with Bilal somehow?" I moved closer, looking deeply into him for some hint.

He looked down at me with softer eyes. "Nanu, I just met the guy. I'm trying to look out for you. You have to cut this last string with Mhammad, or else you'll never be free."

Free. As if any of us could ever be so.

"Fine. I'll go. I'll get the damn divorce. I have to save up some money first," I said.

Before I left for Palestine, Jehad invited us all to his new place for *ghada*. He had moved out not long after returning from Palestine to a rent-free place in exchange for maintaining the landlord's property. He was still cooking when we arrived but would not allow us to help. "I'm not letting you take credit for this feast." He winked his good eye and shooed me out of his kitchen. "Nanu, you can set up the space."

He had a rather elaborate computer setup, like something one would see at a major business enterprise. Until then, I had only seen computers at the Internet cafés popping up around the country. I had heard that rich people had private computers.

"What is all this, Jehad?"

He peeked out from behind the kitchen wall. "It's nothing. I'm fixing up a used system to have my own server."

"What's a server?"

"Forget it. Can you set up for the food? I'm almost done."

Mama and I unfolded a plastic cloth on the floor and arranged floor cushions around it. After half an hour of clanging kitchenware, Jehad emerged with a tray of *maqlooba*—layered eggplant, rice, and chicken in special spices—bowls of cucumber and yogurt sauce, and various salads and pickles. "How is it I never knew you could cook?" I said, surprised how delicious it was.

"I figured I needed to learn before we get ulcers from all the hot spices you put in our food," he teased, his warm smile reminding me how close we used to be.

"Don't you bad-talk your sister," Sitti Wasfiyeh said.

"Ordinarily *you* would take a crack at my terrible cooking," I joked.

"Just eat, my granddaughter," she said, putting more chicken on my plate, her ill-fitting dentures threatening to fall out as she chewed. Sitti Wasfiyeh had grown kinder since our time alone. Jehad smiled at me.

My brother's new home was a small studio apartment on the ground floor of a five-story building in a wealthy Amman neighborhood. Unlike Kuwait, where neighborhoods were segregated by class and nationality, the rich and poor lived cheek-by-jowl in Jordan. Not for some egalitarian ideals, but for the convenience of the rich.

"So this way they have you at their beck and call?" I said, worried that these wealthy Jordanians were taking advantage of my brother.

"They're fine people, Nahr."

"Well, in my experience, the rich buy the poor and then throw them out when they're done."

"They're not all like Kuwaitis, not that Kuwaitis are all the same either. You loved Um Buraq, didn't you?" Jehad said.

"Enough of that. Let's enjoy this meal together without mentioning Kuwait," Mama said. "I am excited that you're going to Palestine, Nahr." She stroked my cheek. "But also eager for you to come back quickly."

Palestine had begun to feel more real since Mama and Jehad had made their trip. Maybe it was the experience of war and exile, or just the passage of time; maybe it was my contemplation of Mama's tatreez, or simply not wanting to be in Amman that made Palestine bloom in my imagination. It was no longer the lost home and heritage trapped in Mama's tin box of old photos from her childhood in Haifa, my parents' wedding, and their life in Ein el-Sultan. As I began planning my trip, I sifted through those pictures with Mama. In one, a ten-year-old version of my mother posed under a fig tree.

"That tree was planted by my grandfather the day my father was born. My grandparents planted a different kind of tree for each of my siblings, my cousins, and me," Mama said. "We used to fight over whose tree was better. My siblings all carved their names on the tree trunks, but I carved mine on a high-up branch." Mama stared at that picture, transported by the past. I was afraid to ask her if those trees were still there, or how she had felt upon seeing her home in Haifa. I listened instead.

"When I was very small, my father used to lift me on his shoulders so I could pluck my own figs." In another photo, she and one of her sisters were teenagers standing in the Al Aqsa compound in front of the Dome of the Rock. "In those days, we could take a bus right to Jerusalem, or we could go by train straight to Beirut, or Damascus, or Cairo even. The world was open." She stared a bit more. "If only we knew then."

"Why are you so depressing?" Sitti Wasfiyeh chimed in from her room. "Doom and gloom, by God! You're going to jinx the girl and make her not want to go to Palestine."

Mama peeked her head through the door. "Hajjeh, we thought you were taking a nap. Come sit with us."

"It looks like I need to. I'm a better storyteller, because I'm older and remember more, because I was in Palestine longer," she said, walking into the family room with her cane. "Make us some tea while I talk to my granddaughter."

There was still a lot of hope and euphoria over the Oslo Accords. A famous Palestinian in America named Edward Said was warning that this agreement was no cause for excitement; it was a trap to buy Israel more time to keep colonizing Palestine. My brother agreed with him and said Bilal did too.

"Nahr, I think you're going to get along well with Bilal," Jehad said. "He headed the Communist Party in Palestine back in the day. He probably hates rich Kuwaitis too."

I didn't know how to answer. The only things I knew about communism were that its color was red and Russians were communists. I made a mental note to find out what I could about the Communist Party. People were talking about how easy it was to research anything on the Internet. I thought I might learn to do the Internet too.

It was around this time that I ran into an old friend at a mall in Amman. Literally, I ran into him. I almost didn't recognize him, until he bent to pick up his bags, which he seemed to have spilled purposely. "I'm very sorry, sister," he said.

It looked like an accident to onlookers, the carelessness of distracted shoppers. But when I looked up, I saw Mohsin, the young man on the balcony in Kuwait, smoking a cigarette, confessing that he preferred boys and asking me to tell him a secret of mine.

"No harm done, brother," I said.

He picked up my bags and handed them to me. I saw in my peripheral vision a woman with children stop to stare at us from a store. His wife.

"Thank you," I said, and walked away to the privacy of the nearest bathroom. As I suspected, he had dropped his business card into my bag. He was a banker. A handwritten note on the back of the card read *Please call me.*

I waited a day to call, confessing, when I finally did, that I had been worried his wife might answer. He laughed, because I had called his personal mobile phone. He had been vacationing with his family at the Dead Sea and had stopped in Amman for a few days before heading back. The woman I'd glimpsed at the mall was indeed his wife.

We made small talk. I told him I was planning to go to Palestine. "I'm so happy for you," he said. "Someday, enshallah, when Jerusalem is liberated, we will all once again be able to visit our holy city."

Then we spoke of the stunning advancement of technology, which seemed to be passing me by. The Internet was everywhere. People could send instant letters electronically through something called e-mail. Jehad had already told me about it, but all I knew was that it wasn't like a fax. "It's amazing, and anyone can have an account for free," Mohsin said, but there were still connection fees at the Internet cafés.

"I have some friends who could show me," I lied for the sake of conversation.

"Let me!" he said. "I can set you up with an e-mail tomorrow if you want."

I agreed, not because I wanted to have e-mail but to see him, and we set a time.

Mama used to get so happy when someone from Palestine visited us in Kuwait, especially if they came from Haifa. She would say they "carried the scent and spirit of my home and youth in Palestine." That's why I wanted so much to visit with Mohsin. He carried the scent and spirit of Kuwait.

I waited the next day among young people sitting at various computer terminals. I had no idea what to do. It was intimidating, and I felt out of place. Mohsin didn't show up. *Such a disappointment*, I thought, and was getting up to leave when a young man rushed in, out of breath. He looked around, then walked up to me. "Are you Madam Yaqoot?" he asked.

I hesitated. "Who wants to know?"

"I have a package for you, and I'm supposed to set you up with an e-mail account," he said, still catching his breath.

"Yes," I said.

"Fine. Before I give you the package, you're supposed to answer a question to verify who you are."

"I'm not answering anything." I turned to leave.

"Okay. You're the only woman here, so I believe you're who I'm supposed to give this to. But just so I can report back—can you just tell me . . ." He unfolded a piece of paper and read from it: "*What is the other name of the girl with two real names?*" He looked up from the paper with pleading eyes.

"The answer is Nahr." I smiled, snatching the package from him, and walked away to open it in the privacy of the café bathroom. There was an envelope with cash in it and a new mobile phone. There was no note, and the money was more than I needed to get to Palestine.

The young man was waiting for me when I emerged. "Madam, I'm very sorry to bother you, but I am supposed to get you on e-mail before you go," he said, explaining that he needed to complete the entire task in order to get paid. The account had already been set up, and he showed me how to open it. "This is the log-in

information. Write it down," he said, then showed me how to
change my password.

"As you can see, you already have one e-mail," he said, pointing
to a line on the screen. He instructed me how to open it and leaned
in when I did. I pushed him out of the way. "I can read on my own,"
I said.

> *Dear Nahr,*
>
> *I hope it's okay to call you by that name. I am sorry I could not
> be there myself today. Something came up with the family, but I
> did my best not to disappoint you. If you're reading this, it means
> that the courier delivered a sealed package for you. I owe you a
> debt and it gives me pleasure to think I might be of some help to
> you now. I believe it was fate that we ran into each other.*
>
> *Your friend,*
>
> *Mohsin*
>
> *P.S. The phone is paid for one year in Jordan. When you get to
> Palestine, you will need to buy a local SIM card.*

I clicked the box labeled Reply and typed with two fingers: *You
never owed me anything. But whatever debt you may have felt, consider it paid in full and more. P.S. The package was still sealed, and
the young man went above and beyond.*

Then I clicked Send.

"Tell me when you're ready to respond, I will show you how," the
young man said.

"Boy, I already did it. I'm good at the Internet," I said. He looked
at me with a blank stare. "But I have some questions. Sit down. I'll
buy you a cup of tea. I told Mohsin you *went above and beyond.*"

The boy relented and sat with me for some tea. He answered

my questions with the limited patience one has for a small child. I learned that I did not have to come back to the same computer forever to access my mailbox. I could do that from any computer in the world. I thought the e-mail I sent would take days to be delivered, but he assured me it was already in the recipient's mailbox. Just like that. I didn't believe him, so he demonstrated with a test e-mail from his own e-mail to mine. Finally he explained what a SIM card was.

"Madam, thank you for the tea, but I really must go," he said. "Best of luck to you."

"Thank you!" I said, contemplating the difference between us. He was not much younger than me, but I was already much older in those days when I was still in my twenties.

IV.
PALESTINE

THE CUBE, SOUTH

A VAULT DOOR on the south side is the only entrance and exit. Food comes through a waist-high rectangular opening. Sometimes books are pushed through the same slot.

The first books I received preceded the first visitors by three bowel movements. One book was about blue whales, one on the cosmos, and another a bad translation of a badly written Western romance novel. I devoured them before the visitors arrived and had begun rereading about blue whales. Such extraordinary creatures. True gentle giants, full of mystery and romance, like the ocean itself.

An expressionless armed guard escorted the visitors into the Cube—a woman in her midtwenties and a man twice her age. He spoke Arabic. She didn't, but was learning, she said. They asked short, simple questions. What did I eat? How frequently? How often did I go outside? Did I communicate with family? Did they give me books to read? Pen and paper?

I find it difficult to look visitors in the eyes. My gaze gravitated to the man's dark, hairy forearm emerging from a rolled-up white sleeve.

All I could think about was touching the dark, hairy forearm.

"Are you interested in blue whales?" the woman asked, nodding at my books. "And outer space?" She smiled as if we were having a normal conversation. I understood her English, but I waited for the man to translate. Information swirled in my head. Blue whales are the largest creatures ever to roam our planet, as long as thirty meters and weighing up to 173,000 kilograms. They have intricate social lives and complex languages. Hunted to near extinction. Less than a few thousand remained before whaling restrictions were introduced, but whalers continue to serve a black market, and these majestic creatures might disappear from the world. Blue whales subsist on krill. *Krill* is a Norwegian word. I wonder what it's like to be Norwegian. What's it like to be a whale? To live in water. To be the biggest creature on earth, still vulnerable to a small man's greed.

Dark, hairy forearm. Rolled-up white sleeves.

"Yes," I said, barely audible. "I'm interested in whales." Her gaze made me more aware of my prison clothes. I had done my best to tidy my hair. Although the man was dressed casually, the woman wore a conservative dark suit, low black heels, and a gray blouse. Blue stones studding her ears accented her blue eyes and, when I focused on them, it seemed as if she had four blue eyes. I wished she had worn glasses. I'd like to see a reflection of myself.

"You seem healthy and well-groomed. I understand your shower comes on automatically. Are you able to shower daily?"

The man did not translate, nor did he realize that I understood her speaking to me as if I were a child. But I wanted him to translate so I could ask her about her hygiene habits too.

"Yaqoot, is there anything else you would like to talk about or bring to our attention? We have ten minutes left," the man said.

"Have you spoken with my family?" If they had, it would have been the first thing they told me. If they had any decency.

The man lowered his eyes. She looked at him, then at me. "No. We didn't," he said. "But we will, and I'll let your mother know you're fine."

Fine?

I put my feet up on my bed and turned my back to them.

Shortly after they left, the same hard-faced guard came in to retrieve the books. I had locked my bracelets facing the room this time, because I wanted to get a last glimpse of the blue whales, the stars and planets and cheap romance before they were taken from me forever.

"Otva`li, mu`dak, b`lyad!" I yelled, bound to the wall by my bracelets.

We were both shocked: me, because she understood.

She turned to me, her hard face replaced with a smile. I smiled too, and said it again. Fuck off, you asshole, fuck!

She laughed, and so did I. She put her hand on her chest and said, "Klara," nodding as she walked out, the metal door closing with an automated clang.

The next day, my whale book was pushed through the door opening.

That's how Klara became my friend, or what could pass for a friend in the Cube. She speaks to me sometimes through the speaker, since the camera doesn't record sound, even though I don't fully understand what she says. She would be reprimanded if they knew. She told me that. I keep my mouth shut because I like her. Sometimes I remember that I should not like her. But I am always excited when she is on duty. She doesn't consider herself Israeli. She's Russian. Her family forced her to leave with them, and she desperately wants to return to her village. She's not even Jewish. She said her father made it all up to get the state subsidies for Jews willing to emigrate to Israel. It was free money, plus her father was close to being caught for embezzling. She hated her father. And she missed her boyfriend. She apologized for not getting more books. I should add that the things she tells me are my interpretations of the broken English, Arabic, and Hebrew we use to communicate. I asked if I could get books about communism. She said, *"Da, naverna."* Yeah, probably.

I fell asleep thinking about the dark, hairy forearm below a rolled-up white sleeve.

THE LAYERS OF ABSENCE

I WAS TOLD to expect difficulties from Israeli border authorities when crossing the Jordan River into Palestine, but it wasn't as bad as I anticipated. I was interrogated. Searched. Searched again. They would not accept the Palestinian ID that Jehad had worked hard to reinstate because it did not appear in their system. They said this was not uncommon because it takes time for new hawiyyas since the Oslo Accords to update in their system. Hours later, they stamped my Jordanian travel document with a three-month tourist visa. One of my interrogators, whose sense of power had been irrepressible and somewhat exhibitionist in the way she ordered me around, pointed to my plump belly and asked, "You have baby?"

Bitch.

In all, I was made to wait six hours. Maybe it was finally getting through, or some spiritual call from my ancestors, but I was overcome with relief—and something akin to belonging—when I emerged on the other side of the crossing terminal. The landscape, topography, weather, and smells were no different from the east side of the Jordan River, but Palestine was nothing like Jordan. There was an immense silence just beyond the bustle of people milling about,

waiting among parked cars, taxis, soldiers, handcarts. I gazed toward the unfolding land, where rolling hills met the sky. Images
began to converge in my chest, deepening my breathing. Memories of two trips we'd taken as children with Baba; Sitti Wasfiyeh's
tales about Ein el-Sultan; stories from Mama, Baba, neighbors, and
friends about Haifa. The ones I thought I'd discarded, tuned out,
dismissed. They were all there to greet me, enfolding me in the
embrace of our collective dislocation from this place where all our
stories go and return. Here is where we began. Where our songs
were born, our ancestors buried. The *adan* sounded from unseen
minarets. It floated through me, raised the hair on my arms, made
me close my eyes and inhale the call to prayer.

A man stood before me. "Salaam, Yaqoot."

I knew who he was, of course. He had told me on the phone he'd
be waiting. His brown face was creased, much older and wearier
than the youthful photos I had seen years ago. I suppose he recognized me from my photos too, and maybe thought the same of
me. We stood that way, in an uncomfortable pause, acknowledging
something shared.

"Hello, Bilal," I said. "You can call me Nahr."

"*Alhamdulillah assalameh*, Nahr." He smiled, taking my bag with
a dark, hairy arm that emerged from the rolled-up sleeve of a white
linen shirt. He looked like Mhammad, with a defined jaw and strong,
dark features, but he was thinner and taller. "Our mother is anxious
to see you and insists that you stay with us, of course," he said.

I knew my mother-in-law only through the telephone, and
would meet her for the first time now as I came seeking a divorce.
She was nearly blind and possessed the limitless generosity and
kindness that often accompanies sightlessness, as if one's love for
the world increases as the ability to see it diminishes. I recalled the

immediate affinity I had felt when we spoke years ago, and now I wished I had come to visit her sooner.

She wore a black embroidered thobe and black hijab in permanent mourning for her husband and, some would say, her eldest son, Mhammad, although he was still living. She had prepared msakhan for my arrival. I didn't know if she knew or if it was a coincidence that she had made my favorite dish. I could smell it when Bilal and I walked into their home, a modest stone structure nestled on the side of a hill in the unplanned, organic style of Palestinian villages, its floors tiled in beautiful granite from nearby quarries in el-Khalil. Their home was accessed only by a narrow, winding footpath, over which Bilal had carried my large bag, and I had struggled to walk in my heels.

"Bilal, may God bestow His favor on him, slaughtered a couple of our chickens and prepared the meal himself. I just watched over it while it baked," she said.

I hid my surprise. This was the second time in one week that men had cooked for me. "Bless both of your hands that made this delicious meal. You humble me with your kindness," I said.

"You are one of us, even though you are here to separate from us," Bilal said kindly.

I looked down, unsure how to respond.

Bilal continued, "We cannot truly know what Mhammad put you through. But we know enough to be ashamed and sorry for how he treated you."

Mention of Mhammad's name clearly wounded Hajjeh Um Mhammad. "May God help him find the path of light wherever he is," she said.

The phone rang. "Probably the neighbors checking up," Hajjeh Um Mhammad said.

"Don't answer, *Yumma*," Bilal pleaded. "Let's have our time with Yaqoot before the busybodies swoop down."

"You must answer. And don't refer to our family and friends as busybodies."

Bilal smiled good-naturedly. *"Ha'ek alay,* Yumma," he said, kissing his mother's hand.

I waited to gather the courage to correct Bilal and finally spoke after a few bites of food. "You can call me Nahr," I reminded him. "Yaqoot is only on my official documents." I didn't mention that I was named after my father's mistress.

"Yes, I'm sorry," he said, embarrassed. "It's just that Yaqoot is such a beautiful name too—but I will not make that mistake again."

"It's fine." I smiled. "Sometime I'll tell you the story behind my having two names. Three, if you count Nanu, which is reserved for Jehad." Almas was long gone by then.

A day or two into my trip, Bilal invited me to early evening tea on a small hilltop overlooking a stretch of cultivated land and a pasture where some sheep roamed. I thought we would just drive to the spot, but I wore my most comfortable shoes for the occasion anyway—sandals with a midsize heel. Instead, we walked for what felt like miles after we parked the car, and my sensible heels were nonsensical. I wobbled over the terrain as best I could, trying to disguise my discomfort, and Bilal caught me around the waist when I almost fell. He suggested I walk barefoot.

"And get stung by scorpions? No thank you."

He chuckled. "No scorpions in these parts."

"Snakes, then," I retorted. "There must be snakes."

"Well, yes. Sometimes." He smiled, then tapped his arm. "Here. At least lean on me if it helps."

"You're enjoying this, aren't you?"

He smiled again, raising one eyebrow—he could do that too! "I am."

"You should have told me my shoes were inappropriate."

"And miss all this?" He laughed.

It was natural to be in Bilal's company, away from the rest of humanity. I balanced myself with a hand on his shoulder; he had his arms poised to catch me again, until we reached a clearing near the top, on the side of the hill. He sat on the dirt under a large olive tree, its low branches extending from its knotted trunk. A cool breeze rustled the leaves and blew my hair into a mess. Bilal began pulling objects out of his bag: a dented tin kettle, a small gas *babbour*, tea glasses, a large water bottle, and plastic bags of loose tea, sage, sugar, and *bizir*—but no blanket to sit on.

He must have read my mind, because he spread the canvas bag on the ground. "Here, you can sit on this," he said. I leaned awkwardly on the tree and lowered myself to the ground, removed my heels, and let out a sigh of relief.

Bilal smiled but didn't say anything. He lit the babbour, poured water into the kettle, and made sweet hot tea with just the right hint of sage.

Ahead, we could see construction activity in a new Jewish-only colony, which, he explained, had started a year before when settlers brought trailers to camp on Bilal's family's land and never left. The trucks were some distance away, however. "They're laying water pipes," Bilal said.

"Why are the pipes aboveground?"

"It's cheaper. They invest just enough to keep these settlers here and attract more who are willing to live a bit ruggedly, until they have enough people to justify greater expenditure on infrastructure. Another reason is to fool international and human rights agencies by giving the impression this arrangement is only temporary."

We sat eating bizir, expertly cracking open the salty roasted watermelon seeds for the fleshy insides. I liked to collect the seeds' entrails in a pile, then eat them all at once, instead of one at a time. Eyeing the small mound of shelled seeds in my lap, Bilal said, "That looks enticing!"

"Don't even think about it. I beat up a neighbor when we were little kids because he stole a pile of shelled bizir that I had been working on for an hour."

He laughed. "Thank you for establishing the red line. I will never cross it. Your bizir pile is safe around me."

Bilal spoke of Areas A, B, and C as the sun began making its way to the sea, painting the sky, land, and life in the colors of its wake. I knew these were designations created by the Oslo Accords, but I couldn't remember their distinctions. He explained that we were in Area C, which was being heavily colonized by Israel, and that my in-laws' home was a prime target. It was the only remaining house for some distance in the village. The nearest homes had been torn down, Bilal told me. "Israel has a lot of excuses. Lack of permits, illegal wells, relatives of fighters, whatever they want."

"How have you managed to keep your property?" I asked, surveying the sylvan terrain stretching before us into the valley.

He turned to me, his gentle brown eyes searching my face. Then he turned back to the land, inhaled from his cigarette, exhaled smoke, and resurrected a name I hadn't heard in many years.

"Tamara," he said.

I had promised Mama to make the rounds to visit our own extended family as soon as I got to Palestine, but I found myself putting it off, spending my time with Bilal and Hajjeh Um Mhammad instead, and contemplating the contradictions of this place, my birthright. The landscape that lived in the hearts of Mama, Baba, and Sitti Wasfiyeh didn't feel like home, though it took hold of me nonetheless. There were no malls everywhere or miles of beaches as I was accustomed to in Kuwait (none that were accessible to Palestinians, at least). No salons on every corner to get my lips and eyebrows threaded, have a full body wax, or get scrubbed in a Turkish bathhouse. Even in depressing Amman, I could still escape to a good lingerie or shoe store. I stumbled awkwardly through the unfamiliar milieu in Palestine, and Bilal was there to pick me up, sometimes literally.

Bilal had been released under the Oslo agreement, but his freedom was conditioned on his never practicing his profession as a chemist in any capacity, not even teaching. He was forbidden to travel outside a specified radius without authorization from the local military authority, could not write or publish any political material, could not under any circumstances enter Jerusalem and, if he ever left the country, could not return.

Bilal complied, as far as I could tell. He had inherited some animals and bought others when he was released. Although he helped care for them, Jandal was their full-time shepherd. Together, Bilal and Jandal sheared them once a year for wool, which they sold to local garment factories. During Eid and for special occasions, people would buy lambs for sacrifice. But Bilal insisted on hiring his own butcher to perform the ritual halal traditions for his sheep. "Because people terrify these animals before killing them. Few butchers actually adhere to halal requirements anymore," he said. "To tell you the truth, I hate that we even eat meat as much as we do. Sheep, cows, fish, whales, goats—they're nations unto themselves. They too deserve to be free." The primacy of humans was only one assumption I had never questioned until I met him.

Most of Bilal's time was spent at the bakery and pastry café, a small business he had started years ago with Ghassan, Jandal's older brother and Bilal's closest friend, who had been his cellmate in prison. Ghassan was a diabetic who spent his time making desserts. People would line up in the mornings for fresh bread, and in the evenings they came for *knafe* and sweet mint tea or Arabic coffee. Bilal and Ghassan seemed to know everyone, and people treated them with respect and the affection reserved for political prisoners.

It shocked me how many checkpoints there were just to go from one village to the next. It seemed Palestinians could not drive more than five minutes without having to wait at yet another. We had to go through two checkpoints on the way to the shop. The first we crossed by car. Typically the wait was about half an hour, but it could be as little as ten minutes or as much as two hours, depending on the mood of the soldiers manning it. Then we would park the car in a lot by the second checkpoint, which could only be crossed on foot. Sometimes we could just drive through the second checkpoint, but usually we had to gather our bags from the car and walk the rest of the way—about half a mile, no matter the weather. Bilal did not want the soldiers to know we were together, and I'd have to wait in line to cross far ahead of him. "Notice, only the elderly couples cross together," Bilal said. I discovered the reason on my own. A soldier groped a teenage girl in line with her father, and when he protested, they threw him to the ground and made them both sit on the side of the road for hours. Bilal knew the father and offered to refrigerate their grocery bags until they were released, but soldiers shoved Bilal to move along.

Before going to the bakery and pastry shop, Bilal and I made daily excursions through the countryside early in the morning. It was exhausting at first, but my time with Bilal was so affirming, I didn't want to miss a moment of it. I set an alarm for 5 a.m., rising daily before the first adan. He would already be making coffee. Then he and Hajjeh Um Mhammad would perform the fajr salat, feed the chickens, and take a light breakfast with the rising sun.

I wasn't particularly fond of the rugged outdoors, but I began to see those rocky hills differently through the sheer force of Bilal's passion for everything they held. Most striking was the silence. Absent was the persistent cacophony of traffic, street vendors, pedestrians, construction, and the buzz of streetlights that filled every space of our tight living quarters both in Kuwait and in Amman. Instead, I awoke to the songs of birds and wind chimes, and I was lulled at night by the orchestras of crickets and the calls of jackals and wolves.

It was disorienting in the beginning, because I didn't know how to be in such openness. I found myself breathing deeply and deliberately in the mornings, inhaling the immensity of that silence. It made me realize how limited my world had been that I could not imagine the need to pack more than house slippers in addition to multiple pairs of heels, even though I knew I would be here at least a couple of months for the divorce proceedings.

My first purchase in Palestine was a pair of green-and-white sneakers, which I wore on my next trek with Bilal. He eyed them with a grin. "Now you don't need to lean on me," he said.

"That's right."

"Pity."

Bilal taught me to identify individual plants we encountered, which usually had associated folklore, culinary uses, and medicinal value. We picked wild za'atar together and plucked the occasional pomegranate wherever we found them. Life didn't grow wild like this in Kuwait, or Amman.

I began joining Hajjeh Um Mhammad and Bilal for morning salat, and then again for the *dhuhr* salat. Soon I was worshipping five times a day. I hadn't done that for years, not since high school, but I wanted to be part of their lives. And I felt they wanted that too.

After breakfast, Hajjeh Um Mhammad would kiss us each on both cheeks. We'd kiss her hand in turn before setting out. We'd walk to Bilal's car, typically parked half a mile down the hill. There was no driveway, as Bilal never carved more than a narrow foot-path to the house, just wide enough for Hajjeh Um Mhammad's motorized cart. "It makes it harder for military jeeps and bull-dozers to get to us," Bilal explained.

Yet despite the difficulty accessing their home, Hajjeh Um Mhammad had visitors nearly daily, a testament to the love and re-spect she attracted. She attended every wedding, birth celebration, and funeral service for miles around. "That's just how it was in my day. It's *osool*. You always showed up for your people," she said. Her life was one of a lost era, in some ways too idyllic to be real.

Once a week, I accompanied Bilal to check on the sheep and goats. "I love watching the flock gather around Jandal when he plays the ney," Bilal said. Then he side-glanced at me. "You're not wearing lipstick anymore, I notice."

"Don't let that fool you. I'm still a city girl," I said, and wore lip-stick the next day to prove it.

Two weeks after I arrived, at my request, Bilal arranged for me to visit my mother's childhood home in Haifa. I wanted to see what Mama would not speak of. "The most the driver can do is take you to the outside of the house. He'll stand by if you want to knock on the door. I wish I could go with you," Bilal said.

I wished I could kiss him.

I traveled with Bakir, the driver, for four hours—two spent waiting to pass one checkpoint. Finally we arrived in Haifa. People call it a "mixed city," but that isn't true. It was clear where Jews lived compared with Palestinians; there was no mixing. We drove around a bit looking for the address, entering an area of modern houses on a hill overlooking the ocean. I thought perhaps Bakir had made a mistake, until a cluster of beautiful stone homes came into view, and he pulled to the side of the road. The homes were different but the same. Their ancient arches, masonry, walled gardens, and grand entrances contrasted with the flat, angular new construction with steel beams, glass walls, and sleek European opulence.

"I think it's this one," Bakir said, pointing to a three-story home with multiple balconies overlooking the street. Next to it was what looked to be a small tree farm surrounded by a low stone wall with an old wooden gate, slightly ajar, barely hanging on its hinges. In Mama's photos, the trees weren't as mature, and the house was more visible from the street. I knew the main entrance was on the side, but one could access the garden from the wooden gate, which used to have an ornate ceramic plaque that read HOME OF EL HAJ ABU IBRAHIM, NASER JAMAL NASRALLAH.

I walked up to the wooden gate. The indentation where the plaque had been was still visible if you knew what to look for. I thought about walking around to the entrance and knocking on the door, but the decrepit gate beckoned me. I stepped into the lush space of our absence. These were the trees my great-grandfather had planted for his children and grandchildren. My grandfather would have planted some for me and Jehad had our destiny not been stolen. I began walking among those trees, looking for the carvings my mother had told me about, but I saw none. At the far edge of the garden was a sycamore fig tree. It bore red fruit close to the bark, unlike the green and brown figs I'd imagined. I looked around before hiking myself up on its trunk to pick one. It was fragrant and much sweeter than regular figs. I climbed as best I could, grabbing fistfuls of fruit and tucking them into my purse as I searched for evidence that this was my mother's tree.

A commotion in the street distracted me, and I grabbed one last bundle of figs. On the branch where the fruit had been were jagged lines. I pulled away some vines and more fruit to reveal the rest. The noise from the street was growing louder as I made out the words: *Rashida, habibit Baba.* Rashida, Daddy's girl. That's how my grandfather had referred to my mother. This was her fig tree. This tree was a member of my family. I belonged to it. All the trees in that garden were my family.

The noise from the street was now upon me—a middle-aged woman screaming up at me in Hebrew. I began climbing down, fruit still in my hand. Bakir was trying to reason with her in Hebrew, at the same time imploring me to hurry up. "She called the police. Hurry!" he warned me in Arabic. Just as I touched the ground, the woman slapped the fruit from my hand and yanked me by my hair. Unthinkingly, I punched her, then again—and again. She was what we used to call in my school days "a princess," someone who had no idea how to fight. I wanted to beat her bloody. For taking away our trees. For pulling the land from under us. But Bakir caught my arm and dragged me away, and we ran together to his car. Neighbors were just beginning to gather and might have overtaken us had we left a moment later. Adrenaline pumped through us as we drove away, slowly, as if we were an ordinary Jewish couple going about our day, just in case we crossed paths with the police. When we were far enough away, convinced we had escaped detection, I pulled some figs from my purse, and we laughed in a way that was somewhat deranged and euphoric.

"You beat the shit out of that woman. Good thing this car has hot plates, so they can't trace it to me," Bakir said.

I turned to him with the shock, admiration, and renewed adrenaline of realizing how much deeper the trouble we escaped could have been.

"What? Bilal didn't tell you? We steal these motherfuckers' cars all the time and mix up their plates," Bakir said, laughing, proud of doing his part to make the lives of the colonizers a little less convenient.

We continued to revel in the thrill of return, escape, and figs. I thought about that woman, the commotion that preceded our confrontation. "What was she saying anyway?" I asked Bakir.

"She started out nice, thinking I was Jewish, but wanting to know what I was doing there parked on the side of the road. I told her I was just admiring the houses because I was thinking of moving into the area. I did my best to sound Jewish, but they can tell from the way we talk, or how we stand or whatever. So she started getting louder, telling me to leave before she called the police. She accused me of plotting to rob her house. She asked if 'the Arab woman' sent me. I didn't know what she meant, but apparently an Arab woman came by a couple of months ago claiming that that was her childhood home. Then she—"

"What else did she say about the Arab woman?" I interrupted him.

"That she was a terrorist. Apparently the Arab woman saw the gate open and helped herself into the garden. The Jewish woman found her there crying and, well, you can imagine the scene. I'm sure the Arab woman left in tears."

Bakir thought for a moment. "I'm such an idiot! Was she talking about your mother? Was your mother here two months ago?"

It was surely Mama. Now I knew why she had refused to speak of it when I asked her in Amman. It was too painful. I wished I had beaten that woman more. I wished I could have walked around the side to see the main entrance, to peek over the mountain and see the ocean as my mother would have done every day of her childhood. I wondered if Mama had done that when she came to see her home, or if she too hadn't made it beyond the garden.

The next morning, Bilal pushed one of his daily newspapers toward me as we sipped our coffee.

"What's this? Did you mean to show me the Hebrew paper?"

"I know you can't read it, but you might want to keep it as a souvenir," he said.

"Really? It's in their newspapers?" I said, leafing through the pages.

"Yeah." Bilal chuckled. "The article is about an Arab woman who assaulted a Jew in her garden. It quotes neighbors and the police saying more should be done to protect Jews who can't even feel safe in their own homes from the Arabs."

"Ugh. There aren't any pictures. I'd like to see what she looks like now." I put the paper down.

"I had no idea you were so scrappy." Bilal smiled at me. "Bakir already got rid of the car. He keeps telling me how insanely fast and powerfully you laid that woman out."

"So long as he's telling just you."

"Don't worry. Bakir is no fool," he said.

————

Most days were spent at the bakery. Bilal and I would arrive in the mornings to find Ghassan and his sister already baking bread for the line of customers. I helped out—cleaning, organizing, serving, and getting to know customers, but Ghassan and his sister remained remote, overly polite to me. I reciprocated their coolness, adding a little sarcasm whenever the spirit moved me.

On one occasion, I noticed two customers disappear into the back room of the shop, as if going to the washroom, only they didn't come back. It had happened once before, and both times the customers exchanged nearly imperceptible nods or glances with Bilal or Ghassan. I instinctively knew not to follow or investigate. Bilal and I closed up the store that evening and delivered a batch of bread to the mosque. The sky was still dusted in twilight as we drove home. Electric lights dotted the illegal colony on the adjacent hilltop.

"Looks like the settlers have electricity now," Bilal remarked.

A small fire flickered outside Bilal's home. "My mother is probably roasting chestnuts with my aunties. Let's go." He locked the car and we walked toward the house.

I awoke late the next morning to find Bilal looking out the window through binoculars. Hajjeh Um Mhammad was tending to the vegetable garden.

"Morning of goodness," I whispered.

"Morning of roses and jasmine," Bilal responded.

"What are you looking at?"

"Come see. The sons of bitches are extending the water pipe," he said, handing me the binoculars.

The work was low in the valley, but I could see the pipe, propped up on cement footings every few meters.

"It's so close," I said.

"Yes. It's actually on our property."

"What will we do?"

"There's nothing we can do," he said.

"Is this the reason for the subversive meetings in the back of the store?"

He hesitated. "I noticed you noticing. I'll explain later."

I wondered if Bilal wasn't still part of the resistance, but he ignored my question about the mysterious meetings. I didn't ask again, disappointed that he didn't trust me, and sulked for the rest of the evening, skipping dinner for an early bed. Hajjeh Um Mhammad thought I wasn't feeling well and made me chamomile tea. "This will settle your body, my daughter," she said.

When I didn't get up with them in the morning, Hajjeh Um Mhammad came into my room, but I feigned sleep. She felt my forehead and walked out quietly. I heard Bilal's voice outside but couldn't make out what he said. A while later, he knocked at my door.

"Are you mad at me?"

I opened the door. "Yes, I am." I put one arm akimbo. "I've been here for more than a month, sharing and helping and living as family. You've made me feel more comfortable and welcome than my own kin in Ein el-Sultan. Why don't you trust me?"

"Let's get going. I'll explain everything. I want to be out of our mother's earshot, because I fear you're going to be even angrier with me when you hear what I tell you."

We agreed to talk in the evening after closing the shop.

It turned out that for a month, Bilal had been spying on me. He'd had me followed and knew where I was at all times. If I took a day off to go to town, he had a spy reporting back my every move as I got my hair fixed, eyebrows threaded, and body waxed. The shady meetings in the back room were for show. To test me. They were actually playing backgammon, night after night, waiting to see if soldiers would raid the pastry shop after a tip-off from me.

He'd set traps and left clues, and I had recognized none of it. He'd pretended to speak in code on calls with his friends, then waited to catch me making a call or sending a message on my mobile phone.

"A call or text to whom?" I stuttered. It was growing dark as we walked home after parking the car, small lights dotting the new settlement on the hilltop.

"Your handler," he said.

"What the hell is a handler?" I was stunned. "You think I would work with *them*?" I pointed toward the lights.

"You have to understand, Nahr, we didn't know you. You showed up with a mobile phone," Bilal said, his right hand quivering. "Suddenly *el khaneeth* calls to give me power of attorney to process your divorce, after we've barely heard from either of you in all this time. Neither of you called my mother first. Someone in my position cannot take chances."

I didn't notice in the moment that he said *khaneeth*. Fag. I was too consumed by anger and humiliation. I had been in contact with one of the girls in Kuwait recently, and she'd sent a text asking if I was still working, because one of my old customers was coming to Amman. Had Bilal seen that? How had I responded to her? Did Bilal know what I was talking about? Surely he did. My face flushed with shame and panic. He had gone through all my communications. Nothing had been private.

"How could you?" I lunged at him. "You and your friends must have had a good laugh! You shit! You fucker!"

He came closer, trying to embrace me. "It wasn't like that. No one talked about you. I wouldn't allow anyone to speak badly of you."

"Fuck you!" I pushed him away. "Fuck your brother. Fuck the divorce. I'm leaving." I sped ahead of him toward the house, but stopped in my tracks and whipped around.

"What about Hajjeh Um Mhammad? Does she know?"

"No. She has no idea, and I must ask that you please do not speak of this in the house. It would devastate her. Her health is too fragile. Please, Nahr. Can we just talk here for a bit? You have every right to be angry. But please, let me speak."

There was a loud thud from the valley. It made me jump, and now I was shaking. I felt weakened by the deceit, but I was relieved to know that at least the love that had formed between my mother-in-law and me was real.

"I know I hurt you. And I know an apology is insufficient, but I am truly sorry, Nahr." He tried again to put his arms around me, and I pushed him away, trying to pull myself together. I wiped my face with trembling hands and ran them through my hair, pushing it back.

"You flatter yourself to think you've hurt me. I'd have to give a shit about you for that to happen," I said, my heart pumping ice.

I stared into the valley. He thought I was colluding with those monsters. All our time together had been a lie. The thought weighed me down, and I lowered myself onto a boulder. He sat next to me.

"Here, put this on." He draped his jacket over my shoulders. "I deserve everything you want to throw at me, Nahr. Your coming here is the best thing that has happened in my life in years. My mother's too. But I had to be sure because lives are at stake and none of us can be sloppy."

We sat in silence for a while, staring at the moving lights in the valley. Despite the emotional trauma of his revelation, I understood why he'd done it. And I believed him when he said he took no pleasure in spying on me.

"Everything that came my way made me admire you all the more," he said, "especially when I heard what you did to that woman occupying your family's home, and when you 'accidentally' exploded a bottle of soda in a soldier's face at a checkpoint."

Eventually we made our way home, and I slept the sleep of depletion. It was only the next morning, when I lay in bed replaying the conversation of the night before, that I remembered the word he'd said. Khaneeth.

Bilal made a large breakfast of *shakshouka*, *mhammara*, labneh, and cucumber along with other mezze that morning. "May God bless you for all your days, my son, and may He send you a kind and beautiful bride," Hajjeh Um Mhammad said. I had to pretend everything was normal in front of her, but I didn't speak much to Bilal.

I packed. Then unpacked. Packed again and kept a few things in the suitcase. But I stayed and went through our routines together. Going to the store, working, cooking, cleaning, driving, walking in the countryside. At night I read through my texts. There was little there, actually. I had responded to the girl that I was not in Amman, nothing more. If Bilal knew about my past, he did not let on. To the contrary, he was especially attentive and contrite.

Wednesday rolled around, the day Bilal typically spent with Jandal and his flock. "What are your plans today?" he asked as we left the house.

"I'm going to get my hair blown out at the salon, then heading back to roll *dawali* with your mother and some of your cousins. I also have that ridiculous appointment with the marriage counselor at the courthouse." Not looking at him, I complained angrily: "I haven't seen my husband in years. I don't know where he is. I want to divorce the shit. He agrees and has given his brother power of attorney. But I *still* have to sit through counseling to *save my marriage*! By myself!"

"It's definitely ridiculous. But I'm glad it takes so long, because it means we get to have you with us longer," Bilal said.

Bilal the Charmer.

"By the way, Mhammad sent word asking about the divorce. It was a few days ago. He called again yesterday. I forgot to tell you."

"He called you?"

"No. We don't speak, as you know. A mutual acquaintance."

"My brother?" I asked.

He turned to me slowly, stared into my eyes, then looked away. "Yes," he said. "What should I tell him?"

"Well, divorce is the reason I came," I said.

He hesitated and with some difficulty said, "Please wait a little longer. . . . I would just like you to stay."

I wanted to leave, and I wanted to stay. "We can talk later. I'm late for my hair appointment," I said, walking away.

Bilal had described the woman who had spied on me, and she was at the hair salon when I arrived. I immediately turned to walk out as she approached me.

"Wait! Please. Can we talk? I'm sorry."

Her name was Jumana. I remembered her. She had seemed smart to me, speaking about Arab feminists and such topics I could not converse in, which, of course, made me dislike her. I'd thought she was another customer, but it turned out she was the owner of the salon. And she was, she said, "with Bilal."

I didn't respond, but she must have seen something in my face that made her add, "No, I mean . . . I'm not *with* him. Not like that."

There was only one other customer, reading a magazine as her hair marinated in foil wraps. Jumana craned her head toward her. "Your hair has to sit twenty more minutes. I'm going to get this lady washed."

She put her hand on my arm, gently trying to nudge me to the back of the salon, but I didn't move. "Look. Bilal trusts you, and I trust Bilal. He asked me to show you something," she said.

Jumana was slender and angular, with a bold face, generous eyes, full brown lips, and a prominent Semitic nose. I had thought her pretty the first time I saw her weeks before. She came from one of the wealthy Palestinian families who had been humbled by the occupation, though she still smelled of money.

"I don't really give a damn what Bilal thinks right now," I said, rolling my eyes dramatically toward my arm. "And *you* need to remove your hand."

"Sorry." She withdrew it. "But please, can I show you something?"

Conquered by curiosity, I followed her into the bathroom. She closed the door, drew out a key, and pulled away a shelving unit by the toilet, revealing a hollow space behind, then nodded toward the void. I craned my neck and saw a knotted rope hanging from the floor into a darkness below. I understood and started to leave.

"Wait!"

She touched my arm again.

"What'd I say about touching me?" My eyes were mean and my fists clenched.

She stepped back, apologizing, and said, "Bilal would like you to join us on Saturday."

"'Us'?"

"A small group," she said, paused, then added, "Down there."

I studied her face, reminding myself that this woman had spied on me, that she was much smarter than me. I turned around and left.

I confronted Bilal that evening. "You can't ask me yourself?" I was still wallowing in the moral superiority of the spied-upon.

"Enough, Nahr! This is not a game." Bilal looked at me with steely eyes. There was more than one Bilal. There was the Bilal of the hills, who would sit alone or lie in the grass for hours with a book, with God, a tree, silence. The Bilal who was a baker, toiling by a hot stone oven. Bilal the Pastry Maker. Bilal the Chemist and Quiet Intellectual. Bilal the Prisoner and National Hero, son of his mother and his country. Bilal the Charmer. This Bilal was a Hard Fighter. A commander who spoke with a deep, meditative resolve.

I felt petty, small in his presence. As I have always done in such moments of hurt or insecurity, I relied on my instinct to be cold, hostile, or sarcastic. I moved closer to Bilal's face and said with what measured indignation I could muster, "You don't ever get to yell at me or tell me how to feel."

I backed away, still holding his gaze. "But I'll come to your hide-out on Saturday with your friends, if that's what Jumana really is."

A WORLD BENEATH
& "OUR SPOT" ABOVE

THERE WAS A city under a city, and maybe another one under that. Maybe more layers still. It had been here for centuries, perhaps millennia. When I descended the rope behind the toilet closet in the salon, I thought I would be entering a carved-out passage, like the drug-smuggling tunnels in America I had seen on television. But this was something else.

I went down first, my path lit by Jumana's flashlight above, and landed a few meters below, shivering in a dank, dark void. It was a corridor as wide as the span of one arm. A small light flickered at the far end.

I became aware of the air, as one does when air is in short supply. "What is this?" I whispered to Jumana, who was now descending the rope.

Jumana reached the bottom and stepped in front of me to lead the way. "You'll see," she said.

Bilal appeared from the shadows. "Salaam, ladies," he said, stepping past us. Jumana held the flashlight for him as he climbed the rope we had just descended, and quickly returned. "I closed the floor behind the toilet," he explained.

"The salon is closed," I reminded them. "No one is there."

"You never know," Jumana said.

I followed Jumana and Bilal about six meters toward the flick-
ering light, where the corridor opened into a room with three
arches and two solid columns holding up stone walls around a
small pool of stagnant black water. The entire space was only
about six by five meters. Two battery flashlights flung a faint light
across ancient stairs in a corner that led farther into the earth,
not yet excavated. Life had once bustled here. I could hardly believe what I was seeing. These had been homes, stalls, and public
spaces. This chamber was another world, a room made of time
and mud.

"Salaam. I'm Samer," said a disembodied voice in a dark corner.
I turned and saw a twentysomething student wearing a Birzeit University T-shirt emerge, extending his hand.

I shook it but did not offer my name. I continued to look
around, seeing as much with my hands as with my eyes. Surfaces
felt clammy, but solid. I crouched by the pool. "Is this oil?" I asked.

Jumana chuckled, but Samer was kind enough to offer an answer, as if I hadn't asked a stupid question.

"No. It's just very old water that hasn't seen daylight in over a
thousand years. But who knows? It could be oil and the joke is on
us," Samer said.

I was already contemplating revenge on Jumana for laughing at
me when two more men materialized. They introduced themselves
as Wadee and Faisal, Jumana's brothers. They emerged with food
bags from what I'd assumed was a hollow crevice in the wall. It was,
in fact, a passage from yet another building. Samer assumed the
tone of a tour guide, showing me around the room, which was no
more than a few paces in each direction. It seemed a bit ridiculous

then, but now, in the Cube, I understand how much space and story one can fit into the smallest footprints.

"We only excavated what we needed," Samer said. "Someday we'll turn it over to archaeologists . . . enshallah." He swept his arm through the airless air. "I am sure this room opens to more and more chambers. It might just be an elaborate cistern. I'm not sure. But we have to be careful not to excavate anything more so we don't unintentionally alter a scene of history or destabilize the structures above."

Samer went on talking, but my attention was on Jumana's brothers. It was easy to see, even in the dimness, that Wadee and Faisal were twins, not merely by their looks but from the way they moved, like two waves of the same ocean. They were setting up the food, each grabbing two corners of a plastic sheet, which they laid on the ground by squatting with outstretched arms like mirror images. One began removing plates of mezze from the bags, the other arranging them on the plastic sheet, lining up hummus, *fuul*, labneh, *fattoush*, and mhammara in two even rows punctuated by plastic bowls with various kinds of pickled vegetables and stacks of bread.

"*Tfadaloo*," the brothers said in unison. Welcome.

I wasn't hungry and couldn't muster an appetite for a picnic in that stifling space. But I joined them on the floor around the food, because I understood that the meal was there for me, a kind of welcoming, apology, and seal of friendship or a shared secret.

Samer was still talking in a low voice, telling me how he'd discovered the underground space. His manner reminded me of an eager schoolboy presenting a science project. From what I gathered, Samer had started digging in the basement apartment of his family home after his brother was killed and his university shut down.

"My brother read about some ancient village and was sure it was exactly where we lived. Except there were no apparent ruins in our town, even though our home was built sometime in the fifteenth century," Samer said. The two of them had talked about it and imagined the buried city based on photographs of ancient underground cities found in Istanbul. "But at the time I didn't believe it could be real," he said.

The group was mostly quiet, eating as they listened to Samer recount the story they had already heard. "My brother loved to read and study." Samer shook his head, reaching for a piece of bread. "I just took a sledgehammer to the floor the day we buried him, busted a hole in it and started digging. It was something to numb my brain. Or maybe I thought I could find my brother by finding this ancient city."

The novelty of the underground space was beginning to wear off. I was both fascinated and ill at ease, wanting to know more but anxious to return to the earth's surface, liking being included but still the outsider.

"I started with small hand tools, carving straight down. Then I used ones with longer and longer handles. I improvised. It became an obsession, and I didn't tell anyone for at least eight months, until I had to figure out what to do with all the boxes of dirt all over the apartment."

I forced myself to eat as Samer went on with his tale. Bilal had brought his dented tin kettle and heated it on a battery-operated burner; he poured tea for us in small glasses and gave the first to me, which I'm sure he meant as a gesture of appreciation, but instead it made me feel like a guest in their secret world. I accepted the glass, sensing a distance grow between us in the confined space.

"I had to do something," Samer said, widening his eyes.

I sipped my tea, tasting the sage. Most people added mint to tea, but Bilal preferred sage as I did. I smiled at the thought, which Samer took as a reaction to the story he was telling.

"There were boxes of dirt everywhere," he repeated, contemplating his tea. "Where I first started digging a hole became a crater as wide as I am tall. It was insane. I wasn't sure if my mind was intact. I either had to tell someone or fill in the hole."

But he kept digging, lowering himself by rope into the pit, now a few meters deep, until the night when he heard dirt fall. Then the bottom gave way and he fell through. "It was absolute terror. I thought the house was collapsing, and we would all be buried alive," he said, finally sipping his tea.

"What about your family? Didn't they hear the banging?" I asked.

"They were used to me building things. The bigger problem was all the dust, but I bought an air scrubber and let it run constantly," Samer said. "I have no doubt this room opens to more chambers under other homes. Who knows how vast it is? Our ancestors built it. I believe they're here now, to help us."

There was still the matter of the excavated, boxed earth. Samer could avoid his family through the apartment's separate basement entrance, but not people in the street. Carrying just one box would be a magnet for curiosity and offers to help; multiple boxes would have brought Israeli soldiers knocking.

For the next month, Samer explored the small cavern. It was sheer luck that he had dug over the open space containing the cistern. He was sure there were adjoining rooms, and the easiest way to excavate was to clear the loose dirt toward Jumana's salon. For the next few months he moved the earth around in the cavern, and found he was right: a small corridor led to another space below the salon.

Samer had known Jumana since he was a small boy playing with her brothers, Wadee and Faisal. Although the boys had drifted apart after Samer went to university, they grew close again when Samer's brother was martyred and the twins came to pay their respects.

The twins' own father had also been killed by Israeli soldiers, and they had separately spent time in Israeli jails. Their friendship revived and spread roots in the terrain of a grief particular to martyrdom, where the anguish of loss mixes with pride, resolve, the desire for vengeance, and camaraderie.

Trust wasn't the only basis for Samer's decision to confide in Wadee and Faisal: the twins worked in construction and had a large pickup truck. Their family owned a nearby hill, forested on one side and farmed on the other, and their sister's salon provided another access for the underground secret.

Wadee and Faisal picked up the story. "We were excited and frightened at the same time. We thought Jumana would know what to do," the brothers said, fluidly taking turns with their words, like a verbal relay.

"We couldn't come up with any good ideas," Wadee said.

"But we agreed that nothing could happen without Jumana," Faisal said.

Samer had not thought beyond the digging. Wadee and Faisal could execute a plan, but not come up with one. That would be Jumana's role. She was the big sister who looked out for them, their only parent after their father died, and she was also a dear childhood friend of both Bilal and Ghassan.

"They said they wanted to install a new bathroom in the salon," Jumana chimed in, twisting her mouth toward her brothers. "I had been begging them to fix a few things for months. Suddenly they were ready to take on a major rehab project." In theory, Jumana was speaking to me, but she didn't look my way, moving her eyes between her brothers, her glass of tea, the food, and Bilal. "I knew something was up, but I never imagined this." She swept her eyes across the walls.

I was twitching, needing to move. The body has its own logic, an impulsivity that betrays emotions running through it. But I held myself steady with a fatiguing determination to hide my discomfort.

"We decided to completely gut the bathroom and expand it," Wadee said, describing how they had measured the precise location to dig, a corner of the underground chamber just outside the existing bathroom stall.

They managed to haul away twelve truckloads of dirt without raising suspicion.

"What about neighbors and spies?" I asked.

"People were curious, yeah. And we knew some of them had to be spies and collaborators. So the first thing we did was to dig through and then obscure the access behind a wall. Then we let people come and look around the renovation of the salon, as if we had nothing to hide."

I turned to Jumana, forcing her to look at me. "And you weren't the least suspicious?"

"Yeah. I was. I did finally demand to know why the simple toilet upgrade I'd asked for became a much bigger bathroom with cabinetry and shelves, why the late-night work, why their neighbor Samer was helping, why they were also redoing other parts of the salon," she said, laughing.

"We had rehearsed ways to tell her, but at that point, we didn't even know where to start," Wadee said. "Instead, we just showed her."

It had been Jumana's idea to bring Bilal into the fold. Ghassan was in prison at the time, doing a stint in administrative detention.

"We grew up together," Jumana said, looking at me now. "I trusted him, and he was the only person I knew who could help us make sense of this, and what to do with it."

Despite the work they had done to excavate and create secret entryways, they had not given much thought to its use. "At least it

would be a place to hide if any of us needed to disappear," Jumana
said. "But it was Bilal's idea to amass weapons here. Between the
army's constant house raids and our own traitors, it's difficult to
hide anything from them." Jumana looked again at Bilal.

My insecurity—probably jealousy—turned into impatience.
Every glance they exchanged was full of their shared kinships and
friendships, family histories, community and political knowledge,
common aspirations and secrets. The more they spoke, the more
irritated I became and the more a question echoed in my head:
What am I doing here?

They told stories about people who had been caught with guns.
I began feeling claustrophobic, anxious to leave. My mind drifted
to Amman. I wondered what Mama was doing. How was Sitti Wasfiyeh's health? I wondered why Jehad hadn't told me he had been
in touch with Mhammad. I missed my brother. The sense of being
an outsider among these people spread homesickness through me.
Why was I still here, with these people who had spied on me? Who
had invaded my privacy, dissected and analyzed my thoughts and
movements? Bilal did not feel familiar to me anymore, and I heard
Um Buraq's voice in my head: *Trust no man.*

". . . and that's why we need your help, Nahr," Bilal said.

"W-what?" I stammered.

"You're the only one who can cross into Jerusalem. None of us
has a permit to enter. We also cannot be caught in a car with yellow
plates," Bilal explained.

One of the first things I'd learned when I arrived in Palestine
was the color code for license plates. White plates denoted Palestinians, restricted to driving on a few roads, most of which were
disconnected and unpaved. Yellow plates were for Israeli citizens,
some Palestinians with Jerusalem IDs, and tourists. One could

travel anywhere with yellow plates, and since I had a tourist visa, I was allowed to enter Jerusalem. Bilal thought someone had made a clerical error in stamping a general tourist visa on my Jordanian travel document, because even tourist visas specifically from Jordan and Egypt could be restricted from entering Jerusalem.

"I have an Israeli contact. He's Russian and will sell us weapons but not risk taking them across checkpoints. We have to transport them ourselves," Bilal said, now softer.

"You're crazy. I can't be a gunrunner!" I said.

"Please just hear us out, Nahr," Samer pleaded. "You're one of us now and—"

"I don't know what that means," I said.

"Stop!" Bilal put his hands up. "Let's all take a deep breath and lower our voices."

Samer apologized. "I was just trying to say, we'll have your back. No matter what happens, we would not let you take the fall. We have sworn loyalty to anyone we bring into this space and expect the same. We've also collected money to pay you."

"There's no need, because I'm not transporting guns and ending up in some Jewish gulag."

"I'm sorry, Nahr. We made a mistake. I'll help you up the rope ladder," Bilal said. It surprised me how much it hurt to hear that he'd made a mistake choosing or trusting me.

As I got up and turned to leave, Jumana's whisper echoed in the chamber: "At least it's an honorable way to earn money."

I hadn't known the extent of the rumors. When I came to Palestine, I'd told myself I didn't care. But there it was, confronting me in this strange place, and I *did* care. What Bilal thought of me mattered, despite myself.

Bilal turned to her before I did. Her brothers too. They all looked shocked. "What did you say?" There was rage and fury in Bilal's question. I could see that his reaction stunned her. She shook her head rapidly, as if trying to erase the past seconds.

They knew.

I walked slowly and deliberately past Bilal toward Jumana, feeling my body quiver with cold rage. Jumana waxed apologetic, but I put my finger to my mouth. "Shhh."

The sense of being an interloper, the insecurity and loneliness I had been feeling, concentrated a chill in my voice, calm, low, and measured. "I don't give a goddamn what you think of me, or what you think you know about me or about honor, for that matter. You act like you're some kind of revolutionary because you found a fucking hole in the ground. You think you're going to liberate Palestine, you stupid, privileged girl? Or maybe you just want to impress Bilal. Maybe you think you're much better than me. That you have a right to kick a woman you believe is beneath you."

Her face changed. She looked more vulnerable in the soft light of our primeval surroundings. But I wasn't speaking only to her, or about her. Something inside of me was unraveling. My thoughts and wounds forming into words.

"What's truly revolutionary in this world is to relinquish the belief that you have a right to an opinion about who another person chooses to fuck and why. That's what we're talking about, isn't it?" I'd thought this since the first time I met Mohsin, the boy who loved boys, but hadn't truly considered it in the context of my own life. I spoke now from my secret shame, the smallness I've always felt and the grand bravado coating it all. It made my face twitch involuntarily, and I was glad for the dimness and shadows that hid my body's betrayals. More than anything, I relished a new freedom blooming in me with every word, and I couldn't stop.

"Those destitute refugees from Iraq and Ethiopia you like to talk about with such feminist fervor—do you know what they do in Amman? They sell their daughters and sons. Honor is an expendable luxury when you have no means or shelter in this fucking world." My legs began trembling, making it hard to stand still, and my voice shook now with suppressed tears. "We are not all blessed to receive a good education and inherit what it takes to live with some dignity. To exist on your own land, in the bosom of your family and your history. To know where you belong in the world and what you're fighting for. To have some goddamn value." I put my face closer to hers. I wanted her to taste my breath. "Some of us, Madam Honor, end up with little choice but to Fuck. For. Money." My head spun behind my eyes. I thought I would faint.

Jumana began to cry, which both surprised and disgusted me. I had expected her to become defensive and lash out with that word: *Whore!* But she was guilt-ridden and ashamed. I swallowed the tears that welled in my throat, turned, and walked to the corridor, leaning against the wall to steady myself. Bilal lit my way and opened the bathroom floor above. He tried to speak, to pull me back, to console. But I was stone. I was heartbroken too, and I shoved him away. No one judged me more harshly than I judged myself.

———

I packed my bags. The belonging and acceptance I had found seemed an illusion. Palestine was my mother's world. It belonged to Sitti Wasfiyeh's stories. Palestine did not want me, nor I her any longer. I was again untethered and vulnerable, a stranger in a place that had felt like home. Needing an anchor and solid ground beneath my feet, I didn't know what to do except go back to Amman. But I had to wait a few days more for the finalized divorce papers, time I spent with Hajjeh Um Mhammad—gardening, cooking, feeding the chickens, watching her favorite soap operas, praying, and talking. Bilal stayed away, returning late in the evenings.

Hajjeh Um Mhammad tried to convince me not to leave. "You made me love you, and now you're leaving. Don't do that to an old woman. This is your home," she said. I wondered if she knew. If she would still want me if she did.

The divorce papers were completed in another two weeks. They were on the table one morning. Bilal had left a letter for me in the package.

Dearest Nahr,

I know there's nothing I can say to convince you to stay, but I want nothing more. Palestine is your home, even if you choose not to live with us.

I would like to speak with you. I fear you have made some false assumptions. It pains me that you will carry them with you. For the sake of our friendship, will you please allow time for me before you go? There are some things you have a right to know, secrets I've carried for too long. I will be in the hills with the flock until sundown. I'll wait in our spot, hoping you will come.

Love, B.

I lingered on the words *our spot*. Now, in this Cube, this chamber of timeless nontime, I ponder why those words touched me as they did. Was I so starved for a place? For a physical and emotional ground that included me? Or maybe what moved me most was to know there was a little clearing on this planet just for Bilal and me, for "love." *Love, B.*

I walked in my green-and-white sneakers—now dirty and worn

from months of walking this terrain—toward the clearing where Bilal and I first shared tea and bizir when I had trekked in heels. We had spent many hours together here since—hiking, picking wild thyme, napping. The quiet of that first day was already a distant memory, gradually replaced by the thuds of jackhammers, the screech of churning cement and drills in the expanding settlement nearby. But Israelis didn't work on the Jewish Shabbat, and the hills were unmolested on that day. I saw Bilal ahead, reading under that old olive tree, resting his head on the belly of a sleeping sheep, man and beast completing each other in perfect laziness.

The sheep heard me first and a few rose to their feet. Bilal closed his book and stood. Jandal, the kind shepherd, was on the other side of the tree. He greeted me: "Salaam, Sitt Yaqoot! You honor me. The land is brighter with your presence."

I didn't correct the name, especially when the flattery continued: "Your name, Yaqoot, is a testament to your precious rarity."

"May God keep you always well, Brother Jandal. You are classy and kind," I replied, and he excused himself, walking farther up the hillside. Bilal had spread a blanket on the ground beside him.

"I'm glad you came." Here was Bilal the Awkward Lover of Life. The Quiet Reader. The Lie-with-Sheep-in-Laziness Bilal.

"Thank you for the papers," I said.

"We're still family, divorce or not. Please sit with me." He motioned to the blanket.

"What did you want to talk about?" I lowered myself beside him.

"Come. Tea first." He pointed to his dented kettle warming over burning embers. From the looks of the fire, he'd been there for some time. He pulled a second tea glass from his knapsack, and we went through the motions performed millions of times through the centuries in this part of the world. Managing a hot kettle on an outdoor fire, adding tea and sage leaves, spooning honey or sugar, pouring, inhaling the warm air hovering over the glass, sipping, feeling hot liquid slide down the throat into one's core. The sweet minted hot tea with sage warmed my insides. I was content to just sit there in the splendid silence of the hills, where the quiet amplified small sounds—the wind rustling trees; sheep chewing, roaming, bleating, breathing; the soft crackle of the fire; the purr of Bilal's breathing. I realized how much I had come to love these hills; how profound was my link to this soil. The turmoil of the days past dissipated. Bilal had once again brought me to this special space where I could breathe deeply, lie on earth, let the crowded, chaotic thoughts colliding in my head recede.

He started to speak, struggling with words.

"Say whatever it is," I said.

He cleared his throat. "I had an inkling of what Jumana was talking about. There had been rumors long before you came. But I want you to know that we never talked about you like that."

I tried to say something, I don't know what, to scramble the uneasiness of the conversation.

"Just let me finish," he said, rubbing his brow, a habit of discomfort. "I haven't stopped thinking about what you said to Jumana. It replays in my mind, and every time I admire you more. There's so much I want to say to you, but now it's all jumbled in my mouth. There are things I want you to know." He looked away, sipped his tea, and began again.

"The way you live your life in our culture, without apology or shame, even if with sadness, makes you extraordinary and special, Nahr. You, more than any of us, are a revolutionary, and the irony is that you don't even see it," he said. The real irony, I thought, was that it was only in that moment with him, when I was truly seen and valued, that I did not feel shame.

"After Mhammad abandoned you, people started to talk. But our mother put a stop to it. I don't know what was said in her presence, but she responded with rare fury and made it clear she would never enter a home where there was gossip about you, nor would those who spoke it enter hers. That was the last I ever heard such talk of you until Jumana . . ."

I was warmed by Hajjeh Um Mhammad's generosity and love, but I did not want to have this conversation with Bilal. Two baby goats playing a game of tag almost landed in the firepit. Bilal knocked over the kettle trying to push them away.

As if reading my mind, he said, "I'm sorry. This isn't even what I wanted to talk about. I want to tell you about Tamara."

"What about her?" I tensed at the name.

"Him." He held me in his stare. "Tamara is a fake name. Itamar is his real name, the man your husband, my brother . . . They were lovers. Are lovers . . . I think. They loved each other. That's what I wanted to tell you. The real story that sent my brother to prison, then to Kuwait; what made him a collaborator."

My body reacted separately from my thoughts. It went limp of its own volition, relieved to hear what it already knew. My body had understood Mhammad's rejection. It knew it had been powerless to seduce him. At the same time, my mind seized with painful memories—the ways I'd tried and failed to be desirable; the sustained erosion of my dignity; my sense of failure and bewildering abandonment. I had been confused by Jamil's tears, the man I'd thought was simply Mhammad's dear friend in Kuwait. But my body knew. My stomach had knotted then. And now I understood. Mhammad had used me. He had robbed me. *He* was my first rapist, not the man on the beach. And he was also a collaborator, a different kind of rapist.

"Habibti, are you okay?" Bilal said.

Bilal called me habibti. "Of course. I'll always be okay," I said.

They met, Bilal said, "on a program that brought Israeli and Palestinian teenagers together when they were in high school. Itamar was an Iraqi Jew. Even back in the seventies, Western do-gooders were trying to bring Palestinian and Israeli kids together, as if our condition was just a matter of two equal sides who didn't like each other, instead of the world's last remaining goddamn settler colonial project."

He stopped, exasperated with himself. "God, I'm trying to tell you something personal, but it all comes out like a political lecture. Sometimes I think I don't even know how to have a normal conversation."

I slipped my hand into his, squeezing it gently. We had held hands before, but this felt physically and emotionally intimate. The two baby goats stopped in their tracks, then made funny sounds, as if they were talking about us. Bilal and I laughed and leaned back against the tree trunk, our fingers still interlaced.

"Mhammad was changed by that camp," Bilal said. "I was only twelve, but I recognized that he was different. He was distant, always gone, and when he was home, he'd just play his oud or write in his diary."

Bilal had found the diary and read it as any nosy little brother would. It had spoken of love and longing for Tamara. "He made a point in his diary to write that Tamara spoke Arabic fluently, which seemed strange, but I didn't think much of it then. They both played the oud, and they bonded over music," Bilal said.

Mhammad and Itamar had been shy and awkward, peeling away from the group at the camp. Rumors ignited, and their isolation brought them closer. Eventually they lost their virginity to each other.

"He wrote about it. I was so curious about this Tamara girl."

At some point, Bilal suspected his brother of being a collaborator. "I observed a strange interaction between him and a soldier at a checkpoint. There was a familiarity in the way they looked at each other . . . like my brother was angry, and the soldier was apologetic."

But it would be another two years before the fateful day that set the course of all our lives.

"Mhammad and I drifted apart," he said. "I was finishing high school, heading to university, and heavily invested in the resistance. Most of us wanted to join the PLO. It was all we talked about. It made us feel like real men. We thought we were going to liberate Palestine within a few years. My brother was already at university and worked at a restaurant in Jerusalem. Back then, Jerusalem wasn't yet closed to us. I suppose he was going to see Itamar too. You know, even when they were together, they still called each other Tamara and Delilah—that was my brother's nickname."

"How do you know? I mean, that he was going to see Itamar?"

Bilal recalled acts of disorganized resistance that had preceded the Intifada. "At first I was just participating in street demonstrations. Later, I did more hard-core planning. Only my comrades knew. We regularly sabotaged shipping trucks and military vehicles with tire-busting nails. At one point, we took out a whole electrical grid to a settlement block."

"But what does that have to do with Mhammad and Tamara—I mean, Itamar?"

"I decided to follow Mhammad once. I needed to be sure he wasn't a collaborator. It was difficult, because he took two taxis, then went into the woods on foot. But I managed, and when I got close enough, I saw him in a passionate embrace with an Israeli soldier, still in uniform. I was still young, naïve enough that I couldn't make sense of what I was seeing. He was kissing a man as he would a woman—and not just a man, but an enemy soldier. Their shirts were off, and they were pawing at one another." There was palpable disgust in Bilal's voice. I wondered if it was because his brother was intimate with another man, or because he was intimate with an Israeli soldier.

Bilal exhaled a cloud of cigarette smoke, watched it dissipate. "Then I heard laughing and clapping.

"Two other soldiers came up on them as they were undoing each other's pants. They stopped close beside me but didn't see me hiding. My heart drummed fast and hard in my chest. I had a *khanjar* knife and quietly pulled it ready. One of the laughing soldiers took a Polaroid of my brother and his lover as they scrambled to put on their shirts. That's when I leapt, unthinkingly, stabbing a soldier, the curve of the khanjar sliding through his neck and back out. Two shots rang out. I thought I was dead, but I was standing. Itamar's gun was pointing at me. My brother tackled him to the ground and another shot was fired. Then everything was still. The two laughing soldiers lay at my feet, one shot dead, the other dying from my knife. My brother and Itamar were also on the ground, stunned. Itamar began to cry. I just froze, leaving my body, until my brother shouted, 'Run! Run away!' So I did, without looking back, not realizing the khanjar was still in my hand, or that my clothes were bloody, until I came upon three women making bread on a *taboon*. They saw me, and for a moment we all stiffened with terror."

Bilal blew out the last hit of his cigarette, fast and hard, his right hand shaking.

He wasn't sure if the women recognized him. They were part of an embroidering club that spanned six villages. His mother had started it two years before, and they met once a month, often at his home. *You're Zareefeh's boy, aren't you?* one finally asked. "I was both relieved and horrified by their recognition," Bilal said. "I collapsed crying, but I couldn't tell them what had happened. I wasn't even sure myself."

It was the first time I heard that Hajjeh Um Mhammad's given name was Zareefeh. It means charming. *Such a pretty name,* I thought.

One woman asked if he had stabbed an animal or a person.

"I told the truth, and they asked if the person was Palestinian; if it was a woman or a man; if the person was dead or alive. I uttered the word 'soldiers' and they didn't ask anything more," Bilal said. Instead they offered him an old black T-shirt one woman had brought to recycle as a rag. He put it on over his bloody shirt. The women packed up their bread and unbaked dough, draped a shawl over Bilal, and walked to their village, where they helped him clean up, washed his clothes, gave him clean ones, and, when it was dark, put him in a taxi to his village. Loading him with fruits, vegetables, and fresh bread, they bade him farewell in front of the driver, as if he had been there all day on an errand for his mother. His wet clothes were tucked at the bottoms of those bags.

"It was late by the time I got home. Our mother was worried I'd been picked up by the military." Bilal sucked air through his teeth. "*Immi* just kissed me and started offering up gratitude and *dua'a* to God, more intensely than usual. Like she knew something was wrong."

I could imagine Hajjeh Um Mhammad's dua'as: "May God bless you, my sons. May He keep you safe always. O Lord, watch over my boys. Keep their path free of evil. . . ." I had heard her daily beg the heavens for her sons and for me. "A mother's dua'as are precious to God's ears," she would say.

Mhammad was already home. Bilal found him in the valley downhill from their house, standing over a fire in a metal barrel. "I walked through the darkness toward him. He turned his face to me, half-illuminated by the flames. We stared at one another for a long while. Didn't say anything, but we communicated in here." Bilal put his hand over his heart. "Then he reached for the bundle of clothes in my hand, told me he had already burned his."

I wanted to hear the rest of this secret, but the sky was dimming around us. Jandal called to the sheep, and they rose, hurrying toward their shepherd's voice.

"It amazes me every time to see this." Bilal watched the flock. "Sheep are nearly blind, but they can distinguish sounds. Jandal's voice is their security. They will always go to him. I could make the same call, but they wouldn't respond."

Bilal began packing up. I had seen him go through these motions often, and my heart ached that this would be the last time. The way he contemplated the landscape as he performed banal tasks was a kind of ritualistic farewell. His eyes roamed the rocky hills, the construction in the distance, and he breathed deeply as he folded the blanket, wiped the kettle, and tamped the embers with fistfuls of dirt, watching their last gasps of smoke rise and dissipate.

The familiar feeling of being alone and lost in the world, unsure of the path forward, had returned to me since that day in the underground. Only bluster and pride concealed the loneliness expanding in me. But now I was overwhelmed by Bilal's pain, the guilt he must have carried, the impotence I knew he felt seeing those settlements, the anguish over his brother, his mother, the years in prison, the torture, the inability to move, teach, or practice his profession. I wanted to take him in my arms and fix everything.

All I could do was help carry the tea glasses as we bade Jandal good night.

We didn't speak further about Mhammad as we hiked home. Bilal instead gave his usual botanical instructions along the way: "... and this is wild Venus-hair, *kuzbarat el ajooz*," he said.

"Yes, I know. I've helped you gather them! How quickly you deny my labor," I quipped.

He laughed and turned to me. "Please don't leave, Nahr."

I didn't respond, except to smile and keep walking.

"At least consider coming back. This is your country and you always have a home with our family."

My decision to leave rested in a clear head. I needed some distance to make sense of events and revelations of the past days. I suppose I had always suspected that Mhammad was gay, but it was real now. What had never occurred to me was that he hadn't actually killed those soldiers but had gone to prison to protect his younger brother. Again, I felt the ground shift beneath me. I needed the steadiness of something real and familiar. There was still more to this tale, but I needed to be with my family, to feel my mother's embrace.

"I know you don't want to hear this, but Jumana is truly sorry. She begged me to convince you to let her apologize in person," Bilal said, interrupting my thoughts.

"No."

"Okay. I'm not going to push it. But you are wanted, loved, and valued here. And that is not going to change." Bilal brought me back with those words. I had laid it all out, and he still accepted me and, maybe, loved me. But that time in the underground and the truth about Mhammad had unhinged something between us. I had to leave, even though I knew there was no future for me in Amman.

The next day I bade Mhammad's family good-bye and headed to the border crossing at the Allenby Bridge to Jordan. In the three hours I spent in Israel's "exit interrogation"—What did I do in "Israel"? Where did I go? Who did I see? What's the name of my mother? My father? My clan? Where was I born? What do I read? What music do I listen to?—I could think of little else but Bilal, imagining going back, running into his outstretched arms.

V.

JORDAN,
AGAIN

THE CUBE, UP & DOWN

A BLACK EYE sits in the center of my sky. A half sphere, dark zit in the ceiling that sees and records everything I do. Hours upon days upon years of me, sleeping, bathing, reading, masturbating, brushing my teeth, braiding my hair, dancing, talking to myself, singing, carving the walls and my skin with my nails, hitting my head against the wall, shitting, pissing, dressing.

That's all there is in my sky. Gray paint with a dome camera. I wonder why the spiders never go there, why they don't weave a web over it.

The floor of my universe is just like the walls, gray concrete, only it slopes slightly toward Attar, where a drain is hidden under a perforated dome.

Klara, the Russian guard, is back after a long absence. I missed her. We don't really talk much. She says a few nice things to me sometimes, and I answer, trying to strike up a conversation, but she usually doesn't answer or simply says she can't talk. She's still trying to get me some books on communism. She once entered my cell when I wasn't locked to the wall, which I took as a gesture of solidarity. If I don't plug my security bracelets in when they buzz, the Cube fills with a high-pitched sound that rings in my brain for hours. I can control only the direction I face when I lock them in.

I suppose wanting some control in my little world is also why I used to try to clog the toilet, to make it overflow, just to make something happen. To make a decision, formulate a plan, implement it, and suffer the results. I took off my shirt, stuffed it in the toilet, but it would not flush until I removed the shirt, as if mocking my effort. I tried again, only I shat in it that time, but it still wouldn't flush. I waited until I felt defeated, and retrieved my shirt from my own excrement. I had to wait for Attar just to wash it out. It took a while—several meals and multiple light/dark cycles. The stench was terrible. Finally the toilet flushed, and everything went back to normal. I lost.

My body rebelled in here too. My muscles shrank to the point that I could close the fingers of both hands around one thigh. Eventually it became too difficult to get up. That's when the guards began taking me out of the Cube, blindfolded. The first few walks were brief and assisted, until I could walk on my own. I take these blindfolded walks regularly now, but I don't know how often or for how long. As I've already said, time is immeasurable in here. I can, however, tell you that sometimes I am taken outdoors, other times somewhere indoors. The light and darkness of this earth are different from that of a building. The first time I felt the sun on my skin, I thought I would sell my soul to feel it again. But I didn't have to. They let me visit the sun again. Even blindfolded, it is glorious. But most of the exercise times are indoors, though I admit I often worry that Attar might arrive while I'm away.

MONEY SOFTENS THE HEART

JEHAD WAS WAITING for me when I emerged from Jordanian customs. We held each other in an embrace made of love and our unspoken yearning for something lost and gone. For home, perhaps, or innocence. For Baba. Or a sense of security, or just to be close the way we were before our secrets and traumas wedged between us. "We've missed you, Sis."

"I missed you more, donkey."

"Aaaah . . . she's back!"

My brother and I chatted on the way back from the crossing, but my mind kept returning to Palestine as he made his way in a rusted 1980 Peugeot through Amman's awful traffic. I hadn't slept well the night before, lying in bed with the fresh memory of the past hours with Bilal and his unfinished story, and I had left early for the border crossing. Bilal had driven me, risking arrest for being outside his designated perimeter. But we hadn't spoken much, our journey to the border oppressed by the weight of much still unsaid.

My brother wanted to hear about my trip, about Bilal, and most of all about my sense of Palestine. Unlike me, he had always felt his roots and longed for the home that was his birthright.

"I have some news. But I'll tell you later," he said. First he wanted to know whether I loved the landscape. Had I gone to Jerusalem and prayed in Al Aqsa or been inside the Dome of the Rock? Did I like Bilal's friends? He said I looked good. He wound his way through the narrow streets of our neighborhood, which felt both familiar and alien. I still disliked Jordan. We had gone there as refugees, and I thought I would forever hold that against the country. Maybe that's how my parents and grandmother had felt about Kuwait.

"Tell me now! You know I can't wait," I said.

Our car interrupted a children's game in the street, and one of the boys cursed profanities at us.

"We're very sorry," my brother yelled back. "I'll take another road next time."

From the side window I could see the boy's surprise. My brother had a way of disarming people. "It's okay!" the boy screamed back, wanting us to hear his forgiveness.

"Impressive," I said.

"Yes, well. You're the one who taught me the power of reacting opposite to expectation." He tilted his head in a sly grin. It was the lesson I had learned from Um Buraq.

"Tell me the news," I said, but he was already pulling up to our building. Piles of uncollected garbage greeted us on the street, a far cry from the pomegranate, orange, almond, and fig trees I had become accustomed to seeing in Palestine. Even in the poorest, most crowded Palestinian neighborhoods, people made a point of planting trees wherever possible, even if only in front-door pots or on rooftops.

A few neighbors walking by embraced me, their children running ahead to alert my mother. Most had been our neighbors in Kuwait who were likewise kicked out when the Americans came. It was that continuity that made life in Jordan bearable.

I rushed to kiss Mama's hand where she waited in the stairwell with more neighbors. Sabah stood behind her, a baby in her arms, waiting to hug me. I missed her too. Sabah had married shortly after our exile from Kuwait and gone to live in Zarqa, about an hour north of Amman. But now her husband had gotten a job in Amman, and they were living nearby.

Sabah and my mother held me tight as we walked up the stairs to our apartment, neighbors and children trailing in our wake. Sitti Wasfiyeh was waiting inside. I bent to kiss her hand three times, then her forehead and cheeks, inhaling her scent—a mixture of old-woman smell, her homemade olive-oil soap, and the cardamom she put in her morning, noon, and evening coffee. "I missed you so much, habibti," she said, tears rolling down her face. My grandmother had never uttered anything so tender to me before. "I missed you, too, Sitti," I said.

Mama and Sabah brought out plates of food, but Sabah couldn't stay to eat. "I'll be here first thing tomorrow after I feed the baby. You're spending the day with me. Don't you dare make other plans," she said, kissed me, and left.

It was wonderful to be with my family again. Mama had lost weight, but she looked radiant and somehow younger. Sitti Wasfiyeh too was thriving physically and uncharacteristically joyful. The interaction between her and my mother was different, kinder and gentler. It seemed much had changed in the nine weeks of my absence.

I turned to my brother and whispered, "Tell me the news!"

"Okay, but not in front of people. Let's eat first," Jehad said.

We had just cleared the meal and were enjoying tea when we heard a knock at the door. In walked my two paternal aunts who had previously wanted little to do with us, who had made every excuse not to take in Sitti Wasfiyeh. They came with baskets of fruit to welcome me home, kissed my cheeks as if we were one big happy family. I was too stunned to protest, and only later thought of better ways I could have reacted. I could at least have asked them what they were doing in our house. My mother rolled her eyes and twisted her lips in my direction, but mostly she played along with the charade, serving them tea and sweets.

Jehad leaned into my ear. "That's the news," he whispered. Even the neighbors seemed disgusted, and politely took their leave, but not without sharing knowing glances with my mother.

Sitti Wasfiyeh, on the other hand, was positively elated, smiling unceasingly. When they left, she said to no one in particular, "They wanted me to stay with them tonight, but I said I'd rather be here, because I didn't want them to start fighting over which of their homes I go to. I said I want to spend time with my granddaughter tonight." My mother, brother, and I exchanged looks, and as soon as we were out of Sitti's earshot, I finally got the "news."

About a month prior, a man had come in search of Sitti Wasfiyeh to talk about her share of an inheritance in thirty *dunums* of land in Ein el-Sultan. My grandmother's village, the oldest town in the world, was being considered as a World Heritage Site, and a team of Palestinian and international archaeologists were seeking permission to create a dig on land that had belonged to her father. Years ago it had been arable farmland, but Israel's siphoning of water had left it nearly barren. It was in Area A, which was under the Palestinian Authority's jurisdiction. A few Palestinian families had bribed their way to build homes on the land, and now had to pay sizable amounts of money to my grandmother and her siblings' heirs for rent and restitution. Universities and institutions funding the excavations were also paying a lot of money for the rights to

dig. There was talk of the Palestinian Authority Ministry of Antiq-
uities wanting to buy the property.

"*Subhan Allah!*" Mama twisted her face to underscore her sarcasm. "How money has softened the hearts of your aunts!"

"How much are we talking about?" I asked.

"I'm not sure overall. But the immediate restitution from the
families who built homes without paying rent or buying is a quarter
of a million dinars!"

Noting my shock, my mother continued, "Yeah, it's crazy. Those
bitches snatched up their mama as soon as they heard." Mama was
rarely so blunt. "They negotiated some type of 'advance' and took
nearly all of it. Suddenly they wanted your grandmother to live with
them, but she kept criticizing their kids and whatnot. You know
how she is. They brought her back after a couple of weeks and offered to pay me to take care of her." Mama twisted her face again.
"Can you believe it? I just asked them what the hell did they think I
had been doing for the past thirty-odd years? Those bitches."

"Mama, that's a lot of money. We can't just let them show up and
take everything!" I protested.

"There's not a lot I can do about it. Luckily, your grandmother
listens to your brother most of all, and he's talking some sense
into her," she said. Still, my mother didn't seem as interested in
the money as I thought she ought to be. I suddenly realized that I
hadn't seen her smoke a single cigarette since I'd returned.

"I quit," she said matter-of-factly.

I looked at my mother more closely, noticing new details. She
was wearing makeup and her nails were painted. Her hijab was different, more modern and colorful. "Are you in love or something?"
I asked.

"No, silly girl!" she protested. She had gotten a "respectable job."

"What are you talking about? You've always worked a respectable job!" I said.

She was employed at a women's crisis center, answering phones, organizing support group meetings, and managing a team of volunteers. "It's a DESK JOB! I'm running the whole place. Can you believe it?"

I had not understood until then how humiliated my mother had felt by her life. The simple dignity of a "desk job," as she called it, had transformed her. I should have said it again, that her embroidery was more special than any "desk job" could be; that she was an artist; that Western images of professional women don't have to apply to us; that concepts of respectability and modernity are manufactured. Instead, I just congratulated her. She added, "They're also training me to use a computer soon. Can you believe it?"

Sabah came the next morning, bearing gifts of food—dates, mangoes, pomegranates, and vegetables that she raised in pots on her balcony. "Look how red it is. Wait until you taste it. I got the seeds from family in Palestine," she said, holding up a tomato. "Let's make breakfast. There's so much to catch up on." She removed her hijab in the kitchen and started peeling cucumbers. I put on the kettle and got a pan to fry eggs.

"You still don't use enough oil, girl," Sabah said, shaking her head. "And you know you shouldn't waste good olive oil on frying."

"You want me to use that American Mazola piss?"

Sabah laughed. "A few months in Palestine and you're sounding like an old peasant."

We set out a tray of food for ourselves and Sitti Wasfiyeh, who had awoken hours before me to perform the dawn salat and had been reading the Quran in her usual spot on a floor cushion. She hated sofas and refused to sit on them. "*Frangie* stupidity," she would say about most things Western. Our sofas were basically backrests for our floor cushions.

Sabah and I laid out the eggs, warmed bread, fresh tomatoes and cucumbers, za'atar, olive oil, labneh, pomegranate, and scalding-hot sweet tea with sage, which we sipped loudly, with exaggerated care, from Arab demitasses.

"I like tea with sage in the winter. Mint in summer," Sitti said. "This is good tea."

"May you drink it in health and joy, Hajjeh," Sabah said.

And Sitti responded, "May God bring enduring joy to you and your child. And may He bring my granddaughter a husband as good as yours."

"There's my grandmother!" I said, glad for the familiarity of her insinuations.

"What?" she protested. "I'm just praying for you to get a husband. I don't know if it's even possible anymore at your age. Shame you didn't even have a child."

I had learned what Mama knew: to be defensive with Sitti Wasfiyeh was silly, because she wasn't actually trying to be mean. It's just who she was. "Take a bite from my hand, my beloved grandmother," I said, extending a bit of bread with labneh and za'atar.

"May God never deny me these sweet hands of my granddaughter," she said, eating from my hand.

Sabah and I left Sitti Wasfiyeh to her daily phone calls to her daughters, her Quran reading, and visits with the neighbors. We chatted in the kitchen while we put the food away and washed dishes. She hadn't married the boy she loved, but a suitor who was a better practical match. Her family had been left penniless and unemployed, as we all had been when Kuwait kicked us out. Her marriage pulled them back from the brink of destitution.

"He's very generous and kind," Sabah said. They'd fallen in love after marriage, but she admitted it didn't feel as gratifying as she thought it would.

"No man is ever as gratifying as we think he will be," I quipped, and she laughed, the two of us standing shoulder to shoulder over the sink, she washing while I rinsed.

Sabah asked about Palestine. We had communicated a bit by phone while I was there and she knew enough to ask specifically about Bilal. Of course, I didn't mention the underground cavern. But I did talk about the bakery, the land, the sheep and goats, Jandal, Jumana—who later sent me a long letter of apology while I was still in Amman—her salon and brothers, the water pipes, the settlements, checkpoints, daily humiliations and indignities. "Israel's occupation is pretty much what you see on the news. But they don't show our weddings, cafés, nightlife, shopping, art and music scenes, universities, landscape, farming, harvests. It's not what I imagined. At the same time, it is everything I imagined."

"Television makes it look like an endless war zone," she said, pulling out a cigarette.

"Oh no. Not you too?" I pointed to the cigarette.

"Why don't you just give in and smoke, Nahr? You're probably the only adult in the country who doesn't smoke."

"I'm quite fond of my lungs and don't appreciate everyone polluting them for me." I yanked her cigarette away and stole the pack.

"Fine. Give them back. I won't smoke," she said.

"I'll give them back before you leave."

"You're a bully!"

"Bilal is a chain-smoker, but he's considerate around me."

"Sounds like love," she teased.

"We do love each other," I said, listening to my own thoughts as I spoke them. "But not how you think. There's no word for it. It's romantic, but without a sexual impulse, at least not an overwhelming kind. It's strangely familiar and comfortable, but not purely friendship either."

"Sounds like you skipped right over the first twenty years of marriage and went straight to old married couple love," she said. "Surely you're going back?"

After a few days catching up with friends, the charms of homecoming tapered off and boredom set in. Sitti Wasfiyeh's inheritance and stories of women at the crisis center dominated conversations at home. I got a job as a cashier at a supermarket in Amman, but the pay was barely enough to cover transportation to and from work. Life in Amman had no substance. Everything and everyone looked the same to me. Every day was a copy of the one before. I went back to threading eyebrows and styling hair on the side. The emptiness of my days was accentuated by the purposeful life my mother was leading. I tried spending more time with my brother at his apartment, but he had a full, busy life. When he wasn't gardening or managing Sitti Wasfiyeh's newfound fortune, he was hitting away at his keyboard, all manner of indecipherable code scrolling on his computer monitors. It was an impressive sight, and it underscored how much our paths had diverged from our beginnings together playing in the streets of Kuwait. The family I knew and loved had been transformed nearly overnight. I found myself a source of joylessness in their midst, dissatisfied with everything around me.

I complained about the grocery stores: "There's so much packaged crap and not enough fresh produce," I said to my mother, holding up a box of a strange pasta. "What is macaroni and cheese? How do you put cheese in a box unrefrigerated?" I complained about the weather: "How can it be so cold here and so hot just a few miles east in Kuwait?" Jehad thought that was a real question and began a science lesson. I complained about the water: "It's making my hair dull"; about the taxis: "They're all cheats"; and, of course, about my aunts: "Why are those two-faced bitches in our house so much?"

"Nahr, don't be so negative," my brother finally reproached me when I suggested, for the millionth time, that my opportunistic aunts were trying to steal Sitti Wasfiyeh's money. "Look how happy our grandmother is. What difference does it make why they visit? They don't have control of her money. Our grandmother is no fool. She's leaving plenty for her daughters and our cousins too. But don't think she doesn't love us," he said.

It turned out Sitti Wasfiyeh was secretly building a home in the Sweifiyeh neighborhood in Amman for my mother. "And for you too, Nahr," Jehad said. Our mother didn't know. *How nice the surprise will be*, I thought.

My life felt aimless, and I blamed the whole of Jordan. Now, because it was not Palestine. Because Bilal was not here. Because no one needed me here. How I would have loved to see Um Buraq at that hour. I could hear her in my mind: *Go fuck his brains out. Wage a revolution together. Fear death, but never fear life. Fall in love if you must, but remember cruelty always has a dick.* How it pained me to think of her caged. It seemed to me the freest individuals were the ones who ended up in state prisons.

Um Buraq would probably tell me that I was the one who had changed, not my family. I'd gone to Palestine to get a divorce, but I'd left with a sense of my worth as a woman who could engage with the world intellectually, who could love and be loved; a woman who could understand that the vast outdoors was more beautiful than anything humans could make. I dared to imagine being part of something as important as resistance and national liberation. The idea of transporting the weapons had settled in me, then morphed into a plan.

In the six months since leaving Palestine, I hadn't received any e-mail. But I continued to visit the Internet café once in a while to check my mailbox. I would compose, then delete, messages to Bilal, until one day my brother alerted me to check my e-mail. "Bilal sent you an e-mail. I didn't even know you had e-mail!" he said.

"You talk to Bilal?"

"Yeah."

"Why hasn't he called me?"

"I don't know. I'm just relaying a message."

Dear Nahr, Everyone here misses you, me especially. I hope you're well and I hope you'll come back, at least to visit. You always have a home here.

I read the e-mail many times.

Dear Bilal, I'm very happy to get this electronic letter from you. I've been thinking a lot about things and I'd love to come back to help you with the harvest to transport your olive oil.

I hoped my letter was discreet enough. He answered immediately.

There is no need to do anything. We have everything covered, but please do come back. You are sorely missed.

I didn't know where I'd live, or what I would do if I went back, but there was no returning to Kuwait, and no place for me in Amman.

I wasn't sure there was in Palestine either, but I longed to return, and gave myself a couple of months to save some money and sort out the logistics.

Finally I had a clear goal, and it felt good to work toward it. I asked for more hours at my job, and booked as many beauty appointments as I could. I made and sold body butters, cleansers, and moisturizers, imagining Bilal would be waiting for me.

At a client's home a week later, I was dyeing and styling the hair of teenage twin sisters in advance of a classmate's fourteenth birthday party. Their mother was paying me to "make them look better than everyone else." She wanted her daughters' hair to be "shiny, silky, and blondy" but didn't want to send them to a salon where "everyone would know they got it done." I charged her extra and made her pay in advance. The girls were pleasant enough, and I was working efficiently as they chatted about school, boys, and girls who were jealous of them. The TV hummed in the background, their younger siblings played noisily, and their mother paced about on the phone, in and out of the room, barking orders periodically for the little ones to behave.

The television presenter said a name that filtered through the ruckus: "Jandal al-Ramli."

"Stop!" I yelled, running to turn up the TV with my gloved hands, getting hair dye on the volume controls.

". . . a simple shepherd. Zionist authorities say he wandered with his flock into a military firing zone, but residents say that's a lie. The village mukhtar said there is no way this was an accident, because they also shot fourteen of his animals and all of them were found where they normally graze. Doctors say it appears he was shot at point-blank range. Meanwhile in Hebron . . ."

My heart dropped. The air felt heavy. Even the rubber gloves weighed on my hands. I pulled them off and tossed them in a wastebasket. I wanted to cry, to speak to Bilal, to bury my face in Mama's chest.

"Where are you going!" my client demanded.

"That one is done. Just wash out this one's hair in five minutes," I said.

"But you haven't blown out their hair or threaded their eyebrows," she protested.

"I'm very sorry. That's my friend on the news. Israel killed him."

"May he rest in peace. But I already paid you and expect you to be honorable."

"What the fuck do you know about honor?" I should have thanked her for that moment of sweet anger that kept me from sobbing right there.

"How dare you spew such dirty-mouthed filth in my house and in front of children!" She demanded her money back.

"Otva`li, mu`dak, b`lyad! I'm keeping my money," I said, and turned to her daughters. "Girls, you are beautiful without all this. And how you look doesn't have much to do with beauty anyway."

My mobile rang as I walked out of her house. "Come to my place. I have something to tell you," Jehad said.

"I'm on my way. I saw the news."

We tried ringing Bilal from Jehad's apartment, but it was no use. The whole village was surely gathered at Ghassan's home, and the funeral procession would follow early the next day.

"We can try again tomorrow." Jehad could see my distress. "If you want to go back sooner than you planned, I can help with money."

Sweet, kind, gentle Jandal was gone. I recalled the last time I'd seen him, the day before I left Palestine—his shy smile, the way his flock responded to his voice and to the music of his ney. The goats that had chased each other in a game of tag that day were likely gone too. Jandal had given continuity to an ancient Palestinian tradition. That was also disappearing, and maybe it was the point of killing Jandal and his animals. He knew those hills like he knew his own body. He would not have wandered into a firing zone, even though Israel endlessly carves out more and more Palestinian spaces for their military training. It was deliberate. Jandal had been murdered. And as with thousands of Palestinians just like him, there would be no accountability for his killers. I bristled with rage that had nowhere to go. The ceaseless accumulation of injustice made me want to fight the world, to lash out somehow, scream. But all I could do was weep in my brother's arms.

I was ready to leave two weeks later, but Bilal e-mailed that I wouldn't be able to enter the village. *It's very tense, and we're still under curfew.*

The army had attacked Jandal's funeral procession the day after they killed him. *Soldiers are still patrolling everywhere,* Bilal wrote. *But, enshallah, things will calm down soon. I can't wait to see you again.*

In another four weeks, Bilal called to tell me the curfew was lifted. I was at the Allenby Bridge the next day, trying to enter Palestine again. This time my residency hawiyya showed up in Israel's "system," and my entry therefore restricted me from entering Jerusalem.

VI.

PALESTINE, ALWAYS

THE CUBE,
THE SPACE BETWEEN

THEN, THERE IS the space between. I lie on my bed, facing the ceiling, trying to remember sky and stars and sun and clouds. In moments like this, time seeps in from the outside and weighs heavily on me. Even when there are no plans or ambitions, no initiatives, intentions, deals, or hope, there remains an irrepressible instinct to account for life.

I improvise calendars, wander in and out of them, destroy and reinvent them. For a time, I marked my existence in menstrual cycles. After one hundred and seventeen periods, represented in bloody dots on the wall, Lena, the interpreter, arrives with representatives of the Red Cross. Israel is bombing Gaza, so there's renewed interest in political prisoners. "We took the opportunity to inquire about you, and . . ." Lena interprets and taps out a message in the 194 method: *Your grandmother passed away.*

A new sort of grief burrows into me, a cloistered, unreachable, immutable ache. I can't see, smell, or embrace it. It just lodges in me, taking up space, a thing within a prison within a prisoner within the Cube.

I long to see Klara. To say, "Otva`li, mu`dak, b`lyad!"—Fuck off, you asshole, fuck!—to someone who would smile in response. But Klara is gone too. I hope for her sake that she has made her way back to Russia. A few other guards come and go, but I rarely see their faces, and none speak to me through the speaker, as Klara used to.

No one visits much anymore. Attar hasn't been on in a while. I would like to take a shower, though I would give up ever showering again just to hear music. The silence of solitary confinement is altogether different than the soothing, promising silence of the sky. The quiet here has a sharp, jagged edge that tears at my mind. I try to take refuge in the sounds on the other side of my skin— conversations and films, stories and cries, sniffles, and fires in my mind. I conjure songs I know. And I dance. But memory, however practiced and refined, is no substitute for actual music.

I start praying, bowing and prostrating. There is no adan in the Cube. I pray when I am moved to do so, though it doesn't deepen my faith or give me anything except something to do. My nails, which used to be strong, good nails, are brittle and cracked. Sitti Wasfiyeh used to get on me for painting them. She said the bright red made me look slutty, that I was asking to be harassed. "Protect your reputation," she used to say. May God rest her soul.

I miss Mama and Jehad. I miss Bilal. They finally gave me a book about communism called *How Communism Will Destroy Humanity*. I read it. It sounds convincing, but I know better, because Bilal— the most complete human being I've ever known—is a communist.

ANATOMY OF HOME

I WAS MET with the aroma of msakhan the day I returned to Hajjeh Um Mhammad's home, where at least twenty people had gathered to welcome me. I rushed first to Hajjeh Um Mhammad and kissed her hand, the top of her head, then her cheeks. "May God bless and keep you, my daughter. May He fill your days with joy and goodness," she said.

I made my way to greet everyone, scanning the room for Bilal. Hajjeh Um Mhammad's sisters and their families were there, and Ghassan and his sister had brought fresh sweets from the bakery.

"May our dear Jandal rest in peace. May his remaining years be added to your life," I said to his sister, to which she responded warmly, "And to your life." I would have hugged Ghassan too, but we both refrained because we knew his traditional sister would not approve. The twins were there, finishing each other's sentences as usual to tell me Wadee had gotten engaged.

"This is Rula, my fiancée," Wadee said, his pride irrepressible. Her hair was dyed blond and she wore green contact lenses. Wadee floated, affectionately waiting on her every need, though I did not get the same sense of devotion from her.

Samer and Jumana arrived together. "Fashionably late, as usual," the twins said as Jumana went to greet Hajjeh Um Mhammad. I had been watching from a corner when she caught my eye and walked toward me, arms outstretched. A few months before, she had sent me another long letter, apologizing again and promising to do whatever it took to earn my forgiveness. She also assured me that I was wrong about her interest in Bilal. She'd promised to tell me something else, which she could not write in a letter, and I believed in her sincerity. If I'm honest, I was glad we'd had that confrontation in the underground. It allowed me to lay bare my life, right on the tip of my middle finger. But that no longer mattered. I suppose Jandal's passing had transformed us all.

"Gratitude for your safe arrival, Nahr," she said.

"And God keep you safe, Jumana," I said, accepting her embrace.

Behind me, I heard the voice I had been waiting for. "Gratitude for your safe arrival, Nahr," he said. My heart leapt at hearing Bilal's voice. I turned to face him, wanting to wrap my arms and legs around him. But all eyes were upon us.

"And God keep you safe, Bilal," I said, shaking his hand as our eyes swam in each other's.

Samer had a nervousness and social awkwardness about him. He was typically fidgety, but that day more than usual. His knees bounced up and down continually when he sat and his hands twitched, tapping on surfaces when he stood. "There's much to tell you," he whispered. "But when people leave." The way he struggled to hold back his news was endearingly childlike.

The first thing I had to do upon arrival in Palestine was to pay my respects to Jandal's family. In fact, it surprised me to see Ghassan and his sister at my welcoming reception, but I supposed life must go on.

"You can ride with us," Ghassan said. "I'm coming back here anyway, so I can also drive you home."

"Bilal, why don't you come with us?" Ghassan's sister added. We all looked at each other. Obviously her suggestion was a way to keep me honest. Maybe she thought I might rape her brother on the way home. I let it pass out of sympathy for her loss.

The formal forty days of mourning had passed, but Ghassan's mother was still steeped in grief. Jandal had been her baby, the youngest of seven, and utterly devoted to his mother. But life has a way of renewing itself. Not long after Jandal passed, a baby boy was born into the family, and Ghassan's mother spent my visit in conversation and in crooning lullabies to the swaddled infant. I didn't stay long. Ghassan's family acknowledged the respect I had shown by visiting immediately upon returning to Palestine.

"*Aseeleh, ya Nahr,*" his mother said. "You are your country's daughter. Times like this reveal the true dignity of people." There were layers of meaning in what she said. I felt it an implicit acceptance of me.

Hajjeh Um Mhammad and her sisters were gone by the time we got back to the house.

"She has her weekly Women's Association meeting," Bilal said.

"What's that?"

"Something they set up in the Intifada back in the eighties. They picked it up again a month ago. They call it Aisha's Army. As far as I know, they help organize and support prison visitation trips for women around the country. But knowing our mother, she could be organizing a revolution herself," Bilal said, smiling so beautifully I felt my face flush.

Faisal and Samer gathered what they needed to make tea on the coals outside, where Ghassan and Bilal were preparing a few argilehs, while Jumana and I washed the dishes. I held no grudge against Jumana, another way I had changed; my former self would have carried the offense until I got sweet revenge.

"Why aren't they doing the dishes?" Jumana joked, nodding toward the men.

"Because we don't trust them to clean what we eat off of," I said.

"Smart girl."

We chatted about her salon and some of the regular customers I knew. The business was growing and she asked if I would be interested in helping her. "You keep eighty percent of whatever you bring in," she offered. It was perfect, as I had actually planned to ask if she needed help at the salon.

When we were finishing the last of the pots, I asked, "What was the thing you could only tell me in person?"

She paused, turned to me, then went back to scrubbing. "When we first met, you were surprised I hadn't already been married at my age. The truth is . . . I never married for the same reason that Ghassan never married."

"You and Ghassan!"

"Since we were kids. He proposed in first grade, actually." She grinned. "But life happened, and when the time came, his family forbade it." She paused again. "People blame my father for the murder of Ghassan's father. Ghassan's father was in hiding . . ." She looked at me. ". . . and my father led the military to him."

I took the overly scrubbed pot from her to rinse. She needed say no more. Her father was a traitor who'd helped Israel assassinate Ghassan's father. His family would never allow them to marry.

"Why is love always so tragic?" I put the pot down and hugged her. "So, who still has to die before the two of you can get married? I'm guessing it's not hopeless, or you wouldn't still be waiting."

She laughed. "Oh, Nahr! You are wonderfully blunt."

"Well?"

She looked away and back at me. "His uncle."

"Just one uncle?"

"Yes. The patriarch. He said he would disown his nephew if he disgraced the family by marrying the daughter of the traitor responsible for his brother's death."

"Well, that's a mouthful!" I said.

She chuckled. "Let's join them," she said, leading me to the terrace.

We sat in a half circle facing the valley. Jumana took the argileh pipe from Ghassan and exhaled smoke with a sigh. I was tuned to them now—the slight brush of their hands, sweet smiles and knowing glances at each other. How had I missed it before?

I caught Bilal watching me, smiling in a way that made my chest warm. I sat back in the chair, drawing the crisp air deep into my lungs. Vivid wild poppies dotted the landscape, announcing the coming of spring. In a few weeks, they would multiply to carpet the land in burgundy velvet. The sky was already streaked with the red and orange ushers of sunset. We took in the beauty of the land, a metastasizing settlement sprawling ever closer, threatening to swallow it all.

Samer sprang up excitedly. "There's something we have to tell you," he said. The others began laughing, checking their watches.

"I won," Ghassan declared. They had taken bets on how long Samer would last without telling the news.

In my absence, they had hatched an elaborate scheme that did not include me as smuggler. "The original idea wasn't good, because everything could unravel if you were caught," Bilal said.

Instead, they set in motion a plot that sounded far more dangerous, with many moving parts and backup plans involving a Russian-Israeli gunrunner, drug dealers, and tourists.

A call to a computer phone—I had never heard of such a thing—from a tour guide in Nazareth would initiate the smuggling operation.

The Nazareth man worked for a bus company that took tourists to biblical sites in the West Bank. His freelance work with small, independent groups was more lucrative, not only for the tips, but because the company's van had secret compartments, which he used to transport dope. The Nazareth tour guide would simply text when and where the car was parked, and someone with an extra set of keys would retrieve the hidden contents while he walked around with his tourist clients. Samer explained that on his next freelance tour gig, the van's secret compartments would transport our guns instead of drugs.

"You're trusting a drug dealer?" I asked, incredulous.

"Technically, a drug smuggler," Faisal said. "But no, the Russians are trusting him." By then Wadee had joined us and completed his brother's thought: "He's their guy."

"If the Russians had an easy way in, why did they wait this long to tell us?" I asked.

"I don't know," Bilal admitted. "My guess is that they wanted to make sure we weren't working with the Israeli police or the Palestinian Authority. But most likely they don't want us to know how they smuggle drugs into Palestinian neighborhoods. They don't want us to spoil their business."

"How do you know they're not undercover units?"

"I don't." Bilal looked at me hard, a reminder that this was no game. I swallowed his stare, letting it germinate resolve inside me too.

Ghassan added, "We have lookouts along the way to alert us if it's a setup."

"What's my job?" I asked.

"If the van is stopped and searched at the checkpoint, you and Jumana need to create a diversion," Ghassan said, and Jumana added, "We'll fight over a man."

"Prepare to have your ass kicked. I'm scrappy," I said, amusing the others. I felt their sincerity. This time around, I wasn't an outsider but a comrade, friend, sister. I thought of Um Buraq and Sabah, the only other friends I had managed to accumulate in three decades of life.

"Nahr?" Jumana touched my hand gently. "You look sad," she whispered.

I squeezed her hand and smiled. "I'm content," I said. The sun was an orange half circle sinking into the land. Samer went inside to set up the table for a card game.

It was nearly ten on a Friday night, three weeks later, when the computer phone beeped. Auntie Um Mhammad wasn't feeling well and had gone to bed after dinner. Bilal and I were cleaning the dishes, craving something sweet, debating whether it was worth it to make an ice cream run. The Nazareth tour guide put an end to those deliberations. Bilal picked up the receiver with wet hands as I listened to his side of the conversation.

"Sabbath is good. Things will be quiet. . . . No. In the Barmal neighborhood. . . . I insist. It has to be in Barmal. I have people there. . . . Enshallah. Salaam. In God's hands."

The Nazareth man was taking a private tour that Saturday. Bilal insisted he park the van in Barmal, a Bethlehem neighborhood with a thriving car-theft business. It was close enough to walking tours of the Church of the Nativity, but insular enough that should anyone see a tourist vehicle being emptied of its contents, they'd know to look the other way.

He hung up. I slipped my arms around his waist and pressed my ear to his chest. His heart was pounding as hard as mine. He leaned into me, enveloping me in his arms and shoulders. "I'm glad you came back," he said, and kissed the top of my head. We had been sleeping under the same roof in separate bedrooms, but I had gone to bed every night imagining him next to me.

I pulled back. "Are you scared?" I asked.

He hesitated, moving slightly closer.

"Yes," he whispered, closing the space between us. I closed my eyes as our lips found each other. I would like to tell you that I was swept away with passion, but it was not so. The disquiet deep within me, an insecurity or fear so constant I barely knew it was there, arose. As our kiss deepened, became more expressive, thirstier, I was overcome by a desire to weep. No one had ever kissed me with such love, and it occurred to me that happiness can reach such depths that it becomes something akin to grief.

———

Each of us was up early the next morning, taking our positions. Jumana and I arrived at the checkpoint at nine. On schedule, the tourist van approached in line with oncoming cars on the other side. She and I queued along the footpath, readying ourselves to create a ruckus, as we noticed the van was weighed down more than it should be with only six tourists, all of whom were white Westerners. To our relief, the soldiers waved them through without inspecting more than their passports.

"I guess our work here is done," Jumana said.

"Damn. I was kinda looking forward to beating your ass in public." I laughed.

"Girl," she said, flexing a muscle, "didn't anyone ever tell you to watch out for the quiet, skinny ones?"

"I'd crush you with one of my ass cheeks before you could do anything with that scrawny muscle."

We laughed, but without mirth, strained by all that could go wrong in the next few hours. Wadee, Faisal, and Samer had the most dangerous job. They had to retrieve the guns from the van's secret compartment, pack them into the sofa in the back of a rented truck, drive to the beauty salon, and unload it. Bringing the sofa into Jumana's salon was the riskiest part, because passersby would surely come to help, as much out of nosiness as generosity, and the weight of the sofa might rouse suspicions, which would surely bring the military at our door. So the twins would have to reject any help, offending would-be helpers and arousing suspicion anyway.

That's where Jumana and I would come in again. We were to be waiting at the salon to help carry the cushions, each packed with weapons and ammunition. No one would think it odd that women couldn't carry more than a cushion at a time. We'd worked out every conceivable detail, even ensuring that Jumana's customers couldn't help, by putting them in hair foils or under the dryers, forcing them to stay put.

Jumana and I had to cross one checkpoint returning to the salon. We didn't expect to get held up, but one of the soldiers decided to scrutinize Jumana's ID. Afraid to lose time, I flirted with the soldier. He was at least a decade my junior, but one could always count on men being distracted by their dicks. The Jewish boy with a big gun allowed us through, smiling, watching my ass jiggle as we walked away.

I grabbed Jumana's hand like she was my lover and warned, "Don't look back."

"You're my hero." She clutched my hand. "I want to be like you when I grow up."

"Bitch, you're older than me." We gave humor another try, but it didn't stop our guts from churning with anxiety. We continued nervously to the salon, about a twenty-minute walk. Jumana loosened her scarf and let it fall with each step until it draped her neck. As we neared the salon, we could see a crowd clogging the street. Jumana grabbed my hand again. We walked a few hurried steps until we realized the crowd was massed around the salon, trying to break the door down. Then we sprinted ahead as the neighborhood children yelled at us, "Hurry, Auntie Jumana! Your shop is burning!"

Pushing through the crowd, we saw smoke foaming out from the door and windows. A siren wailed in the distance, the fire truck parting the crowd with a brain-seizing blast of its horn. We stepped back into the mass of astonished onlookers, clutching each other, watching and listening to the shouting men with the water hose, the hiss and roar of flames, and the black, billowing smoke.

A child's high-pitched voice said, "Looks like your brothers have to do all that work over again." We both turned to the little girl, then to each other, exchanging worried glances. *What if the underground is discovered? What are Samer and the twins to do now? What of Bilal and Ghassan?*

I had a vision of us all being tortured in Israeli prisons, the entire neighborhood razed and taken over by settlers, excavated as yet another Disneyland Jewish archaeology site, the city renamed, its natives ghettoized somewhere else. I felt nauseated.

My mobile phone rang and I flipped it open. "Bilal!"

"Habibti, are you and Jumana okay?"

"We're fine. But the salon—"

"We heard. Ghassan and I are five minutes away. Stay calm. It's all under control."

When the fire truck left and we stood in the charred, drenched salon, Jumana had a meltdown, screaming at everyone to get out. Her hair dryers, Formica counters, and plastic chairs had melted into abstract shapes; her potted plants were blackened and limp; and the ceiling fan hung precariously by a few wires, water dripping from its blades.

"I sold part of my father's farm to create this business. It's all over. They're going to kill us now and take it all," she said to no one, broken glass crackling under her step. I peered into the bathroom. The walls and fixtures, including the cabinet behind the toilet, were blackened but not burned. She slid down with her back against the wall, hugged her knees, and began to sob. I kneeled close to her, worried what was taking Bilal and Ghassan so long.

"Habibti, you have to pull it together. We will find a way to fix up the place, but right now—"

"I'm not crying over the salon. I have no way to get in touch with Faisal and Wadee. I have no idea what happened to them. There's no one to call, no place to look without putting them at more risk." She looked into my eyes. "What have we done?"

"Stop it!" I grabbed and squared her shoulders and said with as much authority as I could collect, keeping my voice low even though she had cleared people out, "Bilal and Ghassan should have been here half an hour ago. For all we know, all the men have been rounded up and soldiers will be here for us soon."

She opened her eyes wider, as if awoken from a bad dream. "What do we do? Should we go underground?"

"No. People will see," I said. "I must go take Auntie Hajjeh Um Mhammad to her sister's house, in case soldiers are on their way to her house. Then you and I can—"

We heard a car engine stop. Bilal and Ghassan were hurrying toward us, Bilal almost slipping on the white fire-extinguisher foam.

We sprang to our feet, Jumana landing in Ghassan's embrace and I in Bilal's. She resumed her sobbing, muffled now against Ghassan's chest.

"What took you so long?" I asked when I caught my breath.

"There's a new checkpoint on Abu Hayyan Street. Two sons of bitches in uniform and a couple of boulders in the middle of the road," he said. Both he and Ghassan were smiling, looking toward the blackened toilet and bathroom walls, all still standing, still hiding our secret.

"What's so funny?" Jumana pushed Ghassan slightly away.

Ghassan hugged her again and apologized. "Nothing is funny. But you don't need to worry. Your brothers and Samer are okay, and we're all going to fix up your salon in no time. I promise."

I gaped at Bilal, the four of us exchanging looks. What began as a small chuckle of relief swelled into laughter that brought passersby peering in.

Finally Ghassan suggested we get out of there. "Come on, let's get something to eat. Bilal and I will seal the windows and door with some of this wood." He pointed to planks from the blackened furniture. "We'll fill you in on what happened when we get to the house."

"No, tell us now," Jumana insisted. "Where are my brothers and Samer?"

"They're safe. They have the shipment. The truck is parked in a garage overnight. Samer had the sense to rent it for a week, and our contact in Barmal is putting them up for the night," Bilal said. Jumana looked at Ghassan for confirmation.

"It's true," Ghassan said. "We're coming early tomorrow morning to repair the outside and replace the door and windows. We'll bring the sofa another day."

Jumana furrowed her brow. "How are you going to replace windows before anything else? What if the whole place collapses?"

Ghassan again chuckled. "It's not as bad as it looks. It just needs some cleaning up and a bit of carpentry. Fire doesn't burn metal and stone, habibti."

"I'm sure she knows that, Ghassan," I instinctively snapped. Men have a way of speaking to women as if we're children.

He looked at Bilal, as though restraining himself on account of their friendship. But I continued, "Just like she knows, as I'm sure you do, that fire can weaken the mortar and make the metal frame shift or even collapse, if it's not repaired." I made that up, but it sounded logical, and I figured Ghassan probably didn't know either. I liked Ghassan, but he had a machismo that provoked me to sarcasm, which provoked him in turn.

"You're both right," Bilal and Jumana chorused to ease the tension. But Ghassan would have the last word.

"Just let the men fix things," he said, pleased with himself as he walked ahead. Bilal signaled pleadingly not to respond. I held my tongue, not because of Bilal, but because of what Ghassan said next.

"It was just an electrical fire, not an explosion. Jumana shouldn't have left that hot plate on," he said.

Jumana immediately put her arm around me, whispering, "I leave that stupid thing on all the time." I realized at that moment what the firemen had told Jumana and then gone around telling everyone else in town. The only "hot plate" was the depilatory wax warming pot that I used for clients. I was the one who had left it on. The fire was my fault. Jumana hadn't told me, or Ghassan. I turned to her, mortified by my mistake, but her eyes told me not to say anything.

I went to bed that night preoccupied with how I was going to apologize and repent. I think it was the first time I had felt such a thing.

Ghassan was correct that the fire hadn't damaged the building, but it destroyed enough to keep the brothers working every evening for a week while Jumana and I cleaned, painted, and repaired what could be salvaged. If there was a silver lining to the fire, it was the trust that formed between Jumana and me. It was my turn to apologize, but she wouldn't hear of it.

"If I blame anyone, and I don't, it's my brothers for faulty wiring," she said.

The hours we spent washing soot from the walls, ceilings, floors, fixtures, and furniture were passed in a redemptive sisterhood. When we had cleaned as much as we could, we painted the walls, the frames of the newly installed front window and the front door, wide open to the springtime air, the radio playing the pop music of Nancy Ajram, Hayfa Wahbe, 'Amr Diab, Sherine, and Ragheb Alama.

"Since you're feeling guilty and need to atone, you can thread my eyebrows later," she said.

"I thread your eyebrows anyway."

"Yeah, but not after a day's worth of scrubbing, hauling, sweeping, and painting at the salon."

"The way you say that makes me feel like I need a raise."

"You said you were trying to atone!"

"I didn't say anything about atoning. I was just apologizing."

A smirk crept onto her face as she flicked her paintbrush, flinging blue paint onto me. Stunned, but fast in my reflexes, I used my roller to paint a blue line from the side of her face down past her waist before she could react, running away, laughing and screaming.

"You did not think this through, girl," I yelled, chasing her with my paint roller. She got a few more swings of paint at me, but her little paintbrush was no match for the long reach of my roller.

That was our state when her brothers arrived to install the counter and shelves they had built in their shop. Nancy Ajram's "Ah We Nos" was playing in the background to our madness.

"What the hell are you crazies doing?" Faisal seemed exasperated. "Sis, you can't do this right now." They had been working for three days straight, both at their regular jobs and later at the salon, neither of them getting much rest, and weren't in the mood for play. Wadee was missing his fiancée. "She thinks I'm cheating on her," he said. Faisal was a nervous wreck, expecting someone to discover the truck at any moment.

"My darling baby brothers. Go home and get some rest. Tomorrow the place will be fully painted and ready for you to install the counter and shelves. Just leave everything over there." Jumana pointed toward the front of the store.

Jumana and I took a break to clean ourselves up and enjoy a glass of tea before getting back to work. Bilal and Ghassan couldn't help out much during the day, since there was so much to do at the bakery, especially with Ramadan fast approaching.

"Is there another reason Ghassan only helps out here in the evenings after I've already gone?" I asked Jumana.

She didn't look up from her tea. "He comes when *I'm* gone. You know how people love to talk."

"That's not the reason, is it?"

She sighed. "Yes."

"Liar."

She didn't respond.

"He doesn't like you being friends with me, does he?" I asked.

"Nahr." She sighed again. "He's a traditional Palestinian man. He's a good man with a big heart."

"But?"

She hesitated. "He's not used to women challenging him so much, that's all."

I sucked air in through my teeth. "Let's get back to work," I said, getting up.

"But he also really respects you. In fact, he admires you."

It both surprised and pleased me to imagine what she said was true. "Really?"

"Yes, he said so more than once."

We worked well into the evening, stopping only once more for sandwiches from the falafel cart across the street. We cleaned and painted in step to whatever played on the radio. We gossiped. We spoke about love, revolution, beauty hacks, food, and loneliness, Bilal, her brothers, Ghassan, the bakery, settlements, menstrual issues, astrology, livestock, stray cats, news from surrounding towns, politics, and why neither of us wanted children.

"I worry enough about my brothers, grown men, in this shitty situation. I don't think I could survive worrying about my children having to deal with soldiers and settlers everywhere they turn," she said. "What about you? Why don't you want kids?"

"Probably the same reason as you. I don't want to bring a life into a world that will despise her existence, and because . . . sometimes the thought of having sex makes me want to throw up."

She turned to me, but I kept my eyes on the task at hand, leaving her to make her own assumptions as to why.

CHAOS THEORY

TWO WEEKS AFTER the smuggling operation, the card games at our house resumed, the truck had long been returned, and the new sofa, emptied of its secret contents, replaced the old, blackened one in the cleaned-up, fixed-up, repainted salon. We were spent, but proud of what we had done. We worked as a team and remained loyal to one another through the worst of surprises. The trust that evolved from that had weight—an immovable thing, like the hills around us, full of stories they'll never tell and life they'll always nurture. Or that's just how I experienced it.

"The fire actually gave us cover to bring in a new sofa, even though the old one wasn't worn out," said Faisal. We could count on him to find something good in misfortune.

Most important, the twins had moved the guns safely underground. Bilal and Ghassan, the only two who knew anything about weapons, still had to inspect the wares. Being watched, they tried not to be together in places other than home and the bakery. The best opportunity to inspect the guns would be during an upcoming local wedding. In the meantime, the most Samer and the twins could offer was: "We counted everything, and it's all there."

Finally Bilal and Ghassan met in the underground, as Jumana
and I ran interference for people asking about them at the wedding. We stuck with Hajjeh Um Mhammad for a while, but she left
early with her sister, who wasn't feeling well. I did the best I could,
but time and again I was pulled to dance and got lost in the music.
Thankfully, Jumana kept her wits and eventually called me away.
"Girl, if you dance one more time, the bride is going to clobber you.
You're sucking all the air and shine away from her," she warned. I
smiled at the bride, who narrowed her eyes and turned away, the
music of Elissa's "Bitmoun" filling the hall.

"On the bright side, you distracted everyone," Jumana whispered.

We saw Samer heading toward our table. It was difficult to read
him because a kind of jittery apprehension never left him, a sheath
of electrical concern, like static that compelled one to always ask,
Are you okay?

"Everything okay, Samer?" Jumana asked.

He signaled he couldn't hear her. The music was loud. Jumana
grabbed a chair and yanked him down between us, the three of us
huddling. "What's wrong?" she said.

"They're not happy," he said. "They said most of the stuff is useless."

We straightened in our seats. I saw Bilal and Ghassan on opposite sides of the room giving a good impression of enjoying the
party. About thirty people were dancing to an 'Amr Diab song; others sat around tables, talking, eating, and watching the dancing.
There was nothing more we could do that night. I started toward
Bilal, but was pulled to the dance floor just as the DJ slowed the
evening with the music of Fairooz. The first notes of her song "Ya
Tayr" always move me. They are simple melodies played on the
flute. But they sound like time. Like all that was good and lost. Oth-

ers on the dance floor linked their arms and began to sway and sing the lyrics. I closed my eyes, the better to soak in the music. Fairooz has the kind of voice that gathers up the heart and takes you somewhere else. I was transported to another time, where I sat on the shores of Kuwait, my bare toes digging in the wet sand of the Arabian Gulf, the tide coming and receding at my feet, hundreds of periwinkle snails burrowing around them. I cruised el-Bahr Street in Salmiya with my friends, flirting with boys, prancing in our newly curved bodies. Silent smiling images of Mama, Sitti Was-fiyeh, Jehad, Sabah, and Baba framed in song lyrics floated gently by. Mhammad's solitude and dishonesty, Um Buraq's cunning and generosity, Deepa and Ajay, Saddam Hussein, American bombs, and finally back to Palestine, to sweet Jandal and baby goats. My hips swirled a spiral of memories that climbed through me into the ether until the song began to subside. I opened my eyes and saw Bilal watching me.

Back at our table, Jumana leaned toward my ear. "I'm pretty sure you just gave every man on this side of the room a hard-on and raised the blood pressure of every woman. We should probably go."

I glanced again at Bilal. He was still watching me. Months later, he would tell me, "Seeing you dance, lost in the music, paralyzed me. I couldn't move or pull my eyes away."

In the end, the planning, risks, fear, and backbreaking work we'd undertaken had been for two useful rifles, one 9 mm pistol, and plenty of ammunition from a Russian-Israeli gangster and a Palestinian dope smuggler. Bilal had spent nearly all his savings to acquire what turned out to be a predominantly useless cache of Cold War–era Russian and American small weaponry. There was nothing we could do about it. Although Bilal and Ghassan were angry initially at having been cheated, by the time we all met again their outlook had changed to optimism. I suppose that's what made them revolutionaries. They were all-in, with everything they had, and that meant rummaging through defeat and disappointment to find a new plan and cause for hope.

We continued our normal routines for the next couple of weeks, during which Ghassan and Bilal managed to sneak away one Saturday for target practice deep in the forest to muffle the sound. Evading watchful eyes wasn't easy, but they had done it before and could cover their tracks, especially on the Jewish Sabbath, when most Israeli workers were either home or anxious to be home. Surveillance was done mostly by Palestinian informers. Bilal and Ghassan constantly investigated suspected informers, and they'd succeeded in identifying several over the years. They would use them to throw Israel off their trail, or they'd see to it that they were "dealt with." The Saturday when they sneaked out for target practice involved them going separately into crowded cities, changing clothes, and disguising themselves as women. "It's easy, but takes time," Bilal had said to me. The twins transported the few usable weapons to specific pickup sites, to which they would be returned and remain underground until they were needed.

They were gone all day. Jumana and I stayed together so as not to worry alone.

"People are talking," she said as I threaded her eyebrows.

"About what?"

"Us."

"They think we're lesbians?"

"No, donkey! Me and Ghassan and you and Bilal."

"I thought they already gossiped about you and Ghassan."

"Not like this. We weren't as much in the open before."

"What do you mean? You're not open now."

"People see us coming to your house a lot. And folks are whispering about you and Bilal living in the house together, even though Hajjeh Um Mhammad is there."

"Does it bother you?"

"Of course! Ouch!"

"Look at you. A revolutionary woman who can't handle the pain of an eyebrow hair getting pulled out."

"I hate you."

"Liar, you love me." I gave her a handheld mirror to inspect my handiwork.

"Looks good."

"It looks great. Why don't you and Ghassan just get married already? Ignore his cranky uncle. It doesn't even make any sense."

"We actually did talk about it. Most of the men in the family are on Ghassan's side. He's going to have a talk with his uncle . . . stand up to him if necessary."

"Finally!"

We didn't acknowledge it, but I suppose we were both thinking that Ghassan's sense of urgency in wanting to marry now had to do with the danger growing closer in our lives.

The weapons remained well hidden for two months until we could meet underground again. It was a late Friday afternoon when the men showed up for their regular card game at Samer's house. Jumana and I closed the salon as usual and helped each other descend the rope behind the toilet. It was dingier than I remembered, suffocating even.

We walked through the dim corridor toward the light of battery torches. The shadows of the men on the dirt walls came into view before they did. We whispered greetings and sat on the blanket spread on the ground. The earth was cold beneath my ass.

"Good idea," Samer said and sat on his hands when he saw me do it. He was chewing gum vigorously.

"Ghassan and I think we have come up with a plan. We want to ensure we're all in agreement . . ." Bilal began.

"We can't tell you the plan, but we need to go over what to say if we're caught." Ghassan paused to let his words sink in.

"If anyone is captured, you must claim innocence and point the finger at me," Bilal said.

"And me," Ghassan added.

"But under no circumstances, no matter what, can any of us divulge this space," Bilal said. Only half of his face was illuminated in the shadowy light. I kept trying to glimpse the other half as his head moved and caught the light intermittently. "If they ever find out, this entire neighborhood and everyone in it will be destroyed. Do you understand?"

Samer began rocking on his hands. "But what are we doing?"

"For now, you're to just go about your normal routines," Ghassan said.

"We can't tell you when or where, but we're going to execute simultaneous operations," Bilal said. The light moved on his face as he leaned forward, bringing all but one eye into view, as if he wore an eye patch.

Bilal explained that a small band of trusted comrades from their days in prison also had limited and isolated roles, but the less we knew, the better.

They had devised a plan to take out Israeli soldiers. "Then what?" I asked. It was a sincere question, but Bilal heard it as something else.

"We have no *then what* here." Bilal the Coldhearted Commander stared me down with a kind of impatience that stung me. "We do what we can to fight them, and endure the consequences, whatever and however heavy they may be." He leaned forward. The fullness of his face was visible now. He didn't blink. "That's it. That's what we can do."

I stared back at him, angry and betrayed. How could he speak to me like that in front of others, especially Ghassan?

Samer pulled his hands out from under him. "The problem is that it's so difficult to organize anything bigger when there are traitors running around."

"You're right," Wadee and Faisal said in unison. Jumana jumped in to say how hard it was to have an organized resistance under the intense surveillance and rampant corruption of the Palestinian Authority.

I was still stewing over Bilal's words, struggling not to be defensive. So I laughed.

"We need chaos, not organization," I said, deliberately not looking at Bilal. "No one is more organized than Palestinians," I began, mockery framing my words. "Look how we all stand so orderly at checkpoints, obediently producing our little green passes for our masters." I looked around the room. Bilal had leaned back into the shadows and only a faint outline of his face was visible. "Remember when I fizzed a soda bottle in a soldier's face? You all thought it was such a big deal, and the soldiers nearly shit their pants. Why?" I answered myself, pushing my neck forward: "Because it was a little bit of chaos in a theater of organization!"

I couldn't tell if they were listening intently because what I was saying was profound, or because it was so ridiculous that they didn't know how to respond.

"Soldiers love facing huge crowds throwing rocks at them, but they panicked at that damn soda fizz. Why? Because they expect rocks and Molotovs. We don't surprise them. We're organized into color-coded spaces, color-coded car plates. Just think of dancing," I continued. "People don't need to be told to dance. You just play music and their bodies know what to do. You can organize them all day to dance, but no one will move until you play the music. We just have to figure out what that music is that will compel individuals and small circles of people to act however they can all over the country, without trying to organize them in advance."

Bilal began rubbing his brow. "You think resistance against a colonizing military occupation is like dancing?" The derisiveness in his voice cut me. Samer, who had slowed his chewing while I spoke but had gone back to audible speed, tried to change the subject.

Fuck this, I thought, and got up to leave.

"Wait," Ghassan spoke. "I think what you're saying makes perfect sense . . . in a strange way." All eyes turned to Ghassan.

A look passed between Ghassan and Jumana. It was almost imperceptible, but it held an unexpressed smile. They had spoken about me in private; perhaps she had admonished him for being too hard on me?

"We don't need a lot of people, not initially at least. We can make use of the few weapons we have for a couple of small operations. Depending on how successful we are, maybe we could confiscate more weapons from soldiers," Ghassan said. "Maybe that should be our first goal, to conduct operations that would allow us to amass guns."

They still don't get it, I thought, though I wasn't sure why and didn't have answers to offer. "I think whatever we start should be with the goal of igniting imaginations for people to act in their own ways, and trust that they will imagine what we've not," I said.

The silence that followed was suffused with possibility and history, like the underground space itself.

"I've been working with our contact in Jordan," Samer said, and for some reason they all turned to me, then looked away. Samer squirmed a bit, but continued, "He—I mean, *they* made connections abroad. We'll be able to set up a website to communicate without being traced."

Jumana and I, and perhaps Ghassan, were not as technically savvy as the others. We used the Internet sparingly and mostly for e-mail, although in the past few months I had learned to use search engines. But I didn't do it much since dial-up Internet service at home and in cafés charged by the minute.

Jumana asked Samer the question in my mind. "What's that for?"

Her brothers answered, finishing each other's sentences. "It's a way for us to broadcast ideas, create message boards throughout Palestine and the rest of the world. The website will be hosted overseas. . . ."

"Why wouldn't you just put up posters or send e-mails?" I asked. They chuckled, which annoyed me.

"Well, e-mails are easily traced. The website can't be traced to us," Samer said.

"Oh." I turned to Jumana. "That makes sense."

Bilal had been quiet, and it was growing late. "We should wrap up," he said. "This has been really good." He turned to Samer: "Let us know about the website"; then to me: "Nahr, you gave us a lot to think about"; then to Samer, Faisal, and Wadee: "Brothers, we have these weapons because of you. We're able to have these plans because of your bravery and your labor."

Just as we couldn't arrive together, we couldn't leave at the same time. Bilal and Ghassan were the first to go. Jumana and I were next, leaving the twins and Samer to tidy up and follow a short while later.

Bilal was already home when Jumana dropped me off. He wasn't the same person at home as he had been in moments past.

"Before you say anything, Nahr, I just want to apologize," he said, taking both my hands in his. "I was wrong, and I knew it immediately." I wanted to ask why he didn't just admit it in the moment, but I let him continue. "I think I just harden when I imagine resistance. Maybe it's feeling the weight of our humiliation in those hours, but I realize I become unsympathetic. It's not who I want to be." He wrapped his arms around me, his embrace more and more my home.

"I also want to tell you that your insight was profound. I understand that now," he said.

I pulled back. "Say that to me while you're looking at me."

"I think you're brilliant," he said. "You have a deep intelligence and natural insight that can't be taught."

My heart ached with love, and I longed for physical closeness as much as I feared it. But we would not disrespect Hajjeh Um Mhammad's trust. So I held him tighter and longer, unsure what to do with my body's yearning.

Samer's website went up. He called it Chaos Orchestra. "I named it after your theory of chaos," he told me. I liked that.

Jumana bought five aerosol cans of wasp and hornet killer. "It's better than Mace, because this stuff will spray up to six meters away." She took credit for having the first creative idea for an isolated confrontation. "I thought we could choose one of the smaller checkpoints without a watchtower. We could take them out, especially if Bilal and Ghassan planted themselves nearby with the rifles."

"You make it sound simple," Wadee said. "You're talking about killing heavily armed soldiers who can summon a whole battalion in a matter of minutes—"

Faisal interrupted. "The Surda checkpoint would be ideal, especially when it starts getting dark and there's hardly anyone passing by. It has only one military jeep and at most four soldiers."

"It's been a while since I've been to Birzeit, but I thought they dismantled that one," Bilal said.

"It's back. We should do it before they dismantle it again," Faisal said.

"If we do, the Jews will set all our towns on fire," Wadee said, obviously having second thoughts, perhaps thinking of his fiancée. We all had doubts, of course, but Wadee was the most willing to express them, now that the possibilities of love, marriage, and family were within his grasp.

Ghassan chimed in: "Wadee, brother, you don't have to be part of this. No one will blame you if you walk away right now. But they'll come for you eventually, and they'll burn our towns whether we fight them or not. And if you're spared, the people you love will not be."

Chaos Orchestra looked harmless enough, reporting news and selecting a "song of the month," which Samer thought was a clever way to pay homage to music, the origin of what he'd dubbed "chaos theory."

"That term is already taken, my friend," Bilal said, sucking on the argileh pipe as we all sat on our terrace overlooking the valley.

"Really?" Samer said, then turned to me. "You plagiarized the whole dance and chaos thing?"

"I have no idea what Bilal is talking about."

Ghassan laughed. "Bro, take it easy on the hash," he said to Bilal, and took a turn on the argileh.

"Hash?" Jumana and I said it at the same time, eyes widening. I wondered if they had been smoking hash all along instead of tobacco.

Ghassan offered the pipe to me, but I declined. "I appreciate my lungs," I said. But Jumana gave it a go. They all did, except Samer and me. "I heard some people get high and never recover," Samer said.

"Anyway, chaos theory is an entire field of mathematics. It is not about disorder. In fact, chaos is not random. It forms predictable patterns," said Bilal the Stoned Professor. "In what appears to be random, there are actually very complex but deterministic systems, with repeating patterns, constant feedback, and organization that is very sensitive to the starting conditions."

I had no idea what he was saying and looked around to see if the others understood. We all appeared lost. But Bilal went on: "It's important to understand that deterministic doesn't mean that it's predictable. And unpredictable doesn't mean random. The weather is an example of chaos theory. The stock market. They are deterministic, they have repeating patterns and constant feedback, and they're self-organizing. Unpredictable, but not random. A butterfly flapping its wings in Japan could initiate a hurricane in the Gulf of Mexico. That's part of chaos theory." Bilal thought for a moment, and added, "You see, Nahr? You were right. Dancing is a good example of a chaotic system, and I believe you are also right that revolution could be as well."

I couldn't restrain myself from beaming.

"I don't understand a word you said, but at the same time it all makes perfect sense, bro," Faisal said.

"Me too," Wadee added, and after a pause, "Y'all, I can't believe Rula is going to marry me."

We laughed and nearly in unison said, "We can't either," except Jumana, who caressed his hair like a mother. "She's lucky to have you, my sweet little brother."

In addition to the news section and song-of-the-month pick, the website was a gateway to a private message board, which was restricted to known and verified individuals. It promised privacy, but the conversations were monitored by "the Contact" in Jordan. They wouldn't tell me who it was, but this person used the chat board to identify potential recruits. I suspected the Jordan Contact might be Jehad, but waited to see how long they would keep it from me.

Essays and political analyses about revolutions throughout the world, and profiles of the revolutionaries behind them, were features that emerged on the website. This part sprouted from the private and public chat boards. Samer and the Contact saved interesting posts into a section that evolved into a repository of historic events and personalities, which became a resource for study groups that began popping up on the message board.

Jumana immersed herself in these posts, and it altered our daily conversations. Talk of chores, customers, money, men, and beauty were slowly replaced with stories about the likes of Dalal Mughrabi, Leila Khaled, Angela Davis, Harriet Tubman, and Kathleen Cleaver. Jumana said, "Most of these women had ordinary lives, but life pulled the extraordinary out of them."

"When is it going to happen?" Faisal asked what we all wanted to know. Wadee had stopped coming to our Friday get-togethers, but no one mentioned it, even though we could see Faisal was only half of himself without his twin.

Ghassan exhaled smoke from the argileh. "When the moment presents itself."

I rolled my eyes but kept it to myself. That kind of cryptic talk annoyed me.

"What about Rosh Hashanah or Yom Kippur?" Faisal pressed. "Like when Gamal Abdel Nasser caught them off guard."

Ghassan said, "Yes, that's the kind of moment we're waiting for." To be fair, Ghassan was stoned. I guessed he was still in touch with the Nazareth tour guide. Bilal wasn't smoking with him that evening. They had tried it together, but Ghassan didn't stop, forming what appeared to be a new habit.

Samer changed the subject. "I've been doing some research about ancient warfare. You'll be amazed how many high-tech weapons there were! Look at this," he said, pointing to a photo printout. "It's an ancient Chinese semiautomatic crossbow called the Zhuge Nu. We could easily reproduce and learn to use it." He looked around at us. "It's already been posted to the online message board. Someone else in the group put up instructions on how to make blowguns. Indigenous tribes in the Americas used them to hunt big game with poison arrows."

He passed another photo around. "This is another powerful crossbow, invented by the Greeks in the fifth century BC. Something else, called a polybolos, is a repeating artillery system they invented in the third century BC. And, of course, the ninjas, invented by the Palestinians in the twentieth century's Intifada." Samer laughed and pointed to a photo of the tire-puncturing devices made from large iron nails inserted into rubber discs from used tires.

Bilal grabbed the picture. "I remember these. I was already in prison, but during the Intifada people would throw them all over the street in advance of the military and watch their jeeps run off the road with flat tires."

The sun had been gone for a while and we sat under a marquee of stars against a thick darkness that sent our imaginations and fears roaming. They could put Jandal and thousands like him in their crosshairs and pull the trigger, but we were not powerless. The possibilities for creative armed resistance were vast.

Bilal and I picnicked in a tent nestled among trees at the outer edge of his family's olive groves one Friday evening, not far from "our spot." We hadn't gone back there since Jandal was killed, even though some of his flock remained. One of Jandal's cousins had taken over shepherding, a way to continue Jandal's legacy. But it wasn't the same for Bilal, and he rarely checked on the animals anymore.

"I want you to know in case anything happens to me. Only Ghassan knows," Bilal said, sipping tea.

I waited.

"You see how the almond trees are dying?"

I did. We had talked about it before. Israel rationed water to Palestinians, especially farmers, and would then move in to confiscate farms and groves of dying trees for being neglected. "Are you afraid the Jews are going to take the groves?" I asked.

He took a deep breath and looked away, thinking about how to say something. "One of the laborers who worked on the settlement water pipeline is an old friend. He took the job out of desperation, so I don't fault him. But I paid him to drill two holes in the pipe and run narrow tubing from it to water the almonds," he said.

"That's brilliant!"

"The tubes run down the side of the footings into the ground and spring up about three meters out. He couldn't take them farther without getting caught. I have to run them the rest of the way to connect with our watering system here," he said, showing me where he had buried an underground hose from the tent. "I've been pretending to weed around the trees and turn over the soil to extend the tubing, but the last bit is still out of reach without being detected."

I listened, waiting to hear the rest, the tarps of the tent flapping gently in the breeze. The tent had only three sides and a roof. The fourth side opened to the hillsides of trees and a green valley. An old rug carpeted the tarp floor, and heavy Bedouin wool lined the walls inside to muffle the tarps. I sat cross-legged, toying with the frayed edge of the rug.

"Can I help connect the hoses?" I said finally.

He was on the edge of words, but didn't speak.

"Whatever it is, I'll do it," I said.

"We're sure they have surveillance of some sort, but they're not established enough yet to have fixed cameras. From what I can tell, they just have one station of soldiers on lookout since it's still a relatively small settlement," Bilal began. "I need you to connect the tubing while I distract the soldiers. I'll tell you exactly what to do."

"How are you going to distract them?" I asked, but he didn't answer. "Will it get you arrested?"

"Possibly."

I thought for a moment. "It sounds like you've thought this through, and I trust you. Tell me when and what you need."

"Tonight," he said, and proceeded to explain the plan, step by step, before leaving me in the tent with a handheld motorized spiral digger, tubing, plastic tape, and a timer—alone.

Night fell, and I understood why Bilal had insisted I bring along a sweater and jacket. Even though the weather was still warm, winter came at night. I shivered inside the tent, waiting for the signal, a bonfire in the distance on the lower slopes of hills behind Ghassan's home.

A symphony of crickets filled the darkness as my anxiety rose. Alone in the open outdoors, the memory of Kuwait came back to me, the long-ago place in a long-ago time on the beach, when a broken shard of glass dug deeper and deeper into my back with each thrust of the man on top of me. I felt shooting pain from the scar that marked that night on my body forever, and it occurred to me how much my life had changed. Two frightful nights alone in nature, one fraught with despair and a sense of endings, the other ripe with possibility, life, love, anticipation, and power—both personal and collective.

There it was. I sprang to my feet as firecrackers popped like a thousand fiery eyes blinking in the darkness. My heart pounding in my chest, I started the timer, grabbed the tubing, and measured forty paces from the tree he had marked; then I dropped to the ground, feeling for a mound of small rocks, as Bilal had instructed. I checked the timer and panicked. I was already too slow. I felt around more frantically without luck, but just as I almost gave up, I found the rocks and dug until I found the plastic. The tubing attached easily. Bilal had worried the ends would not fit and instructed me to improvise with the roll of tape, but I didn't need to. I crawled a few paces to the right and felt for the second tube. Nothing. Then I remembered that I had to go left.

The firecrackers were still going off, spaced between a few seconds of quiet. I found the second mound and attached the tube. Now I had to dig two small trenches to bury both tubes the length of the forbidden zone between the water pipeline and the edge of the groves. I held my breath and waited for the firecrackers to intensify so I could start the digger. This was the dangerous part. The motor was noisy. I turned the lever, pushed the digger slanted into the ground as it came on, and ran with it toward the tree line. It was surprisingly easy, because the force of the digger pulled me along. I quickly buried the first tube and rolled my body down the hill to pack in the dirt. I felt my way to the second tube and waited for another burst of firecrackers before repeating the same procedure.

The firecrackers stopped. The fire on the hillside went out. And I began walking along the road toward the house. I couldn't see much but I was sure I was covered in dirt, sweat, and possibly bugs. If Bilal was arrested, I'd have to walk the rest of the way alone, which was the riskiest part of his plan. My heart beat faster and harder than I thought possible.

I didn't get far before Bilal pulled up alongside me on the road. "Get in," he yelled.

"It's done," I said, and he grinned as I had never seen him. He grabbed my face and kissed me square on the lips, almost driving off the road before swerving back, laughing all the while.

We thought the Israeli military would come that night, but they didn't. They didn't come the next day, or the day after, or the one after that. They didn't come for Ghassan either for the firecrackers, which aren't allowed for Palestinians, and it made us all nervous that they were planning something big.

"Or maybe they just don't know who did it," Ghassan said.

"Did what?" I asked.

Ghassan laughed approvingly.

Bilal and I returned to the groves, pretending to prune and weed while we connected the tubes I had planted to what Bilal had already run underground. He looked out toward the pipeline. The two trenches I had dug and filled in were still visible, but only if you knew what to look for.

"You did a nice job," he said.

An irrigation system had long been in place, supplied from a water barrel at the top of the hill, just behind the tent, which Bilal sometimes filled from costly water-truck deliveries when rainfall wasn't enough. But now, as we sat with a tray of snacks, sipping hot tea, a small pump siphoned water from the underground tube into the barrel, from which it then trickled to the trees.

"Stealing from thieves," I said.

"I'm just taking back a bit of what's ours," he said. Bilal wasn't much for humor.

He showed me how to connect the pump. "Bring it with you whenever you come," he said.

"Do you think they just don't know it was you?" I asked. "Or maybe they didn't think the firecrackers were a big deal."

"Trust me, they know, and they'll come."

"Why don't you just hide out?"

"It'll be worse if I do. They'll demolish the house or do something else to hurt the people I love."

The hum of the pump gave me an idea. "When the tank is full, we should reverse the pump and send our sewage into their pipeline," I said.

Soldiers came at four thirty in the morning on Wednesday. Bilal was sleeping, but Hajjeh Um Mhammad was performing wudu cleansing in preparation for the fajr prayer. I woke to an explosion busting down the courtyard gate and hurried to pull on a sweater over my pajamas. By the time I made it to the door, soldiers were already rushing in and dragging Bilal outside, shirtless, wrists tied behind his back. Hajjeh Um Mhammad began screaming, and a soldier pushed her to the ground. As I ran to help her up, one of them yanked me back and bound my wrists too, the plastic ties cutting into my skin. Hajjeh Um Mhammad threw everything within arm's reach at the soldiers—an ashtray, a carved wooden trinket, a shoe, the argileh. When she rose to her feet, one of them raised a threatening open hand to her, and she spat at him, her curses unceasing. Another soldier pulled him away and, perhaps to save face, grabbed me instead, dragging me by the hair outside with Bilal.

The early morning was still dark and cool. I was glad for my sweater. Bilal stood across the front yard guarded, as I was, by two soldiers. Light from the moon and porch lamp misted his body. I had never seen him without a shirt, though I had imagined it. He was thin, his chest muscular with a triangular tuft of black hair tapering to a line that ran down the center of him to his belly button into his pants. His belly was slightly soft. I had felt it many times when we embraced. He was staring at me, mutual anguish, lust, fear, and rage moving between us. Our eyes locked as we listened to things breaking inside. Lights in nearby homes came on. People would gather soon. Some were already walking through the olive groves to avoid soldiers stationed on the road. They came for solidarity, curiosity, to bear witness, and because they would want people to show up when their time came.

Daylight slowly washed out the moon and stars as more soldiers appeared walking up the pathway.

Bilal gave a scornful laugh. "Well, well! Look who's here! To what do we owe the honor, Commander?" he jeered at the approaching uniformed Israeli. The two men stood face-to-face. I heard Bilal whisper, "Hello, Tama—" before the Israeli struck him unconscious with the butt of his rifle. I knew. At last. Here was Tamara.

Four soldiers scooped Bilal from the ground, dragging him along the path toward the road, each holding one of Bilal's limbs, his limp head bobbing with their steps.

The commander turned to me, contemplating my face. Then he looked away and ordered them to cut me loose. By this time a crowd had gathered. Soldiers were pushing them back, firing bullets into the air and throwing tear gas canisters toward villagers approaching on the hill. I heard Jumana before I saw her. A soldier moving past her had pushed her to the ground. *"Sharmoot! Ibn sharmoota,"* she cried out. Whore! Son of a whore!

The sun was up by the time the Israelis left, taking Bilal with them. Although it was bound to happen, I was tormented by his arrest, and later by his absence, spending sleepless nights wondering what interrogators were doing to him.

Jumana and I fetched Hajjeh Um Mhammad's heart and blood pressure pills and made her a small breakfast, which she refused to eat. All the cabinets throughout the house had been opened, some broken, their contents spilled onto the floor. A regiment of neighbors and kinfolk surrounded Hajjeh Um Mhammad, who hurled curses at the vanished soldiers. I saw then the formidable woman who had endured a lifetime of military occupation, toil, and widowhood. She alternated between curses and entreaties to God to strike Israelis down, to bring the wicked to their knees, as all oppressors must be punished and the victims avenged. But she shed not one tear. She was a rock. A wall. A force. A woman. She would cry later, anguished and bitter tears, but only in solitude or in the company of her sisters and dearest friends. I thought of my mother and Sitti Wasfiyeh, Um Buraq and all the women of our *hara* in Kuwait who had endured these traumas of colonialism.

Jumana put her arm around me. "Bilal is a warrior. He'll be fine. Let's fix this mess," and we began another cleanup. We refolded and organized scattered clothes, gathered spilled foods, salvaged what we could of the rice flung across the kitchen floor, vacuumed the sugar and flour off the furniture and wiped it off the walls.

The following day brought news of Ghassan's arrest. Hajjeh Um

Mhammad cooked a meal for his family, and we piled into Bilal's car to drive to their home, which had also been ransacked. Many were already there cleaning up, but Jumana and I stayed to help before returning with Hajjeh Um Mhammad to finish putting our own home back together.

In another day's time, a local carpenter had mended broken cupboards, drawers, and shelves. Over the following weeks Hajjeh Um Mhammad's sisters, and the multitude of families who loved her, brought more food than we could eat. We refrigerated some and gave away the rest. The sun went down and rose again, as if nothing had happened, indifferent to Bilal's and Ghassan's absence, to the knowledge that they were being harmed in ways we couldn't bear to imagine. There was no charge. No trial. Both were held in "administrative detention." All of this just to secure a bit of water for the trees.

The tenacity of heartache can take a toll on the body. Hajjeh Um Mhammad grew thin in the months after Bilal's arrest, and I stayed to care for her. Jumana split her time between her own house, ours, and the salon. Once a week, she also accompanied me to run the pump and fill the water barrel. Ghassan's sister and other family members took over running the bakery. Continuing Bilal and Ghassan's work was how we all coped with their imprisonment.

Their administrative detention orders were renewed twice at six-month intervals. Neither Bilal nor Ghassan was charged with a crime. In those eighteen months, Wadee married his fiancée, Samer got a scholarship to study in Russia, Hajjeh Um Mhammad spent a week in the hospital, and the olive harvest came and went without her and me, as I remained by her side while the whole village picked, sorted, and pressed the olives. Settler attacks increased, but in all it was a good crop, I was told. It was the first harvest Hajjeh Um Mhammad had ever missed in all her life.

It was late October again, another harvest season, when news came that Bilal would be released. Hajjeh Um Mhammad's joy was effusive. "Praise and gratitude to you, Almighty. Praise Him!" she sang, laughing and crying at the same time. Giddy for the rest of the day, she moved about the house in song. Her sisters and friends arrived to help make *mansaf*, Bilal's favorite lamb dish. We didn't know exactly when he'd be released, but his lawyer assured us today was the day. Hajjeh Um Mhammad busied herself all morning preparing the meat and the *jameed*, fermented dried yogurt. She sent Jumana and me out to source the best and freshest lamb cuts.

"If it has a gamy smell, it was slaughtered too old, and the meat is no good. Same with color. Make sure you look for meat that has a lighter pink color. Red meat is too rough and won't be as tender when I cook it," she instructed.

"*Haader, ya sit el kol,*" we both replied. Yes, ma'am.

"Get some fresh cardamom too. I'll grind it here."

"*Haader, ya sit el kol.*"

"And make sure you get it from Abu Abdelkarim. He's my favorite spice seller. And make sure you tell them who it's for."

She tried to give us money, but we refused, of course. Since I'd stopped working to take care of Hajjeh Um Mhammad, cash was low, but Jehad had come through for me with enough to last for a couple of months. Between his job, the computer freelancing he did, and managing Sitti Wasfiyeh's newfound fortune, my brother was doing well.

"At least take these for Abu Farooq and Abu Abdelkarim," she said, handing us bags of fruits and vegetables to gift the butcher and spice merchant. "I always take them a few things from my garden."

News had spread fast. People stopped Jumana and me on the

street to ask if it was true Bilal was coming home. When they asked about Ghassan, Jumana's eyes would betray her private despair over his continued detention.

The butcher gave us extra cuts of meat, and the spice merchant loaded us with gifts of coffee beans, cashews, and fresh turmeric, "for the hajjeh and our hero Bilal."

Hajjeh Um Mhammad had already soaked the rice and dissolved the jameed by the time we got back. The other women had worked a bit in her garden and gone home, taking a few vegetables and fruits with them, keeping to their habit of sharing from home gardens. Jumana and I watched eagerly while Hajjeh Um Mhammad went through the bags we brought, sniffing the spices and inspecting the meat.

"You did good, girls!" She smiled at us from the kitchen table. Relieved that we had executed the task satisfactorily, Jumana and I washed the meat repeatedly as she instructed. Arthritis had taken the vigor from Hajjeh Um Mhammad's hands and her movements were fitful, but she insisted on prepping the meat with spices herself.

"You have to coat each piece separately," she said, rubbing the spice mixture into the lamb. "And recite Quran in your heart when you do it . . . or at least think about blessed things. Give thanks to God and to the animal whose life will nurture us. O Lord, bless this day. We thank you for all things. Praise you, Lord."

Jumana helped spice the rest of the lamb while I beat the cardamom to powder with the mortar and pestle. Then Hajjeh Um Mhammad added the lamb to the pot of boiling water and poured in the cardamom, bay leaves, *mistika*, salt, black pepper, and cloves. The smells of a loving home waiting for its son wafted through the house. When the meat was cooked almost to perfect tenderness, we set up another vat to cook the sauce. Jumana and I took turns continuously stirring the jameed yogurt as Hajjeh Um Mhammad slowly added the pieces of cooked meat. She pinched turmeric and sprinkled it onto the white sauce. "It needs a bit more salt," or a bit more of this or that, she'd say, tasting her work. "Are the almonds roasted?" she asked.

"Yes. And the parsley is chopped," I answered.

"You're such good girls, you two. God has given me the daughters I never had. Praise Him. Praise His wisdom and His mercy." She looked up at the clock on the wall. "O Lord in your infinite mercy, bring my son home soon. O my God and my Master, please clear his path of the evil and malice of those people."

Jumana and I looked at each other. Bilal should have been home by now. We continued helping with the cooking and cleaning. Several people arrived to check in and wish us blessings. Most stayed, and when it looked like Bilal might not be coming home, more visitors, including Hajjeh Um Mhammad's sisters and friends, returned to help bear the disappointment.

"He's coming today. By the Almighty's will, he is coming home," Hajjeh Um Mhammad insisted, refusing to accept anything less. She asked us to fetch her motor chair. As we did so, we heard the roar of a crowd, then saw a group of thirty or forty men hurrying up the walkway, carrying Bilal on their shoulders. He was smiling, but I knew it embarrassed him to be the focus of such adoration, and I could see weariness beneath the smile. He went first to his mother, kneeling to kiss her feet as she struggled to pull him to her face. He kissed her hands, then her forehead, then her cheeks. He pulled his aunts and others into an embrace. Then Jumana and me. It didn't matter that we weren't related; people accepted the physical affection as if we were his sisters. Before anything else, we were the dearest of friends, and his homecoming filled me with a happiness not unlike the day Jehad was returned to us from a Kuwaiti prison.

I heard him whisper to Jumana, "Ghassan sends his love."

Hajjeh Um Mhammad rushed all the women into the kitchen to heat the food and begin assembling the layers onto the dishes. Heaps of saffron rice were molded into small hills on four large trays. Hajjeh Um Mhammad picked out the chunks of lamb and arranged them on top of each rice hill. As she sprinkled the parsley and roasted almonds on top, Ghassan's mother arrived at the house, and Hajjeh Um Mhammad moved as hurriedly as her arthritic body would allow to embrace her friend. The two hajjehs held each other for a long and poignant moment. When they let go, Bilal kissed the hand of Ghassan's mother.

"Let me kiss your face, my son. You are as dear to me as Ghassan and Jandal, God rest his soul. Praise God for your safe return, my son. Praise God," she said.

"Ghassan is in good spirits, Auntie. They moved us to the same detention center last week, and I got to see him a lot. He sends his love," Bilal told her. His words gave her some comfort, and she filled the room with more and more prayers for both men and for all Palestinian prisoners.

"Come, come, Sister." Hajjeh Um Mhammad pulled her friend away. "Let's eat. By God's will, we will eat our next meal together soon in celebration of Ghassan's return." She began ladling sauce on the rice and instructed us to bring the rest in bowls to place around the central trays. We set out the hot trays of mansaf, tender lamb in spicy white yogurt broth on a bed of saffron rice, topped with roasted almonds, parsley, and pine nuts.

There were too many people to fit indoors. A group took one of the trays to the terrace and ate in the crisp, cool breeze of October in Palestine.

Mansaf was always a dish for large gatherings or holidays in my youth. Eating it by hand makes it all the more cherished. The continuity of these traditions helped bridge the spaces between dislocation and the home I had forged in my birthright homeland, but I knew I could never again be complete in one place. This was what it meant to be exiled and disinherited—to straddle closed borders, never whole anywhere. To remain in one place meant tearing one's limbs from another. I missed my mother. My brother and grandmother. I balled a bite of mansaf in my hand and looked around the room. Bilal, Jumana, Samer, Wadee and Faisal, other friends, Hajjeh Um Mhammad and her sisters, neighbors, and more family. This was where I belonged, but so much of me was still scattered elsewhere.

HARVEST

NOT WANTING TO give people more fodder for gossip, especially with Hajjeh Um Mhammad's fragile health, I moved in with Jumana after Bilal returned. But I was there daily for the hajjeh, even though she had plenty of people caring for her.

"May God brighten your days and clear your path of wickedness, my daughter. You always check on me. May God's angels always check on you. Amen," Hajjeh Um Mhammad would say.

A couple of days after Bilal's homecoming, Hajjeh Um Mhammad collapsed in the kitchen. The doctor said it was exhaustion, probably a combination of excitement over Bilal's homecoming and preparations for the harvest in the coming week. Age had stolen her strength and agility and she hadn't been able to do as much as she used to at harvest, but there was no way she would miss it again, especially with Bilal home, though the doctor had ordered her to rest.

The evening before the big day, Jumana and I prepared salads and mezze dishes to take to the groves. Hajjeh Um Mhammad and her friends kneaded dough to make fresh *khobz* bread, which they would bake outdoors on a hot taboon. We started the first day of harvest early, packing for a long day, and began hiking to the groves before the sun made it over land. I even carried a basket on my head as the elders did, and as I imagined my ancestors had done.

Although Hajjeh Um Mhammad could not walk well, she had always insisted on making this annual trek to the olive groves. This year she relented and allowed Bilal to drive her to the top of the hill, where she could walk a short distance to join the elder kinfolk and friends gathered to sort the olives, bake bread, and prepare food. The women who managed to balance a load atop their heads and converse with one another while simultaneously walking the steep, rocky paths, sometimes carrying a child too, were a marvel to behold. I struggled to keep the basket from falling off my head, holding it in place with one arm. Then I had to use both arms, which provoked some children (and adults) to laughter.

"Accept who you are, city girl," Faisal teased. "We're taking bets when and where the basket is going to fall." Wadee laughed, and so did the children.

"Whose side are you on, Jumana?"

"Well, ordinarily I'd be on a sister's side. But there's a prize involved. I have to go with the safe bet that the basket is going to fall off your head before you reach the trees."

"And if I make it? Will I get the prize?" I asked.

"Nope. This one here gets it. She's betting you're going to make it just fine," Jumana said, pointing to a little girl of nine or ten. Her name was Amna, a relative of Bilal's.

"Come here, beautiful Amna," I said. "You're my only true friend. We'll show them, won't we?"

"Yeah." The little girl looked up at me, smiling sweetly.

The prize was a bag of M&M's, which Amna won and put aside for dessert after lunch and a hard day's work. "Want to share with them?" I asked her.

Amna grinned sheepishly. "Only if they work hard. And they have to show me how many olives they picked and sorted!"

Bilal had already laid the tarps by the time we arrived. We got to work right away, toiling among those ancient trees as the sun inched along its arc. Amna taught me the proper way to pick olives. "Some of the lazy boys try to just shake and hit the branches to make the olives fall, but that's wrong. My father says it's wrong to beat a tree that's giving you blessings. Do it like this," Amna said, picking one olive at a time with rapid dexterity, letting them fall onto the tarp laid beneath the tree. The plop of hundreds of olives falling at once from the trees all around made music like rain from clear blue skies.

Five or six people toiled at each tree, picking as far as we could reach. Some, like Amna, climbed on ladders and filled buckets of olives from the high branches. Some sat on the tarps, sorting the olives into baskets according to color and ripeness. Children too small to pick ferried the baskets to and from piles destined for the olive press. Jumana, Amna, and I worked alongside each other on one side, Bilal, Wadee, and Faisal on the other, listening to a radio another family had brought. We talked. Sang. My arms grew sore and moist patches darkened the underarms of my shirt. The air was refreshingly cool against my face, even as beads of sweat rolled steadily down the groove of my back. I had never known the pleasure of such physical toil. Soon the smell of fresh bread wafted between the trees. It was nearing time to pause for the food being spread at the top of the hill, not far from the road where Bilal's car was parked.

"I stink!" Jumana sniffed her armpits.

"Who's the city girl now?" I smirked.

Amna suddenly made a strange sound in her throat and dropped her bucket from atop the ladder, spilling its contents on the ground. The sun was in my eyes. I couldn't see her, but Jumana would later describe the fear on Amna's face. Before we could say anything, a little boy a few tiers up the hill screamed, "The Jews! The Jews!"

People scrambled to their feet, gathering as many olives as possible. I ran to Amna. Her legs were trembling, and I reached up to help her down the ladder as Bilal ran past us up the hill. Wadee and Faisal followed, ordering us to "wrap up the olives."

"*Allah yustor*," Jumana prayed, hands shaking as she scooped the olives into buckets.

We could see them now, settler children throwing rocks. Behind them, their fathers pointed rifles at us while soldiers guarded their flanks. Amna was reciting the Quran, still trembling, when her mother called to her. I watched mother and daughter flee holding hands. Clouds of tear gas crept menacingly through the trees, forcing people into the valley.

Can something expected still be a surprise? We knew that Israelis were especially menacing during the harvest season. They know olives have been the mainstay and centerpiece of our social, economic, and cultural presence for millennia, and it infuriated them—still does—to watch the unbroken continuity of our indigenous traditions. So they came with their big guns, and the colonial logic of interlopers who cannot abide our presence or our joy.

Two shots rang out.

"Hurry!" Jumana urged.

I ran behind her up the hill. The settlers appeared to be retreating, firing from farther and farther away. Hajjeh Um Mhammad had collapsed to the ground amid smashed plates of food and someone's blood. Bilal was screaming to help his mother as a horde of soldiers bound and dragged him away. Faisal too was arrested. Wadee carried a boy who had been shot in the abdomen toward an approaching ambulance. The boy would die in the hospital that night.

Hajjeh Um Mhammad was having trouble breathing, but she was conscious. As soldiers hauled Bilal away, I shouted as loudly as I could that his mother was okay, we would get her to the hospital, and prayed he heard me.

The streets shook with mourning the next day as large crowds carried the body of the slain boy to his burial. He was eight years old. But there was still work in the fields, and we all went back to finish as much as we could. What had been delightful yesterday was unbearable now. Clouds dimmed the sky. No one spoke. There were no radios or songs. The sound of plopping olives was bitter and mournful. Hajjeh Um Mhammad's kin took turns caring for her. She had recovered physically, but heavy grief anchored her to her bed.

We left in the afternoon to pay our respects to the boy's family. Some internationals came to help pick olives and offer their bodies and cameras as shields against another attack. They came again on the third day, but could do nothing but film when masked settlers arrived, once more protected by soldiers. I was engrossed in a robotic rhythm of picking, my mind emptied of thought. The ability to become vacuous was a skill I had honed over years. The slow stream of sweat trickling down the groove of my back brought me in and out of awareness. I was there, but not there.

Pandemonium suddenly brought me to my senses—wails, fire, smoke, laughing settlers running away, and soldiers preventing the sole fire truck from reaching us. I saw those soldiers in the distance; their languid posture seemed to say they were bored by our swelling panic as the fire spread.

Villagers converged from everywhere to extinguish the flames. Jumana and I grabbed our buckets and ran to fill them with dirt that we hurled into the inferno. It was like trying to mop up the sea with sponges, but to stand and watch the land burn would have been more painful than the burns on our skin and smoke in our lungs.

God intervened, or so everyone later said. More clouds gathered, and a bolt of lightning cracked open the sky. Rain poured. Jumana fell to the ground crying as the fire slowly died, a ground of embers hissing wherever raindrops landed. We stood there, covered in soot, rain streaking our skin black. We were waiting for the next thing—for rescuers, for settlers to return and shoot us, for lightning to set their colony alight. But there was nothing now. Only rain. I pulled the scarf from my head and wiped Jumana's face. She finally stopped sobbing, and together we waded through the mud and char.

We went to her house to clean up. I should have gone immediately to see Hajjeh Um Mhammad. Surely neighborhood children had already spread news of the fire. I should have been there when she found out, to give her a reassuring eyewitness account of the miraculous rain that contained the fire, to tell her that only a small part of the grove was lost. But I couldn't. Selfishly, I retreated. I could do no more than wash the day from my body.

Jumana and I bandaged each other's burns, and we fell asleep where we sat on the sofa. When I opened my eyes again, someone was banging on the door. It was six the next morning. Jumana lifted her head at the opposite end of the sofa, our legs still tangled in the middle. It was her brother Wadee. His fiancée had called to tell him that Hajjeh Um Mhammad had been taken to the hospital in an ambulance.

I wasn't ready for another day of turmoil. I needed more time on the sofa, doing nothing at all. Yet just as I was pulling myself together to go to the hospital, another whirlwind of news sent our heads spinning: Ghassan had just been released.

Bilal's rearrest, the torched fields, and Hajjeh Um Mhammad's hospital stay made the hours stretch and fold in on themselves, holding time hostage to different iterations of the same day that would not end. We got word that Bilal had begun a hunger strike. At the same time, doctors informed us Hajjeh Um Mhammad had suffered a stroke. The right side of her body was paralyzed. Doctors said there was also a problem with her heart, that it had grown too large to pump sufficient blood through her body. There was nothing more they could do. "It's in God's hands," they said. Her sisters took turns at her bedside and a steady stream of visitors came and went. Hajjeh Um Mhammad was awake and talking, but only her sisters could understand what she was saying.

Israeli settlers setting fire to trees during the harvest had become so commonplace in the past ten years that international aid organizations had been established for the sole purpose of defending Palestinian farmers. The group that came to pick with us also pledged to replenish the soil and replant trees. I showed up as much as I could to help with replanting and turning over the soil, but I was not accustomed to such successive trauma without respite. I needed time to mourn, time to recover.

I went back to working at the salon and helped at the bakery sometimes, though Ghassan didn't really need me. I visited Hajjeh Um Mhammad every day, but I'm ashamed to say it became more of a chore than something I truly wanted to do. It was hard to watch her deterioration. My heart was perpetually stuck in my throat.

Realizing I couldn't understand her words, Hajjeh Um Mhammad mostly squeezed my hand as I relayed news from the village. There were some good days, when she was more alert. On one such occasion, she pulled me closer, insisting I comprehend. Two of her sisters helped make out her words. She wanted Bilal and me to marry. It wasn't the first time she had suggested this, but now it had the gravity of a dying woman's request. I knew our living arrangement was not sustainable in our conservative culture, and I wanted to stay close to Bilal. But marriage unsettled me. The physical intimacy of it. Its permanence. The ownership of belonging to a man. People would surely gossip that I had married both brothers.

"You're good for each other. Take it from an old lady who knows more about the world than you," she whispered hoarsely. Her sisters concurred. They had all spoken of it. Of her four sisters, Hajjeh Um Mhammad was the only one who had given birth to fewer than five children, the only one without daughters and grandchildren. The only widow among them now would be the first to die, though she was not the oldest.

She envied the abundance her sisters had produced—sons and daughters, grandchildren and great-grandchildren. She'd once confided in me that she sometimes wondered if God was displeased with her for some offense she might have committed. Then she shooed away the thought, begged God's pardon, and thanked Him for all she had and did not have. "One must always be grateful to God for one's fate, alhamdulillah," she had said.

I looked into Hajjeh Um Mhammad's eyes, unsure what to say. She spoke again, and I understood perfectly. "He loves you. And I know you love him," she said. How strange to be brought into this family as the wife of one brother, only to fall in love with the other and receive benediction from their mother to marry him after divorcing the first.

I did love Bilal, though those words seemed too small for his expansive presence in my heart. He saw me in the fullness of my shame and broken parts, and didn't look away. Through his eyes,

I saw and maybe became another version of myself—a thoughtful, powerful, intellectual woman who could love, be loved, affect the world, and maybe be touched again by a man.

"Your elders know best, daughter," her sister whispered. "Bilal will honor you. Ease our sister's heart before she dies, darling Nahr. You are the nearest she has to a daughter in her final days."

I leaned toward Hajjeh Um Mhammad's face and kissed her forehead, her hands, her cheeks. Then I nestled my face by her ear, tears gathering behind my eyes, and whispered, "I will take care of Bilal. If it is God's will, I will marry him."

I felt her body relax, and I stayed there, allowing my tears to fall. I told her how much I loved her. How grateful I was for the kindness she had shown me. That her place in my heart was like that of my own mother.

Someone entered the room, but I didn't look up, continuing to speak to Hajjeh Um Mhammad's ear. But when her sisters asked, "Who are you?" I lifted my head and came face-to-face with a skinny woman wearing *niqab*. She pulled off the veil and lowered the abaya, and we could see she was a man. His hair was too long for a Palestinian from these parts. A goatee framed his mouth. He had a quality of illness. But there was no mistaking Mhammad's face. Hajjeh Um Mhammad let out an audible cry, and her sisters jumped out of their seats to embrace him. I froze.

The sisters hushed and hurried to close the door, looking about to check whether anyone had seen him walk in. He kneeled by Hajjeh Um Mhammad's bed, kissing her hand. Quiet tears ran down the faces of mother and son.

"May God look upon you with favor, my son," Hajjeh Um Mhammad repeated. Her sisters too were crying. I stood in astonishment and confusion, almost forgetting that they could see me.

One of his aunts said to the other, "Such a brave son. He figured out how to sneak back into the country just to see his mama. . . ."

The other sister: "Here from Canada. I didn't think we'd ever see the boy again. He's very brave and resourceful. God give him long life, amen."

Canada? They think he's living in Canada?

"Hello, Nahr." His voice sounded raspier than I remembered. His eyes were red and distant. There had been a time in my life when I longed for this man to return to me, but that discarded girl was gone, and now he repulsed me.

I kissed Hajjeh Um Mhammad. "I'll be back later to check on you," I whispered. As I reached to open the door, Mhammad said behind me, "It goes without saying that no one can know I'm here."

I suppressed the urge to slap him.

Hajjeh Um Mhammad demanded to go home the day Mhammad visited. He had stayed with her until early evening before donning his disguise and leaving. "I want to die in my own home," she said. Her kidneys were producing very little urine, and doctors said it would not be long before other systems failed.

"While I can still talk, I demand to go home," she said with as much force as her frail voice could muster.

Her sisters brought Hajjeh Um Mhammad home from the hospital, and we began the vigil. Jumana and I were there when she went to sleep that night, surrounded by some twenty family members, and we were there when her sister let out a long wail at five o'clock the next morning. News traveled quickly as Hajjeh Um Mhammad's sisters performed the ritual washing of the body.

Jumana, Hajjeh Um Mhammad's nieces, and I managed the flow of people to the house during the funeral and the following weeks

of mourning. I don't recall who said it first, but people began refer-
ring to me as "Bilal's fiancée." Thousands came to pay their respects
after the funeral, the men gathered daily outdoors on the terrace
while the women kept their sacred space indoors—Hajjeh Um
Mhammad's sisters, nieces and nephews, their children, spouses,
grandchildren and in-laws; the hajjeh's own in-laws and their families; her friends and their families; her neighbors (even those whose
homes had been demolished and who had been forced to move far
away); merchants she frequented in various towns; farmers who
delivered her produce; carpenters and plumbers who had worked
in her house; Ghassan and his family; other friends of her sons and
their families; prison mates of her sons and their families. Everyone
was there—except her sons.

"Praise God, Mhammad managed to elude the Jews to comfort
her in her last hours. At least she saw him one last time. But I know
it burned her heart not to see Bilal. May God burn the hearts of the
Jews. Amen," one of the sisters whispered to us. Another shushed
her: "Lower your voice! Mhammad might not be safely out of the
country yet."

I turned to Jumana for answers. She caught my eye but looked
away. I wondered what she knew, but it wasn't the time to ask.

Once again, Bilal's detention turned into weeks, then months.
Over the forty days of mourning, with people paying their respects
streaming in and out of the house, Bilal's hunger strike started to
attract attention. Israel's English newspaper published an article
about his deterioration, which spurred several international media
outlets to follow suit. Telesur, Al Jazeera, and the BBC did stories
about Bilal's detention without charge or trial. I filled those dark
days with an exhausting determination to keep some continuity.
I cooked and cleaned for the mourners, worked in the salon daily,

and picnicked with Jumana in the groves at least once a week, to keep up Bilal's watering scheme.

Years before, when the almonds were dying off, Bilal had changed the configuration of the trees so most of the water-intensive almonds were replanted behind the more drought-resistant olives to prevent Israel from seizing the land on the pretext of dying trees. The irrigation tubing he'd devised ran from the center outward, so most water went to the almonds, and now they appeared healthy again with delicate white flowers, although not yet with nuts. The cousin who had taken over Jandal's job brought the sheep to graze regularly to ensure the soil would get enough nitrogen. Even the burned patch was showing signs of life, with weeds sprouting here and there. We had wrapped the burned trees with white cloth—a bandage to reflect the sun and hold in moisture—and I extended a hose to the area to soak the soil as much as possible from the water tank, which we were still siphoning from the settlers' water pipe. Trees aren't much different from people in that way. You protect the burned parts from the elements, keep hydrating and nourishing the body, and wait for life to heal itself.

"I want Bilal to find this place alive when he comes out," I said to Jumana. "I know it must kill him to not have been here when she passed. . . ."

She looked away, out at the trees.

"Something's on your mind. Just say it," I said.

"What if they don't let him out this time?" she finally asked.

"You can be such a downer! What if aliens invade us tomorrow?"

She laughed. "Okay, remind me again how this works, in case aliens invade and snatch you up," she said, reaching for the pump.

I showed her the valves on the barrel. "When the pump is on, turn it this way to fill it. When you shut off the pump, turn the valve this way, so the water will drip through the tubes. And this is the neutral position where water doesn't go in or out. Leave it here when it rains or if the soil looks too wet. The soil has to be well drained."

"Wow, look at you," Jumana said. "There's a peasant in the city girl after all!"

"Stick with me. I'll teach you a few things," I said. "Now listen, smartass. You have to monitor carefully. It's tricky because the almonds need a lot of water but not wet soil. And the olives can't get too much water because their oil will have a diluted taste. Got it?"

"Yes, boss."

International media attention grew as Bilal's health deteriorated. A European delegation was dispatched to negotiate his release when it was leaked that Bilal had been transferred to a military hospital, possibly in critical condition. Two weeks later, more than four months after Bilal's arrest and nearly ten weeks into his hunger strike, Israel agreed to negotiated terms for his release, and they broadcast his first bite: a spoonful of soup. The phones rang off the hook at the house, the salon, and the bakery.

Ghassan called me at the salon. "Thanks to the Almighty our brother is coming home," he said. "You should stop by the pastry shop this evening. Join us for dinner."

It wasn't so much an invitation as an urgent request, but our calls were monitored, and there was only so much we could say. "Yes, of course, brother. I'm sorry I've not been by sooner. Jumana and I will come straight there after closing the salon, enshallah."

"See you soon. We want to hear about the wedding plans too. Everyone's looking forward to the honor of celebrating the two of you," he said, and we hung up.

My wedding was growing in local imagination, even though Bilal and I hadn't yet actually spoken of it. For the first time since my girlhood in Kuwait, I fantasized about a life of my own making, a story Bilal and I would create on our own terms. I dared to imagine a forever with him. I dared, even, to wish for a child, a life born of love, to be loved hard and always.

I turned to Jumana. "You think Bilal knows of his own impending wedding?"

"He has probably been fantasizing about it from the day your divorce was finalized," she said.

"He's not like that."

"All men are like that," she said, reminding me of Um Buraq.

Ghassan's sister was at the bakery when we arrived. She worked there less frequently since Ghassan had returned, because her incessant lectures were intolerable: he wasn't pious enough; he should be married by now, should have kids; he didn't associate with pious friends; why was he so stubborn. Worst of all was her disdain for Jumana.

We were surprised to see her, and she us.

"Welcome, ladies. Ghassan didn't tell me we were having company," she said. She eyed Jumana up and down, stopping at her hair. "Still not wearing a hijab, I see."

I stepped forward, putting every nasty curse word into my stare. Ghassan appeared in the periphery, and I whispered, "Something is wrong with you," before he came near to greet us.

She didn't like him shaking Jumana's hand and kissing her on each cheek, but she held her tongue as Ghassan congratulated us on Bilal's triumph and on the wedding.

"Oh, Ghassan. This is the strangest wedding in the history of Palestine," I said. "Bilal is going to be—"

"Did he even ask for your hand?" Ghassan's sister interrupted.

Before I could sink my claws into her eyeballs, Ghassan snapped,

"What are you still doing here? Your husband called you home half an hour ago. Go!"

As she walked away in a huff, Ghassan turned to us. "I was just making some fresh bread while dinner gets here. I sent for a few *mashawi* and mezze plates," he said.

"You shouldn't have troubled yourself," Jumana said.

He smiled at her, repeating an old saying: "For the ones we love, nothing is ever trouble, and everything is never enough."

"Ugh. You two are ridiculous." I rolled my eyes. "We should be talking about *your* wedding."

Ghassan leaned in. "Looks like we have extra ears," he said, motioning to a group of young men sitting at a table across the room. They were the only remaining customers, and we spoke superficially until they left.

Ghassan got up to lock the door after them.

"Do you think they're spies?" Jumana asked.

"Who knows anymore. They're from the village, but they don't come here often," he said. "Listen, we have some inventory. We need to move it tomorrow," Ghassan added. "Two women are going to come to your salon in the late afternoon to get their hair fixed. Make sure your parking spot is available. And get rid of other customers when they arrive. We'll take care of everything else."

I looked at Jumana. Neither of us knew what to say. Ghassan admonished us. "Try to seem as if we're just having a friendly conversation. Anyone walking by can see us." We complied, adjusting our expressions for the large storefront window.

We had not been back to the underground for more than two years, although Ghassan might have come and gone on his own a few times. Samer was home from Moscow on break from university. With more to lose, he had grown paranoid that his mother or one of his snoopy nephews would find the passage to the underground.

Wadee told Jumana and me, "Samer thinks he's putting his family at risk for some delusion that we can actually mount a resistance because we found a hole in the ground."

Jumana examined her brother's face. "Is that Samer or you speaking?"

Wadee looked away nervously, then turned back to us. "No one except Ghassan has been there in years. We have to forget about it."

Jumana began pacing. "All right. Listen, we don't have to make any decisions right now. We only have to ensure that the passageways are well concealed, even if the military raid our homes. I think it would give Samer some assurance to somehow fortify the passage in his basement."

"How about if he built a wardrobe over the space, with a false floor like the one at the salon?" I said.

"Soldiers usually just knock those over," Wadee said.

Annoyed, Jumana threw her hands up. "Then he builds it into the room, with plastered walls, like a closet! Why are you complicating matters unnecessarily?"

The closet idea proved to be the right solution for Samer. He, Faisal, and Wadee spent a few days building a wardrobe with a complicated floor that could be opened and closed from both above- and belowground. "It's amazing. You have to know what you're looking for to figure it out," Faisal told us proudly.

Around the same time, the negotiated terms of Bilal's release were made public. He would serve only five more weeks.

When we finally met two weeks before Bilal's release, we were stunned to see what Ghassan had deposited underground: shelves stacking a cache of twenty crossbows with more than four hundred arrows. Some were more complicated than others, some made of wood, others of plastic or metal. The most complex of them had multiple wire strings, levers, and a scope, and were made of fiberglass and metal alloys. They seemed expertly crafted. None of us knew Ghassan had been commissioning them, nor how he'd paid for them.

"Whoever made this one is an artist," Faisal said, running his fingers in awe along the smooth metal and taut wires of one crossbow. The arrows were also expertly made and varied. Some looked like long steel pencils, while others were more conventional, with feathered tails and metal arrowheads.

"This must be because of those posts about ancient warfare," Jumana said. "It's amazing Israel hasn't infiltrated the website."

All eyes shifted to me. "Why does everyone always look at me whenever there's mention of the website?" I asked. "Is my brother behind it?"

"Yes!" Wadee exclaimed. He surveyed the others, protesting, "Why are you looking at me? She already knows!"

"Habibti," Jumana said to me, "we all thought you should know and wanted to tell you, but your brother was adamant that you not know. I guess he wanted to protect you. But I don't think he understands how involved you are."

HOMECOMING

WE WEREN'T SURE how to celebrate Bilal's homecoming this time. It would be his first confrontation with Hajjeh Um Mhammad's death, and he was still ill from the prolonged hunger strike. His organs had suffered permanent damage during the ten weeks without food. Kidneys, I think. And heart. I hoped it had all been rumors. Ghassan and Bilal's aunts and their clan were gathered at the house waiting for news. The military typically dropped off prisoners wherever they fancied, and we didn't know when or where he'd be. A group of little boys came running to the house first, yelling over one another, each wanting to be the first to deliver the news.

"Take a deep breath," I said, ready with sweets in my hands. "Each of you take one of these. You"—I pointed to the smallest of them—"tell me."

"Ammo Bilal was walking and all the men went with him," he said.

"Okay. Now you." I pointed to another.

"They went to the cemetery to read the Fatiha for Hajjeh Um Mhammad."

"How did he look?"

They exchanged confused looks. One said, "He looked like Ammo Bilal."

"Okay. Thank you, boys. Here, have more sweets."

Ghassan rushed out the door, I supposed heading for the cemetery, but just then we heard chanting and singing. Then we saw them, Bilal carried on the sturdy shoulders of his comrades. His aunts said to me, "Enshallah, the next time he's carried like this will be on your wedding day!"

Ghassan ran to them as Bilal was lowered slowly to meet him. The two friends held each other, their faces buried in the other's shoulders. When Ghassan lifted his head, tears glistened in his eyes, surely the bitter joy of holding the thin, fragile body of a friend who had been so strong. Seeing Bilal make his way to me, I thought there could never be words big enough to hold such love and desire for one person. His arms circled around me, and I put mine around him. Love eclipsed propriety this time. I could feel his ribs beneath the sweater, but he was the whole world in my arms. He whispered in my ear, "You are everything, Nahr."

Reluctantly I went back to living with Jumana. Rectitude had to win until we were married. Bilal's aunts took turns staying overnight while he recovered, and I came during the day, which no one seemed to mind.

"Maybe they think sex only happens in the dark," Bilal joked.

"I guess they didn't consider our thick curtains."

But mostly we didn't speak much, especially in the first few days of his return. *You are everything, Nahr* filled all the rooms and the silence echoed with those words when we were together.

The first morning after his return, I arrived just as one of his aunts was making coffee. "Good morning, daughter!" she said. "I'm glad you're here early. I have to get home. My grandson is sick. Here, take over the coffee."

Bilal was sitting on the terrace looking out upon the valley. The Jewish-only settlement jutted on the hill in the distance like a tumor, acres of olive and fruit trees separating us from them. He looked like an old man, with sunken eyes and protruding cheekbones. His head had been shaved. I approached slowly, not wanting to intrude. "Morning of goodness," he said, a smile in his eyes.

"Morning of light and jasmine." I joined him with coffee and a kiss. Now, in the Cube, I conjure those glorious, quiet mornings with Bilal and the morning sun, the land, the threats, and the breeze caressing our faces.

I carried the coffee tray back to the kitchen and prepared a simple breakfast. Bilal made his way inside. The wind hummed from the terrace, rustling the leaves, playing the chimes and merging with the small sounds of our breakfast—the swish of water from the faucet, the whistle of the teakettle, the occasional clank of a plate or knife, the squeak of the oven door, the rhythmic thump of Bilal's cane as he moved, then the sipping of hot mint tea, the tearing of hot bread. I hadn't wanted to disturb the symphony of our silence, but Bilal's voice was a welcome interlude. "Why didn't you remarry? You could have gotten a divorce for abandonment a long time ago without having to come here."

I continued to eat, considering my answer.

Moments passed. Finally I said, "I don't know why. Why didn't you ever marry?"

"I didn't want to have anything to lose. Did you want to remarry?"

"No."

"Did you imagine being unmarried forever?"

"Technically, I'd be a divorcée forever."

He chuckled. "Smartass. Is that how you saw your future?"

"What are you trying to get at?"

"Nothing in particular. I just want to understand you. I'm wondering if you were happy without a partner."

"Are you withdrawing your proposal?"

"Technically, I never proposed."

I didn't like that he said that, even though I knew he was joking. "According to the whole town, you did," I said.

"Well, I am honored, and over the moon that we're getting married." He grabbed my hand.

"*Technically*, I never accepted."

He laughed. "According to the whole town, you did."

We let the lovely quiet move in again. Then he said, "You don't mind that I'm . . ." He hesitated, looking at his own body. ". . . that I'm like this?"

This was a good opening to broach the conversation we needed to have, but I was afraid. "There's something I have to tell you," I began.

"Don't tell me you're divorcing me already."

I smiled awkwardly and spit out the words: "I don't think I can have sex with you."

He looked shocked and hurt.

"I mean, not you. Not just you. I don't know that I can have sex with any man," I said.

"Do you prefer women?"

"No. I'm just . . ." I struggled to find the words I had rehearsed. "I don't know why, Bilal. I'm just damaged."

His face softened and he pulled me gently toward him. I slipped my arms around his waist and we stayed that way, my head nestled at his neck, the rhythm of his breath lulling me to a sense of home.

"We can be damaged together," he whispered. "As long as I can hold you like this, I will be a happy man."

Within mere days of being home, Bilal began to regain weight and color returned to his face. He still found it difficult to walk without a cane.

"How was it to see Mhammad?" he asked me one morning on the terrace.

"I wondered when you were going to bring it up." I sipped my tea.

"We don't have to talk about it if you don't want to."

"Well, for starters, it surprised me that some people thought Mhammad was living in Canada. From the whispers in town, I can't tell if he's a hero or a traitor."

"He's both. And he's neither," he said, cryptic language that made me sigh. "I'm not trying to be obscure," he assured me. "The truth is, I don't know who or what my brother is."

"Then finish the rest of the story you told me before I went back to Amman," I said.

Later that evening, he did.

Mhammad and Bilal had watched their clothes burn in the barrel on that day so many years ago that set the course for all of our lives. The night, tranquil and beautiful, hid their frightened bodies, and belied their shattered futures. The crackle of flames gave no hint of the inferno to come, as Israel would exact vengeance from all Palestinians for the deaths of the two soldiers in the woods.

Bilal hesitated as he spoke, opening and closing his right fist, trying to control its tremor. "The memory of sinking a knife into a man's neck is embedded in my hand. Even after my body stopped shaking that night, my hand didn't. It never really stopped.

"Mhammad was calm as we stood over the barrel burning the

evidence. He asked for the knife, warned me never to speak of what I had seen in the woods, and demanded that I leave for Jordan first thing the next morning. I assumed all the borders would be closed, but my brother assured me it would be a while before anyone found the bodies.

"That's how I knew that he and Itamar . . . I knew they had a plan. That they were working together," Bilal said. "I went inside our home, showered, and packed."

Bilal had lain there that night, a young man waiting for the sky to fall, crying, replaying the last few hours in his mind. His brother and the Israeli soldier. Their aggressive lust for each other. The laughter of the other soldiers. The camera. The knife in and out of a man's neck. He had to leave before his mother awoke.

"I went downstairs around four thirty a.m., feeling my way in the dark, and put my things by the door. Suddenly a small table lamp came on, illuminating my brother in a chair. He must have been there all night. His eyes were weary and dark. I could tell he had been crying and wondered if he saw the same in my face."

Mhammad handed him a box. In it was a book containing several Polaroid photos embedded in the cover. The camera itself was also in the box. "He told me to find someplace safe to hide them, and to rescue the photos if anything ever were to happen. He didn't say what. Just that I'd know."

They were the Polaroids of Mhammad and Itamar together, taken by the laughing Israeli soldiers, which Mhammad had taken from the bloody scene as leverage to keep his family safe. Mhammad and Itamar had cooked up a plan that spared Bilal and his family, landed Mhammad in prison, and earned Itamar a promotion, putting him on track to becoming a high-ranking commander.

"It sounds like Mhammad sacrificed himself to save you and the rest of the family."

"He did. But he's not innocent either. Everyone's hands are bloody and dirty in this place," Bilal said. He continued, "I stayed in Amman for a few years. Went to college and then worked as a chemist for a plastics company in Kuwait."

"What? You were in Kuwait?"

"Just for a couple of years." He swept his arm through the air, indicating the green landscape before us. "Kuwait was all concrete and sand. I hated it. I've never been as lonely as I was there, not even when I was in prison."

"My God! We could have passed each other in the streets," I said.

To make their story believable, Mhammad had stabbed Itamar superficially in the soft tissue of his abdomen with his own military knife, and had hit him on the head with a rock, just hard enough to leave marks and swelling to prove he was unconscious, unable to go for help. Several hours passed before the soldiers were reported missing and a search began. When they reached the woods, a bloody and dazed Itamar emerged an instant hero—but not because he'd survived an attack.

"Only Arab-killers are Israeli heroes," Bilal said.

"I don't understand," I said.

Bilal sucked on a cigarette, the tip lighting up brighter. His right hand trembled.

"Two brothers we knew growing up lived nearby. Haj Ayman's boys. They were rumored to be collaborators. I don't think it was true, but they'd been a disgrace to their family, did drugs, went to Israeli bars and had sex with foreign women. Stuff like that. But they weren't traitors." He sucked on his cigarette again. "Or maybe they were. I don't know."

I waited quietly, remembering the newspaper stories claiming Mhammad had two accomplices found dead at the scene along with the Israeli soldiers.

Bilal looked at me. "Mhammad and Itamar knew Haj Ayman's boys suspected them of being lovers. Mhammad sacrificed those boys, two Palestinians, for his Jewish lover."

I was taking it all in, trying to make sense of my brief time with Mhammad, seeing the man I'd married in another light. "Or maybe he did it for you?" I asked.

He exhaled and ran his fingers through the bristles of his graying hair, cupping his temples as if to hold his thoughts in place. "Yes. He was trying to protect me," he said, tearing up.

"I don't know how Haj Ayman's boys came to be at the scene. I guessed that Mhammad or Itamar lured them. Maybe with drugs. I don't know," Bilal said. "I don't want to know. Itamar murdered them there. He staged the scene to support his heroic tale that he shot the Palestinian attackers before passing out from his injuries."

"Does anyone else know?" I asked.

"No."

"Not even Ghassan?"

"No."

"Why me?"

He hesitated and turned back to the landscape. "You should know who you married . . . and who you're planning to marry now."

Something I could not name lodged in my throat. I had no language for such overlapping love, disappointment, disgust, and sympathy.

Their deceit, once planted in the public imagination—like the epic fabrication of a Jewish nation returning to its homeland—had grown into a living, breathing narrative that shaped lives as if it were truth.

Heroes, Palestinian and Israeli, were made from their lies that day. Israel honored its fallen soldiers and decorated Itamar for killing two Palestinians. Haj Ayman could hold his head high in the country now because his sons had chosen the righteous path of resistance and died martyrs. People came to pay their respects and honor his fallen sons. The community's blessings lessened the pain of watching Israel demolish his home and make of him a homeless old man.

Israel wreaked havoc throughout Palestine and needed a live suspect to show for the massive destruction they inflicted on thousands of innocent Palestinians. The authorities always suspected Bilal, because he'd disappeared overnight and later emerged as a leader in exile. But someone had to pay. The day after Mhammad was tried and sentenced, the military demolished Bilal's home too.

"I had no idea," I said.

"This isn't the house we grew up in," he said. "When my father died, my paternal uncles took our inheritance. We were just kids. Our mother was illiterate and trusting. She signed some things, or possibly they forged documents. They took as much as they could. But we kept our childhood home, the orchards, and the rest of the land. We couldn't do much with it. It cost more to hold on to it, but selling was unthinkable. We managed as best we could. My mother's younger brother, our uncle who lived in Chile with a Chilean wife, sent us money every month to help out. When Israel demolished our house, he deeded his and my mother's childhood home to her. He had plenty in Chile and wasn't ever coming back. He just asked us to let his children live there if ever they visited, or, if Palestine was liberated in their lifetime, to let them return if they wanted."

Mosquitoes were starting to bite. I wanted to go inside, but feared interrupting Bilal. I endured the bugs while we watched the serenity of a tired sun ignite the sky and paint the hillside with a palette of reds, oranges, and yellows. "How did they catch Mhammad?"

"They found a repair-shop receipt with his name on it at the scene. When they arrested him, he denied being there, of course. His precious Tamara didn't back him up, though. He said he didn't recognize the Arab, that he only remembered two attackers, but possibly there had been a third. Then Israel tortured some little Palestinian boys into confessing that they had seen Mhammad with Haj Ayman's boys that day."

Bilal closed his eyes with a sigh, perhaps remembering his boyhood when the military had tortured him too.

"I don't think Mhammad and Itamar ever intended for him to go to prison. All the blame was to fall on Haj Ayman's boys. But they hadn't counted on that receipt at the scene."

By the time the Israeli military found Itamar, the two dead soldiers, and the bodies of Haj Ayman's boys, Israel had already raided hundreds of Palestinian homes, arrested more than 1,800 Palestinians, mostly young men and boys, and terrorized whole towns looking for them.

"What did he say about why they were in the woods in the first place?" I asked.

"Itamar's story was that he and the dead soldiers had spotted and followed a Palestinian carrying a rifle. They couldn't radio for help—their equipment wasn't working. He claimed someone knocked him out as he and his fellow soldiers were handcuffing the terrorist. When he regained consciousness, the two Palestinian attackers were standing over bleeding soldiers. Then Itamar reached for his gun, like in a goddamned James Bond movie, I guess, and shot them dead. Itamar and Mhammad staged the scene so the evidence supported the testimony he gave to his superiors."

"How did they miss the receipt if they staged the scene?" I asked.

"I've thought about that for years. There are only two explanations. One, they truly didn't notice it. Two, Itamar planted it. Just like my brother took the Polaroids for leverage, maybe Itamar wanted his own leverage."

It was getting late. Bilal's aunts should have arrived by now. As I helped him inside, he turned to me. "You still want to marry me?"

The telephone rang. It was Bilal's aunts calling to check on him. They couldn't come to stay because the military had imposed a curfew unexpectedly until 5 a.m. On his side of the conversation, I heard, "Thank you, Auntie. But it is not necessary for you to come anyway. I can take care of myself. . . . Yes, Auntie. . . . Thank you, Auntie. She left some time ago. Yes. . . . Thank you, Auntie. Good night."

"She wanted to know if I left?"

"How did you guess?"

We laughed. The phone rang again. It was Jumana calling to say that Bilal's aunts had called her to check on me.

"What did you tell them?"

"I said you were with Bilal, surely committing terrible sin," Jumana said.

"Okay. Good."

"See you tomorrow. I hope you commit sin."

"Really, what did you tell them?"

"I said you had a terrible headache and were already in bed."

Mosquitoes had left little red welts on my arms. "Wait here." Bilal hobbled to the kitchen and returned with a saucer of olive oil. "Here," he said, taking my hand. He dipped his fingers in the oil and rubbed it into my skin. That sweet silence I had come to know in his presence settled around us. When he was done, we lay in each other's arms and slept.

A TIME FOR US

A LITTLE MORE than four months after Hajjeh Um Mhammad passed away, Bilal and I got married in a memorable *fallahi* wedding. We had wanted only a small celebration with family and friends. In part, it was all we could afford, but mostly it didn't seem proper to have a wedding at that time; the Second Intifada was in its second year and Israelis had elected Ariel Sharon, the Butcher of Beirut, as their prime minister, and his brutal legacy was already being felt. But my mother and Bilal's aunts would have none of that.

"Exactly the opposite. We show those monsters how we will continue to live and love on our land, no matter what they do to us," Ghassan said to Bilal.

Mama, Jehad, and Sitti Wasfiyeh made the journey from Jordan. "I agreed to get a visa from the sons of Satan at their godforsaken embassy just for you," Sitti said. "Your mother tried to make me miss the wedding on account of the doctor claiming my heart is too weak. But my heart feels fine." Then she turned to Bilal. "Nahr's mother gets jealous because my son's children love me more than her. You're a good man for marrying my granddaughter, even though she was married before and couldn't keep her husband very long."

"He already knows, Sitti," I assured her. "Mhammad is his brother, remember?"

"Yeah, that's right," she said. "I forgot."

She turned again to Bilal. "Nothing is the same without her. I wish we were all still in Kuwait with my son. Or how about if we could all be here forever again?" She wiped tears away with her hijab. Mama consoled her. Sitti was losing her mind and these reveries happened often, Mama had told me.

Mama had been trying to pull me away all day. When I finally had a moment, she made me close my eyes and guided me into the guest bedroom.

"Open your eyes," she said.

What I saw took my breath away. I flung my arms around my mother's neck and began sobbing. "Habibti, Mama. May God keep you always. May He extend your life and presence in mine for all our days. This is the best present I have received from anyone, ever. Thank you, Mama."

Laid out on the bed was a stunning, elegant embroidered wedding thobe, and an equally striking headpiece.

"Come, let's try it on," she said. As I moved to pick it up, Mama explained her creation. "I thought a lot about this and decided to use the basic patterns of a Jerusalem thobe, because we're being erased from her story and her stone," she said. Even the way she described her embroidery was poetic.

"Ordinarily I would use white silk for this thobe, but I found this gorgeous terra-cotta silk that harkens to Jericho. You see here on the chest piece: this is a collar worn by Canaanite queens. I added these geometric patterns typical of Romi thobes from the Ramallah area to show the olive, almond, and pomegranate trees. On the sides here is the crucifixion from when the Crusaders ruled over us, and here, you see, is the crescent for the return of Jerusalem to Muslim rule since the time of Salah Eddein."

I was in awe. "This is a treasure, Mama."

"You're the treasure," she said. "And here, look closely at these shapes. Verse twenty-one from Surat el Rum in the Quran. A prayer for marriage."

It was hard to make out the convoluted script, but Mama read it to me.

"And of His wisdom is that He created for you from yourselves mates that you may find tranquility in them; and He placed between you affection and mercy. Indeed, for in these are wisdoms for those who think."

I ran my fingers over the intricate stiches of cyan, terra-cotta, emerald, maroon, and apricot. Life was sweeping me up in an unexpected dream.

Jumana stayed by my side on my wedding day, helping me prepare. Mama had invited cousins I didn't know from Ein el-Sultan and Haifa. It seemed entire villages showed up to celebrate. Even news cameras from Palestine TV were there to report on the wedding of a national hero. The day turned into evening and into night in a blur of song, dance, food, revelry, *zaghareet*, prayers, wellwishers, and gifts. My brother footed most of the bill. He knew Bilal and I could not afford it. "Actually, it's mostly from our grandmother," he said. Bilal was uneasy about accepting. Jehad said, "Consider it my contribution to the revolution."

"As if you're not running websites." I grinned at him. He smiled too. That was all we had the opportunity to say on the matter of his being our Jordan Contact.

Bilal and I were exhausted at the end of the night. We wanted to have a romantic ending to our wedding, but we barely got out of our clothes and washed up before collapsing to sleep in each other's arms. I suppose such an uneventful wedding night would concern most couples, but it felt natural and precious. Besides, we still had guests in the house, and we were mindful of making noise.

We were the last to awake the next day, forced to get up by the commotion in the kitchen. "So much for a quiet, romantic morning after," he whispered to me. My mother and grandmother were arguing in the kitchen. "It's the opposite of romance," I said with a grin.

We greeted Sitti Wasfiyeh and Mama. Jehad was on the terrace drinking coffee. "Your mother is making the eggs wrong," Sitti Wasfiyeh complained.

"Please, Hajjeh. I've been making your eggs for at least thirty-five years," Mama said.

Sitti raised her brows, signaling a thought she wanted to share. She shuffled toward me, the curve in her back pushing her head downward. "I forgot to tell you about your friend. Did you hear?" she said.

"What friend, Sitti? Hear what?"

"The crazy one that almost killed us with her driving when we left Kuwait."

"Um Buraq?"

"How should I know her name? She's your friend!"

I laughed. "What about her?"

"I forget. Ask your mother. Something happened in the newspaper."

I looked at Mama, who was frying garlic and tomatoes. "I don't know much, habibti. The article said she might be released soon on humanitarian grounds." Apparently, Um Buraq had cancer, and

Kuwaiti officials were urging the justice department to release her on the condition she relinquish her Kuwaiti citizenship and be deported to Iraq, where she had family ties. It distressed me to think of my old friend like that, sick and penniless at the doorstep of distant relatives in Iraq, asking for charity. I remembered her parting words to me in Kuwait: *Whatever happens in this ungenerous world, we will meet again, my sister.*

The five of us ate breakfast on the terrace—Sitti Wasfiyeh, Mama, Jehad, Bilal, and me together in Palestine. The winter rains of December and January had been heavier than usual, ushering in a dense and diverse cover of wildflowers across the hillside. Red, white, and purple anemones and pink and white cyclamen carpeted the eastern hills rolling around us. Poppies, buttercups, and red everlastings overlapped in random pockets. Rare wild tulips rose here and there. Bull mallow, Jerusalem sage, mustard, and thyme found their places around rocks and boulders.

Soon the blue lupine and yellow corn marigold would replace the anemones. The crocuses and squill were waiting dormant in their bulbs to bloom in summer. The honeysuckle had already begun creeping over the bushes and trees, and the hyacinths, daisies, and narcissus bloomed on the higher ground.

Mama and Jehad were impressed that I knew so much about the local flora. Hajjeh Um Mhammad, God rest her soul, had taught me the names of plants and their medicinal values. I couldn't remember everything she'd imparted and wished I had written it all down, though Bilal also had much indigenous knowledge of our botanical heritage. Hajjeh Um Mhammad used to say there was no illness on this earth for which God had not also given us a medicine.

"Palestine suits you," Jehad whispered. "You look the most radiant and alive I've ever seen you."

"More than when we were in Kuwait?" I asked.

"Kuwait was another lifetime. We were too young. Too different."

It was true. Jehad had changed. We both had. There was a gravity to his presence, a kind of solid, sturdy thing I could depend on. He and Bilal were similar in that way.

"I suppose you're right. We're a long way from our little apartment in Hawalli. Remember our summer business ventures, your science experiments, and my girl gangs?"

"Who can forget? Nobody messed with me because of you and your girl gangs." My baby brother laughed, putting his arm around me.

As I take stock of my life, as one does in the Cube, I realize that my wedding, surrounded by family in February of 2002, began the happiest days of my life. My family didn't stay long after the wedding because they planned to take Sitti Wasfiyeh to spend a few days in Ein el-Sultan before heading back to Amman.

"I'll come back in two months," Mama promised. She had more time off coming up. We kissed and hugged farewell at dusk. Sitti Wasfiyeh used Hajjeh Um Mhammad's old motor cart to get to the car, though she seemed slower on it than if she had walked.

"You can make it go faster, Hajjeh," Mama urged.

"You're trying to get me killed," Sitti shot back.

"Hajjeh, you're indestructible. Give that thing a little more gas," Mama said.

"I curse your gray hairs, woman! Stop rushing me!" Sitti waved her off.

Before they drove away, Sitti whispered to me, "May God bless you both and bless your marriage and bring you many babies. Don't mess this one up like you did the first one. God loves you and we all love you."

Bilal made a fire outside as it grew dark. He could walk without a cane now, but his gait was still not what it had been. We curled up together, wrapped in a blanket by the glow of the firepit. "Alone at last." He kissed me. The closeness was familiar, as if we had always been together. It was hard to remember life without Bilal.

We gazed at the blackness of the sky lighting up an incomprehensible universe.

"Everything I worry about feels impossibly small and unimportant when I'm confronted with a sky like this," Bilal said softly.

I snuggled against his shoulder, kissed his neck. "I got in so much trouble in second grade for trying to fathom the universe," I said.

"What do you mean?" Bilal pulled away to look at me.

"My religion teacher told the class how big and vast God made the universe. She said He made millions of planets and some might even have life like earth. Of course, I asked perfectly logical questions, like: Why does God only care about people on earth? How does He manage to keep track of everyone everywhere and account for who might eat pork? Did little alien girls have to wear hijab too? And finally, the straw that broke my teacher's back: Why would He really care what we eat or wear? Doesn't He have more important things to deal with?"

Bilal laughed. "Most people live their whole lives without having such obvious questions."

"The principal suspended me for a week."

"These stupid school systems beat the curiosity and creativity out of kids," he said.

"But no one holds a grudge like I do. When I got to fourth grade, I slit the tires on both of their cars. No one ever knew," I confessed.

Bilal roared with laughter. "I love it! You've been a rebel and revolutionary your whole life, woman!"

"True. And you're the lucky man who married me."

"Indeed I am."

We stayed that way for a while, talking, laughing, sharing, making out. I wanted to make love, but my body did not. Or maybe it was the other way around, my body wanted it, but I didn't. He too seemed lost in his own internal conflict.

He spoke first. "We're both thinking about it, aren't we?"

I smiled.

"I respect and accept your wishes, Nahr. You already told me and don't have to tell me twice. What I wanted to say then is that only we will determine how our relationship should be. We can be whatever we want to each other. We don't have to make love now, and maybe never, as long as it's what we desire. All I ask is honesty. I will give you the same, and I will always work to earn and keep your love, respect, and loyalty," he said.

I burrowed my face in his neck, fulfilled, grateful for this life, and impossibly in love.

He shifted awkwardly. "There's something else I want to tell you."

I waited as he searched for the right words.

"I wanted to tell you this the day you confided in me. But I didn't have your courage," he began. "When I was in prison the last time, they tortured me in different ways. Years ago, they beat me all over, especially my groin, but this time they hit me over and over in my genitals. I was vomiting constantly, and everything was swollen between my legs. They left me alone after that, but it became infected and they wouldn't take me to a doctor. That was when I started the hunger strike. By the time they transferred me to the military clinic, the infection was too far gone and the damage could not be repaired." He shifted again in his seat, holding me hard. "They had to remove one of my testicles."

He was nearly in tears. I tightened my arms around him.

"I was too ashamed to tell you. I'm sorry I didn't." He paused, ran his palm over his face. "And here I am asking you for honesty." He sucked air through his teeth. "I wanted to tell you then. That I'm only half a man . . . and I don't know if I am physically able to make love." His jaw muscles were contracting under his skin. He wouldn't meet my eyes.

I kissed him gently on his lips. "Don't do this to yourself." I kissed the side of his face. "I love you, Bilal. People are complicated, you said that yourself. We'll figure out what works for us, and we'll do that as we go along." I cupped his face in my hands. "For now, we have honesty, trust, and love." I wanted to describe to him how the emotional intimacy growing between us was shattering my heart in the most life-affirming ways, but I didn't have the right words, except to say that I loved him, which wasn't nearly enough.

We spent that night, and every night together after, in a closeness I had never known, or even thought possible with another person. I was happy. Truly content.

Drifting to sleep in Bilal's arms, I thought about the hills beyond the terrace. Soon wild plum, peach, pear, fig, medlar, mulberry, date, and almond trees would bloom. I would tend to Hajjeh Um Mhammad's loquats and pomegranates in the summer.

Mama and Jehad had returned to Jordan just before Ariel Sharon ripped through the land and tore the sun apart, less than two months into our marriage. He bombed all of our major cities to push up his domestic approval ratings. He pulverized Gaza's airport and tore up the runway, which had been a small symbol of Palestinian sovereignty. Their military executed our leaders, made rubble of schools and universities, stole population databases and student statistics, and put us all under months of curfew, during which we could not leave our homes at any time, for any reason, unless specifically announced by the military.

Bilal still wasn't fully healed, and doctors thought he might never walk without a limp because some of the musculature in his groin and hip had also been removed to take out the infection. But he had regained weight and strength. He spoke infrequently on the phone because our calls were monitored, but he worked for hours from his computer. We were luckier than most to have a home computer. It kept us from dying of boredom inside the house twenty-four hours a day, with no relief in sight. Ours was called a Dell. I only used it to check e-mail once a week, but Bilal was on it daily researching chemistry topics I didn't understand, and using chemistry software to do with the brews he cooked up in the kitchen sometimes.

"What are you making?" I asked him.

"Just tinkering to pass the time."

But when I started to make a snack for us in the kitchen, he wouldn't allow it until he had scrubbed, rinsed, and wiped the entire kitchen. "I need another space for this stuff," he mumbled to himself.

"I'm guessing those aren't new pastry recipes?"

He pulled me by the waist. "Your sarcasm is so sexy."

The next day he made a work space in the second-floor bathroom and modified the fan to an exhaust hood over his work surface. My curiosity grew.

He read a lot too, and although I tried to read with him, abstract political theories didn't hold my interest. I preferred stories, human dramas. Sometimes we cuddled on the sofa for hours, watching television or doing nothing at all. Other times he read aloud to me. It started with an essay by an American named James Baldwin. It was a letter to his nephew, Big James. "Go back. Can you please read the last line again?" I asked.

"You can only be destroyed by believing that you really are what the white world calls a *nigger*."

There were others in the world who, like us, were seen as worthless, not expected to aspire or excel, for whom mediocrity was predestined, and who should expect to be told where to go, what to do, whom to marry, and where to live. Mr. Baldwin tells Big James:

"Here you were: to be loved. To be loved, baby, hard, at once, and forever, to strengthen you against the loveless world."

Bilal continued reading, but my mind lingered on that sentence because I knew that, despite everything, I was loved. I was loved hard. At once and forever against the loveless world. I missed my family. Um Buraq too. But I was home here.

"Habibi, I'm sorry, can you reread that last bit? I was thinking about previous lines."

"I know what you mean. Reading Baldwin ought to be slow. Every sentence beckons not only the mind, but also one's heart, history, and future." He paused.

". . . if we had not loved each other none of us would have survived."

"Do you think that's how we've survived?" I asked.

He put the book down, thought for a moment, and looked at me.

"I don't see how else anyone can survive colonialism. Understanding our own condition, I think in saying 'loved each other,' Baldwin doesn't just mean the living. To survive by loving each other means to love our ancestors too. To know their pain, struggles, and joys. It means to love our collective memory, who we are, where we come from," he said, and after a silence for both of us to soak up that thought, he continued reading.

"There is no reason for you to try to become like white people and there is no basis whatever for their impertinent assumption that *they* must accept *you*. The really terrible thing, old buddy, is that *you* must accept *them*. And I mean that very seriously. You must accept them and accept them with love. For these innocent people have no other hope. They are, in effect, still trapped in a history which they do not understand; and until they understand it, they cannot be released from it. They have had to believe for many years, and for innumerable reasons, that black men are inferior to white men. Many of them, indeed, know better, but, as you will discover, people find it very difficult to act on what they know. To act is to be committed, and to be committed is to be in danger."

To be committed is to be in danger. I have never forgotten those words.

Reading Mr. Baldwin together was how we passed our time for the next few days under curfew when he wasn't doing chemistry experiments upstairs. I never told anyone, not even Bilal, that the first book I ever read cover to cover was the first one we read together—*The Fire Next Time*, by James Baldwin—when I was thirty-four years old.

"Do you think Baldwin would say we should love Israelis?"

"I don't think that's necessarily what Baldwin is saying. I think he just means that we should fortify ourselves with love when we approach them. It's more about our own state of grace, of protecting our spirits from their denigration of us; about knowing that our struggle is rooted in morality, and that the struggle itself is not against them as a people, but against what infects them—the idea that they are a better form of human, that God prefers them, that they are inherently a superior race, and we are disposable."

Next we read Ghassan Kanafani—I loved him too—starting with his book *Men in the Sun*, which we finished in one day. In this story, Palestinian men inside a water tanker being smuggled into Kuwait die quietly from the scorching desert heat. "Why didn't they knock on the tanker wall to get out?" is the question that haunts the book and haunted me.

Baldwin and Kanafani were contemporaries thousands of miles apart, who never met but lived parallel lives. They wrote with the same passion, the same irreverence and defiance; with overlapping wounds and bottomless love for their people. Baldwin was forced into self-imposed exile and Kanafani was assassinated by Israel. *To be committed is to be in danger.*

Those weeks cloistered together in the house, alone, unable to leave or receive guests, having to sneak into the garden for fresh air and a bit of food, were perhaps the most profound honeymoon anyone could ask for. We packed a few years into a couple of months. We roamed inside each other—our memories, insecurities, and dreams. We explored each other's bodies, inching toward an enchanted precipice that was both frightening and irresistible. Behind me, he ran his fingers along the scar on my back.

"Is this it?" he asked.

"Yes," I whispered.

He took his time kissing all my parts, his lips lingering around the scar. Bilal changed everything, rearranged my world. I think it was the first time I desired a man truly. My body desired him emotionally, psychologically, intellectually, and, at last, physically.

We made love many times before we made love. Our bodies often melted together when he read to me, when we kissed, talked, hugged, undressed, bathed, slept. And when it finally happened, when he slid inside of me, I fell into the sublime abyss of him. The rush of fire through me made me sob.

"Shall I stop?" he said.

"No," I whispered, still crying. He kissed me hungrily, pushing himself deeper into me. I consumed him and learned a sexual yearning made insatiable by love so vast, as if a sky.

We barely left our bed for the next few days. We read, listened to the radio, watched television, made food, ate and bathed together. Ariel Sharon was still laying waste to the country. Now they were invading the refugee camp of Jenin. Bilal was on and off the phone with comrades, speaking in code, planning from powerlessness. Then we made love again. We found ways to love despite his physical limitations, which frustrated him but not me. I was almost grateful for it, because each time he could not have an erection or an orgasm, it seemed to push us closer, deeper into love and trust. Five million people like us were locked inside their homes, and perhaps they too were oscillating between rage and love.

It is not easy for me to speak of those weeks of my life without slipping into clichés, mostly because I don't have the right language. I don't have sufficient words to explain how thoroughly and exquisitely I unraveled in love.

I know, even now in the Cube, that he stayed with me, unseen, loving me still. I know the things they told me about him weren't true. I know he didn't give me up. I know. I know. And that knowing will not yield, not even now in this unnatural gray place.

Food had dwindled significantly by the third week of the curfew. But we were still luckier than most. We had a vegetable garden within reach and enough olive oil to last a year or more. Once a week, Bilal made bread dough, and we baked it together.

"This reminds me of when Saddam occupied Kuwait. There was a bread shortage and we baked whatever we could at home," I said as I flattened a sphere of dough with the roller. "That feels like a lifetime ago now. Almost like it happened to someone else."

He continued kneading the dough, balling it into spheres, listening.

I grabbed more dough, rolling it out. "Um Buraq is the one who got me into it."

He looked at me inquisitively.

"She used to book appointments and take us to parties with men," I said.

Bilal stopped midmotion. His right hand quivered. He kept his eyes on the dough. I held my breath.

He said, "I won't lie to you, it's hard to hear some things. But I love you, Nahr, more than you can imagine. Whatever you want to tell me will go into that well of love."

I told him everything. Not then, but later. I wanted him to know what I could never tell anyone. All of it. I couldn't stop myself. Abu Nasser, the panty sniffer. Abu Moathe, my rapist. Saddam Hussein, my savior. The money. Um Buraq, my procuress, my friend. How I hid it from my family. Why I did it. Why I stopped. Why I went back. I told it as I tell it now. As if it were someone else's life, something distant from me. I didn't feel the shame, pleasure, or trauma of it. I wasn't holding back tears. There simply were none.

Bilal listened, intermittently stroking my hair, without sympathy or empathy. With patience, and at times maybe with judgment, though he didn't say.

It grew dark. We had missed the television news and didn't eat. Finally I got up to go to the bathroom, but he pulled me back. "I love you all the more for what you survived, what you did to support your family, and for trusting me," he said.

Bilal put on a kettle to make tea, just enough for two small cups because our water tank on the roof was low. We made a mezze dinner with the fresh bread we had baked earlier—fried tomatoes, garlic and zucchini from the garden, boiled eggs, the last of our Nabulsi cheese, zeit-o-za'atar, labneh with olive oil and paprika, sliced cucumber, beets, and pickled vegetables. We spread the plates on the floor by the terrace door to feel the cool breeze of the outdoors we could not roam, lest unseen snipers spot us with their night vision. We ate in the dark, by the glow of a small candle, and listened to the news report on the radio.

The Israeli military hinted we might be granted a two-hour reprieve from curfew the following day to stock up on food. The announcement was followed by a stern warning that anyone outside at the end of the reprieve would be shot on sight. Bilal and I made bread dough, timing it to rise sufficiently to bake it fresh at the bakery when the curfew was lifted. He ventured into the garden to collect as much as he could to share with friends and family. An announcement came the next day that the reprieve was canceled until further notice.

Fighters in Jenin had heroically resisted Israel's invasion of the camp, killing dozens of soldiers. But the fighting was over and Israeli soldiers were on the rampage in the camp, exacting vengeance. Bilal turned off the radio. It was dark now, and we didn't turn on the lights. No one did unless the windows were blacked out. Bullets and missiles, like moths, were attracted to light.

We took the food tray through the darkness to the kitchen. "Leave it," Bilal said when I started to wipe the dishes (only enough water remained for consumption). He kissed me, lifting me onto the counter as I wrapped my legs around his waist. When our kisses deepened, he pulled back, stroking my cheek. I could see the contours of his face in the moonlight filtering through a window. "Will you dance for me?" he whispered.

He carried me into our bedroom, still limping but strong, pulled the heavy dark drapes across the window, gathered as many candles as he could find, and lit them around us. He put a tape mix into the boom box and played it low. It wasn't dance music, but *tarab*, the classical Arabic songs from the Levant and North Africa. He tied a *kuffiyeh* around my hips. I danced first for him, but quickly, as always happened, I danced for the music, for the sake of dance, for the sake of my body, the air, and the night. For the sake of memory and the moon. For love of Bilal and longing for my family. It felt good to dance. I gathered up the hours past with my hips, rolled them into my body. Bilal's hands brushed against me, but I wasn't yet ready for him. I wanted time with the music. It had been too long since I had danced. I shed my clothes, my dishdasha falling with a swoosh to the floor. Naked now, but for the kuffiyeh Bilal retied around my hips, I returned to the music and danced. He watched. For a long time. There's music that I can hear, listen to, enjoy. Then there's something else. It's when the deft, small movements of instruments invoke a kind of beauty that fills the room. It calls on history to join in. Centuries gone and maybe time yet to come arrive. It takes my breath away. And all I can do is let it seep into my skin, close my eyes, watch beauty expand inside of me, and feel it animate every part of me. At some point, it always happens, the music closes its eyes too. It takes a breath too—maybe with the plaint of a violin, the call of the ney, or the quiver of an oud—and settles so gently on my heart.

Bilal whispered, "You are the most magnificent woman I have ever laid eyes upon." As Abdel Halim Hafez sang from the speakers the lyrics of "El Hawa Hawaya," Bilal kneeled next to me and held my leg, kissing my ankles, calves, knees, taking his time moving up my thighs, between my legs. The music kept playing. Candles flickered and burned out as we made love under curfew, behind blacked-out windows, hidden from the tanks and jeeps and snipers hemming in our town.

Temperatures soared, and we struggled to keep ourselves cool. I worried about the trees in this sun without rain, especially the vulnerable burned trees still recovering and the saplings with shallow roots.

As we sat drinking our morning coffee the fourth week of curfew, the radio broadcast: *"International condemnation of the Zionist entity is increasing. Zionist occupation forces are rumored to be planning to lift curfew for a few hours to allow evacuation of the sick, burial of the dead, and for people to buy supplies."*

"When they lift the curfew, one of us should go water the almonds and olives," I said to Bilal.

He looked searchingly into my eyes. I could feel words gathering on his tongue.

"What's going on?" I asked.

"We'll water the trees, but then I am going to reverse the pump," he said.

"What do you mean?"

"Sit down." He touched my shoulder gently. He began rambling about chemical compounds with names I couldn't pronounce and scientific terms like *anti-androgenic* that were meaningless to my ears.

"Stop. The only thing I understood is that you've been making compounds in the upstairs bathroom," I said.

He took a breath and started again.

"Wait." I stopped him again. "I have to go make my own compounds in the bathroom."

He laughed as I hurried off.

This is what I finally understood: The compounds he was cooking up were called phthalates. They are anti-androgenic, which means they will feminize men and weaken their sperm. Androgens are male hormones. Phthalic anhydride is a phthalate. Phthalates are found in nearly everything we use, from glues and home cleaning supplies to personal care products, building materials, children's toys, paint, and medical supplies. Years ago Bilal had synthesized a variation that turned out to be too toxic for consumer use.

"The right phthalates in high enough concentrations disrupt endocrine functions, and—"

"What are endocrine functions?"

"It's the system of hormones in your body," he said, adding, "Like androgens."

"Okay, go on."

He looked blankly at me. I stared back, until I saw behind his eyes and understood. "Are you going to pump your special phthalates into their water?"

"Shhh." He put a finger to his lips and came close. "Don't say that out loud. But, yes, that's what I'm going to do."

"Will it kill them?"

"No. But it might fuck them up." He didn't wait for my reaction before launching into a defense. "These people are trying to wipe away all traces of us. I'm going to do whatever it takes. Even though they pump poison and sewage into our wells and springs, all I'm trying to do is spook them enough to make them leave. So, yes, that's what I'm doing, and I thank you for having the brilliant idea in the first place."

I remembered the day we had picnicked, when I had suggested pumping our sewage into their water.

Bilal and I split up during the three-hour window when Israel finally lifted the curfew. It hadn't rained in weeks. One of us had to get to the orchard. The whole southern edge had to be watered more intensively because the saplings there were struggling to survive. I thought he would do it, but instead he wanted to bake the bread at the store and go to town for food and supplies. The plan was for me to drop him off in town and take the car to the tree groves, then pick him up at the bakery. In part, he thought it would look suspicious if he went to the trees instead of the bakery, when the reprieve from the curfew was so short. They would think he was up to something. But there was another reason, which I would only learn later.

We loaded the car with four empty five-gallon water jugs, the buckets of dough, and bags of vegetables from our garden. Then we unloaded everything but the empty jugs at the bakery, and I left as lines of people formed for fresh bread. Foreign reporters scurried around the town like bugs with cameras, zooming in on faces scribbled with misery and on people shopping frantically, trying to get as much as they could in preparation for another uncertain stretch of curfew.

The tree groves were about a ten-minute drive away, and luckily I didn't have to go through any checkpoints. But the streets had been torn up by tanks. Electric pylons were broken everywhere, and I had to watch out for sparking, jumping wires. Pipes were busted up and precious water poured into the streets. Cars parked on the streets had been smashed like toys by the tanks.

I parked our car at the top of the hill and walked to the tent. The water tank had been knocked over, which meant either soldiers or settlers had been there. But the rock formation where the tubes were hidden was undisturbed. I pulled the tank upright and activated the pump to fill it with water. I put on a show of struggling to lift the empty water jugs from the car, as if they were full, and, to the best of my acting ability, emptied their heavy make-believe water into the tank. One could never be sure when and where soldiers were watching, but we knew they had eyes on Bilal and everything he did. The last thing we needed was for them to discover a full water tank without an explanation of how it got that way.

When the tank had filled sufficiently from the pipe, I switched tubes so the water would trickle to the trees, and pushed the other tubes back into the ground, under the small rock formation.

It took me two hours to finish, mostly because I decided to walk the length of the hill to check on the trees at the far edges. I was happy to see the saplings were still alive, and below the crust of sunbaked earth, the soil was moist enough to sustain worms.

There were still lines of people at the bakery when I arrived, with less than forty minutes before curfew. Bilal hadn't had time to buy supplies, but there were bags set aside for us. He had distributed the vegetables to his aunts and to Ghassan, and they had brought cheeses and pickles for us, and some spices and rice. Ghassan's sister and I tended to the last customers while Bilal and Ghassan loaded our car. There was just enough time for me to hurry down the street for ice cream, and I got enough for us all.

"Thank you, my sister, you made me a happy man!" Ghassan said. It was rare to see Ghassan effusive. Who knew ice cream was all it took?

There was not enough time to see Jumana, but we talked on

the phone. She had checked on the salon and actually found one woman who wanted to spend her precious three hours getting her hair colored and fixed, her face waxed, and her nails done.

"I told her the salon wasn't open, but she was so pitiful I changed my mind," Jumana said. "She paid me well, but I wasn't able to do what was on my own list. Luckily Faisal stocked up on food for us. I didn't even get to see Wadee. His wife is pregnant, and she's having a hard time with the nausea. I had planned to check in on her, but I suppose the woman at the salon needed me more."

I would have liked to get pampered at the salon, and tried to thread my own eyebrows when I got home. But it was no use. Threading isn't the kind of thing you can do to your own face. My hair had been graying, and I wanted to dye it. I was in need of a full body wax, and though I could do that on my own, depilatory sessions had always been social events with friends. I began to plan how I would spend the next three-hour curfew reprieve, and realized I had stopped thinking about a total lifting of the curfew. Tragic, how we adjusted our sense of normal.

"You're brilliant, my wife!" Bilal said, pulling out the ice cream. "This is what I love about you. We're all fighting and rushing for the basics, but you have enough sense to remember the sweetness."

"*El hilw ma byinsa el halawa,*" I said. The sweet do not forget the sweets.

Bilal turned on the television news as I unpacked the bags. The reporter was interviewing a young woman when the military came through with loudspeakers on their jeeps. The girl immediately ran away. The reporter argued with the soldier that they still had fifteen minutes, but the footage ended abruptly with the camera being thrown. The announcer came on just as I pulled some strange white plastic containers from one of the bags.

The latest statistics were being read off on the television. The body count, the number of injured; people who'd died under curfew and had to be kept in their houses until the curfew was lifted; the number of people transferred to the hospital during the last three hours; how many doctors and nurses were living at hospitals during curfew to take care of their patients. A teenager in Nablus had been shot only moments before for remaining in the streets after curfew was over. It turned out he was mentally disabled, and his family didn't realize he was out. Soldiers shot people even when we were allowed out. Yousef Iyad and his wife, Jameleh, left their children in the Dheishe refugee camp to buy food when Israel lifted the curfew there the previous day. On their way, soldiers shot up their car and the couple ran to the nearest house for refuge. The curfew was reimposed, and the couple were now separated from their children, the youngest of whom was a breast-fed two-month-old who hadn't been fed in eighteen hours. The reporter was interviewing the eldest sibling over the phone and we could hear the baby crying.

"What are these?" I held up the plastic containers of white powder. The English label said: PHTHALIC ANHYDRIDE.

"An Israeli professor brought them." He put the containers back in the bag.

"It's a little annoying how you say things that make no sense and expect me to understand," I said as he walked upstairs with the bag. I followed him. "Bilal, where did the professor deliver them to?"

"The bakery."

"Does that mean Ghassan knows?"

"I had to tell him for practical reasons, but also because if he knows how you're helping he'll stop doubting your commitment," Bilal said. I figured that's why Ghassan had been extra friendly to me. I had thought it was the ice cream.

Moments later Bilal went to the kitchen and emerged with a large bowl and two spoons in one hand and the other behind his back.

"If that's ice cream in there, you're not getting your fair share, darling. You might as well go get yourself a separate bowl because I'm an ice cream eating machine. I have to work hard to get thighs and an ass this big," I said.

"I knew you were going to say that." He revealed another bowl in the other hand.

"Habibti," he said. "That Israeli professor used to send me reagents for my lab when I taught chemistry, because we didn't have the budget at our university. In return, I gave him data to publish under his name from time to time. He's a total shit, but I can depend on him to get me reagents and compounds without asking questions. Phthalate anhydride is an inert and harmless compound. He has no idea what I'm using it for. But now I have enough to make up a large enough batch of what I need in high concentration."

We ate so much ice cream that night we skipped dinner.

REDEEMING HISTORY

THE PEOPLE OF Nablus were the first to leave their homes en masse. On Monday, July 29, 2002, the fortieth day of curfew, thousands of young men and women took to the streets, throwing stones at Israeli soldiers. Jenin had inflicted casualties on the Israeli military; Nablus was openly challenging their curfew; and Bethlehem fighters were hunkered down in the Church of the Nativity, refusing to surrender despite a terrible siege around them. Ramallah endured the heaviest military presence, because Yasser Arafat was holed up there in the Palestinian Authority's headquarters. Each district had its own stories of what was ultimately nearly sixty terrible days of confinement that turned homes and cities into prisons.

Some younger activists said Bilal and Ghassan "did nothing"—that the leaders they looked up to "hid like rabbits" when needed. Their words hurt Bilal deeply. I suspect he felt no small measure of guilt for not doing more, for passing the hours in the decadence of love instead. He didn't talk about it, but for a time he was not himself, as if he blamed me. It wasn't long, though, before he returned to being the man of days past. But these vacillations would become a pattern, a tangible manifestation of the clash inside him, between the fighter who gave his life to national liberation and the husband who simply wanted love and family.

He worked longer hours in his bathroom laboratory during the two weeks after we received the powdered phthalic anhydride. He made gallons and gallons of other phthalates to pump into the water pipe flowing to the settlement once curfew was lifted.

When we were finally let out of our home prisons, the statistics were ominous. Hundreds of Palestinians dead, thousands arrested, untold disappeared, thousands more wounded or crippled, hundreds of homes demolished . . . and on it went. It was hard not to become numb to the violence and those sadistic numbers. I could not exist in a constant state of outrage and mourning, unlike Bilal. He sought out the individual lives, the families left behind.

"Look at this." He showed me a *Sunday Digest* clipping from June 30, 1957, quoting excerpts from a diary at the American Colony Hotel in Jerusalem. "Read the next to last paragraph," he said.

After the massacre of the Arab village or Deir Yaseen, I took fifty babies into our nursing home. As I stood talking to the frightened women and registering the babies, a boy between three and four years of age looked at me and seeing that I was not an Arab gave a shriek and fell in a faint. I hastened to get water to revive him, but he was dead. What horrible sights had he seen to bring on heart failure?

"Deir Yaseen wasn't just a massacre, an abstract word with numbers and grainy photos of a long-ago time. To me, Deir Yaseen is this little boy. There are stories like this for every pogrom they committed against us," he said. Bilal surrounded himself with stories, stacked shelves of them to collect people's pain and paste it into historic events and political analyses.

I listened, helped him work out plans, and pumped high concentrations of phthalates into the settlement's water pipe.

We monitored Israeli media, searching for relevant news about that particular Israeli colony on Bilal's land. After five months of pumping phthalates into the pipe, an article appeared in a local Hebrew-language newspaper describing strange symptoms among the residents. Bilal translated that the health ministry was coming under criticism for ignoring their request for an investigation. But officials fired back that the reported symptoms did not raise alarm. "Some men are growing tits. Okay, maybe they go on a diet," a source from the ministry was quoted as saying. But there were other issues. Women were having difficulty getting pregnant. The source replied that "this happens to people sometimes. They have to keep trying or go to fertility. Plenty of other women there are pregnant." It was true that there were a few pregnant women. But there was more: asthmatics having frequent flare-ups, new cases of wheezing and other respiratory issues.

The article was perfect. It gave us warning the authorities would come soon to investigate. We used the next few days to reverse the pump, to siphon and store as much clean water as we could; and when we saw water department trucks ride into the settlement, the pipe had been clear for four days. Nothing would show up if they tested the water. And that's what happened. The only noteworthy result that came up in their tests was slightly elevated levels of pesticides, which had nothing to do with us. But they weren't high enough to convincingly be the culprit, according to the article.

The settlers' health problems persisted, however, because we went back to sabotaging the pipe when it was safe to do so.

Another article reflected the authorities' annoyance with the settlement's residents. They were newcomers, mostly from the United States, who had been given government subsidies to live on confiscated Palestinian land. Most could barely speak Hebrew, and Israelis saw them as soft and feckless—Jews who had not yet been hardened by the military or the realities of the country.

"These people hate each other. If they didn't have us to brutalize, they'd be killing each other," Bilal said.

Now Bilal increased the concentrations of phthalates until doctors complained and major media began reporting it. Religious leaders issued authoritative assessments that the area had been cursed. Finally we had our results: settlers were moving out of the colony.

We stopped pumping phthalates. Vans of scientists tested the water, soil, building materials, roads, houseplants. By coincidence, the colony had been obtaining its produce almost exclusively from a community farm, which had been confiscated from three of Bilal's uncles and cousins. Unusually high concentrations of pesticides were found in the soil and in urine samples from individuals tested. That was it. They identified the source and remedied the situation by reducing the use of pesticides. Case closed. But the damage was done. No one would buy anything from the farm after that.

Residents weren't satisfied with the official report and continued moving out. The farm struggled to sustain itself. News articles reported that some of the residents who remained believed "the Arabs" had cast black-magic spells to curse them. They intended to remain, confident that God was on their side. For them, it was a battle between God and the devil. But the colony was emptying by the day.

We read it all and celebrated. We also prepared for renewed raids.

I moved Bilal's reagents, flasks, and tubes to the underground, taking a few things at a time every day when I went to work at the salon. Jumana didn't know, because I did it on days when I opened the store, before she arrived. I didn't like keeping it from her, but I'd learned from Bilal that the less everyone knew in general, the safer we all were.

The military came, of course. Itamar made it a point to come himself to oversee the ransacking of our home. Bilal and I watched, our arms bound with plastic ties. Itamar spoke to us in Arabic, shadows of weariness tinting his face. "I don't want to do this, Bilal. But I will get information from you one way or another."

"Information on what? You cunts watch us twenty-four/seven. You know when I take a shit." Bilal pretended indignation.

Maybe Itamar was pretending too when he squeezed his hand around Bilal's throat and warned, "You know what we can do. If I have to, I'll bring your wife in and make you watch my men fuck her one after the other."

Bilal held Itamar's gaze, clearly unable to breathe, his face turning red. When Itamar loosened his grip, Bilal doubled over, coughing, sucking in gulps of air.

"You are a sick and cruel man from a sick and cruel society," Bilal said. "You forget I know what rotten garbage you really are."

I thought Itamar would beat him, maybe shoot him. But he just stood there, breathing Bilal's words, staring long into Bilal's face, a mixture of sorrow, rage, and defeat in his posture.

"There is nothing here," he said to his soldiers, ordering them out. When two of them began to pull at Bilal and me, Itamar ordered them to leave us. The soldiers hesitated, confused. Itamar screamed, "Cut their cuffs! Leave them!"

In 2003, the third year of the Second Intifada, the horrors of Israel's crackdown incubated whole cities in humiliation and despair. But nine months after those harsh months of curfew, Palestinian babies were popping out of hospitals like popcorn. Most folks had obviously done exactly what Bilal and I had. When you can't leave the house and there's little food or water, fucking is all there is. Even as percolating anger and the solidifying plans of the resistance were as sure as the eyes and ears of traitors in our midst, families everywhere distributed sweets in celebration of baby girls and baby boys.

Ghassan said, "Those stupid motherfuckers are terrified we'll outnumber them, so what do they do? They imprison everybody at home for months with nothing to do but make babies. And now there are thousands of little demographic threats. It's damned poetic!"

Farmers lost their crops, families lost sons and daughters, towns lost electricity and roads, Israel's jails were packed with young and old, jobs were nowhere to be found, but all those babies brought people together, gave hope and something to do, pushed us to visit each other, to eat together, live again, and plot the next moves of an unrelenting national liberation struggle.

My period was three weeks late.

What followed was no surprise. Protests and strikes intensified, rock-throwing confrontations with soldiers increased, and a few suicide bombings rocked Israel. Bilal and Ghassan busied themselves planning. Jumana and I knew little and were not to be involved unless necessary. With Samer gone off to graduate school in Moscow, we were the sole guardians of the underground and kept Wadee and Faisal in the dark on most things. Whatever Bilal and Ghassan were planning would involve nearly all the weapons. Jumana and I knew that much, because we helped smuggle pieces and ammunition out of the underground one by one. We took them wherever instructed; usually it was just to the trash dumpster down the road, where someone we didn't know would pick it up. Once, we wrapped one of the crossbows like a giant present that we took to a baby shower. We didn't even know the expectant mother, but her brother took the gift box and we pretended to be friends in front of their guests.

On a cool February evening when we all gathered at our house, Bilal and Ghassan gave us a bit more information.

"Listen," Bilal started. "Many people are involved in what's going down. Some will be caught, even killed. They know the risks, as do Ghassan and I." Bilal looked at me, Ghassan at Jumana, the twins at each other—looks suffused with love and the terrifying realities of our fates.

"We're covering our tracks, but it's likely they will arrest us. That includes all of you by mere association." They focused on the twins now. Wadee had joined this meeting reluctantly. He had made it clear he wanted nothing to do with any more plans, creating a rift with his twin that was painful to watch. He was desperately in love with his very pregnant wife, and though it was still clear to all of us that she did not reciprocate his affection in the same way, he had refocused his energy into winning her heart.

Wadee plunged his head into his hands. "Why am I here? What does this have to do with me?" he pleaded. Faisal turned to him in disgust, but Ghassan interrupted.

"Most likely they're going to arrest us all," Ghassan said.

Wadee flung his head back, exasperated. Faisal looked ready to punch his brother. I don't think he was truly angry at Wadee for wanting out. Faisal was incomplete without his other half, who seemed oblivious to everyone but his wife.

Ghassan continued, "They'll torture us. They'll ransack our

homes, the shop, and the salon too." He paused to let that sink in. "It would be unrealistic to expect anyone to withstand torture without talking. None of us is superhuman. We're not trying to be heroes. We have to give them something." Nodding to Bilal to take over, he took out a cigarette, lit it, and puffed away as Bilal began describing all we had done with the pipeline, the phthalates, the pump, the trees.

"You mean you're the reason they abandoned that settlement?" Wadee exclaimed.

"Technically, I am," I chimed in, wanting credit for my hard work filling the barrels and running the pump for hours every day. But Bilal shot me a terrible look.

"Ignore what she said. When you feel it's time to confess, you tell them about the water pipeline, and that I alone did it. Nahr had no idea what was happening. None of you did at the time. If everyone confesses to hearing or finding out about it somehow, it will be convincing enough. But under no circumstances can any of you *ever* reveal the underground."

Bilal took in a long breath. "I need to say that again. Give up anything you want. Make shit up if you have to. But never, ever the underground."

We all nodded in agreement and proceeded to align our stories—specifically, how, when, and where each of us learned about poisoning the settlement's water pipeline.

All of it was to fall on Bilal. "We have a plan," he said. "It may or may not work. But in any case, use this information to give them something if you're tortured."

"Each of you will get a call about five hours in advance of anything happening. You have to make sure that you get a solid public alibi for the next few hours after you get the call," Ghassan added.

"When is it happening?" It was the first thing Faisal had said.

"We can't tell you that. Even the people executing the plan will not know until five hours in advance," Bilal said.

Two elderly Egyptian women walk me down a dark corridor. They look familiar and I remember where I've seen them before. "No." I tell them I don't want to abort my child. But they just laugh and say, "We've already been paid."

I woke up from a nightmare gripped with panic and sat in bed sweating, Bilal still sleeping next to me. The clock read 3:48 a.m. It was Friday, the day we usually slept in. I tiptoed to the bathroom and peed on the pregnancy test filament, as the instructions indicated. I watched the line of my urine travel up the filament. It crossed the first window on the test, revealing a single red line, the "control," to make sure the kit was working properly. The edge of my urine advanced to the next window, and slowly a pair of lines appeared. The insert's interpretation said, *Positive: Congratulations! You're pregnant.*

I sat on the toilet thinking that the pregnancy-test makers should stick to the facts without assuming they know what is or isn't cause for congratulations. Fucking patriarchy. I wrapped the test stick in tissue and tossed it, got back in bed, and fell asleep until I was assaulted by sunlight coming through the window. I had forgotten to close the heavy shades the night before.

Bilal was already awake and dressed, making breakfast. "Morning of goodness and jasmine, my beautiful wife," he said, unusually cheerful, as if he were in a movie scene. He didn't normally like to talk in the morning. Mostly he grunted until he had had his coffee on the terrace.

"*Sabaho*, my love," I said, kissing him.

The movie-scene cheer of that morning quickly slumped into ordinary quiet, and we went through the motions of our Friday routine. Coffee, a light breakfast for him, big one for me, newspaper on the terrace, lazy hours at home, and—although he didn't believe in God—afternoon prayer at the mosque. It was something he looked forward to all week. I rather loved his contradictions. I went sometimes, but mostly Jumana and I would get together to cook, maybe take a few clients at the salon, go shopping, play cards. Then Bilal would take his shift at the bakery. Later all of us might gather at our house, or we'd go hiking and spend time with the flock (Bilal had eventually gone back to visiting with Jandal's animals and their new shepherd). Fridays were sacred.

The house phone rang. I ignored it because Bilal liked to answer. Instead, he turned to me. "Aren't you going to answer?"

How odd, I thought. It was Jehad!

"Habibi, little brother! I miss you so much! Hearing your voice is the perfect way to start this Friday!"

"I miss you, too, Sis . . . but sit down. I have some bad news."

I steadied myself. "What?"

"Our grandmother passed away," he said somberly. "She died peacefully in her sleep."

Now, lying on my bed in the Cube, I remember the call and the click of the receiver when he hung up. I remember the shock of it, then questioning how it is that death can be life's only assurance and yet also its greatest, most devastating surprise.

Bilal put his arms around me. He said he would get cash from the bank and arrange a car for my travel to Amman for the funeral.

"What about—"

"Don't worry. It's not going to happen for another couple of weeks," he interrupted my question.

"I thought you said no one could know except five hours in advance."

"Well, I just told you. Now, you should start packing and go to your family."

He's right, I thought and went to pack. I was taking my time, assuming I would leave the next morning, but Bilal surprised me less than half an hour later with cash, informing me he had arranged for a car to the border.

"I wish I could go with you, or at least drive you to the border, habibti," he said, holding my face. The terms of his last release had curtailed his movements to an even smaller radius. He'd have been arrested if he drove me.

I tried calling Jumana, to no avail. My brother called again, urging me to get there as soon as possible. He said our mother needed me, though he wouldn't put her on the phone, which was odd.

"You should leave right away, darling, because they close the border early on Fridays," Bilal urged. Before I could process it all, a taxi was waiting outside, only a few short hours after I woke up to what I thought was going to be an ordinary lazy Friday.

Bilal held me in a long, strong embrace and kissed me hard, like he wanted to pull me inside of him.

"Don't worry, my love. I'll be back in a few days. At most I'll be gone a week or two," I said. He studied my face, as if trying to record every detail.

"Take this." He pulled a sealed envelope from his back pocket. "Give this to Jehad when you get to Amman."

"What is it?"

"A coded letter. He'll understand. But don't open it before you're in Jordan."

I put the envelope in my purse, slipped my arms around his

waist, and rested my head on his chest, tuning myself to the rhythm of his heartbeat. He squeezed me again.

"I love you, Nahr. You've given me the best days of my life," he said.

I got into the taxi, kissed my husband once more through the window, and set off.

That was the last time I ever saw Bilal.

I love you, Nahr. You've given me the best days of my life. Those words bounce around in my head now; their letters fall apart and float in my eyes, behind my face, in my throat, and I scramble to reassemble it all, afraid I have forgotten the sound of Bilal's voice or the thuds of his heart in my ear against his chest. I lie on my bed in the Cube, concentrating to put it all together to replay: *I love you, Nahr. You've given me the best days of my life.* Sometimes I can't and am seized by panic. I'm terrified of forgetting.

A longing to see my family in Amman tugged at me as the taxi set off. Sadness curled in my heart, imagining the apartment without Sitti Wasfiyeh. I had not experienced death so close since our father passed away. The incomprehensibility of death, the finality of it, settled on me. My grandmother had been an unbroken presence throughout my life. In that taxi nearly halfway to the border, I saw Sitti Wasfiyeh with a new clarity—a refugee four times, a mother who lost her only son, whose daughters could not tolerate her, who defended herself and protected her pain by hurling insults, who spent her life chasing the home Zionists chased her out of. I had a desperate yearning to feel my mother's big-bosomed embrace. And Jehad, how sweet it would be to have time together alone. We could at last speak about his role in the resistance, and why he had wanted to keep it from me. I checked my purse for the letter. I pulled it out, then returned it unopened.

The unusual quiet in the streets pierced my reverie. There was barely any traffic, even in town where honking horns were a mainstay of life. Surprisingly few people were walking around, especially for a Friday. Come to think of it, the entire day had been strange. I replayed the morning, starting with Bilal.

Why did he want me to answer the phone? Did he know it was for me? He must have. He must have already spoken with Jehad before I woke up. Why was he so insistent I leave so quickly? He was anxious that I took so long to pack. Why didn't Jumana answer her telephone?

Something was happening. I realized that the driver had been driving in silence. I asked him to turn on the radio news. Instead, he put on music.

"No, please put on a news channel. Don't you think things around us seem strange?"

"I'm sorry, daughter. I am not allowed. I'm supposed to just drive you straight to the border," he said.

"What do you mean, you're *not allowed*?" I scooted myself up and leaned over the seat.

He didn't answer, but hesitatingly changed the channel. "You're right. Something is going on," he said, turning up the volume.

The broadcaster was in midsentence: *". . . due to heavy military presence. We don't yet know what happened, but eyewitness reports are coming in. In the meantime, the military has cordoned off the area. It seems they cut off all telephone communication because no calls are getting through to residents in the area."*

I dialed Bilal on my mobile. There was no answer at the house or the bakery. The driver pulled over in front of a blacksmith shop. People were clearing the streets and shops were closing. The driver leaned toward the radio, as if the better to hear. My heart raced as

pieces of the day came together in my head. I yanked out Bilal's letter to my brother and ripped it open, and was shocked to discover
it was addressed to me!

To my darling, beautiful, dear wife. Habibti, Nahr, I pray you are
reading this letter in the safety of your family in Amman and that
you will remain there to raise our child . . .

I realized he knew. I hadn't concealed the test kit well in the
wastebasket!

. . . until we are reunited again. I write this as you are sleeping in
our bed. I have already spoken with Jehad. I'm sure you know this
by now, and I hope you have forgiven us both. I cannot bear . . .

"Turn around!" I shouted at the driver. "Take me back, now!"

I'm sure you know . . . I already read that. I couldn't find where I'd
left off.

"*Ya Sater!*" The driver turned up the volume with trembling
hands. "*. . . just moments ago. We now have confirmation that two*
operations have been carried out by the resistance, twenty minutes
apart. It appears they were accomplished in the manner of the hero
Tha'ir Hamad. We are hearing that . . ."

The driver suddenly turned the radio off, threw himself down
across the front seat, and ordered me to put my head down. I saw
military jeeps racing toward us in the distance and I quickly lay
down. The car shook as they sped past us. I looked up slowly and
saw the driver's eyes staring at me from the front armrest. His eyes

were swimming in their sockets, as if he didn't really see me. "Keep your head down," he ordered, terrified. We heard helicopters roaring overhead and more shopkeepers shuttering their stores. "God help us," the driver said. "If this is another Tha'ir Hamad operation, they're going to rain hell on us."

Tha'ir Hamad was a twenty-two-year-old lone Palestinian sniper who'd carried out an attack on soldiers at a checkpoint at the beginning of the Second Intifada. All he had was an old WWII Mauser rifle and thirty rounds of ammunition. Before dawn on the morning of March 3, 2002, Tha'ir Hamad dug a hiding place under some olive trees on a hilltop overlooking Wadi al Haramiya—the Valley of Thieves—and waited for the Israeli reserve company manning the checkpoint at Uyoun al Haramiya. He fired four times, killing four soldiers. The two soldiers who emerged to locate the shooter and assist the fallen soldiers were also shot dead. He fired at reinforcements when they arrived, killing the sergeant and wounding several of his men. An Israeli woman with her children arrived to pass through the checkpoint, but he yelled at her to leave, refraining from harming them. He finally left when the rifle jammed on the last bullet, twenty-five minutes after he started firing. The Israelis dispatched helicopters and canine search units to find the shooter, but they didn't even manage to find his hiding place. He would have gotten away with it, had he not made the mistake of confiding in a friend. His name became synonymous with precision and expert marksmanship.

I kept my head down, strangely calm, running the previous days through my head. I knew Bilal and Ghassan had something to do with this. We were all to find out five hours before they put their plan into action, but the pregnancy stick had hastened a change in plans to get me out of the country. *Did he tell Jumana not to answer my calls? Did she know?*

I looked back at the letter.

. . . forgiven us both. I cannot bear the thought of what they would do to you while you're pregnant with our child. So I am . . .

The driver turned the radio back on, keeping the volume low.

". . . third site, and now we're told there are sirens at Huwwara, making this the fourth checkpoint ambush in half an hour. This is incredible! Incredible! No one has taken responsibility, as far as we know. We've received calls from eyewitnesses who told us that some of the soldiers were hit with arrows."

The voice of a caller crackled through poor cell reception: *"I saw it with my own eyes at Huwwara. Long live the resistance! A group of* shabab *looked like they had gotten into a fight, and the soldiers all came out with their guns drawn to break up the chaos. All those boys and about ten more came up on them pointing aerosol cans—it turned out to be hornet spray—and released it in streams on their faces. The soldiers started scampering back when all these arrows— like American Indian arrows!—rained down on them. Praise God! Praise God! God bless our warriors! God bless the resistance. God protect them. Allahu akbar."* God is bigger.

The driver and I listened in disbelief. "Praise God. Allahu akbar," he said.

My heart hammered at my chest now. "I think we should get out of the car and try to walk to the nearest house," I said. "The street will be crawling with tanks soon, and they're going to run right over this car. If you try to drive away, we'll probably get hit with a missile from one of the helicopters."

"Yes, yes. O God. Have mercy, O God." We poked our heads up slowly. The street was quiet. People had disappeared into their homes or shops and the helicopter noise was receding. Our best option was an apartment building five meters away. Although we could not detect immediate danger in walking such a short distance, the eerie quiet was frightening. We could not be sure there were no Israeli snipers on rooftops. Slowly we opened the car doors. The driver began crawling out through the passenger's side and I did the same from the backseat, just as a helicopter appeared overhead.

"Helicopter!" the driver yelled. We reacted in opposite ways. He rushed out of the car toward the building, leaving open the front passenger door. I pulled myself back inside the car, closing the door. As he ran, the helicopter came overhead and military jeeps sped down the street. I cowered low in the car, and heard several shots before something smashed hard into the car, jarring and disorienting me. There was blood. The car was upside down. Soldiers were pointing big guns at me, dragging me first by the neck, then by the arm from the shattered window, which cut the entire right side of my body as they pulled me through.

"Yaqoot? Are you Yaqoot?" they barked in accented Arabic.

The letter was still in my hand, still not fully read.

The letter! I wanted to read the rest of it. *I cannot let them get the letter!*

As they dragged me along the street, I rolled over and stuffed the paper into my mouth, the asphalt grating the side of my face. I kept my mouth shut, slowly trying to chew the letter to manageable pieces as they bound my hands and arms, threw me in the back of a jeep, and rummaged through my belongings. There was blood in my eyes. I didn't know where I was bleeding from or if it was even mine.

One of the soldiers noticed me chewing. "What's in your mouth?" he demanded, and I swallowed as much as I could. He yelled something in Hebrew to other soldiers, and within seconds several of them were on top of me prying open my mouth. I bit flesh and drew blood. There wasn't much left of the letter.

The next thing I remember is waking up in a hospital, my wrist handcuffed to the bed. A soldier sat in a plastic chair reading a magazine. I must have mumbled, because she called a nurse. The rest was a blur. I was in constant strange and variable pain, at times sharp, then muddled by the drugs in a way that made my head feel thick, cloudy, and heavy to the point that moving it required herculean strength in my neck. I could not reposition my body either, because of the handcuffs. When I tried to pull out my IV line, they shackled the other wrist. Then I remembered that Sitti Wasfiyeh was dead. *Or is she? Oh God, Bilal!*

I don't know how long I was in the hospital. They transferred me a few times to what I thought were other wards. When I finally regained my senses, I was in a prison clinic. I learned that I had suffered a head injury and fallen into a coma for two days.

"There's no baby," was the only response I could get to my repeated question. Suddenly my womb was a cavern, a carved-out emptiness in the place where love, life, hope, and future had been planted. Even now in the Cube, sometimes I hear baby cries echoing from my belly.

The initial interrogation was mild compared to what I expected. I was taken into a room, my head bandaged, various cuts and bruises at different stages of healing. I had a long red scar with stitches that spanned the side of my torso. The small room's dingy walls were spattered with crimson specks. A used latex glove lay on the floor in a small puddle of dirty water. Two men in jeans sat me in a metal chair at a metal table. One wore a white T-shirt, the other a black one. Another man, in a suit, paced slowly around the room, all of us under the clink and hum of an old ceiling fan.

White T-shirt asked how I was feeling and whether I would like a cigarette. I said I didn't smoke. "A glass of tea then?"

"No thank you," I said.

"She's polite, this one," said Black T-shirt.

White T-shirt pretended to disapprove of Black T-shirt and said, "We have a lot of questions for you, Yaqoot. But first you have to tell us, where is Bilal?"

I saw that he immediately regretted asking me, because I must have smiled or somehow betrayed a sense of relief.

"I don't know," I said.

He tried but could not conceal his ire. Instead of getting information, he'd inadvertently told me Bilal had gotten away. All three men were rattled by my satisfaction. They unknowingly gave away one more bit of information.

Black T-shirt began aggressively questioning me, his anger rising each time I would not answer or if I gave a nonanswer, while White T-shirt pretended to calm him, faking compassion for me, until Black T-shirt slapped me. I was momentarily stunned. I didn't even realize it was happening until I picked myself off the ground. This time, White T-shirt genuinely rebuked Black T-shirt. They spoke to each other in Hebrew, but I picked up on two words that explained his reaction: *zeekaroon* and *zokheret*.

Bilal had once explained to me that Hebrew is a simple language, without many conjugations and with many verbs and nouns similar to Arabic. *Zeekaroon* and *zokheret* sounded like the Arabic root word *zakira*, meaning "memory." I had a head injury, and I figured White T-shirt worried I might have memory loss and didn't want to exacerbate it. From that moment on, I pretended to remember very little, even insignificant things.

"Yaqoot, I am sorry for my colleague's bad manners," said White T-shirt. "Tell me where you were going the day we arrested you."

"I don't remember being arrested," I said. "In fact, I'm not really sure how I got here. To prison, I mean."

"Do you remember your grandmother dying?"

"My grandmother is dead? Sitti Wasfiyeh is dead?"

"Actually, no. She's alive and well," said White T-shirt.

Here I may have revealed my confusion. "Why would you say such a thing to me if she is fine? Thank God she's alive!" *They know about Sitti Wasfiyeh from monitoring our telephone calls. Surely that's the only way. Unless they captured Jumana and she told them, if she knew.* I surmised that Israel had been hit hard. Their intelligence hadn't expected such sophistication and coordination. My interrogators let me know that they were ripping through our neighborhoods with a fury "you cannot imagine." I thought it was probably only a matter of time before they discovered the water-pipe rig we had set up.

"I have no idea what you're talking about," I said.

The T-shirts exchanged a look and Black T-shirt slammed his hand on the table with a frightful bang that made me jump. I began to cry, cupping my face.

"We're trying to help you," White T-shirt said. "We already know what you did to the water supply."

I was grateful to have been crying into my palms, or they might have seen my shock. I played along as well as I could. I said I didn't know what they were talking about.

"We already have enough evidence against you. Your accomplices confessed."

This went on for days, hours upon hours of waiting, then questions, threats, and yelling. They bound me in a painful position with my back arched abnormally across a chair for so long that my whole body spasmed when they finally untied me. Eventually I confessed to helping sabotage the water pipe. I refused to implicate Bilal on principle. But I did sign a confession in Hebrew, and who knows what the confession actually stated.

They sent me back to prison, where I resided in a room with four others. It was not at all like Bilal's imprisonment where, despite everything, there was camaraderie and brotherhood among Palestinian political prisoners. Instead, they locked me up with Israeli criminals who despised me. One of them spoke Arabic and later tried to befriend me, warning me about this or that, advising me how to get the best food, and which guards or inmates to avoid. She claimed she was a Palestinian from the Galilee, in prison for "resistance activities." She seemed a cartoon of what Bilal had once explained were "birds," Palestinian collaborators who befriended new arrivals to extract information. She claimed she knew Bilal. "Well, I don't actually know him. I've heard of him. Everyone has. You're so lucky to be married to a hero," she said.

I nodded. She smiled.

"I just want you to know that I don't believe the things that were said about you. I hate it when people let their jealousy ruin a girl's reputation," she said.

I didn't react. She wasn't a very good bird and could barely contain her impatience to get me to talk. She eventually left me alone and soon disappeared from the prison. That's when harassment by other inmates and guards started. I was terrified but did my best to hide it, until two Israeli women came to my defense the second time I was beaten. They weren't interested in being my friends, but they made it clear that there could be consequences if others didn't stop attacking me. I don't know why they did that, but I have learned one can be surprised by the presence of humanity in many guises and languages, and in the most inhuman of places.

My trial was in Hebrew and lasted two days. It would have been shorter, but I had "wasted the court's time and made things worse."

The first time Israel sentenced Bilal to prison, he was tried in absentia. They locked him up when he traded himself for his brother. Every subsequent imprisonment was for violating the terms of his release or simply administrative detention. He never had a trial in a courtroom. He once told me he would never have cooperated with their judiciary because that would mean recognition of Israel's authority.

I did exactly what he would have. I wanted to make him proud, wherever he was. Maybe he would see or read about it in the news. I took Bilal's imagined defiance a step further. I sang, even though I don't have a good voice. I started with "Yumma Mweil elHawa," to set the mood. The judge admonished me. I waited a while, then sang every Abdel Halim Hafez song I could think of. "El Hawa Hawaya" followed by my favorite, "Qariatol Fingan." The judge was baffled, then irate, yelling at me, at the prosecutors, lawyers, bailiffs. She ordered the guards to silence me. I sang "Mawood," another of my favorites. The judge had allowed reporters into the courtroom. But now she motioned for them to leave, and on their way out, they snapped photos and videos, for which I posed as best I could.

I did what Bilal would have done. I colonized the colonizer's space of authority. I made myself free in chains and held that courtroom captive to my freedom. I felt Bilal's presence with me. For those hours, it gave me comfort and strength to imagine he was watching. When I would not stop singing, the judge ordered guards to escort me out and "make sure she's civilized tomorrow."

I continued to sing as they hauled me out into the hallway, where reporters clamored and were pushed back by police. I was singing "Gabbar" at that point, stretching out the interminably long note of the last syllable, "*Gabbaaaaaaaaaaaaaaaaaaaaaaaaar*," until one of the guards cupped my mouth. I licked his palm, faithful to Um Buraq's lesson not to react predictably. He removed his hand reflexively, then gripped my jaw so tightly my cheeks bruised.

They put me in a metal vault, with bright lights and loud music that blared until the next morning, when they lugged me back to military court. My head drooped from the weight of the dark bags under my eyes. The room was empty on that second day, except for officers of the court. I hummed quietly to myself, but guards stuffed a rag into my mouth and sealed it with tape. The judge opened the proceedings by expelling the press, but not before holding them responsible for giving a platform to a terrorist to hijack the sanctity of her courtroom in particular and Israel's democracy in general. But, she added, she was pleased to see me behaving now.

I tried to muster energy to hum through the gag, but the freedom of my defiance got stuck in my throat, and I choked on it. My body filled with silence and exhaustion. I was grateful not to be under bright lights and blaring music. My heavy head fell, my eyes closed, and when I opened them again, I was in a van, then inside the Cube.

For a long time, I didn't know the precise reason for my imprisonment since all the proceedings were in Hebrew, but I supposed it at least had to do with the water pipe and phthalates. During my early time in the Cube, Arabic newspaper clippings were slipped through the door, maybe to demoralize me. There they were, long-forgotten photos of my nineteen-year-old self, dancing in the midst of hungry men, one of whom was showering me with money. Their faces were obscured, but not by the newspaper. Um Buraq had done that many years ago when I forced her to hand over the photos to Abu Moathe. I don't know how Israeli intelligence managed to get them, but I suppose they simply followed rumors right to Abu Moathe's door. And maybe Abu Moathe saw an opportunity to finally get revenge on me for cleaning out his bank account all those years ago.

I stared at those pictures, not even noticing the headline initially. I thought how hurt my family would be. How ashamed. The thought made me glad to be locked up, even though I ached to see them.

Then I noticed the headline: "Heroic or Heinous?" It seemed the media had reported on my trial, and some were inspired by the spectacle I had created of the proceedings. Israel had not been able to censor the footage that showed their court humiliated and their authority diminished by a Palestinian woman in shackles. I hadn't known any of this until I read the article. And it was in that same report that I learned for the first time that my crime had been "terrorism." Of course, I already knew that and understood the specifics from the interrogation, but this was the confirmation. It said I aided Bilal in planning multiple terrorist attacks, one of which they referred to as "silent terrorism." That's what they called the water-pipe setup.

Israel tried to conceal many of the details, lest others get ideas.

Bilal's legend grew among Palestinians, especially as he remained at large. Israel concluded publicly that he was most likely dead, and that it was a good thing because he was a "rising Hitler." They said Saddam was Hitler too. Any leader they don't like is a Hitler.

If Israel knew the extent of what we did with the pipe, they didn't let on publicly, because the media downplayed the effect of our sabotage at the same time that they hyped the crime. A reporter was allowed to show me an article during an interview in the Cube. It said,

> *Although the terrorists succeeded in breaching the water pipe, the cause of illness among our brave settlers was the misuse of pesticides. The original investigation into this matter still stands.*

Bilal and I had accepted the consequences long ago (though how could we truly?), which was complete destruction of the tree groves and orchards, as well as the demolition of our home, all of which happened before my trial. It was a small price compared to what happened to others.

VII.

BETWEEN FREEDOM

THE CUBE,
THE UNREACHABLE BEYOND

THE INITIAL SHOCK of seeing the newspaper clippings dissipated quickly. Feelings erode in here. Memories wear off. All that's left are facts without the emotion that once accompanied them. I don't cry in this place. There isn't room enough for the heart to move. There are no winds to rustle it. Silence here is not the absence of sound, but the presence of a dense, unshakable stillness. Like dark matter in space, silence here is a living force that slides into all corners and seams. I have come to depend on it.

I've been here long enough for my hair—almost entirely gray now—to grow down to my back three times, after being cut just a few centimeters from my head. I still wonder whether Bilal is alive. If Israel knew, I think I would too, because that kind of news seeps through every permeable point. What I learned over time—from smuggled notes and occasional conversations—is that Bilal's coordinated assaults on their military killed twenty-four Israeli soldiers and wounded twelve on that stunning day. It was a staggering toll for Israel that caught them by surprise. They'd never imagined guerrilla resistance with such unconventional weaponry as crossbows and hornet spray. Some of the arrowheads were poisoned with plant oils, all of which were found in Ghassan's home. Soldiers had raided his house many times before, not realizing the weapons he would use against them were there in the potted plants they ransacked, and which Ghassan simply replanted. It was those plants that gave plausibility to Israel's claim that Ghassan had been the sole mastermind of the attacks. They knew it wasn't true, but they needed to sustain a narrative of strength, because admitting that the leader of this offensive had slipped through their grip would have been a humiliating sign of their vulnerability.

The first attack had been a decoy to divert resources from subsequent ones. It occurred at a remote checkpoint. Two soldiers were killed with a torrent of arrows from three comrades. This checkpoint was only minutes away from a military outpost, but our comrades piled large stones in the road to delay rescue and backup. The automatic weapons and hand grenades seized from the dead soldiers were used to attack the Israeli reinforcements. The second checkpoint assault was the same as the first. With Israel's resources diverted to those areas, Ghassan and six others attacked a third checkpoint, one of the largest and most heavily manned. They used what working guns they had obtained from the Russian smugglers. As Israeli soldiers began to retreat inside the fortified terminal, Ghassan's brigade descended upon them. About twenty Palestinians who had simply been waiting to pass through the checkpoint spontaneously joined the fighters, overwhelming the few soldiers who had not had time to hide behind bulletproof walls. There was a fourth attack similar to the first two.

Israel killed Ghassan that day. Military backup arrived on the scene and sprayed the Palestinian fighters with hails of bullets. A newspaper clipping quoted Ghassan's mother pleading for the return of her son's body, so she could bury him next to his father and younger brother, Jandal. One of my interrogators showed me a photo of Ghassan, lifeless and bloodied on the side of the road. I vomited, and vomited again imagining Jumana seeing it, then felt relief that it wasn't Bilal, then shame for feeling relief.

Bilal had been with Ghassan at the third checkpoint. There were even rumors that Mhammad was there too. It shocked me to hear that, and I don't know if it was true. It became clear, however, that Mhammad hadn't been in Canada all those years. It was reported he had been living in Tel Aviv, working as a bartender. Whatever the truth, Mhammad turned up dead weeks after my arrest, his corpse still bearing the marks of torture, perhaps because they believed he was hiding Bilal.

Israel lost its mind and launched an all-out war against all Palestinians, including those with Israeli citizenship inside the 1948 territories, the so-called Green Line. Their fighter planes dropped bombs on schools, mosques, business centers, and factories in the West Bank and Gaza. They rounded up thousands of men and women, exacting vengeance. Five million people were subjected to curfews and various collective punishments. And Israel became consumed by a national scandal involving a top general named Itamar who, it turned out, had had an affair with an Arab named Mhammad, the older brother of their most-wanted man. Israeli authorities accused him of unwittingly aiding Bilal's escape. They blamed his "oriental roots," because he was an Iraqi Jew. They blamed the Jewish tendency for kindness toward non-Jews, and let it stand as a warning to whoever trusted Arabs.

Itamar is still in prison. I find it poetic that both Tamara and I are imprisoned. Jumana was arrested, tortured, and raped even after she confessed to knowledge that Bilal was "stealing" water for his trees. She maintained she knew nothing about the phthalates. She spent four years in prison. Faisal likewise confessed to the water-pipe breach and pointed to Bilal as the mastermind. He was released from prison after agreeing to be deported to Gaza. At some point in my confinement, Gaza became a giant prison camp. Samer remained in Moscow, where he continued to run the website with Jehad, and expanded it to multiple networks. Israel tried unsuccessfully to get him on Interpol's list. Jehad's name never came up except in news reports that I had a brother who was a disabled gardener with one eye and a lame hand. Wadee, whom we all imagined was the weakest link, turned out to be the toughest. He confessed to nothing.

The most bizarre oddity in all this was that Wadee's wife had been part of another resistance cell. A year and one daughter into their marriage, they learned each other's secrets in an Israeli interrogation room. The military didn't suspect her of anything but brought her to be raped in front of her husband to prod his confession. Wadee didn't suspect either, but when she shouted to him, professing for the first time, "My husband, my true love," he found the courage he needed. She fell deeply in love with her husband on that day, when they saw each other at last in the fullness of who they were. (I don't actually know this, but it is how I imagine happiness for Wadee.) She was released after a few days, but Wadee remained, first for two years without charge, then a life sentence after an ad hoc terrorism charge and speedy military conviction. Like my prosecution, it took two days from charge to conviction. His wife and daughter can visit him in prison once every two months for thirty minutes.

As for Bilal, no one knew where he ended up, or whether he was still alive. The way Israel pummeled Palestine and arrested most of the men left everyone dazed, but it was not long before the resistance regrouped and a Third Intifada ignited, even capturing two

Israeli soldiers and holding the remains of two dead ones. It happened not so long ago.

The underground city has remained our secret.

———

Here I am now. My story is written and this is all I know. I stare again at the paper, perhaps three thousand written pages stacked along the Cube walls. In every direction there are papers. The prison warders have not tried to confiscate any of it. I suppose they are waiting until I'm done. But if they do, it will read like the gibberish of a madwoman—nonsensical attempts at an endless children's parable. It's coded in our 194 method.

I don't know what compelled me to write it all. To set the record straight? To lay bare with love what others find offensive? To pass the time? To mark my place in the world? To inject life into this lifeless box? To declare simply that I survived? To keep Bilal near me?

Perhaps I will destroy it all and start over. Maybe I'll soak all the pages in water. But Attar has not been here for some time. The musk under my arms and between my legs ripens and I do my best at the sink.

The alarm signals me to shackle my bracelets to the wall. A guard arrives carrying a chair, which tells me a visitor is coming. She places it in the center of the Cube and beckons another guard, who ushers in an Israeli reporter, a middle-aged white woman with kind eyes, unruly brown hair, no makeup, freckles, glasses, old jeans, and sneakers. I know her.

"Hello, Nahr," she says as my arms are released from the wall. She was the only visitor who didn't call me Yaqoot. "Is it okay if I sit?" She speaks accented Arabic.

I nod. "Hello, Nira."

"Is this all your writing?" She sweeps her hand through the air over the stacks of paper.

"Yes."

She has in her hand a small yellow notepad, a pen, and a newspaper clipping, which she begins to unfold. "I obtained permission to show this to you. They will not allow me to give it to you, but I can show you and read it. Would you like me to do that?"

"What is it about?"

"You might be released in a prisoner exchange."

It wasn't the first time I had heard such a thing during the time it had taken for my breasts to sag and my hair to turn to ash. "Is that right?"

"I think it's real this time. An exchange. Six hundred Palestinian prisoners for the four captured Israeli soldiers, two of them dead."

I laugh, not really believing. Israel never stopped trying to trick me into giving them information on Bilal, as if I knew anything anyway. "And you're going around to all six hundred prisoners to deliver the news?"

"No. Only you." She removes her glasses. "The negotiations are a year in the making. We're told they have been concluded and the releases are set to take place over the next three weeks. Israel and the Palestinian Authority have turned the country upside down searching for the missing soldiers, to no avail, and it is believed they were smuggled out of the country somehow. A new organization took credit and has been demanding this prisoner exchange since the soldiers were captured," she says. I think about what I have been doing in all that time, reading (when they gave me books), waiting for Attar, for Klara, dancing. I cannot bring myself to care, or feel.

"You are the only prisoner singled out to be released to Jordan."

I search her face and begin to believe her.

"I am writing a feature on the exchange."

The edges of my vision dim. They do that sometimes. I blink hard, shaking my head to restore my senses.

"Are you all right?"

I nod.

"Is it okay if I ask you a few questions?"

As I contemplate saying no, she asks, "Can you think of a reason why you're the only prisoner they want released in Jordan?"

We stare at each other. She tries to hold benevolence in her eyes, but I can see it slipping away, and she knows I see it. She puts her glasses back on. A name percolates between us. She wants me to say it first. Her breathing changes, her chest rises higher and collapses harder. It is slightly mesmerizing.

"I don't know," I say, unintentionally raising one eyebrow. I am already lost in thoughts of what it all means. I roam my mind, unearthing faces and voices in the vast terrain of memory.

Her eyelids gently close and slide open. She takes a deep breath and lets it out calmly. "Do you think your Bilal is alive?"

I return to my honeymoon, Bilal and I locked inside our home under curfew in the spring of 2002.

"Nahr?"

"Are you going to read that?" I say, motioning to the partially unfolded newspaper article.

She straightens it and begins to read aloud. It's a long article, rehashing the now legendary crossbow attacks, the hornet spray, the recent kidnapping of Israeli soldiers, the inability to get them back, the new Palestinian resistance inside Palestine and in the diaspora, the international boycott campaign called BDS. It quotes an Israeli general who says the prisoner release is a necessary sacrifice, and hints that they'll eventually round them up again. "Terrorists always end up back in prison where they belong," he says. The article mentions my name.

"... She is the wife of Bilal Jalal AbuJabal, and the only prisoner for whom a demand was made for release to Jordan. This has led to widespread conjecture that the infamous terrorist is still alive. To Palestinians, AbuJabal is revered as a hero and beloved fighter. The general laughs at this. 'His wife is a whore,' he said."

Nira looks at me.
"Continue," I say.

"'... His wife is a whore,' he said. But when challenged that Palestinians consider her a revolutionary as much as her husband, the general laughs again and says, 'A revolutionary whore.'"

I know now, as I have always felt, as this Israeli general knows, as Nira knows, as the world now knows, that Bilal is alive. I know too that even if I am freed, I may never see him again. I recline and lie flat on the bed, gazing at my concrete sky. Thoughts and questions and images and memories race and collide in my mind. Nira says she would like to read my writings, maybe publish them. She believes she could get permission to take them out of the Cube. She keeps talking. It's too much sound. I turn on my side, my back to her, and I close my eyes. There is motion and voices. I am raised to shackle my bracelets and I stand facing the wall until I hear the clang of my prison door and my bracelets are released. Soon the red flash of Attar comes on. I turn around and watch the water fall from the shower, but I do not move. Fuck Attar.

DAY ONE

I WALK WITH cuffs and shackles to a waiting black vehicle. It is so far, the farthest I have walked since I first came to the Cube. My legs are quickly exhausted, and I must breathe deeper and faster. People in uniform escort me to people in suits. Men and women, tall and short, somehow they all look the same. I close my eyes wearily.

Finally I am in the vehicle, a large SUV. It is the fanciest, most unusual vehicle I have ever seen. The driver demands directions to the Jordanian embassy in Hebrew. No one answers, but a screen in the front lights up with a map, and I realize he is talking to the car. It is difficult to comprehend. The men and women in suits—one in the front, one on each side of me in the next row, and two in the row behind me—all have what I surmise are mobile phones. One of them puts hers to her ear and speaks.

The world has changed. The realization exhausts me. I want to sleep. The next hours are marked by interminable waiting. We arrive at the Jordanian embassy, an ugly, checkered building called Oz, where different people in the same suits and uniforms scurry about as I am led from one room to the next. Fashion has changed.

Men's suits are tighter, their ties narrower. Lipstick colors are muted, skirts shorter. The guards unshackle my legs, but I do not move. People come in and out and look at me. They want to see Bilal Jalal AbuJabal's wife. The only prisoner released to Jordan. The whore hero terrorist. I lift my legs onto the sofa and lie down, missing the Cube.

WEEK TWO

I AM IN Jordan now. Time here moves along a calendar, and I calculate having been in the Cube for sixteen years. They take me to a government ministry, where my picture is snapped with more suited men and women. On the way out, exhausting hours later, a crowd meets me with shouts. They are divided between those who see a hero and those who see a whore. Their calls ring in my head. A blinding sun bears down on my shoulders. I faint. At my family's home—a contemporary stone house with large windows and modern furnishings—I am told my brother carried me away. "Thank you," I tell him, studying the large framed photo of Sitti Wasfiyeh hanging on the wall next to the framed photo of my father that used to hang on our wall in Kuwait. I don't ask when or how she died. I know this is the house she built for my mother.

The noise is unbearable. Cars, horns, sirens, doors opening and closing, people talking to each other, and worse, to me. Even the hum of the refrigerator and air conditioner vibrate my brain. Mama looks old. She learns to leave me alone to lie on my side. I cannot convince her that I am not depressed. I can see in the eyes of those around me that I am not the person they remember. I have no feelings on that or any other matter.

WEEK THREE

DAYS ARE MORE of the same. So much noise. The best time is
when my mother leaves for her job. Well-wishers come to welcome
me back, but I pretend no one is home and don't answer the door. I
thought by now they would stop coming. But they are relentless. It
is hell in the evenings when Mama is home. She opens the door for
them. They arrive in droves with sweets and smiles and kisses and
so much goddamn chatter. But I put up with it because my mother
is doing the best she knows how.

Still, I gravitate to the bed in the corner of my room and find no
peace until I can lie on my side facing the wall. I assure Mama again
that I am not depressed, that "yes, I know you are proud of me, and
yes, I know you think I am a hero, and yes, I know you don't think
I am *that other* word." But I tell her that I am not a hero either, that
language is absurd, life is absurd, this theater of visitors is absurd,
and the hum of the goddamned refrigerator is grating my bones,
and "please trust me that I need solitude. I'm not bothering anyone,
just please give me some peace, some quiet."

WEEKS FOUR & FIVE

MAMA INSTALLS PADDING around the window and door of my room to dampen the noise. Visitors stop coming.

Mama knocks gently on my door, walks in. She sits at the edge of the bed and lays her hand on my shin. "Darling, there's someone here to see you."

Before I beg her to make them leave, she says, "It's Um Buraq," and leaves the room.

I turn around to chase a memory. A crazy car ride away from Kuwait for the last time. Laughter and sorrow colliding. Sitti Wasfiyeh making us pull over so she can get in the backseat. My brother's silence. Words from another life scramble and hit against my body from the inside, and I hear a whisper in my mind: *Whatever happens in this ungenerous world, we will meet again, my sister.*

I sit up, looking at a small, thin woman in a black abaya leaning forward on a cane. She smiles. There is no mistaking that massive, gap-toothed smile. I get up, walk to her, slip my arms quietly around her. She wraps her free arm around me, lets out a sigh, and the decades we have crossed wrap around us both.

She smells like an old woman. I can feel the bones of her ribs beneath the loose abaya.

"*Waleh, ma ajmal shooftitsh*," she says. Gurl! How beautiful the sight of you. "Now help me sit down," she demands.

For the first time in many years, an irrepressible smile takes me over. I am grateful not to be handled delicately. I thought I would never see Um Buraq again. But here we are, the frayed strings of our lives closing a circle. I can see that life has trampled her too. But fate feels generous in this moment, and something in me is restored. I feel color and texture transform what is dull and desiccated.

"Looks like you got old too," she says, that enormous tooth gap pumping sunshine through me.

WEEKS SIX, SEVEN, EIGHT & NINE

I STEP ON Mama's scales and see that I have put on three kilograms. Last week Um Buraq took me to a Turkish bathhouse, and we sat together naked in the steam while attendants scrubbed our bodies. It was my first time out of the house since I arrived. Tomorrow we will go there again. But today, she says we will go to a park. "Don't worry, it's out of the city and quiet. Hardly anyone will be there and the only noise is from birds and wind," she says, shaking her head and adding, "You're as difficult as your grandmother, may God rest her soul."

"You didn't even know my grandmother," I say.

"Of course I did. That crazy old woman made me pull over just to dramatize that I was a bad driver. Don't you remember?"

I laugh. "She had a point, though."

The park isn't really a park, but an open landscape of hills and valleys dotted with trees and rocks. It looks so much like the landscape of Palestine. Like the view over the orchards Bilal and I used to look upon. I indulge an illicit fantasy of a world that would have allowed us to simply live, raise children, hold jobs, move freely on earth, and grow old together. I allow myself to imagine that the dignities of home and freedom might be the purview of the wretched of this earth. Bilal and I would be in a place like this, perhaps hiking with at least one grown child, a teenage girl. Her father would teach her the names and benefits of all the plants we'd encounter. I would listen to stories of her life—her friends, romantic interests, dreams, and plans. We would eat together as a family and go home tired after a long day of being whole and free on earth. I feel the loss of what we never had, and it feels good to know that my heart stirs.

Um Buraq's cancer has returned. It is her third recurrence, and doctors tell her the treatment isn't working this time. "It's the reason Kuwait let me out of prison and deported me to Iraq through Jordan," she told me the first day she came to our apartment. "Some of our old clients advocated for me." In Iraq, she lived with distant family.

"It was terrible to be at their mercy, but thankfully Saddam still ensured free health care and social services even under American sanctions. So at least I could have a little bit of my own money from the state and got a little shack to live in."

But American warplanes and war plans followed her to Iraq years later, under a US president who was the son of the president who bombed Iraq when we still lived in Kuwait. This time they reduced Babylon, that once splendid, sophisticated, ancient civilization, to nothing. They made beggars of her teachers, taxi drivers of her doctors; and they made off with her treasures and artifacts. Um Buraq had arrived in Jordan in that thick human stream of refugees in the spring of 2003. "Americans are the devil," she said.

Bitterness is hard to keep away. Um Buraq sighs, flashing the gap in her teeth. "It sure is a beautiful world, though," she says, surveying the grandeur of our planet, knowing her days are few.

That is all we say about sickness and war.

"Do you think it means anything that we both ended up imprisoned?" Um Buraq asks.

"It means fate lacks imagination," I say, but I sit with the question. "Or maybe it just proves the state will always find a way to imprison those who are truly free, who do not accept social, economic, or political chains."

That is all we say about prison. We return home, where I paint her nails and give her a facial.

I spend more time outside of my room. I return to making body creams from olive and coconut oils, and I rub them into Um Buraq's papery skin. Her hair has fallen out, and she doesn't need eyebrow threading or hair dye. Or waxing. "Look at your bare pussy," I say. "Like a little baby girl's."

"Goddamn pussy brings nothing but shit. It might as well be another asshole," she says. "Just rub that good lotion on my thighs and leave my business alone."

My mother and I speak more. I fix her hair, thread her brows, and care for her as I do for Um Buraq. We go for a walk every day around the neighborhood. Sound bothers me less.

Twice a week, Um Buraq and I go to the hammam bathhouse, and when we've been scrubbed and oiled, I paint her nails, draw her eyebrows, and outline her eyes with kohl. The hammam attendant knows and likes us. She gives us the best hot rooms, and we tip her well. Um Buraq gets money from some of her old clients in Kuwait who softened over the years as they watched helplessly the devastation of Iraq and Palestine, and who now are moved to act in the service of their guilt and nostalgia.

"No matter what happened, we're still Arabs. We're still brothers and sisters. Despite everything, I still love Kuwait, and consider myself Kuwaiti despite the revocation of my citizenship. We're all part of each other. When you see what the Americans have done to us, what they've done to Iraq, Libya . . . And it breaks our hearts, all of us. That's how you know we're incomplete without each other," Um Buraq says, reminding me of Bilal when he spoke of pan-Arabism and pan-Africanism.

"Did you see the other day how Marzouq al-Ghanim kicked the Israeli representative out of that international meeting? What a man! I was so proud of Kuwait. Did you see it?" she asks.

I shook my head. "Who is Marzouq al-Ghanim?"

"You are starting to piss me off. Don't you watch the news? He's a Kuwaiti diplomat."

"I think I can find it on these computers," I say. "Jehad will know how."

We talk about computers, "smart" phones, and the alienating technology that makes us feel like intruders in the world. We talk about Kuwait.

"Those were good times," she says.

"The beaches were magical, weren't they?" I say. "What I'd give to be at an evening concert by the water in Salmiya, tasting the salty air, looking up at that starry desert sky, transported by music." I enjoy this reverie.

"We didn't know how good we had it," Um Buraq says. "Remember how the receding tide would uncover thousands of crabs scampering along the shoreline? And Ala'a Eddin ice cream parlor. Damn! I'd love some of that ice cream right now, and to just go back to my old house and watch hours and hours of soap operas."

"Remember the night we met?" I ask.

"How could I forget? You were the finest dancer I had ever seen," she says.

We both feel the weight of that day, and all the words unsaid begin to push through.

Um Buraq speaks first. "I'm sorry for what I did. It was a terrible thing. Can you ever forgive me?"

I pull her near, kiss the top of her head. "There was a part of me that wasn't afraid of your blackmail because I think I knew you wouldn't show those pictures to anyone. I made the choice to go along. I wanted the validation and worth that came with having a bit of money and being able to help my family. I liked breaking rules I had no say in making, at the same time that I hated how I did it." I take her old face in my hands. "You don't need my forgiveness, but if you want it, consider it granted."

JOY

UM BURAQ IS in a wheelchair now. We arrive at the bathhouse as usual and I push her to the front desk. Our friendly attendant is there. She takes the money and hands us the receipt, but there is something else with it. An envelope. She looks around and whispers, "Someone dropped this off and told me to give it to you. As you can see, it's unopened."

I thank her and wheel Um Buraq into the changing room. "Open it!" Um Buraq demands.

It is a typed story letter, like a children's fairy tale. It's strange and makes no sense. "Let me see." Um Buraq takes it from me.

As she grabs it, something occurs to me, and I snatch it back from her, quickly wheeling her into a private steam room. I rummage frantically in my purse for a pen. I can only find an eyeliner, but it'll do. My heart begins to race as I lay a towel on the bench and spread the paper on it. I circle the first word. Um Buraq has no idea what is happening, but she knows not to ask. I count nine words and circle the ninth. I count four words and circle the fourth. I start over: 1-9-4, 1-9-4, until the letter runs out. I put the eyeliner down and read what I've circled.

But I can barely make out the words through the steam, and the paper is already wet. Fumbling, I manage to turn off the mister and I open the window.

> my . . . darling . . . wife . . . I . . . have . . . spent . . . these . . . years . . . trying . . . to . . . make . . . my . . . way . . . back . . . to . . . you . . . if . . . you . . . will . . . have . . . me . . . I . . . will . . . come . . . to . . . you . . . there . . . is . . . a . . . tree . . . in . . . the . . . valley . . . where . . . you . . . go . . . and . . . sit . . . tomorrow . . . I . . . will . . . leave . . . a . . . letter . . . under . . . a . . . rock . . . there . . . enshallah . . . we . . . will . . . meet . . . again . . . my . . . love.

I crumple on the bench, sweat and tears pouring down my face. I am overwhelmed by the possibility of seeing Bilal, electrified by the thought of him.

Bilal is alive. Israel knew it all along. They've been trying to find him all these years. It's why they made me their special prisoner. Why I got the Cube. Why they displayed me to the world. I was the bait then, and I still am.

Um Buraq watches me knowingly. "It's him, isn't it?" she asks, but she can see the answer on my face.

She struggles to get out of her chair, and I help her sit next to me. "Turn that steam back on and close the window," she says. "Keep it normal."

I put my arm around her to whisper in her ear, even though we're alone in total privacy. "He survived," I say. "We survived them all."

Her lips slowly stretch and out comes that massive laughter. It is the only part of her that has not been diminished. I know she will be gone soon, taking her magnificent laughter with her. I don't know when and how I will see Bilal, though I know we can't ever be together openly. I may never find a place in this world, but for now, in this moment, I feel the purest, most perfect joy.

ACKNOWLEDGMENTS

I'VE BEEN WRITING this story in my mind for over twenty years. Like my other novels, some of it came from direct personal experience. Some of it from research. Some, imagined. In my research, I interviewed several individuals I am not at liberty to acknowledge by name. But I wish to make a space of gratitude for them here, something tender for all girls (and boys) and women everywhere who've had to sell their bodies to survive, or to escape or perpetuate demons that cannot be dislodged.

I want to thank political prisoners whose extraordinary lives and writings helped me understand (though I know I cannot fully understand) what it means to be a political prisoner: Khalida Jarrar, Ahmad Sa'adat, Mumia Abu-Jamal, Albert Woodfox, and members of the MOVE family. In particular, I wish to thank Janet Holloway Africa, Janine Phillips Africa, and Ria Africa, who were recently released after being imprisoned for more than forty years, and who graciously spoke to me about their lives in prison. I am in awe of their fortitude, generosity, and commitment to the world and to each other, and of the love they give despite enduring sustained indignities most of us cannot imagine.

Not long after I finished a readable draft of this novel, I found Anjali Singh, a brilliant agent at Ayesha Pande Literary Agency. I'm grateful for the ways she helped improve the manuscript, and I'm excited to begin a new journey in my literary career with her by my side. Because of the shuffle between agencies, it ended up that the German and Swedish translations were published ahead of the English, which meant that my editors at Diana Verlag Random House and Norstedts had to work extra hard to edit the translations. So, thank you, Britta Hansen and Gunilla Sondell.

Of course, thank you to Martha Hughes, my trusted editor who sees my work from stream-of-consciousness writing until it's recognizable as a story. Other than my dear friend Mame, Martha is the only person I've trusted to read the early drafts of my books, and I'm grateful for her encouragement and keen editorial eye.

To my editors at Simon & Schuster and Bloomsbury, Michelle Herrera Mulligan, Alexandra Pringle, and Allegra Le Fanu: thank you for believing in me and in Nahr. I am fortunate to launch this book with such powerful women.

I want to thank members of my family who provided guidance and insight into the conditions in Kuwait during the Iraqi occupation and subsequent US invasion, which they lived through. They prefer not to be named. I am grateful to Dr. Salman Abu Sitta and Ibrahim Nasrallah for providing me with or pointing me to textbooks and other materials I needed in my research where it came to specific historic audits, local topography, and political chronologies. Thank you to Dr. Richard Falk, Rachel Holmes, Adab Ibrahim, Eric Larsen, Linda Hanna, Ghada Dajani, and Raja Shehadeh for reading and offering encouragement on early drafts. Thank you to Dr. George Zahr for his consult on questions relating to organic and inorganic chemistry.

In addition to Norstedts and Diana Verlag, I want to thank all of my other international publishers, especially Aschehoug (Norway) and Feltrinelli (Italy), who have been so good to me over the years.

Mame Lambeth, my dearest and oldest friend, read all my books multiple times at different stages. I turned to her because she was brilliant and creative, but mostly because she loved me, and I trusted her more than anyone else in the world. She read a rough draft of this novel before she passed away on June 12, 2018, the night after her seventy-fifth birthday. I spent the next several months revising this manuscript with the profound grief of losing the person who had been my only anchor in life spanning the past thirty-two years. In both of my previous novels, I inserted tributes to her that only she would recognize. Her daughter Erin Caldwell, my former high school classmate, recognizes them too. Mame taught me many things, among which was how to live my truth even (and especially) when it was at odds with social conventions. She showed me how to love and appreciate solitude, how to connect with the natural world and forge emotional relationships with animals. She didn't like many people and let very few into her life. It was my privilege to be loved by her. She never let me down, never disappointed me, though I'm sure I let her down and disappointed her plenty. This novel is dedicated to her memory, and as with my previous novels, there are bits written for her. I am glad that I was able to tell her how much I loved her and what her enduring and unwavering friendship meant to me over the years since we first met, when I was a lost and troubled sixteen-year-old high school student. But I am still left feeling that I did not do or say enough. She gave me far more than I gave her. Dedicating this novel to her memory is only fitting, however insufficient or late it might be. My life is dimmer without her. I still have not adjusted to the reality that our daily online Scrabble games are no more; or that I cannot pick up the phone to call her whenever I want, to ask about her garden, her dogs, her shoulder problems, her kids and grandkids; or to tell her about my days, to gossip, complain, rejoice, and generally indulge in the most profound friendship I've ever known.

Then, just as the galleys were printed, I learned that my birth mother, Aminah Abulhawa, was critically ill. We spoke for the first time in ten years. She was in a hospital bed unable to breathe well, but we saw each other on FaceTime, and her eyes smiled behind the oxygen mask when I told her I was coming to Kuwait to see her. By the time my plane landed a couple of days later, she was already in the ICU, heavily sedated, unaware of my presence or of her body's struggle to hold on.

I had always wondered what that moment would feel like. But it was like nothing I had ever imagined. It was an immensely sad, lonely land, littered with shards of ancient hurt, ancient anger, the corpses of so many unsaid words and unanswered questions, and memories without stories—meeting my mother for the first time in 1975. I was five years old. She was beautiful, with long shiny black hair, silky olive skin, and groovy bellbottom jeans. A hot wind across my face coming off the airplane in Kuwait. Black marks on my white shorts from the luggage conveyer belt. Aminah said "I told you not to sit there." A photo of a mother and daughter cuddled, smiling in bed. I looked happy. She did too. I was her first born, and her only child then. The others (five more girls) would come much later. No one in the family knew the abyss that bound us. They think they do, and they have their own narratives—bad daughter, wicked sister, a mother's tough choices, and so it goes. The truth is that I would have liked to know her as a woman. She didn't have it easy, thwarted by terrible men, first my father then my stepfather. I have always had compassion for that. But she and I could not cross that abyss. It was too big, too deep, too dark, though we both tried, teetering on its edges at different times.

Six months prior, she sent me a friend request on Facebook, which I accepted. Then she sent me a message: "Hi." Nothing more. I didn't know what to do with it, and though I came back to that message many times, I never responded. I thought I had more time.

Her lungs couldn't take one more cigarette and just stopped. Her other organs followed one by one. I watched in the hospital as edema slowly dissolved her wrinkles and restored her face to the smoothness of her youth. We looked so much alike. Everyone said so. Some people who hadn't seen me in a while thought I was her. One of her grandchildren, a nephew I had just met, thought his "teta" was out of the hospital when he first saw me. I liked that, thought it was poetic.

I know enough about vital signs and blood markers to realize she would be gone in a day or two. I said a final farewell by her bed and went to the airport to leave her memory—and days of condolences and the stream of well-wishers that arrive after Muslim burials—to the daughters she raised, whose love for her was not complicated. I left them to grieve together, without the distraction of the estranged older daughter in America and the curiosity that always provokes.

Alone with my grief and regrets, I stared at the Facebook message Aminah sent to me—"Hi"—the only written note I ever received from the woman who gave me life. I realized for the first time that she had been a powerful driving force in so many of my decisions and achievements—driven by a desire to hurt her, to make her see me, make her proud. She is present in all three of my novels, in the complicated mother daughter relationships of my first two, then simplified in this novel.